INDIES INFERNO

Indies Inferno

EDWARD HOCHSMANN

Main Characters

Haley Reardon, Lieutenant, U.S. Coast Guard. Haley is a superbly competent, hard-charging young officer working her dream job—command of the patrol boat *Kauai* on the front lines of Coast Guard operations. She is realizing that having a loving relationship is not necessarily a liability for a commander and is exploring a relationship with DIA Agent Simmons.

Benjamin "Ben" Wyporek, Lieutenant, U.S. Coast Guard. Ben is the executive officer or second in command of the Coast Guard cutter *Kauai*. He is a young but experienced and heroic officer, holding the complete trust of both Haley and the crew. Ben is trying to balance his extremely demanding and dangerous job with his devotion to his new) wife Victoria, the love of his life.

Victoria Carpenter Wyporek. Victoria is a neuro-diverse mathematical genius, formerly an analyst with the Defense Intelligence Agency, who met Ben during a joint operation almost a year ago. Her mild autism condition makes some ordinary life activities challenging. She is deeply in love with Ben, who helped her leave her safe but sheltered and unfulfilling existence. She struggles with her fear for Ben's safety when he is out on missions.

Dr. Peter Simmons. Simmons is a field agent with the Defense Intelligence Agency. He has a talent for deception, which has led to his success as a DIA field agent but is the antithesis of Ben's ethos. Simmons also has a risk-seeking bent that borders on pathology. He shares a cordial relationship with Ben and is supportive of his relationship with Victoria, his protégé and sister of his beloved late fiancée. He met Haley at Ben and Victoria's wedding and has been becoming closer to her since then.

Marcus Porter, Cadet First Class, U.S. Coast Guard. Marcus is a young officer trainee on an Academy summer intern program with the Coast Guard UAV team on the island of St. Ignatius. He is in for far more adventure than he expected.

Isabelle Jones. The beautiful young deputy administrator of St. Ignatius. Just a couple of years out of college, she is the youngest elected official in the island's history and is the liaison with the Coast Guard and U.S. Geological Survey teams.

Select Technical Terms	
ASAP	As Soon As Possible
CARE	Climate Annihilation Response Emergency
CO	Commanding Officer
DIA	Defense Intelligence Agency
DNI	Director of National Intelligence
EMCON	Emissions Control
EPIRB	Emergency Position-Indicating Radiobeacon
FC3	Fire Control/Command and Control
Gitmo	Naval Station Guantanamo Bay, Cuba
GPS	Global Positioning System
MEDEVAC	Medical Evacuation
NSA	National Security Agency
OBS	Ocean Bottom Seismometer
OOD	Officer of the Deck
Port (side)	To the left when facing forward on a boat
Quarterdeck	Entry point for a ship/boat when moored
RHIB	Rigid Hull Inflatable Boat
SCIF	Special Compartmented Information Facility
Starboard (side)	To the right when facing forward on a boat
UAV	Unmanned Aerial Vehicle
USCG	United States Coast Guard
USGS	United States Geological Survey
WILCO	Will Comply
XO	Executive Officer

Dedication

This book is dedicated to my parents, who successfully managed to raise a son in challenging times and become a good friend to him after he left home to join the service. It is also dedicated to the Coast Guard, the oldest continuous seagoing service of the United States, and its complement of supremely skilled, committed, and courageous professionals. They stand the watch and lay their lives on the line every day to save others, defend the homeland, protect the environment, and promote maritime commerce.

Semper Paratus

Contents

Prologue

The environmental extremist group Climate Annihilation Response Emergency, or CARE, began as the U.S. version of similar movements in Europe dedicated to ending petroleum production. The U.S. group's members were as fervent in their beliefs that the world's end from climate change was nigh as their European counterparts and started off employing their tactics of vandalizing artwork and disrupting traffic in major cities. But the U.S. is not Europe, and it was only a matter of time before activities such as these escalated into deadly violence. The break point involved a grieving father whose young daughter had died in an ambulance blocked from reaching a hospital by a CARE protest. Outraged by their public, unrepentant dismissal of her death, he gunned down and killed six of the group at another CARE protest the following week before being killed by the police.

It was a galvanizing development. The public, the mainstream press, and the government had already had their fill of the group's sanctimonious rhetoric and intransigent behavior, and this new threat to public safety was the last straw. A zero-tolerance policy was quickly enacted by municipalities across the country, dusting off and vigorously enforcing existing permit regulations for public gatherings. CARE members who attempted further disruptions were instantly arrested, removed by force, and held for prosecution to the maximum extent of the law.

The litigation normally attending such heavy-handed government policy was conspicuously absent—not even the American Civil Liberties Union would take CARE's phone calls by this point.

Rational people would take stock of the event and the intense and near-universal negative reaction to their approach to engage in some self-reflection. Many CARE members did and quickly disassociated themselves from the movement. Unfortunately, this left a rump of the most fanatical members, dedicated to the furtherance of the cause by any means available. They were well-supported in this by wealthy dilettantes, industrialists seeking profits in "green" products, and other shadowy organizations interested in the destabilization of society. Unlike the radical groups of the late 1960s and early 1970s, CARE did not have to support itself via bank robberies or other illegal activities that would draw the attention of law enforcement. They could lie low, planning and gathering the resources needed for a first strike of maximum impact.

As CARE's membership dwindled and activity subsided, law enforcement interest in the group waned and intelligence focus shifted to higher-priority threats. Plans to infiltrate undercover officers into the organization were shelved and operations scaled back to passive monitoring of the social media activity of known group members. The law enforcement community missed the relocation of CARE's center of gravity to Florida and the group's research into potential targets for direct action.

The planners managing CARE knew they had only one shot—after any attack, the terrorist designation would quickly follow and end any chance of further operations in the U.S. The first one had to be big, not some trivial pinprick like blowing up a gas station or two. They considered and discarded options for attacks on airports and airliners, railroads, and key land-based infrastructure. The chief problem was the one enduring legacy of the aftermath of the 9/11 attacks: the hardening of such targets against threats posed by foreign and domestic terrorists. These were not invulnerable, but security was thorough and resilient enough to defeat any but the most dedicated and skilled attackers. Besides, mass casualties would just intensify the public animus toward the organization with no chance of advancing the cause.

Like an airport attack, an assault on a vessel moored in a U.S. port was considered and discarded—security in the significant harbors was as tight as a major airport and few were close enough to highly populated areas to achieve the desired audience factor. Besides, the firefighting and response capabilities of these facilities were substantial and likely to contain and extinguish any fires started in the attack.

Vessels underway, on the other hand, were far more vulnerable. If one could be effectively attacked within sight of a large population area, the impact could be huge. The problems were timing and firepower. A ship is generally in sight of land only for brief windows of time while entering and leaving port, leaving little room for error in the attack's timing. The other problem is that ships are very large, heavy things, designed to survive damage from most natural threats. Gunfire, small rockets, and even direct impact by explosive-laden UAVs were unlikely to cause much damage. A large amount of explosives, positioned right next to the hull on detonation, would be required. This left a small, fast vessel acting as a powerful torpedo as the best option.

After resolving the question of the delivery vehicle, manning became the next problem. There was no question that this would be a one-way mission, and the planners were worried about leaving its success to the resolve of a human operator, even among the fanatics of CARE. Early on, they decided that a remotely piloted boat was the best option, teamed with another vessel that would guide the boat to its target via on-board video camera and radio control. The purchase and clandestine rigging of a large recreational boat for remote control was an easy undertaking.

For the payload, the planners knew authorities would be watching for purchases of explosives and even large quantities of precursors. They carefully sent CARE operatives to purchase small amounts of ammonium nitrate, ostensibly for agricultural use. Over time, they accumulated enough of the compound and powdered aluminum to fill four out of five of the fuel tanks on the boat. These were sealed, awaiting the time of launch, when gasoline would be added as the boat was fueled for the mission.

For the target, the planners considered and discarded the idea of attacking a cruise ship. It could kill many people, but the ships were so big that sinking or even disabling one would be highly unlikely. Like an attack on an airport or airliner, it would hurt more than help the cause. Likewise, the idea of an attack on a large cargo vessel was dismissed. They eventually decided that an attack on a medium-sized tanker bringing in refined fuel would provide a spectacular visual and the clean-up would remind everyone of the horrors of continued dependence on oil.

Now, they had the plan and weapon available. It was only a matter of awaiting the arrival of a suitable target.

Canto V of *Inferno*, Part I of *Divine Comedy*

by Dante Alighieri

Part I

Chapter 1

Dilemma

USCG Cutter Kauai, North Atlantic Ocean, eleven nautical miles southeast of Port Canaveral, Florida
11:13 EDT, 12 June

Haley

Please, God. I don't want to have to kill anyone today!

Lieutenant Haley Reardon, commanding officer of the Coast Guard Cutter *Kauai*, took another long look at the suspect boat through her binoculars and then swung her gaze back to the tactical screen. They were closing to five hundred yards range and Chief Hopkins had already given the helm order to bring them on a parallel course with the target. Within one minute, Haley would have to make the most difficult decision of her career.

Every sensor they had, from the hyperspectral imaging camera on the unmanned aircraft flying overhead, the high-resolution electro-optical camera on *Kauai*'s mast, and now her own eyes screamed this boat was loaded with explosives and unmanned—essentially, a robotic improvised explosive device aimed straight at the tanker they were there to protect.

Her hands shook as she thought, *but what if I'm wrong and this turns out to be just another boat with a bunch of CARE loons hiding somewhere aboard?*

It would not be the first time she had given the order for lethal fire—the other occurred six months previously at the Haitian island of Ile Ste. Michel. They were shooting back in self-defense on that occasion, protecting *Kauai*'s retreating small boat from machine gun fire from a Chinese armored car. This was different—an American boat that was not shooting at them, but giving every sign of being a deadly bomb. She wondered at how in such a short time this turned from just another ordinary patrol to a matter of life and death.

Fifteen minutes earlier...

For the third time in the last two weeks, the *Kauai* was at General Quarters Condition One with her crew in combat helmets and ballistic vests and weapons manned and loaded. It was sunny and getting quite warm already, typical June weather for Florida's Atlantic Coast. Haley was thankful to be inside the air-conditioned bridge when wearing the heavy protective equipment and felt sorry for the two crewmen standing outside at their fifty-caliber machine guns.

Haley leaned forward in her command chair on the bridge, scanning between the video screens on the Fire

Control/Command and Control console, known as the FC3. The left-hand screen showed the real-time video feed from the electro-optical camera on the cutter's mast—it was trained on the tanker *Paul Morris*, following three hundred yards behind them. *Kauai*'s position and any targets being tracked in the vicinity were shown superimposed on the local geography on the tactical display on the right-hand screen. The FC3 system fused information from multiple sources into the target display, both the feeds from *Kauai*'s radar and the AeroVironment T-20 unmanned aerial vehicle currently loitering overhead.

The mission was close escort, this time leading a pair of response boats from Station Cape Canaveral and shepherding a medium-sized tanker of fifty-two thousand tons carrying a split load of diesel fuel and unleaded gasoline for offload ashore, conveniently in *Kauai*'s homeport of Port Canaveral, Florida. This was normally a job for a single response boat or maybe the eighty-seven-foot patrol boat homeported in Cape Canaveral, not a highly equipped, special operations cutter. But these were not normal times.

The environmental extremist group CARE had become a genuine physical threat over the past month, and special intelligence suggested they were preparing for a public act of extreme violence somewhere in Florida to focus attention on their cause. Forcibly boarding and setting a sizeable tanker afire within sight of the beaches and generating a massive cleanup effort would make a significant impression, both psychologically and economically. This made industrial ports like Tampa, Jacksonville, and Port Canaveral prime targets, and internal security was beefed-up accordingly. Meanwhile, the Coast Guard, along with Brevard County Sherriff and port authority police patrol boats, covered the port approaches and internal waters to intercept and ward off any suspected attackers of transiting vessels. Haley shook her head at the thought that anyone with a functioning brain would conclude this would be a sound approach to combat climate change, but it was a sign of the pervasive and increasing insanity of the world.

Haley was typical of a Coast Guard officer in command of a patrol boat. Just shy of her thirty-first birthday, she received her commission eight years previously on graduation from the Coast Guard Academy. A tallish five-foot-eight with shoulder-length dark hair and gray eyes, she was extremely fit, with a slim, athletic build. She had taken command of *Kauai* a little over six months ago, overcoming the challenge of succeeding an extremely successful, almost beloved predecessor, and quickly winning the respect and affection of the crew as they had won hers.

Kauai was an Island Class (Block D) patrol boat, one-hundred-ten feet long with a crew of two officers and fourteen enlisted personnel. She was an old boat, beyond twenty-five years on a design meant to last only fifteen, and was among the last of her class still in commission. She should have been decommissioned by now, but a year and a half previously, she received a stay of execution after being swept up into an extremely classified mission in the Florida Keys.

During a law enforcement patrol off Key West, *Kauai* had discovered a wrecked and derelict sailboat laden with illegal drugs. After reporting the find, they were drawn into a search for a lost Russian nuclear-tipped missile, launched by accident after a mid-air collision between a Russian bomber and U.S. fighter off-shore of Miami. Realizing the boat had been wrecked by a near-miss by the missile, *Kauai*'s crew, teamed up with a Defense Intelligence Agency operative, traced its drift back to the impact point. After a vicious firefight with the wrecked boat's crime syndicate owners, *Kauai*'s crew secured the live nuclear warhead, preventing a devastating explosion that would have likely ignited a nuclear war between the U.S. and Russia.

Recognizing the high caliber of her crew and *Kauai*'s potential to respond quickly and discreetly to similar national crises, the Director of National Intelligence invested a considerable sum of money to extend the cutter's life, upgrade her powerplant and electronics, and cycle select members of her crew through advanced tactical training. The boat's homeport was moved from Miami to Port Canaveral, nominally to serve as the permanent range safety cutter for the Cape Canaveral rocket launch facility, but actually as the on-call platform for sensitive and covert intelligence missions in South Florida, The Bahamas, and the Caribbean. There had been two such missions since the upgrade. The first occurred about eight months before Haley's arrival and the second, the mission to the Haitian island, within days of Haley's assumption of command.

Haley glanced again at the FC3's tactical display, now showing two small targets to their north and nearly two dozen to their south. The map also showed the boundary line of the temporary security zone established for the arrival of the tanker, extending two miles on either side of the channel leading into Port Canaveral. This area was no stranger to security zones—one was always established from the shore to around twelve miles downrange during rocket launches from Cape Canaveral to provide safe clearance from falling debris in the event of a post-launch malfunction or abort. However, needing to impose one to prevent a terrorist act was unsettling enough—to do it for the third time in a fortnight was downright disturbing.

They had to regard any of those targets milling around seemingly at random just south of the security zone boundary as a potential threat, and nearly all displayed the infuriating white abbreviation "UNK" indicating that their name or registration numbers had not been determined. Haley knew most, if not all, those contacts were innocent sport fishers, recreational boats, and daysailers. Their behavior thus far had suggested nothing else and, despite the boredom associated with this type of operation, Haley hoped it would continue to be a quiet day.

The two Station Cape Canaveral response boats were cruising in line about a mile south of *Kauai*'s track, halfway to the zone boundary. These were the "pouncers"

Haley would dispatch to close rapidly on any boat penetrating the zone to warn them off or, if necessary, try to stop them. *Kauai* was the last line of defense and would engage any non-compliant boats getting past the response boats. Haley's orders were clear: with the terrorism threat posed by CARE, this was a national defense mission. Any vessel breaking through the response boats would be considered as having disclosed deadly intent—Haley would use non-lethal means to stop it, if practicable. But, one way or another, that vessel would be stopped before it reached the tanker.

Haley looked up as Chief Operations Specialist Emilia Hopkins strolled across the bridge deck to check the radar display on her normal Officer-of-the-Deck sweep. Hopkins was the "old hand" on *Kauai*, the crewmember with the longest tenure, having joined some three years earlier as a petty officer first class and remaining on board after being promoted to chief petty officer. She was tall—she had two inches on Haley—and was a fit thirty-four-year-old widowed mother of thirteen- and eleven-year-old sons. Hopkins shared a house with her mother, who looked after the boys when she was at sea. She led the Operations Division and was the premier ship driver on *Kauai*—like now, she was the go-to OOD for any unusual situation. Haley smiled and nodded when Hopkins glanced her way, receiving a smile and a nod.

"Captain, I have three contacts moving into the buffer zone from the south," Electronics Technician First Class Joe Williams said from his seat at the center position of the FC3 console. As the commanding officer, Haley was addressed as "Captain" aboard *Kauai*.

"Let's move one down. Whose turn is it, Williams?"

"Four-Two-Three, ma'am," Williams replied, referring to the boat's hull number.

"Very well. Send him down to the line."

"Aye, aye, ma'am." Williams keyed the transmit button for his headset and said, "Four-Two-Three, Orchid, head two-one-five for the intercept of targets bearing one-eight-three, two-zero-seven, and two-four-one from you. Hold at the security zone boundary. Over." They had set up an area stretching a mile beyond the security zone boundary to the south as a buffer zone to allow Haley time to position the station boats to intercept a contact before it entered the security zone proper. The protocol was for the boat to activate its flashing blue law enforcement light and begin audio warnings for a target approaching within a quarter mile of the security zone boundary. If the target did not stop, the boat would execute a non-compliant stop-and-board.

After three seconds, the reply came from the speaker. "Orchid, Four-Two-Three, WILCO, heading two-one-five. I have three rec boats in sight on those bearings. Over."

"Four-Two-Three, Orchid, roger, those are your bogies," Williams replied. Williams was also an old hand on *Kauai*—only Hopkins and Chief Machinery Technician James Drake had been aboard longer. He was a solid performer who loved his work maintaining electronics and, especially, being the fire control master operating the cutter's automated weapon systems—the non-lethal entangling weapon colloquially known as "the Squid" and the twenty-five-millimeter auto-cannon mounted on the cutter's forward deck. Both were loaded and "hot" right now, ready to be directed against a potential target by Williams with a few keystrokes and slight movements of his joystick.

To Williams's right sat Operations Specialist Third Class Natalya Zuccaro, performing quartermaster duties of navigation and keeping the electronic logbook. Zuccaro was among the newer members of the crew and one of the youngest at twenty-one. She was not a top performer in Haley's estimation—good enough to remain on board, but not much more. Haley knew Hopkins shared this opinion and when they occasionally discussed the young petty officer, she would usually roll her eyes or shake her head, and simply say, "It's Gen Z, Captain. They're hit or miss!" The thought that Haley had, like Hopkins, become a member of the "older generation" at the ripe old age of thirty never failed to amuse her.

Chief Avionics Electrical Technician Erich "Fritz" Deffler occupied the third and last seat at the FC3 console to Williams's left. He was the Air Mission Commander for the UAV, controlling its movements and sensors as it orbited lazily over the security zone's southern boundary line. Deffler was not part of *Kauai*'s standing crew, but was assigned to the Coast Guard's aviation deployment center in Jacksonville. When *Kauai* needed UAV support, he usually led the aviation team, allowing him to be together with Hopkins. They had met in his first deployment on *Kauai* eighteen months ago and had built a romantic relationship since. Haley was not keen on romance between members aboard the same boat, but, technically, Deffler was not one of her guys. As with Hopkins, Haley liked Deffler personally and deeply respected and appreciated his skills. So, as long as he and Hopkins remained consummate professionals when aboard the boat, she could live with it—when they were off duty ashore, they could do as they pleased as far as she was concerned.

Haley's second-in-command, Lieutenant Ben Wyporek, stood silently on her right, where he could see the tactical display. He was a supernumerary on the bridge during the operation, there to maintain "situational awareness" in case he had to fill in for Haley or Hopkins or lead a boarding crew in a non-compliant vessel situation. Ben's official title was Executive Officer, but he was generally referred to by the position's abbreviation "XO." He was of average size, about five-foot-ten, clean-shaven with his sandy brown hair cut to regulation length and startlingly blue eyes.

Ben's primary job as XO was to handle the load of administration for the unit to free up the commanding officer to keep "the big picture." But Ben was far more than an administrative manager to Haley. He was the tactical lead for the unit, combat trained for expeditionary missions ashore during *Kauai*'s "black bag" operations. Although subordinate in position and several years her junior, he was the person she leaned on for advice, to bounce ideas off, and to handle problems before they turned into crises. He had wisdom and common sense well beyond what one could normally expect of a twenty-five-year-old junior officer and the crew deeply respected and admired him. He and Haley were not friends in the conventional sense—it was difficult to maintain a friendship within the hierarchy of a military command cadre—but they were partners in leadership on *Kauai*, and Haley had grown to trust him more than any other person she had ever known.

Haley glanced over and, noting Ben's grim expression, whispered, "What's on your mind, XO?"

Ben returned her gaze briefly before turning back to the display and replied, "It's probably nothing, Captain, but I don't like how those three just decided to make a run north." He pointed to one contact on the screen. "And this one in the middle, it was keeping pace with the others before, but now it's dropping back. Why is that?" He turned to Haley again and, noting her slight smile, grinned back and added, "Sorry. I guess I'm getting a little jumpy."

"No, no. Let's pull the thread. Not like we have anything else going on. What are you thinking here?"

Ben's frown returned. "We're getting close to the jetties—maybe twenty minutes at this pace, so the window is closing. It's now or never. They've had two chances before today to watch our tactics. We've had a couple of intercepts on those, so if they were around, they know how we roll: we go to the closest threat. So, if this is the real deal, I would expect one or both boats in front to be decoys, with the third carrying the threat."

Haley's smile disappeared. "So, what would you suggest?"

"Let's move down half the distance. If it is nothing, then no harm done. If one of those guys is just screwing with us for setting up another security zone, a show of force might make them think twice."

"And if this is the real deal?"

Ben turned with a grim expression. "Then we have twice the distance to engage and...defeat them."

That's a carefully chosen word, "defeat," Haley thought. *He knows if this is the real thing, it will probably end up in a gunfight.* "What about those two to the north? It would be an excellent tactic to decoy us away in one direction while they come in from one-eighty out."

"Yes, ma'am." Ben nodded. "We should pull the second response boat up to backfill us here and tell him to focus north. If anything looks hinky, we can hustle back here to deal with it."

This was becoming one of those conversations with Ben that Haley dreaded, one of those calling for a decision on a life-or-death situation, the likes of which she could not even have imagined before she arrived on *Kauai*. As always, Ben had presented a straightforward case and logical solution, but Haley hesitated, willing for it to just go away.

"Captain?" Ben asked, quietly pressing the issue.

Well, girl, you wanted to be the boss. Time to do some of that captain shit. "OK. As usual, you've sold me, XO." She turned to Hopkins across the bridge and said, "Chief, let's move south smartly. Make it half the distance to the boundary line."

"Aye, aye, Captain," Hopkins replied as she advanced the thrust levers. "Helm, left ten degrees rudder, steer two-four-five."

"Chief, my rudder is left ten, coming to two four five," Seaman Mitchell Pickins, the helmsman, replied.

"Very well. Zuccaro, give me a heads up when we come onto the new trackline."

"Yes, Chief," the young petty officer responded.

Haley switched her communications panel setting to "Radio 1" and pressed the transmit button for her headset. "Five-zero-six, Orchid Actual, close on the tanker and take the lead," Haley said, directing the second response boat into *Kauai*'s former position leading the tanker.

"Orchid, five-zero-six, WILCO, out," replied the coxswain on the second response boat.

As *Kauai* heeled to the right in her turn toward the new course, Haley smiled ruefully at Ben, getting a sympathetic smile in return. "Hey, it breaks up the monotony, Captain."

"I suppose. Hopefully, we have reached peak paranoia for today."

"Captain, the bogie furthest east has turned and is heading southeast," Williams interrupted. "The other two are continuing on an intercept track for the tanker, and the one furthest west is accelerating."

"Right. Are any of the other contacts moving this way?"

"Negative, ma'am," Williams replied.

The news troubled Haley. *This is bad. That target must see the response boat by now, and he's behaving more aggressively. That can't be a coincidence.* "Williams, give me an intercept course for the target lagging behind."

"Yes, ma'am."

Haley activated her radio again. "Four-two-three, Orchid Actual, close on, stop, and board the vessel on your port bow," she said, referring to the now-speeding boat. "We'll take the other northbound target."

"Orchid, four-two-three, WILCO, out," came the disembodied voice from the radio receiver.

Haley watched on the tactical screen as the course vectors associated with *Kauai* and her two companions grew and rotated. She turned to Deffler and said, "Chief Deffler, I need closeups on those two northbounds ASAP. Start with the one running further west."

"On it, Captain," Deffler replied. "Going to max continuous power, ETA one minute, fifteen seconds."

"Good. Make it one pass, then proceed to the second target. Pass data directly to the boat as it comes in on Radio One."

"Yes, ma'am," Deffler replied, keeping his eyes on the split screen showing the UAV's flight telemetry and its on-board camera view. After slewing the camera to the target's azimuth and down-angle, he selected the lock function as soon as the boat entered the field of view. It was a white recreational boat with green trim, about thirty-five feet long. Deffler keyed the transmit button and said, "Four-Two-Three, Orchid Air. How do you read?"

"Loud and clear."

"Roger. I'm coming up on your target now. I see three people on board, all adults. From the clothing, it looks like two males and one female. No weapons in sight. I'm running hyperspectral. Give me a sec while it processes."

"Roger, copy all."

Less than three seconds later, the results of the hyperspectral imaging popped onto the screen: "Explosives: Negative; Chemical Agents: Negative; Radiological Agents: Negative; Confidence: High."

"Four-Two-Three, Orchid Air, negative for explosives, chem, and radiologicals, confidence high," Deffler radioed.

"Roger. Thanks for the assist!"

"Good luck, Four-Two-Three," Deffler said, directing the UAV toward the second target. Turning to Haley, he added, "One minute to the next target, Captain."

"Very well. Same as before, please."

"Yes, ma'am," Deffler replied and turned back to the screen.

Haley glanced at the tactical display. The response boat had reached the target vessel, and both were slowing down, she was relieved to see. She did not want to have to break off from the second target to support the smaller boat. She glanced at the icon for their target again—still motoring steadily on a collision course with the tanker at eighteen knots. The UAV was approaching from the west. *We should have something on them by now.* "What's happening, Chief?" she asked impatiently.

"Um, I'm not reading any POBs, ma'am. Nothing showing on either visual or infrared."

This was a very ominous development—they should at least be seeing the heat signature from any people on board at this point. Haley stood and stepped over to the aviation station. "Can you put the camera on the second screen, please?"

"Yes, ma'am," Deffler replied, pressing a button to bring up the electro-optical camera feed onto the righthand screen. A fast-cruising recreational boat appeared also white, but with blue trim, trailing a thick, white wake with regular splashes of waves under the bows. The deck area and mezzanine behind the enclosed helm were covered by a dark blue canopy.

OK. Maybe they're inside or under the canopy, Haley thought hopefully. At the same time, an icy ball was forming in her stomach at the thought the boat might be uninhabited. "How soon on the hyperspectral, Chief?"

"Just completing the initial scan now, Captain. It will take about five more seconds to process." After that length of time passed, the readout popped onto the lefthand screen. "Holy shit!"

In flashing red letters, the top line read: "Explosives: POSITIVE [AN]."

Deffler turned a wide-eyed look to Haley and said, "Positive for explosives, Ammonium Nitrate, confidence high, Captain!"

OK, there it is! Haley took a deep breath to steady herself and replied quietly, "Very well. Get as close as you can. If you see anything that could be alive on that boat, shout it out."

"Will do, ma'am," Deffler said, turning back to his control panel.

Haley turned to Ben and swallowed hard. "XO, you handle comms with the command center. Tell them there is a rec boat, positive for explosives and apparently unmanned heading for a collision with the *Paul Morris* at eighteen knots, distance four thousand five hundred yards. Unless it changes course, I intend to engage with the twenty-five before it gets within fifteen hundred yards."

"Aye, aye, Captain," Ben replied grimly, then leaned over to dictate the message to a pale and wide-eyed Zuccaro.

"Chief Hopkins, close to five hundred yards from the target and assume a parallel course at eighteen knots."

"Aye, aye, Captain," Hopkins replied. She stepped over to Ben's right to watch the tactical and radar displays as *Kauai* approached the target.

Haley returned to her seat and took another deep breath to calm her thundering heart. Finally, she looked at Williams with as neutral an expression as she could muster and said, "Williams, surface action port. Weapon select mount twenty-five. Load high explosive incendiary. Target is the rec boat at two-five-six and nine hundred yards. Weapons tight."

"Yes, ma'am," Williams replied coolly. "Loading high explosive." He entered a command into his keyboard and the twenty-five-millimeter auto-cannon on the foredeck emitted a series of "clanks" as the autoloader put a shell into the breech. As soon as the green "Ready" status appeared on the auto-cannon's status board, he selected the recreational boat from the tracking list and clicked on the "target select" button on his screen. The auto-cannon came alive and pivoted onto the bearing of the target, after which "selected" and "tracking" appeared next to the boat's listing. "Target identified, target selected, on target and tracking, Captain."

"Very well. We can't have any overs in this environment, Williams," Haley warned. The odds against a stray shot reaching far enough to cause collateral damage or injury among the other boats in the area were enormous, but she was taking no chances.

"Yes, ma'am," Williams replied, as he selected another option on the screen. "I'm going to manual now. I'll pitch the first shot fifty yards short and walk them up into the hull."

"Good. Hold for now."

"Yes, ma'am."

Haley raised her binoculars and took a last intense scan of the target boat. She could see no movement whatsoever or anything bearing a resemblance to a human being. After lowering the binoculars, she turned back to the tactical screen. They were closing to five hundred yards range and Chief Hopkins had already given the helm order to bring them on a parallel course with the target. Two thousand one hundred yards to the tanker. Maybe a minute to decide. Keeping her eyes on the screen, she asked, "Chief Deffler, are you still reading no people on that boat?"

"Affirmative, Captain," Deffler replied. "I've still got nothing on visual or infrared."

"Any chance they are there, and we are just not seeing them?"

"There's a chance, ma'am, but they would have to be hiding using pretty sophisticated gear." He turned toward her. "I'll go on record that there's no one aboard."

Haley smiled grimly. "Thanks, Chief. Zuccaro, anything from the command center?"

"Just an acknowledgement of our last message, ma'am."

Figures. You're on your own, as usual. Stopping that boat will not be a problem. One command from me and the high explosive shells from the twenty-five-millimeter will start punching holes in the hull—just a few hits will slow her immediately and then sink her.

And probably kill anyone on board.

Haley watched the range to the tanker tick down with each passing second. *Everything we have says this is an unmanned bomb and the only correct action is to sink it before it hits that tanker. But what if we're wrong?* She paused a few more seconds, wishing the boat would just turn around. "Right. Zuccaro, log that I have determined this vessel is an unmanned improvised explosive device targeting the tanker *Paul Morris* and I am engaging with twenty-five-millimeter gunfire."

Zuccaro furiously typed on her keyboard and then said, "Log entry complete, Captain."

Haley swallowed hard, her heart pounding in her ears. "Very well. Williams, batteries release, commence fire!"

Chapter 2

Hot Pursuit

USCG Cutter Kauai, North Atlantic Ocean, nine nautical miles southeast of Port Canaveral, Florida
11:15 EDT, 12 June

Haley

Haley stared at the image of the recreational boat on the gunsight monitor. In the fraction of the second that had passed since she gave Williams the order to fire, time seemed to stand still. Nothing intruded on her consciousness other than the image of that boat, surrounded by motion and fire control data readouts, monotone gray but crystal clear, every detail of the hull, windows, even the deck fittings, burning into her memory.

"Firing," Williams announced, pressing the trigger button. The auto-cannon emitted a loud "bang" and the first shell exploded in the water about fifty yards short of the target. The second did the same at about half that distance. The third vanished, exploding in an empty area in the boat's bilges, and the fourth round was another hit that failed to explode.

Immediately after the fifth round penetrated the hull, the target boat vanished in a bright flash, briefly obscured by the white fog of an expanding shock wave. Haley reflexively gasped when the wave struck *Kauai* with a sharp, ear-splitting "boom" a second later that rattled everything on the bridge.

"Holy shit!" Ben muttered from his position at the console as Haley stared mutely at the camera display, watching the billowing brown and gray smoke cloud spreading slowly over the water amid the small splashes of falling fragments of the disintegrated boat. The initial shock of the explosion had faded, replaced by an almost intense relief that the decision to fire on the boat had proven to be correct.

"Target destroyed," Williams announced, snapping her out of her reverie.

"Cease fire," Haley said, then sat upright. "Alright everybody, give me a systems check. Williams?"

"Fire control and EO/IR, no damage, Captain."

"Zuccaro?"

"Radar and nav systems are normal, ma'am," Zuccaro replied with a shaking voice.

"Chief Deffler, how's the bird?"

"No damage, Captain. I have set it to orbit the debris field."

"Good. Keep it there for now." Haley turned to Hopkins. "Chief?"

"Just checked with Main Control," Hopkins replied as she hung up the telephone. "No powerplant damage and COB has Brown checking the hull for penetrations or shock damage."

Haley exhaled; her relief complete. *I'm half surprised we're normal after that blast.* "Zuccaro, send the following to the command center: have engaged an unmanned, non-compliant target with twenty-five-millimeter gunfire. Target destroyed by secondary explosion, estimate one-plus tons of ANFO. No injuries to Coast Guard or third-party personnel. No damage to Coast Guard or third-party property."

"Yes, ma'am," Zuccaro answered, then turned back to her screen.

"Chief Hopkins, continue on course for the tanker for now and take station five hundred yards southeast of her. We'll hold that until she gets to the jetties."

"Yes, Captain," Hopkins replied with a nod.

"Coast Guard, this is the *Paul Morris*. What's going on? Do we need to turn around?" a panicked voice came from the radio speaker on the console.

"I've got this," Haley said, then keyed her transmitter. "*Paul Morris, Cutter Kauai.* Negative, continue your approach. The only threat vessel is neutralized. Over."

"Roger. Thank you," the slightly calmer voice replied after a brief delay.

Probably thinks I'm bullshitting him, Haley thought. *Hopefully, he won't do anything stupid.* She switched to the Coast Guard private channel and keyed her radio transmitter again. "Four-Two-Three, Orchid Actual."

"Orchid, Four-Two-Three, roger, that was some show," the boat's coxswain replied. "Are you guys OK?"

Haley smiled, realizing for the first time what a shock the explosion must have been for their response boat teammates. "Affirmative, no dents or bruises. Did your guys find anything that looks like a control device? The boat was unmanned and we need to find who was driving it."

"Standby, ma'am," the petty officer replied. After half a minute, he came on again. "Negative on the controller. They're CARE people alright. They were laying all the enviro-whacko crap on us until that boat blew, then they got real quiet. But none of them were jiggling anything and we don't see anything that looks like a control station."

"Roger, that. Arrest them for conspiracy and seize the boat. Head in as soon as you can. We'll hang around out here and have a look for their buddies."

"Roger, Orchid. Good luck. Out."

Ben straightened up and stepped over to stand by Haley and asked in a quiet voice, "What now, skipper?"

Haley turned to look him in the eye. "We find the boat controlling that thing. We need to present a straightforward case if they want to roll up CARE for good. I suspect the people on the boat four-two-three bagged were just cannon fodder and probably told this was just another protest action. Otherwise, they would have put up more resistance in the stop and board."

"That other boat, the one that peeled off early, you think?" Ben asked.

"Could be." She turned to Williams. "Williams, let's put up the tactical playback. I want to see who was hanging around the bomb boat before they started their run."

"Yes, ma'am," the petty officer replied. "Coming up on screen two. I'm going to put a tracking marker on the contact."

"Excellent, carry on," Haley replied, gazing at the screen. The playback showed the tactical picture in reverse, with the attack boat's pip surrounded by a red circle. As she and Ben watched, the third boat, the one that broke off to the southeast early in the engagement, was clearly maneuvering in conjunction with the other two.

"That settles it," Ben said. "Where is that boat now, Williams?"

The petty officer made another selection and a second red circle appeared around the suspect boat. He then put the playback on fast forward and quickly brought the display up to the present moment. "There, sir. One-four-three and six-point-two miles, heading one-six-five at twenty-one knots. I'm about to lose him on radar."

Haley nodded. *Heading for The Bahamas. He must have figured we'd be searching any boats coming in for a CARE connection.* "Chief Deffler, put the bird on that contact. I want high-res visual and full hyperspectral as soon as you can get it."

"Understood, Captain. Heading out now," Deffler replied and made the needed inputs to the UAV controls.

Haley returned her gaze to the tactical display. The tanker was nearly over the line crossing between the jetties that marked the internal waters of the port. She saw from the speed readout that the tanker had increased speed to fifteen knots, undoubtedly because of her captain's alarm over the explosion. *Hope he doesn't run her aground in his panic—that would be worse than getting hit with the bomb.* She keyed her radio again. "Five-zero-six, Orchid Actual."

"This is Five-zero-six. Go ahead, Actual," the second response boat's coxswain replied.

"Are you up with the sheriff and port authority?"

"Affirmative. They're coming out now."

"Roger. Continue with the escort until mooring. We are breaking off in pursuit of a second suspect. Acknowledge."

"Orchid, Five-zero-six, copy all. Good luck, ma'am. Out."

Haley looked over to Hopkins and said, "Chief, we've got a stern chase through a gaggle of civilians. Can you handle it?"

Hopkins tilted her head and affected a mock injured expression. "Puh-lease, Captain. Williams, I'll take an intercept course as soon as you can work one up."

"On it, Chief," Williams said.

"Left twenty degrees rudder, steer one-four-five," she ordered.

"Chief, my rudder is left twenty. Steer one-four-five," Pickins replied.

As *Kauai* passed through due south on her turn to the southeast, Hopkins slowly pushed the thrust levers ahead to full speed. Haley smiled as the patrol boat kicked up onto the step, planing through the water at her maximum continuous speed of twenty-eight knots. With the lead the other boat had, it would take over an hour for *Kauai* to catch up to her, but they would still be far from any foreign sanctuary.

"What's the plan, skipper?" Ben asked.

Haley shrugged and said, "It's up to them, XO. Let's just say they 'disclosed intent' back there. Hopefully, they're not looking for a gunfight. But gunfight or not, they won't motor out of this one." After Ben looked down and shook his head, she added, "Is there something else?"

Ben turned to her with a sad smile. "No, Boss. I was just thinking that the paperwork on this one is going to be a world-class bitch!"

USCG Cutter Kauai, North Atlantic Ocean, thirty-two nautical miles southeast of Port

Canaveral, Florida
12:43 EDT, 12 June

Ben

Ben was taking advantage of the time spent in the pursuit to change from his combat gear to his law enforcement kit in his stateroom. He had a few minutes to spare before he needed to return to the bridge and spent them looking at the pictures of Victoria mounted on the wall above his small desk. She was the love of his life and, for the last three weeks, his wife, a fact to which he was still getting accustomed. They had met eighteen months previously during the mission to recover the Russian warhead. Ben had come ashore to serve as liaison, while *Kauai* remained offshore in support.

Victoria was the protégé of Ben's DIA teammate, Peter Simmons, who warned him before their meeting that Victoria was mildly autistic and that he should expect some unusual behavior. Expecting to meet some geeky neurotic, Ben was surprised to find a beautiful, extraordinarily charming young woman who made him feel like the most exceptional person in the world during their first conversation. The interest was mutual, and although separated by their duties, Ben's in South Florida with *Kauai* and Victoria's in Washington, DC with the DIA, they shared the details of their lives on the phone each night when Ben was not out on patrol.

She had a surprisingly deep voice for someone so petite and her elocution was precise, even in casual conversations. Victoria never used contractions or diminutives; even at the most intimate times, he was "Benjamin" to her. They were aspects of her neurodiverse condition, but he loved listening to her talk and would never wish her to change.

With each passing day, these conversations became more precious to Ben, and he chafed at the operational pace that kept them apart. After three months of this quirky pre-courtship, they moved in together, and a little over a year later, they were man and wife and heading to Yellowstone for a week's honeymoon.

Reluctantly tearing himself away from the pictures and memories, Ben was now back on the bridge, awaiting the moment to start the engagement with the fleeing suspect boat. He was watching the boat on the two screens of the FC3, the left showing real-time video from the UAV and the right displaying the view from the powerful electro-optical camera on *Kauai*'s mast. The UAV had quickly caught up to the suspect boat, and Deffler had it tracing lazy S-curves to keep it five hundred feet overhead while *Kauai* closed the distance between them. They had pretty detailed information on the boat by this time, a forty-two-foot recreational boat, white with blue trim, named *Pelican's Pride*, cruising steadily southeastward at twenty-one knots, leaving a creamy white trail in the deep blue water of the Atlantic off *Kauai*'s port bow.

He could make out three people on the boat right now. One was female, lounging on the afterdeck in a brief bikini and sunglasses. He could not get a read on the other two, who were simply shadowy figures inside the boat's enclosed cockpit. The *Pelican's Pride* looked like a thousand other innocent boats Ben had seen over the years. *Just out for a cruise, nothing to see here, officer.*

The *Pelican's Pride* was owned by a company in Fort Pierce and was one day into a four-day rental to one Bridget Morehouse of Concord, Massachusetts. Initial checks of her background yielded no red flags—a twenty-year-old undergraduate art major at Wellesley College with no criminal history. She was not on any watch list or other law enforcement database. According to the owners, Morehouse had declined to employ one of their usual captains and instead provided her own licensed master, Terrell Pollack, who, while having no convictions, had been held on suspicion of smuggling and other minor charges. The curious combination of a presumably wealthy young undergrad with a thirty-two-year-old ne'er-do-well boat skipper was not lost on Ben and added to the suspicion that they had the correct target.

Their pursuit had taken them far away from the scene of the attack on the tanker, and from the radio traffic they were hearing, absolute pandemonium was breaking out. The powerful explosion was easily heard on the crowded beaches and that, along with the swift lockdown of the port, would soon draw swarms of media looking for a story on an otherwise quiet June day. Although stopping and boarding a boat suspected of involvement in a terrorist act would be hard, dangerous work, Ben was glad to be out here rather than fending off newspeople at the dockside. Like most military officers, Ben disliked reporters in general, but he had a particular loathing for the TV and internet "journalists" who would crawl over every pier asking the most inane and confrontational questions imaginable.

Ben glanced at the tactical display. Four hundred fifty yards to the *Pelican's Pride*, a little under a quarter-mile. Haley, Hopkins, and Ben had discussed the situation and decided that the risk of armed conflict with the *Pelican's Pride* was low—there were no guns visible on the boat and the UAV's hyperspectral imaging camera had detected no chemical signatures of explosives. So, they would close to one hundred yards and assume a parallel course and pacing speed and attempt to persuade them to stop. They did not expect any armed resistance or aggressive maneuvering, although *Kauai* was prepared in case that came to pass.

Haley had briefed their bosses in the Operations Center at the Seventh Coast Guard District Office in Miami on secure chat and they were also getting a real-time video feed from both *Kauai* and the UAV. They concurred with her decision to pursue and stop the *Pelican's Pride*, authorizing the use of non-lethal force if needed. Going beyond that to warning shots or direct gunfire would require a separate, specific authorization. Ben had no problem with that decision. The adrenaline from the terrorist attack had worn off and, as far as he or anyone else knew, there was no proof yet that anyone on the *Pelican's Pride* was involved.

Assuming these were the people controlling the attack boat, Ben reckoned they knew there was no point in trying to shoot it out with the Coast Guard and were opting to run out the clock before *Kauai* worked through all the levels of permissions required to use disabling gunfire. If they could reach West End, the closest point in The Bahamas and about four-and-a-half hours away at this speed, they would be home free. Their best option would be to hold a steady course and not do anything that would provoke a lethal response. Ben smiled. *No doubt Miss Morehouse's presence in a highly revealing swimsuit is intended as a further inducement for a boatload of Coasties to hold off on shooting.*

It would have been an excellent strategy in dealing with another Coast Guard patrol boat, but not with *Kauai*. They were quite correct that the Coast Guard would be reluctant to employ lethal fire without provocation, even in the wake of a terrorist attack. What they did not know was that *Kauai* had a non-lethal ace in the hole. Ben glanced down to the foredeck to a device mounted just forward of the main gun. It was still a prototype system, with the official title Non-lethal Arresting System Projector, but it was colloquially known aboard *Kauai* by its nickname: "the Squid."

The Squid was essentially a three-barreled recoilless cannon mounted on a pivoting and elevating cradle that fired a pattern of three Kevlar nets into the path of a fleeing suspect boat. The boat could not avoid all three and any one of them would foul the propellers and bring the boat to a halt with no lethal gunfire. It was a very useful addition to *Kauai*'s bag of tricks and had been used successfully several times, but it also had limitations. Its range was only two hundred meters, and the relative motion between *Kauai* and the target had to be stable—an erratically moving target could defeat the system.

So far, the *Pelican's Pride* had held a steady course and speed. Ben supposed her operators knew they could not lose the patrol boat by maneuvering alone and that any maneuvers slowed their progress toward the imagined safety of The Bahamas. Ben hoped the current situation would continue. He glanced again at the image showing the young woman lounging in the back of the boat and tried to suppress his dread of where this day could lead. Before coming to the bridge, he had taken the time to brief his boarding team and the boat coxswain. It would be a complex operation on the *Pelican's Pride*, because of the risk of dealing with people who may have just tried to blow up a tanker. He smiled to himself in confidence—his people could handle this, and far worse.

His assistant on this operation would be Boatswain's Mate First Class John Bondurant. Six-foot-three and 240 pounds, with a muscular frame that reminded Ben of an NFL tight end, he was the first choice on any risky boarding, where his size would give most hotheads pause. He was a surprisingly quiet and thoughtful man, a thirty-five-year-old devoted father of two high school-aged boys. His intelligence and outstanding performance aboard *Kauai* had earned him a spot in Officer Candidate School, and he would leave in two months, much to the regret of Haley, Ben, and his other shipmates.

Because of the presence of a female on board the *Pelican's Pride*, Ben had included Boatswain's Mate Second Class Shelley Lee as the second member of his boarding party. Lee was short for a boatswain's mate at five-foot-three, but she was very athletic and, like Ben and Bondurant, highly trained in personal combat. She was *Kauai*'s premier coxswain and lived to drive the cutter's Rigid Hull Inflatable Boat, known as "the rib" for its acronym RHIB. She was the most heroic individual Ben had ever known, most recently volunteering for a death-defying drive of the RHIB during a hurricane to save a young family from a disabled sailboat. At twenty-five, they were close in age and shared interests, temperament, and deep personal respect.

Law Enforcement Specialist Third Class James "Jimmy" Chen was the last member of the boarding party. He was a young twenty years of age, about Ben's height and size, and the newest member of the crew. He had come aboard three months ago, in the unenviable position of replacing the crewman killed in the Haiti operation, and had impressed everyone since with his dedication, competence, and sense of humor. His predecessor Juan Lopez still had their hearts, but Chen had won their confidence.

"Four hundred yards to target, Captain," Williams announced, snapping Ben from his thoughts. Williams had switched his panel to fire control mode, providing updated information to both the main twenty-five-millimeter gun on *Kauai*'s foredeck and the Squid system. Neither was targeting the *Pelican's Pride* at present, but could, within seconds of an order from Haley.

"Thank you," Haley replied. "Chief Hopkins, assume parallel course and speed at one hundred yards."

"Aye, aye, ma'am." Hopkins kept her eyes on the fleeing boat with binoculars during the approach. The risk of an accidental collision was low at this distance, although it increased exponentially as they closed with the target. That risk could change in seconds should the *Pelican's Pride* suddenly turn to the right. As OOD, Hopkins's first responsibility in this situation was safety, and she knew even a few seconds could make a difference. "Williams, when we get within two hundred, I want a callout every twenty-five yards with the *Pelican's Pride* course and speed."

"Yes, Chief," Williams replied.

Ben turned to Haley and said quietly, "Captain, we'll be in position in less than two minutes. Recommend I initiate contact."

"Agreed. Proceed, XO."

"Yes, ma'am." He stepped over to the communications panel above Zucarro's display and plugged in his headset. After checking that VHF-FM Channel 16 was selected as "active," he pressed his transmit switch and said, "Motor Vessel *Pelican's Pride*, this is the United States Coast Guard on Channel 16, over." After standing by for about ten seconds, he repeated the call. "Motor Vessel *Pelican's Pride*, this is the United States Coast Guard. Please respond on Channel 16, over."

The silence continued for a few seconds, then was broken by Williams. "Two hundred yards, Chief. Target course one-six-four, speed twenty point eight."

"Very, well," Hopkins replied.

In the next thirty seconds, Ben made two more attempts at radio contact without success while Williams ticked off the closure to the *Pelican's Pride*. Finally, he announced, "One hundred yards, Chief. Target is still at one-six-four and twenty point eight."

"Very well. Cease reports," Hopkins replied as she retarded the thrust levers to bring *Kauai* to a matching speed. "Paralleling target at one hundred yards, Captain."

"Very well," Haley replied. "Lights and siren, XO."

"Yes, ma'am," Ben responded. He flipped the switch activating the flashing blue light on *Kauai*'s mast, then selected "Loudhailer" on the communication panel and pressed the "siren" button. After twenty seconds of a shockingly loud police "howler" sound, the system returned control to Ben, and he pressed his transmit switch. "Motor Vessel *Pelican's Pride*, this is the United States Coast Guard. You are ordered to stop your vessel immediately." After five seconds, with no response from the fleeing vessel, Ben repeated the order with the same effect.

"No response, Captain," Ben said finally.

"Very well. Williams, surface action port. Target Squid on the motor vessel *Pelican's Pride* and standby."

"Aye, aye, Captain," Williams replied, pressing a few buttons on his console to activate the squid system. Electronic data from the radar, the laser rangefinder on *Kauai*'s electro-optical camera, GPS, and environmental sensors all started feeding directly into the Squid's targeting system. The artificial intelligence resident in the system immediately generated and began updating a firing solution for optimal placement of the nets.

"Give them a last warning, XO," Haley said with a nod.

"Yes, ma'am," Ben replied, then pressed his transmit switch. "Motor Vessel *Pelican's Pride*, this is the United States Coast Guard. This is your final warning. Stop your vessel immediately or we will use force to stop you. Repeat, stop immediately or we will use force." As Ben watched on the monitor, the woman lounging on the stern suddenly jumped up and stepped quickly into the cockpit. *OK, maybe we can do this the easy way,* he thought hopefully. His hopes were dashed less than ten seconds later when the woman returned hesitatingly to her post on the afterdeck and resumed sitting. *Crap!* He shook his head and turned to Haley. "No joy, Captain."

Haley nodded and in a firm voice said, "Zucarro, log 'Motor Vessel *Pelican's Pride* has ignored radio, visual, and audio signals to halt and is continuing on course one-six-four degrees true, speed of advance twenty point eight knots in position,' add our GPS position. 'Employing NASP system to stop the vessel.'"

After a few seconds of furious typing, Zucarro said, "Log entry complete, Captain."

"Very well. Williams, Squid status, please."

"On target and tracking, targeting solution achieved, Captain."

"Match generated bearings and shoot!"

Chapter 3

Accessory

M/V Pelican's Pride, North Atlantic Ocean, thirty-two nautical miles southeast of Port Canaveral, Florida
12:52 EDT, 12 June

Bridget

For the first time in her life, Bridget was genuinely afraid. This was not the glorious act of civil disobedience she had expected—public, delightfully confrontational with the promise of wine and recreational drugs at the end of the day and a viral media presence the next day and beyond. They were running away, running for their lives, with an American Coast Guard boat hot on their heels and growing closer by the minute.

Bridget glanced at the approaching boat again, then looked down at the ridiculous crimson bikini Terrell had insisted she wear and flaunt during the trip. He said the view would make any law enforcement skeptical of their involvement in the operation or, at least, resistant to take any positive action. The approaching white boat with the red racing stripe was concrete proof that the plan was a failure, and it wasn't just that. The idea that a pack of horny sailors was gawking at her right now through binoculars or cameras on the drone they had parked overhead made her skin crawl. Her mind raced through a litany of indignities that would surely follow if she were arrested.

******

Bridget Morehouse was the eldest daughter of one of the richest hedge fund managers in Boston. Average height with brown hair and eyes, she was an attractive young woman halfway through her twenty-first year. Her family came from old money, although her father had struck out on his own at an early age and the fortune he enjoyed with his young family was self-made. Bridget did not inherit her father's drive for self-reliance—just wandered through prep school with no desire for achievement. She had a brief flirtation with hard drugs, stamped out by a trip to rehab and her father making it credibly known throughout the drug community that dealing to any of his children would be the last mistake any of them would ever make.

Her mediocre grades would probably have kept her out of any other high-end college, but she was destined for Wellesley, her mother's alma mater, almost from the day she was born. Her father paved over any concerns of academic deficiency via a substantial donation toward a new wing in the art school building. Bridget was made aware of her parents' expectations with crystal clarity—stay clean and graduate with the promise of a comfortable life or fail at either and be cut off. She was resentful of her parents' perceived heavy-handedness, but she was no fool and trudged off to Wellesley to make the best of it.

By the end of Bridget's first year, she had mastered the routine of classes, social climbing, and partying and was utterly, insufferably bored, resolving to get involved with one of the many causes suffusing the campus when she returned from summer break. She was not a dedicated revolutionary, in fact, she barely qualified as a dilettante. The problem was she had no interest in any of the social causes—she could barely conceal her contempt for most of *those* people and could never fit in at the meetings or events. On the other hand, CARE provided the niche she was looking for: showy and "in your face" activism literally intended to save the planet.

Bridget had fallen in with them eight months previously, shortly after the beginning of her sophomore year. She had been furious when the movement apparently folded before she even had a chance to engage in a single protest and made her frustration known to her organizational contacts. They assured her that CARE was not dead, just lying low while building for a major upcoming action and she could be a big part if she quietly stood by and waited for direction.

Excited to be a part of an underground activist organization, Bridget did her best to fade into the background on campus. She kept her nose to the grindstone in classes and intermural sports, feigning envy for her classmates' advocacy for XYZ+ rights, anti-[fill in the blank] privilege, and whatever, while studying the CARE propaganda in secret. The concomitant jump in her grades delighted her parents. Her father, whom she had wrapped around her little finger by this time, rewarded her with her own American Express Black Card as a Christmas gift. It took all her willpower not to spend like mad with a card having no credit limit, but it was important to keep herself and her resources ready for the call.

That call came shortly after the spring semester. She was to fly down to West Palm Beach, Florida, and meet up with a man at one of the high-end hotels. When she asked what she would do, the voice told her to expect to rent a boat to take part in the biggest protest event ever. Bridget was giddy as she packed her bags and then headed to Boston's Logan Airport for the flight down to Palm Beach International.

Shortly after Bridget checked into the luxurious hotel in West Palm Beach, there was a knock on her door, which proved to be her contact, Terrell Pollack. She was not impressed—he was much older than she was, deeply tanned and tattooed, with unkempt, shoulder-length dark hair and a scruffy beard. However, her initial revulsion faded as he enthusiastically shared the plan for her to rent the boat to take part in a mass civil disobedience event. "What will it be?" she asked excitedly.

"We are going to stop a large oil tanker from entering port. The coverage will be awesome!"

"When?" she asked breathlessly.

"Tomorrow morning. We will pick up the boat at a marina in Fort Pierce," Terrell answered. "It will just be a couple of hours up the coast from there."

"Don't I need to call for a reservation or something?" Bridget asked.

"Naw. They have plenty of boats available on a weekday. It will be no problem as long as you have plenty of money to put down. You *did* bring your black card, right?"

"Yeah! I could buy a boat if I wanted to!"

Terrell smiled. "No need for that. You wouldn't be able to do it in time to help, what with titling, licenses, yadda, yadda. A rental is perfect."

"OK," Bridget said. "What are we going to do in the meantime?"

"Well, I have a lot of business to attend to, so I'm outta here. You need to hang around, relax, and order a buttload of room service." He winked at her. "I'll pick you up at six-thirty tomorrow morning."

"Six-thirty?" Bridget said, wrinkling her nose and trying her best to conceal her relief that Terrell would not be staying in her room that night. She had very little interest in sex right now, particularly with someone so old and...*common*.

"Yes, we are slaves to the tanker's schedule, and it gets in at noon." His smile disappeared, and he gazed meaningfully at her. "One more thing. It's really important that you not tell anybody what's going on until we are done tomorrow. No family, friends, nobody! If the feds get on to us, they'll shut everything down and all of this will be for nothing. Understand?"

"Sure." Bridget nodded furiously. She had been hoping to tip off some of her classmates to monitor the news feeds so they could watch in real-time, but the need for security thrilled her even more.

Terrell arrived promptly at six-thirty the following morning and they drove an hour north to the marina in Fort Pierce to pick up the boat. At Terrell's suggestion, he did the haggling while she sat back, looking disinterested. Terrell had a master's license, so they could get the boat just for themselves, albeit with a substantial deposit and an extra fee for not using one of the company's preferred captains. An hour after they arrived, they were speeding northward aboard the lovely white and blue recreational boat *Pelican's Pride*, a couple of miles off the beach.

At Terrell's suggestion, she was wearing a brief bikini underneath an oversized orange tee-shirt with the CARE logo printed on the back and "I CARE!" printed in yellow on the front. If they encountered any law enforcement, Bridget was expected to take off the shirt to distract the presumably male cops—a suggestion she found thoroughly disgusting, but reluctantly agreed to do. At least the weather was perfect, a wonderful sunny day, with the breeze from their speed keeping the temperature very comfortable. Bridget was relieved to see the seas were very light. She had only been boating once before, in Nantucket Sound during a family vacation at Martha's Vineyard, and had been deathly seasick. This was much more pleasant, with the boat gently rocking and pitching in the deep blue Atlantic Ocean and the occasional small wave breaking into beautiful rainbows of spray over the bow. After a short time, Bridget became bored with the unchanging seascape and retreated to her iPhone to watch TikTok videos.

A little over two hours later, they slowed down, and Bridget stood from her seat on the afterdeck and stepped over next to Terrell at the helm. "Will we go straight to the tanker?" she asked.

Terrell shook his head. "No, we need to meet up with a couple of other boats first, then we all go up together." He pointed forward. "There they are now."

Bridget looked where he was pointing and saw two more recreational boats, both stopped. They looked like the *Pelican's Pride*, only a little smaller. She could see three people waving at them from one boat. They were pulling up to the other, on which she could only see one person in the cockpit. As they moved alongside with a bump and a squeak from the bumpers hanging over the side, this person stepped aboard the *Pelican's Pride*, carrying a computer bag and what looked like a long pole attached to a spherical base. It was a man, younger looking than Terrell, but still older than Bridget, with short blonde hair and wire-rimmed glasses. He was dressed in a tee-shirt and shorts, like Terrell, but wore a camouflaged base-ball cap.

The visitor gave Bridget a brief, completely indifferent glance, then turned to the cockpit, exchanged nods with Terrell, set down the computer case, and began attaching the pole to the cockpit overhead, using a clamp at its bottom. When he finished, the pole stood erect about four feet over the top of the boat's cockpit. He then pulled a laptop computer out of the bag, plugged a wire dangling from the pole into a USB port, and began typing.

Bridget stepped beside him and said, "I'm Bridget."

The man continued typing without looking up and said, "Good for you."

Bridget turned to Terrell and got a shrug in return. Then she tried again. "It's usually polite to introduce yourself."

"Not where I'm from," the man replied, still gazing at the screen and typing. After a few seconds, he said. "OK, we're ready. Head north-northwest at fifteen."

Terrell turned to Bridget. "Better take a seat." After she resumed her seat above the transom, Terrell pushed the throttle forward and the *Pelican's Pride* resumed her northerly course.

"Are we just going to leave the other boat here?" Bridget asked.

"No," the nameless man replied, then typed briefly on the keyboard.

As Bridget turned to look at the empty boat, it started moving and turning toward them. Within a minute, it was keeping pace with them on their left side. "It's a drone!"

The nameless man turned to her with a contemptuous expression and then glanced at Terrell. "Do we really need her?"

"Yes," Terrell replied. He turned to smile at her and said, "She's our camouflage."

"Fine," the man replied, then turned to Bridget. "It isn't a *drone*. It's a remotely piloted vessel."

"And you're driving it?"

"No, I'm *piloting* it. When I'm not distracted by damn fool questions."

"Screw you! Remember, I'm paying for this boat!"

He turned toward her and said, "You mean your *daddy* is paying for this boat. You're an art major. The only way you could earn any money would be to take your top off on OnlyFans!" He slowly scanned her from head to foot. "And I think you'd be lucky to earn enough on there to rent a rowboat. Now, are you going to go back where you belong, or do I need to slap you?" he asked with an icy look.

Bridget felt her face flush with raw anger, but she stepped back. "What's going on here, Terrell? I thought we were going to block that ship."

"Honey, we couldn't slow that tanker down with twenty *Pelican's Pride*s—they'd run us down without getting any more than a little scratched paint. That RPV is going to give them something to think about."

"You're going to crash it into the ship? Is it filled with paint?"

Terrell and the man exchanged glances, and the man snorted. "Yeah, *tons* of paint."

Bridget turned to look at the automatic boat again and noticed that the other boat, the one with three people on it, was also cruising northward. They cruised together for a short time, and then the nameless man pulled out a cell-phone and spoke into it. "They're coming. Buy us some time."

Bridget looked over at the other boats again. The one with the people suddenly picked up speed and raced ahead of them, turning a little toward the shore. She then caught sight of another boat, a small gray one travel-ing at high speed toward their speeding companion, its blue light flashing. "It's the police! They're after the other boat!"

Neither of the two men acknowledged her, just con-tinued looking forward. Finally, Terrell pointed forward. "Here comes the other one!"

The nameless man nodded and said, "OK, we're close enough. Haul ass!"

"I hear ya!" Terrell turned the wheel and *Pelican's Pride* swung into a right turn. They were going roughly in the opposite direction when he straightened out and pushed the throttle all the way forward.

"Where are we going?" Bridget shouted over the engine. "Aren't we going to stay for the show?!"

Terrell turned to face her. "We can't hang around, honey! Things are going to get mighty hot around here in a few minutes!"

"So, we're heading back to Fort Pierce?"

"No, The Bahamas!"

"The Bahamas? What are we going to do there?!"

"Hang around a few days until things chill out, then head back!"

"Oh!" she said, looking back at the boats receding in the distance.

"And now's the time to take that shirt off. We need to look real innocent from here on out!"

Bridget's mouth clamped shut, and she stepped back to the afterdeck. She was furious about having to go half-naked after that dweeb called her an OnlyFans whore. After a brief hesitation, she pulled off the shirt, folded and set it carefully beside her chair, and then stretched out on the flat area above the engine compartment. She knew little about The Bahamas, although she heard it discussed in school as the poor man's Bermuda. *Great, they probably don't even have decent hotels!*

Bridget had been ruminating for a few minutes over the likely absence of quality accommodations at their destination when the nameless man suddenly shouted, "Shit!" and slammed his fist on the keyboard. She puzzled over this for about half a minute when a loud "thud" from behind them drew her attention and she could see a cloud of smoke in the distance. She turned back to see the nameless man unscrewing the pole from the overhead. As soon as it was loose, he tossed it overboard, followed by the laptop computer. He turned to her with a furious look and shouted, "If you want to live through this, keep your mouth shut!" He then turned and disappeared into the cabin. Terrell did not even turn to look at her.

Bridget turned for another look at the smoke cloud rising in the distance. *This is not how it was supposed to be!*

******

The Coast Guard boat had stopped approaching and was now pacing them, behind and slightly to their right, a few hundred feet away. The sound of a police siren made her jump, but she maintained her provocative sunbathing pose, despite the growing fear. After a short time, the siren stopped and a few seconds later, a voice boomed over the water, "Motor Vessel *Pelican's Pride*, this is the United States Coast Guard. You are ordered to stop your vessel immediately." After five seconds, the voice repeated the announcement.

"Terrell!" Bridget cried out.

"Sit tight! They won't do anything as long as we don't do anything stupid!" Terrell replied.

Bridget remained prone, trying not to stare at the white boat. After a minute passed with no change, she was calming down when the voice boomed out, "Motor Vessel *Pelican's Pride*, this is the United States Coast Guard. This is your final warning. Stop your vessel immediately or we will use force to stop you. Repeat, stop immediately or we will use force."

Bridget jumped up and trotted forward to Terrell. Her voice quavered in terror as she said, "They're going to shoot at us!"

Terrell turned on her in wide-eyed fury. "I told you they can't shoot at us unless we shoot at them! They're just trying to scare us! Now, get your ass back down!"

Bridget turned and walked stiffly back through the cockpit and laid back down. She was about to turn to look at the Coast Guard boat again when three loud bangs sounded in quick succession. She screamed, threw herself face-first on the deck, and covered her head with her arms. *They're shooting their cannon at us! They're going to kill us!*

After a couple of seconds, she peeked up and saw Terrell looking behind them in astonishment. She sat up and turned her head to follow his gaze. The Coast Guard boat had turned away and was dropping behind. *What the hell?* A series of soft pops sounded ahead of them, and she turned just in time to see something fall into the water. There was a thump, and the deck jumped slightly, followed immediately by a staccato of thuds and a grinding of metal as the engine suddenly stopped.

The *Pelican's Pride* slowed to a stop and the nameless man suddenly appeared from the cabin. "What the hell happened?!"

Terrell hung his head. "They shot some kind of net ahead of us and fouled the prop."

"Well? What are you doing? Get down there and fix it!"

"Are you high, man? That's it, game over!"

The man turned toward Bridget and said menacingly, "Then we'd better shut her up."

As Bridget cowered in terror, Terrell stepped between them. "You try laying a finger on her and I'll kill you. Besides..." He pointed up at the drone flying overhead. "What's the point of committing a murder on camera?"

The man looked up and his hands fell to his sides when he saw the small aircraft. He turned slowly and ducked back into the cabin. After he was out of sight, Terrell turned and walked over to her. "You might as well put that shirt back on." He looked past her toward the Coast Guard boat. "Stick to the story and you'll be OK."

Bridget slipped into the tee, then turned to look. The Coast Guard boat had circled around and was now coming slowly toward them. At that ominous sight, the relief of being saved from the nameless man was displaced by an icy feeling of dread that spread outward from her stomach and consumed her every thought.

It was not going to be *"OK."*

******

Bridget was still processing the anxiety she had been feeling since the Coast Guard boat had appeared. She was now manacled to a steel bunk bed in the corner of a tiny room on that Coast Guard boat, wearing this hideous dark blue coverall, and staring across the room at the short black woman left to watch over her. The woman had been one of three Coast Guard people who came aboard and had been the one who searched and handcuffed her. Being pawed over and manhandled into and out of the small boat they used to transport them to the Coast Guard boat was degrading. It was nothing like the glorious stories of civil disobedience she had devoured during her prep school and freshman days at Wellesley.

The woman had been wearing a helmet and bullet-proof vest during the boarding and had threatened Bridget after she started reciting her CARE catechism. She would never forget the woman's fierce expression as she leaned in and said, "For your safety and ours, we need it quiet during the transfer. After you get over to the cutter, you can talk your head off. But if you open your yap before then, I'll tase your ass. Understand?" Bridget was furious about being talked down to like this by someone who could be serving her latte at the Emporium on campus but had the good sense to nod and keep her mouth shut.

The woman, whose nametag on her dark blue utilities read "Lee" had shed the helmet and vest but was still wearing her gun belt and she stared at Bridget with folded arms and an indifferent expression. Bridget decided it couldn't hurt to try to reach her now that they were alone. "Can I ask your name?"

"Sure," the woman replied. "My name is Lee."

"You have a first name, don't you?"

Her right eyebrow raised. "Two, actually: Petty...Officer."

"OK, Petty...Officer Lee, what is going to happen here?"

"As soon as Lieutenant Wyporek is finished with your shipmates, he'll be in to read you your rights and interview you."

"Interview? You mean 'interrogate', don't you?"

Lee shrugged. "Whatever."

There was a brief knock and a young man entered the room carrying a clipboard in one hand and a steel chair in the other. After he sat, Bridget realized it was the young officer who had led the team boarding the *Pelican's Pride* after it had been stopped. It was a shame really that he had become a fascist for the government, as without his helmet he was kind of cute with his slim, tanned face, curly dark blonde hair, and those lovely blue eyes.

"Miss Morehouse, I am Lieutenant Wyporek. I have placed you under arrest on suspicion of violating Title 18, United States Code, Section 2291, Destruction of a Vessel or Maritime Facility. I am going to explain your rights again, then I'll ask you some questions. Do you understand?" After she nodded, the officer continued, reading her the same explanation of rights she had heard countless times on TV shows. On finishing, he looked up at her and said, "Having the rights I explained to you in mind, would you wish to talk to me about this charge?" he asked.

"What are you talking about? I didn't destroy any vessel or...or...What was the other thing?"

"Maritime facility. Miss Morehouse, your vessel, the *Pelican's Pride*, rented in your name, was operating with two other vessels, one of which turned out to be a remotely piloted bomb aimed at the tanker *Paul Morris*. Fortunately, we were able to detonate that bomb before it could crash into the tanker, or you would also have been looking at a murder charge on top of the charge of blowing up that boat."

"I don't believe you. I never saw any bomb. I think you blew that boat up yourselves!" she shouted defiantly.

The officer leaned forward with an intent expression. "Our gunfire might have set it off, but rest assured, that vessel was carrying a large quantity of explosives intended for a terrorist act. What did you think you would accomplish with this bit of mayhem?"

"I am not admitting to any 'mayhem.' What do you think you're accomplishing by propping up the oil companies and their corrupt cronies in the government? How many people have to starve to death, coastal villages be inundated by sea level rise, species be rendered extinct before you and your...your fellow nazis see the light?" she asked with a defiant glare.

The officer sat back and said calmly, "I take it you do not wish to discuss the charge against you—am I correct?"

"Yes. I have nothing to say about any bullshit charge. Particularly to some petty bureaucrat who couldn't even get a real job!"

"Right," he said with a smile as he stood and picked up the chair. "If you change your mind, let Petty Officer Lee know and she can have someone fetch me." He turned and stepped toward the door, closing it behind him.

The staredown with Lee resumed and continued in silence for what seemed like hours but was probably only fifteen or twenty minutes. Then there was another brief knock and this time a woman entered, exchanged nods with Lee, and then sat down in a chair she brought with her. The woman was tallish, maybe five-nine with an athletic build, wearing just the dark blue tee-shirt, pants, and boots, without the shirt with nametag and insignia Lee and the officer wore. She was older, Bridget estimated her to be around thirty, with gray eyes and dark hair hanging down to her shoulders, unlike the tight bun in which Lee had her hair. The woman looked at Bridget with a warm smile and said, "Hi. I'm Haley. Can I call you Bridget, or do you prefer Miss Morehouse?"

"Bridget will be fine," she answered.

"Oh, good! Thank you! I'm here to make sure you are OK and see if you need anything. I'm sorry about those restraints, by the way. It's regulations," she said, rolling her eyes at the last word. "Oh, yeah, speaking of that, before we can talk, I have to remind you of your rights." She started searching the many pockets in her pants with a perplexed look. "Now, where did I put that Miranda card? I know I had it this morning!"

At last! Someone who is not a raving fascist! "That's OK, I remember my rights," Bridget said, smiling at the other woman's confusion.

"Oh, good, good, good!" She nodded vigorously, her smile even wider than before. "Thank you for your understanding. I was worried about you because those two men you were with looked pretty rough. I told Ben...he's the officer who was in here before. Anyway, I told Ben that those two might be holding you captive and that you might be afraid to talk. He said I was crazy, and I shouldn't waste my time over some snotty tree hugger."

"Girl, wherever you find them, men are pigs," Bridget said with disgust.

"I *know!*" Haley said, her eyes widening at the last word. "You're from Boston, I hear. I'm from Newport myself."

"Really?" Bridget asked. *One of us. Better and better!* She glanced at Lee and then back. "Maybe we can talk in private?"

Haley winked and nodded, then turned. "Petty Officer Lee, would you excuse us, please?"

Lee looked down at Haley with surprise. "Um, I don't know, ma'am."

"I do. You're dismissed, petty officer!"

"Yes, ma'am," Lee said, giving Bridget one last glare before leaving the room.

"OK, just us now," Haley said after the door closed.

"How did you get involved with these...*people*?" Bridget asked with a scowl.

"Oh, my dad and his trophy wife were hard over on my marrying some other inbred rich fool in Newport after college so they could keep their thumb on me. I decided this was the best way to spite them, so I signed up as soon as I graduated. My stepmom's meltdown was absolutely *epic!*" She shook her head with a chuckle.

"Oh, that is awesome! But it must be hard to deal with all this BS, every day."

"Yeah, but it's fun when I get a twist on them." Her smile faded and her face took on a serious look. "So, back to you. Did those guys have you as a hostage on this thing?"

"No, nothing like that. I think the guy with the glasses wanted to hurt or kill me at the end, but Terrell stood up to him and backed him down."

"Really?" Haley said, leaning forward in interest. "Why would the other man, not Terrell, want to do that?"

"I think he was afraid I would talk about the laptop and pole. I guess it was some sort of antenna."

"Wow! Do you think it had something to do with the boat that blew up?"

"I'm pretty sure. He was so hostile, I didn't get close enough to see the screen. But after he set it up, the boat started driving on its own."

"That is *so cool*!" Haley nodded appreciatively. "Did he hide it somewhere on the boat? I heard Ben saying that they couldn't find anything like that."

"No, he tossed it overboard after the boat blew."

"Oh well, that explains it. That was a hell of a bang, by the way. I nearly wet my pants when it happened. It must have been one massive bomb on that thing."

"Haley, I didn't know about any bomb. I thought we were going to block the ship from coming in. Then Terrell and the other man said it was too big, and we were going to run the boat into it to splash paint on it."

"So you had nothing to do with the other boat?"

"No way! What do I know about bombs? I just rented the *Pelican's Pride!*"

Haley nodded and sat back. "I see."

"So, you can see I had nothing to do with whatever happened. You can tell the captain, right? Explain I had nothing to do with this?"

Haley stood, her face suddenly cold. "No need. I *am* the captain."

Bridget felt like she was about to faint. "What? You're with *them*? You *bitch!*"

"If by *them*, you mean decent, brave people trying to keep the world safe from the likes of *you*, then absolutely, I'm with them." She picked up the chair and stepped toward the door, then stopped and turned back. "You accused Ben of conspiring in the extinction of species. Speaking of endangered species, have you heard of the North Atlantic Right Whale?"

Bridget was taken off guard. "No. What about it?"

"It is about as critically endangered as it gets. Estimates are there are only about three hundred and fifty left in the entire world. Since you didn't know of them, I imagine you also didn't know their calving grounds run from just north of here through the Georgia coast. Do know what would have happened if your plot had succeeded? That tanker would have been ripped open and sunk with forty thousand tons of gasoline and diesel fuel we could not hope to contain. It would have been carried along the shore by the Gulf Stream and wiped out the coastal biosphere from here to North Carolina. We've been working hard to protect those whales and everything else around here for decades—you and your buddies could have killed them all off in *one day*! You think about that, you stupid, spoiled child!"

Bridget's stomach flipped, and her eyes filled with tears as Haley opened the door and said, "We're done." She stood aside as Lee came back in and resumed her post. "I'll get someone down to relieve you for chow."

"Thank you, ma'am," Lee responded with a nod. After the door closed, Lee folded her arms again and gave Bridget a smile that chilled her to her bones. "Long time, no see, *girlfriend*."

Chapter 4

New Mission

***USCG Cutter Kauai, North Atlantic Ocean,
thirty-eight nautical miles south-southeast
of Port Canaveral, Florida
16:43 EDT, 12 June***

Haley

Haley was just finishing putting up her hair when there was a knock at the door. "Come in!"

Ben stepped inside and beamed. "That was masterful, Skipper! Although the biosphere catastrophe bit was kinda overblown."

"Thanks, Number One. A little hyperbole is good for a CO now and then. If it makes her think a little from now on when she is going for TikTok likes, it was worth it. Anyway, it was fun. And Lee? The indignation she faked on being shown the door was perfect! It totally sold the con."

"I'll be sure to tell her. So, you think that girl will do hard time?"

"No. She's obviously not the brains, and I believe what she said about not knowing about the bomb. Her old man will hire a crack legal team and, if she cooperates, she'll probably get off with probation."

"Really? He would spend that much after she tried to chuck away everything he did for her?"

Haley turned to him. "Oh, yes. It's a father-daughter thing. If I had ever done something like that, my dad would stop at nothing to get me off the hook, legal or otherwise! Good thing I ended up on the side of truth and justice, eh?"

"Not a day goes by that I don't thank the fates that placed you on our side of the law, boss!"

"How gratifying. Now, have we gotten anything out of her chums?"

"Not a peep. I don't suppose you could school me on working those guys up like you did, Miss Bridget?"

"Way different situation. You see, she and I have a lot in common, much more than I'd like to admit. There's no common ground at all between you and those thugs."

Ben's face twisted into a half smile. "Thanks, I guess."

She reached over and patted him on the upper arm. "Don't get wrapped up in it, XO. These idiots will be the FBI's problem once we hit Miami and they can worry about wringing information out of them. Now let's head to the messdeck and see what Chef has on the menu tonight."

Office of the Chief of Staff, Seventh Coast Guard District, Brickell Plaza Federal Building, Miami Florida
09:37 EDT, 13 June

Haley

Haley's interview had taken a little over an hour and was held in a small anteroom adjoining the main conference room. She knew that the fact-finding associated with the tanker incident would be extensive and, despite the confidence that they had made the correct decisions at the right times, there was always the chance that someone in authority would not see things the same way. The lieutenant commander from the legal office doing the interview had been non-committal, jotting down her answers largely without comment. When he finished and was packing up his notebook, Haley asked him directly if he saw any issues. The man's answer left her chilled.

"It's not for me to say, Lieutenant," the man replied, then stepped through and closed the door to the room.

After a ten-minute wait that seemed more like ten hours, Ben came into the room and sat down. "Dare I ask how it went?" Haley asked.

"It was not for her to say," Ben replied with as neutral an expression as he could muster. "And you?"

Haley briefly stared back, then burst out into laughter. "My God! They even say the same things!"

"Really?" Ben asked, the relief apparent on his face.

"Word for word," Haley said with a smile. "OK, I'm officially not worried, and neither should you be."

"I'll get back to you on that after we meet with Captain Mercier." Ben nodded.

The meeting with Seventh District Chief of Staff, Captain Jane Mercier, was the second act in their ordeal this morning. She was behind the original conversion of *Kauai* into a special operations unit while she was the District's Chief of Response and kept control afterward when she was promoted to Chief of Staff. Mercier was a supremely competent, no-nonsense senior officer, destined for promotion to admiral shortly if she continued on her current path.

Haley's first meeting with the captain, more of an interview for consideration for *Kauai*'s command, had ended so poorly that she was almost surprised she got the job. Haley had stupidly let slip a wiseass comment during a frank discussion with Rear Admiral Pennington, the Seventh District Commander, and Mercier's boss. The admiral was a forgiving man who laughed it off. Mercier, on the other hand, was furious and ripped into Haley thoroughly after the admiral departed. It was a terrible start, but Mercier had a soft spot for *Kauai* and her crew. If she held any ill will toward Haley, it was quickly swept aside after her first mission aboard.

Haley had been convinced she would be summarily relieved of command after Ile Ste. Michel. They had succeeded in their mission of supporting the DIA team and rescued two more innocent syndicate victims to boot. But

Haley had violated explicit orders to avoid contact with the Chinese and had gotten her boat shot up and one of her men killed. Mercier's quiet but enthusiastic support in the mission's aftermath was as decisive as it was surprising to Haley. Mercier was never friendly to the two junior officers on *Kauai*—it was not her way, but there was also no doubt she held them in high regard and had their backs.

After a few more minutes of small talk, the phone in the room rang and Ben picked it up. "Lieutenant Wyporek. Yes, ma'am, we'll be right there." He hung up the phone, turned to Haley, and said, "Showtime."

"Right," Haley said as she stood to lead Ben out of the room. It was a short walk to Captain Mercier's office, where they found Haley's boss standing behind her desk. Mercier was a stockily built woman in her late forties, about average height, her graying brown hair cut short. Like Ben and Haley, she wore the tropical blue uniform with a light blue shirt and dark blue epaulets with the four stripes of a captain and the gold wings of an aviator over a single row of ribbons.

"Haley, Ben, get in here!" Mercier said, extending her hand to shake theirs.

"Good morning, ma'am," Haley said with palpable relief as Mercier pumped her hand.

"Have a seat, please," Mercier said, continuing after they sat in the two chairs in front of her spacious desk. "That was great work yesterday. Sorry for the third degree this morning, but, as you know, that's part of the drill."

"We get it, Captain," Haley replied with a nod.

"Good. Well, besides lavishing praise on you two, I wanted to give you a head's up on your next special gig. Have you heard of St. Ignatius?"

Ben shrugged and looked at Haley, who said, "Do you mean that little island in the Virgin Islands south of St. Croix?"

"Yes, indeed. What do you know about it?"

"Never been there, but it is supposedly very beautiful. It's super small, maybe a couple miles across. Largely unspoiled because it's so hard to get to. I think you could get into the harbor with an eighty-seven-footer, but it was too shallow for a Fast Response Cutter or anything bigger and you need a short takeoff and landing bird to use the airport. Most of the tourist traffic is by a small ferry from Frederiksted on St. Croix."

"Very good. Did you know it is also an active volcano?"

"No. I'm surprised I haven't heard that, given I was stationed in San Juan."

"Not really surprising, since it hasn't erupted in over four hundred years."

"Hmm. I guess I have a different definition of 'active' than others." Haley shared another glance with Ben. "What has this to do with us, ma'am?"

"There have been some rumbles there and the U.S. Geological Survey has requested we support one of their teams going down for a look-see. The gear they are taking is too big and heavy for an eighty-seven and, as you said, the harbor is too shallow for a buoy tender or FRC. *Kauai* is, in fact, the Goldilocks boat for this mission. You can plan on operating down there for about a month, staging out of San Juan for logistics."

"Okay, Captain," Haley said. "Not that I'm complaining about a low-key mission to a lovely little Caribbean island, particularly after yesterday. But I'm a bit surprised we're signing off on this—shouldn't the USGS be contracting something like this out to the private sector?"

Mercier's face slowly spread into a broad smile. "Very sharp and perfectly correct. They're not the reason we are sending you down there, they're just the excuse. We needed a cover story for having you guys hanging around the Leeward Islands. It seems our friends from the DIA are running a covert op down there that needs your special talents."

Haley leaned forward. "What's the mission, ma'am?"

Mercier shook her head. "Not here. We'll head down to the SCIF to meet with the DIA reps in about five minutes," she said, referring to the Sensitive Compartmented Information Facility, where it was safe to discuss matters at the most secret levels. "Agent Lamonde from DIA and Dr. Simmons from the DNI's office have already checked in and will be waiting for us. Dr. Simmons and Ben are old friends from previous missions, but I don't think you have met him, Haley."

Mercier was wrong, and Haley had to suppress a jump at the mention of Peter Simmons's name. She and Pete had met at Ben and Victoria's wedding the previous month, where he was acting as "father of the bride" for the orphaned Victoria. Although her predecessor on *Kauai* had ill feelings bordering on outright hatred for him, Haley found Pete to be the most fascinating man she had ever met. He was brilliant, charming, funny, very attractive, and their conversation over drinks at the reception turned into a night together, then two more wonderful days and nights. In the back of her mind, a little voice was warning her he was an intelligence field agent, a spy who compromised people for a living. But the pleasure and excitement of being with this intelligent and interesting, although dangerous man, spoke louder.

Their association thus far had been just that short fling, followed by a very cordial parting—no strings attached. Haley had been fine with that arrangement at the time but had had second thoughts since. She was single and had been comfortable with the choice. Haley found out early that you didn't hook up with other officers in the Service—the job was too competitive for any relationship to work, and the wreckage afterward was bad for everyone, not just the couple. Likewise, she had no success with men outside the Service. The interesting ones moved on when they learned what her career entailed, and those who did not move on were inevitably needy.

Peter Simmons was a different animal. Like Haley, he was in a challenging profession in the service of his country, but being with him lacked the baggage of sharing a relationship with a fellow officer. Although Pete didn't speak of his work with the DIA when they were together, Haley had heard enough from Ben beforehand to know it involved some of the most important and physically dangerous operations the organization conducted. Her curiosity about him grew over time, resolved most satisfactorily during the reception after the wedding. It surprised her to learn during their sojourn afterward that he had been as curious about her as she was about him—her reputation among the DIA rank-and-file was sky-high after she had risked everything to rescue one of their teams.

The holiday with Peter had given Haley pause. The pressures of command were far more than she had expected, and she envied the emotional backstop Ben and Hopkins had with their respective partners. Now, suddenly, here was a man who understood her, with whom she could share her joys, concerns, and fears without judgment or competition, and Haley was considering what had been unthinkable before might be possible now.

She knew it was too early to pitch a relationship with Pete—even if she believed he shared her level of interest, she would not take the risk of ruining what was shaping up to be a very enjoyable thing. For now, she had to accept an agreement to get together occasionally when their jobs permitted it. They also agreed to keep their association confidential for professional reasons—even Ben and Victoria were kept in the dark about it. This was the first time the issue had come up, and Haley was eager to keep the details under wraps without lying to her boss.

"Actually, we have met, ma'am. I ran into him at Ben and Victoria's wedding. But don't worry, Sam Powell gave me the full download on him."

"I see. In that case, I won't have to tell you to be careful with him."

"No, ma'am," Haley replied, wishing the conversation would move on.

"How about you Ben? Any problems with this assignment?"

Ben shook his head. "I'll just be sure my life insurance is paid up, since every time I have been with DIA guys, I've almost had my head shot off." After the chuckling ended, he added, "It's up to you, ma'am. He's basically like a brother-in-law to me, but I can keep it professional."

"Good enough," Mercier replied as they all stood. "Let's head down."

Peter

Peter Simmons, Ph.D. and special assistant to the Director of National Intelligence, sat at the SCIF meeting table with his teammate for this mission, Special Agent Gregory Lamonde of the Defense Intelligence Agency's Defense Clandestine Service. Technically, Peter was also a special agent of the DCS, but he had been detailed to the DNI's staff for over a year now. Officially, it was to provide close advice and assistance to the Director on sensitive operations, particularly those involving the employment of *Kauai* and her crew. Unofficially, Peter was being screened from reprisals by Vice Admiral Jennifer Irving, the current director of the DIA, with whom he had publicly fought following the Honduras mission. He had determined to leave the service and return to his previous academic career for his own safety and sanity, but a personal appeal from the DNI and a promise to keep him safely ensconced until Irving moved on had kept him in the fold.

He looked across the table at Lamonde, who was leafing through a reference binder he had brought to the briefing. Like Peter and most other successful agents, Lamonde was "average" in height, weight, and appearance. Both men had medium short hair, Peter's brown and Lamonde's black. Facial hair was their chief physical difference—Peter sported a scruffy anchor beard while Lamonde was clean-shaven.

They had traveled separately to the meeting today and had met for the first time in this room. After a brief handshake and mutual introductions, they had sat at the table and not exchanged a word since. Peter was fine with this. Although he had never worked with Lamonde before, he had heard things about him, whispered things between agents after both had looked around to ensure no one could overhear.

The records of many of the operations Peter had taken part in were concealed in the highest security within "Special Access" or "Codeword" programs, accessible only through specific authorization on an absolute need-to-know basis. The word on Lamonde was that many of his missions were beyond that level—there were no records of these to access because, officially, they never happened.

Lamonde was a government-employed expert in untraceable murder.

Peter knew Lamonde was also highly talented in the more conventional professional skills employed in the field and the fact he was working with a partner suggested that this mission was not simply wet work. For now, he was prepared to accept that the mission was the one he had been assigned by the DNI. Nonetheless, Peter was on his guard as rumors also suggested that Lamonde was Irving's go-to man for "personal" work, and he would not put it past her to settle a score via a mission assignment.

They both stood when the door opened after a brief knock and Captain Mercier entered the room, followed by Ben and Haley. This was an extremely delicate moment for Peter, requiring the utmost concentration to maintain the pretense of nonchalance. He stepped over to Mercier immediately for a professional handshake. They had met several times previously, before and after *Kauai*'s missions with the DIA, and this was purely routine. "Good morning, Captain," he greeted her with a professional smile.

"Doctor Simmons, it's good to see you again." She turned to Lamonde and offered her hand. "Agent Lamonde, I'm Jane Mercier."

"Pleased to meet you, Captain," Lamonde replied, shaking her hand while wearing what Peter assumed was his professional smile.

"Likewise. May I present Lieutenants Haley Reardon and Ben Wyporek? They are the captain and second-in-command of *Kauai*." After Lamonde had exchanged greetings and handshakes with the two officers, she turned back to Peter and continued. "And you all know each other, of course."

"Yes, indeed," Peter said, gripping Ben's hand firmly with a warm smile. "Hello, Ben! How's married life?"

"Better every day, Pete." Ben smiled back.

Now comes the tricky part. He extended his hand to Haley with his professional smile. "It's good to see you again, Captain Reardon. I hope you have been well?"

"Yes, indeed, thank you, Doctor. And you?" Haley replied.

Peter was relieved to see she was showing her professional rather than personal smile—he was familiar with both—that and the words told him their secret was still a secret. "Excellent! Particularly now that I have a chance to work with you all again."

Mercier stepped to the head of the table and sat. "I'm sorry to interrupt the socializing, but we might as well get down to business. Haley and Ben are completely in the dark about the mission other than their cover will be babysitting a pack of egghead volcanologists." She turned to Peter with a wry smile. "No offense, Doctor."

"None taken, Captain," Peter replied. Turning to Haley and Ben, he said, "Well, where to begin?" After a brief pause, he continued. "We have had a mole epidemic in D.C. for the past year. Three found so far, but we are pretty sure there are a bunch more. They were scattered over different agencies, and, as far as we can tell, they were not coordinating with each other. The interrogations are ongoing, but we do know they are not cases of greed or political disenchantment—these three individuals have been personally compromised. One has already admitted as much."

"Do we know who is blackmailing them?" Haley asked.

"We are pretty sure it is the Chinese," Peter replied. "It's circumstantial, as the moles have been supplying the information via dead drops and cutouts and don't appear to know themselves. But the nature of the information they provided would not be of much use to anyone else. Also, the only reason we got on to these three was that the Chinese had crossed us up on several operations and initiatives, clearly with knowledge that went well beyond open source and targeted intelligence efforts. We were able to trace the compromised information back to the three moles we found.

"The one suspect who has confessed was a senior executive at the State Department's Bureau of Intelligence and Research. He apparently has a...*thing* for pre-pubescent boys and somebody got some pictures of him during some pretty nasty behavior. Needless to say, the Marshals Service has him on a suicide watch through his trial."

"This is all very interesting, Doctor," Mercier interrupted with a little irritation. "But I wonder if you could fast forward to where we fit in, please."

Peter nodded. "Yes, ma'am. Sorry about that. As it turns out, these pictures were taken surreptitiously during a visit to Île Oiseaux. Have you heard of it?"

After a glance at the two junior officers which received shaking heads in return, Mercier replied, "Apparently not. Please enlighten us."

"Yes, Île Oiseaux is a small island in the Îles des Saintes group south of Guadeloupe. It's privately owned and run as a super-exclusive resort called L'hôtel Caraïbe. The facilities there are supposedly first class, and their rates are unknown because it is invitation only. It is a haven for the hyper-rich and otherwise well-connected who have, shall we say, *unconventional* tastes. It is a place you can go to get anything, and I mean *anything* your heart desires, be it S-and-M, pedophilia, or even snuff sex. As you might imagine, getting an invitation requires a rather rigorous screening for any law-enforcement connection and all guests sign up for a non-disclosure that amounts to a mutually assured destruction pact."

"The French tolerate this?" Ben asked incredulously. "Surely pedophilia and murder for fun must cross the line, even for them."

Peter nodded in return. "You'd think so, but they let it go on. We are not sure why but suspect certain high-ranking government and military officials are involved, either as participants or because they know someone who is. Those not involved probably rationalize it as something that would exist anyway, and better offshore than in *La Belle France*. I can tell you their intelligence people at my level are madder than hell and frustrated by their inability to do anything about it.

"Anyway, the place is run by an ex-Foreign Legionnaire named Renard Laurent, who joined one of the *Le Milieu*, which is what the French call their organized crime gangs, after completing his enlistment. He brought a variety of military skills, the utter ruthlessness of a sociopath, and the discipline of a soldier, which served him well in his quick trip up the organizational ladder. The Île Oiseaux resort was his innovation and has been an under-the-public-radar success for his gang. Up to now, they had been collecting hefty fees from their clientele without posing a threat to France.

"The Chinese connection is a new wrinkle—Laurent and the gang must be collecting a huge payoff from them to take that risk. We also suspect the Chinese are subsidizing the "fees" Laurent charges to people they are targeting to get them in the door and keep their compromise from being picked up in the normal financial surveillance we keep on high-level clearance holders. We have gone through the normal channels with the evidence we have to point out that French higher-ups would be just as vulnerable to '*Kompromat*' as Americans, but the powers that be over there don't buy it. 'They wouldn't screw with us like that' seems to be the prevailing opinion. So, we are going to go in there and take out the proof."

"Doctor, there must be better alternatives than an op inside French territory," Mercier said. "If the blackmail fodder is electronic, why not hack our way in? Surely the NSA has tools that are fit for the job."

"No, Captain. Laurent might have started as a *Le Milieu* thug, but he was one of the first cyber ops guys in the Legion and knows all the tricks. That skill was one reason he moved up so quickly in the gang. The NSA has hit that island with everything in the toolbag and got bupkis. Whatever they have must be air-gapped as well as locked down. That leaves the good old-fashioned HUMINT approach."

"So, you've turned one of their gang members?" Mercier asked.

Peter turned to Lamonde. "Why don't you take this one?"

Lamonde nodded. "No, Captain. The management and security guys on the island are all old Legion buddies of Laurent. They'd kill their own children before they'd give him up. The good news is that, except for the big boss himself, none of the gang is very tech-savvy. They had to hire the guys that set up and manage the IT on the island. Of course, they check those guys pretty closely—much more thoroughly than their guests—before they get in the door and none of them get on or off the island without a complete body cavity search. Plus, they have a list of all close friends and relatives who will be murdered if they decide to make a run for it. Since they control all access to the island, they are well-positioned to make that stick."

"Are you telling us you flipped one of them? How did you manage that?" Haley asked.

Lamonde sat back with a sly smile. "Simple. We found one hanging out in an online hacker's collective who is as much a sociopath as Laurent. We offered him the standard ten-million dollars and a new life for him and his family if he could give us a flash drive with a list of who Laurent sold out to the Chinese—he countered with twenty-million and the gang could do what they pleased to his family."

"That's some serious evil," Ben said. "What makes you think you can trust a man who would abandon his family to these animals?"

"Our scout asked the same question. His reply was they were a liability, now and later, and he didn't feel like staying with anyone who might lead the gang to him someday."

"Amazing," Ben replied, shaking his head. "So, are we supposed to pick this guy up from the island?"

"Yes, but it will take careful timing and handling. We can't communicate with him directly; he's too closely watched. We have to get one of our people in there to dead drop the pickup info and then do the lift." Lamonde gave a shrug, as if it would be easy.

"Our people? You are not going in?" Mercier asked.

"No, that would be me," Peter interrupted. He noted reactions of surprise from Mercier, deep concern from Ben, and just a flicker of movement in Haley's eyes. He smiled inside. *Yes, admirable control, but you do feel something for me, my lovely captain!* "I'll slip in there as a guest. We have already arranged a series of dead drops and codes. When the time comes for the extraction, I'll rendezvous with him and escort him to the extraction point for the pickup."

"You said this place has top security and is by invitation only. How will you manage that?" Haley asked with a steady voice.

"I have a few close friends in the Crime and Security Branch of Garda Síochána, the Irish national police, from some joint operations we ran to keep the 252 Syndicate out of Ireland. In general, the Irish like the French—same religion, enemies, *etcetera* across history—but the Garda are definitely not fans of *Le Milieu*. When we briefed them on the situation, they offered one of their standby legends for me to use on the operation, and I have already made contact with the gang on the dark web using this alias. I requested a stay conveniently overlapping a state event in Guadeloupe that will account for your presence in the area. I'll be flying to Dublin in a few days to burn into the alias, one Declan Shea, in advance of my guest 'interview' a week from now."

"Interview?" Ben asked.

"Yes, they didn't call it that, and most interviews aren't conducted in a secret location after a trip with a bag over your head. But it's the final step where they make a physical check that you match your bona fides and verify which particular depravity you have a yen to experience and settle on a final price. I imagine it will end with the 21st-century equivalent of a blood oath and an explanation in minute detail of the gruesome fate that awaits anyone who betrays them. You know, the usual." Peter grinned.

"Indeed. And which 'depravity' are you signing up for?" Ben asked, his face moving from a look of deep concern to one of amusement.

"I haven't decided yet," Peter replied. "I'll need some time walking around in Declan's shoes to get a feel for his perversions. Whatever I come up with needs to pass the smell test or this will be a mighty short op." He glanced at Haley, getting a studiedly indifferent look in return. *Yes, very cool indeed.*

Haley turned to Mercier and asked, "What's our schedule, ma'am?"

"You have seven days of CHARLIE status, starting tomorrow," Mercier replied with a smile. "No operations, and don't get distracted on your way home today. Obviously, give everyone as much time off as you can. You and Ben need to be available on the day after tomorrow to meet with the USGS lead, Professor Lydia Hernandez. She'll be flying into Orlando from Aguadilla to brief you guys on the St. Ignatius mission and answer any questions."

"Will she be coming down with us, ma'am?" Ben asked.

"No, she will fly back. I made it clear that no berthing space is available on *Kauai*, so the plan is for you guys to pick up her and her team in Mayagüez. It's only a seven- or eight-hour trip from there to St. Ignatius. She was all over that idea since she and her students are from the University of Puerto Rico campus there."

"I'm relieved to hear it, ma'am," Ben said. He turned to Peter. "So, can we expect any DIA passengers?"

"Yes, me," Lamonde said. After the others turned to him, he said, "I will accompany the landing party and be making the linkup with Peter. The state event you will attend is the inauguration of the new Prefect of Guadeloupe and will be held at noon on the first of July. I'll meet you in San Juan on your last port call before you head down south. After the pickup, we will head directly back to San Juan, where you will drop the defector and us off. Then you can get back to your little scientific field trip." He finished with a smug smile.

"Well, I guess that covers it," Mercier said after an awkward pause. "Anybody have anything else?"

"Yes," Peter said. "Captain Reardon, would you mind if I hitched a ride up to Canaveral with you guys? I'll be flying out of Orlando and it would save me a lot of hassle getting up there."

"I have no objection, ma'am," Haley said after turning to Mercier.

"Consider it done," Mercier said. "Now, last call. Anything else?" After a second of head shaking around the room, she stood, followed immediately by the others, and said, "Then I will wish everybody good luck and a safe return." After handshakes around the table, she turned and walked out the door, followed by Lamonde.

"Would you like to ride back to the boat with us?" Ben asked.

"If you don't mind," Peter replied. "Let me get my bag and I'll meet you in the garage."

As they turned and walked through the door, Ben asked, "Do you have a hotel? I'm sure Victoria would be delighted if you could stay with us."

"I'd like that," Peter said.

"Excellent!" Ben said. "We could all go out to dinner tomorrow night." He turned to Haley. "What do you think, skipper?"

Peter studied Haley's expression as it changed from neutral to her professional smile. *Ah, even more interesting!*

"I think that's a fine idea," she answered.

"Great! I'll call Victoria and get her started on it," Ben concluded as they continued down the hallway to the elevators.

Chapter 5

Guardian

***USCG Cutter Kauai, North Atlantic Ocean,
nine nautical miles east of Jupiter, Florida
16:03 EDT, 13 June***

Haley

Haley's anger had calmed to a slow boil in the four hours since they departed the Coast Guard Base in Miami Beach. Being underway on this beautiful sunny day with the people she held in the highest regard was a soothing influence, mitigating, though not eliminating the source of her anger hanging out in Ben's stateroom ten feet below her. It had taken every ounce of self-control to conceal from her boss the shock of learning of Pete's involvement in the mission, and then her anger at him as he blithely outlined the extremely hazardous role he was to play. She was rapidly gaining a much deeper understanding of her predecessor's animus toward the man.

"Captain, when would you like to sit down for the discussion?" Ben asked, breaking into her thoughts. During the car trip from the District Office to the base, Pete had asked for a private chat concerning the upcoming mission once they were safely underway. Her cabin had been soundproofed during *Kauai*'s upgrades to facilitate classified discussions such as this.

Haley turned to look at Ben. It was clear he picked up that something was wrong, but he was too professional to inquire into the moods of his CO. *He really is a fine man, and it's not fair for him to be wondering what the hell is wrong with me today.* She gave him a genuine, warm smile and said, "Might as well get it done, XO. Let's head down and I'll meet you in the cabin."

"Yes, ma'am," Ben replied.

He stepped aside as she stood from the captain's chair and then fell in behind her as she moved to the ladder in the rear of the bridge. It was a short walk to her cabin, and she sat at her desk to await Ben and Pete's arrival. She gazed around the small room that served as her sanctum while they were underway. It was decorated now, far more personal than it had been when she first took command and launched on the fateful mission to Ile Ste. Michel the next day. Her eye fixed on the plaque displaying *Kauai*'s crest mounted above her bunk—at the time of that mission, it was the only decoration in the room.

She liked the design far more than any ship's crest she had seen before. It was simple, featuring the escutcheon of the Kingdom of Hawaii overlaying a silver fouled anchor with the phase *Fortier et Fideliter*, Latin for "Bravely and Faithfully" inscribed on a scroll across the bottom. She remembered when she stared hard at the plaque during the critical point of that first mission, the phrase inspiring her to abandon the safe play and go to the rescue of the DIA team and the two captives they had liberated from the 252 Syndicate thugs. As it always did, her sense of satisfaction dimmed to sadness when she recalled the cost. The condolence visit she made to the father of the crewman who had been killed to deliver his personal effects was the most heart-wrenching experience of her life. She blinked away a tear as a knock sounded on her door. *Not now, buck up, girl.* "Come in," she called.

The door opened and Ben stepped into the room, followed closely by Pete, who closed the door behind him. "Captain," Ben said with a nod.

"Welcome, gents. Have a seat where you can," Haley said. After they were seated, Ben in the spare chair and Pete on her bunk, she continued. "Alright, Doctor, what can we do for you?"

Pete nodded with a slight smile and said, "Thank you, Captain. Sorry for the cloak and dagger, but I have some concerns about this mission I wanted to share with you while I could."

Ben glanced at Haley, then turned back. "Seems relatively low-key to me, Pete. I can see that if we're caught by the French, it might be embarrassing, but it's nothing like the fights for our lives we have had before."

"Granted, but something is off on this one. First, after Irving pitched this thing, the DNI pulled me aside and told me to get involved quote, 'to keep an eye on things,' unquote. He knows she is after his job and is looking for an opportunity to show off, make him look bad, or, preferably, both. Second concern is the selection of Lamonde for this op. There are a bunch of guys more experienced for an extraction than he is. Frankly, he is not the type."

"Oh? And what is his particular specialty?" Haley asked, more than a little relieved to hear that Pete had been assigned and not volunteered for this job.

Pete glanced at Ben and then back before answering. "Murder. He is Irving's go-to guy to take care of, shall we say, *difficult* issues."

"*What*? That's really a thing?" Ben exclaimed.

"Not officially, of course. But yes, it's a thing. And let me assure you, I am not one of those. I've fought my way out occasionally, as you well know, but I never went in with the mission of assassination. Given the tool assigned, one wonders what the job really is. It could be to eliminate this defector, maybe even take a shot at Laurent himself, or maybe me."

"Are you *serious*?" Ben asked incredulously. "No way!"

"Yes. Irving and I tangled in front of the JUBILEE committee after the Barbello operation. She had expected me to grab the computers with the production formulas and process for the gas. When I pointed out that our stated purpose to the military commanders was the destruction of the gas and not taking it for ourselves, she berated me for my naivete in front of the committee. After I responded by implying she was little different from the 252s with expectations like that, it was game on and the DNI had to step in. I not only foiled her attempt to embarrass the DNI through an over-delivery on the mission, but I also made her look like a fool in front of the committee. I was going to chuck it then and there, but the DNI convinced me to stay on in a detail position on his staff until Irving moved on to another job at the end of her term. Given this history, I would not be at all surprised to learn Lamonde has collateral orders to punch my ticket as well."

Ben looked at Haley, who said, "Alright, what does this mean for us on this mission?"

"Nothing. Just watch your backs and don't trust him any more than you have to."

Ben smiled. "Funny, that was the same advice Sam gave me about you on our first go-around."

Pete smiled in return. "With that pedigree, you know the advice is rock-solid." He turned to Haley again. "That's about it, Captain. Do you have any questions for me?"

Haley smiled. "No, but I would like you to hang around a minute for a private chat."

"Of course."

"Thanks, XO," Haley said to Ben. "I'll see you in a bit."

"Yes, Captain," Ben said, then stood and closed the door behind him as he left.

They stared at each other for a good five seconds before Pete finally broke. "I presume this is not the prelude to a pre-dinner quicky," he said with a smile.

"You are not as dumb as you look," Haley shot back icily. "Care to explain why my boss was the one delivering the news we would be working together?"

His smile faded. "It's a classified mission. What was I supposed to do, ring you up on your cellphone?"

"Yes! You could have done that without revealing anything sensitive. Do you realize the position you put me in?"

"No, I don't. We had a good time together and my understanding is we parted as friends. Well, friends with benefits, perhaps. I am at a loss as to why you're learning of an operation with me working with you would be so discombobulating. Explain, please."

Haley could feel her rage building as she balled her fists. She took a deep breath and let it out slowly, willing herself to calm down. "Screw you. You are supposed to be some kind of genius—figure it out for yourself."

He sat back with what looked like an injured expression. *Probably fake as can be*, Haley thought. "Alright, I think we are done here," she said, nodding toward the cabin door.

"Would you like me to put a stop to Ben's dinner plans? I can explain that something has come up and I have to cancel."

"No. He'll see right through that. He's smarter than you give him credit for, you know."

"You're wrong. I apprehend you'd love to chuck me overboard right now, but it better not be because you think I look down on Ben. Quite the contrary. He's the best man I've ever known, and I'd take a bullet for him any day of the week. I was simply trying to keep him out of the middle of whatever the hell is going on here."

Haley smiled coldly. "Good. Do so by leveraging your beguiling personality to convince him and Victoria there is nothing to see here. I'll do the same."

Pete stood. "Very well. I'll do my best." He turned toward the door, took a step, then stopped and turned back. "Look, I'm completely at a loss how we got here. But, for whatever my part in it was, I'm sorry."

"Acknowledged," Haley replied. "Now, please leave."

He nodded, turned, and stepped out of the room, closing the door without another word.

Haley stared at the door for some time. How long, she could not say. This was the moment she had geared herself up for since leaving Mercier's office—she had laid the guilt on him and he had acknowledged it.

She was triumphant.

So, why do I feel like I just took a fastball square on the chest? What is WRONG with me? She thought as her eyes welled up with tears. *No. No, you don't! You wanted this job, lived for this job. Now you have to live up to it! How did you think this would go, like some damn romance novel?*

The humorous thought of being the subject of some chick-lit paperback partially pulled Haley back from her funk. She imagined the cover with some big-haired bimbo in a cosplay uniform looking up into the eyes of a shirtless, muscle-bound idiot and a sappy back-cover blurb.

Let me see. Oh yes: "Dangerous Tides of Love *is a captivating romance novel that intertwines the worlds of a fearless female Coast Guard officer and a dashing secret agent, where duty and desire collide in an exhilarating tale of love, danger, and the strength to overcome. Will Haley and Peter find a way to reconcile their divergent lives and build a future together? Or will the turbulent tides of their professions force them to choose between their love and the call of duty?"*

Haley chuckled softly as she wiped her eyes with the back of her hand. *OK, girl. At least you know you have a fall-back profession writing ready to go in case this Coast Guard thing doesn't work out.* She stood from her desk, and after a last, sad look at the spot on her bunk where Pete had been sitting, grabbed her ball cap and headed out the door.

3532 Slidergate Drive, Rockledge, Florida
21:47 EDT, 13 June

Victoria

Victoria checked her watch again, then walked across the room again for the eighth time to straighten the wine glasses she had arranged for Peter and Benjamin's arrival. They had, of course, not moved in the four checks since she had achieved the optimal placement. She was fully cognizant that this was abnormal, obsessive behavior, a symptom of her thankfully mild neurodivergence. But the act made her feel more comfortable, and after all, she had nothing better to do while she awaited the arrival of the two most important men in her life. This was Peter's first visit to her and Benjamin's home, and everything needed to be as orderly as possible.

Peter had come into her life fifteen years previously, first as a boyfriend, then as fiancé to her older sister, Julie. At the time, Peter was an Astrophysics Ph.D. student at Princeton, where Julie was working through her undergraduate degree in English Literature. Julie was her guardian, their parents having been killed in an automobile crash when Victoria was eight. The demands of school, work, and caring for a special needs adolescent left little time for male companionship in Julie's life. Most of her beaus were short-term, particularly after they met her "challenged" little sister. Peter was different.

Peter was a fellow genius with a talent for mathematics, although not at Victoria's level, but he had a gift for languages that was beyond even her comprehension. Julie's academic interest opened a whole new world for him and, rather than being repelled by her home life, he embraced it. Victoria came to love Peter dearly as an older brother figure, not just for his kindness and good humor, but for the joy he brought into Julie's life. The three of them had built a happy life together at Princeton over several years, with Peter moving on to post-doctoral studies, Julie to her master's, and Victoria matriculating into the Data Science program at age fifteen. Julie and Peter planned to marry shortly after her graduation, but the wedding was not to be.

Julie had flown to Paris, both for some last details in her thesis research and for a last "fling" with some of her friends, while Peter had reluctantly stayed behind. A few days after Julie left, Peter appeared outside Victoria's classroom unexpectedly and asked that she accompany him. He looked terribly worried, which thoroughly frightened Victoria. Once they were out of earshot, he explained that there had been an explosion outside a museum in Paris and that Julie was not answering her phone. They hurried back to their apartment to await a response to Peter's frantic inquiries to the embassy in Paris. Hours later, their worst fears were realized: Julie had been killed in the explosion.

It was a devastating loss for Victoria, far worse than her parents' deaths had been. Julie was much more than her sister. She was her best friend and hero for how she had put her own life aside to care for her. And as terrible as Julie's death was for Victoria, it had been worse for Peter. She watched helplessly as the man she loved like a brother vanished before her eyes, replaced by a broken shell. Victoria was convinced that if it had not been for his sense of duty to see her through school, Peter would have killed himself. For her, it was like dealing with two deaths.

During this personal tragedy, the DIA, who had been aware of Peter's peculiar talent with languages for many years, made their pitch to him. They were the government agency with the lead on dealing with the 252 Syndicate, the multi-national criminal organization responsible for Julie's death. "Come with us," they said. "And you can help take the fight to them." Peter grasped this proposal like a man dying of thirst offered a glass of cool water. He extracted two conditions before signing up: that the agency would allow him to see Victoria through to her graduation from Princeton the following year and that they would make a position in the agency available to her. The DIA gladly accepted the counteroffer, acquiring both a talented field agent and a genius data scientist in a single transaction.

After her graduation, Peter helped Victoria move into her new position at the DIA's Data Analysis Division within the National Intelligence University in Bethesda, Maryland, with an apartment within convenient walking distance. Victoria's condition made many mundane life activities very challenging for her, but once she had established a routine of home-work-home, coping became easier and she could function on her own. Peter was delighted that the thing he worried about the most, Victoria's ability to integrate with her coworkers, proved to be a non-issue. Her curiosity about everyone she met was very disarming, and her immense analytical talent and absence of ego won her many admirers at work.

Time passed and Victoria and Peter settled into their respective roles within the DIA. Experience honed Peter's skills to the degree that he became a scourge to his 252

Syndicate nemesis. Victoria's talents and good nature made her the go-to data scientist for quick solutions to seemingly intractable analytical problems. This static but satisfying arrangement had continued for several years and she had accepted it would continue that way indefinitely. Then Benjamin came into her life.

Victoria sat at her desk and picked up the picture of Benjamin taken over a year ago in the early days of their relationship. It sat next to one of them both strolling arm in arm on the Washington DC Mall, a candid shot taken by the same photographer after they had toured the National Museum of Art. Benjamin knew she feared having her picture taken and went immediately to confront the photographer. It ended well for all concerned—Victoria persuaded the man to take this solo shot of Benjamin after he had agreed to sell them the other picture and was delighted with the result. The photo was comprehensively perfect in her mind: the lighting, venue, composition, and ideal subject. She loved the picture as a tangible mark of what she still regarded as her most perfect day, rivaled only by their wedding day. It was the perfect day followed by the perfect night when she and Benjamin made love for the first time in her apartment.

Benjamin had been as much a surprise to Victoria as she was to him. They met by chance on the only occasion Victoria had gone into the field from her office job. Peter needed her support to process UAV imagery data, and she appreciated the challenge of working in the austere environment of a hotel room. The location of the Florida Keys was also agreeable, particularly in January. Even the journey was tolerable—because of their sensitive and highly classified equipment, they traveled on a government plane, avoiding the horror of the commercial airport terminals with their crowds, confined spaces, noise, and all those people *touching* you.

Later in the week, Peter notified her he was coming ashore and bringing one officer, Benjamin, with him as a liaison. Victoria had pulled Benjamin's record for Peter's review before the operation, and she was decidedly unimpressed. Benjamin was a mediocre performer at the Coast Guard Academy, had an uneventful tour of duty aboard USCG Cutter *Dependable* in Little Creek, Virginia, then was assigned to *Kauai* as second in command. There was something unusual—he had been awarded the Coast Guard Commendation Medal for heroism in saving three lives after a traffic accident. She noted this with approval as she pulled his official photo, which was also unimpressive.

The young man who arrived with Peter for the team meeting that first night was nothing Victoria expected. Some height, but not overly tall, with a slim, athletic build and the most captivating blue eyes she had ever seen. Benjamin was not the militaristic buffoon Victoria took him for after reading his personnel file, but a modest, almost shy, intelligent young man who provided fascinating conversation. She suspected he was also attracted to her—she caught glimpses of him looking at her while she worked at her computer during the team discussions.

After the team meeting, they had a long conversation, mainly with Benjamin describing and answering her questions about his life aboard ship. The next morning Victoria had to return to Bethesda, but they continued their association after Benjamin returned from the mission, settling into a routine of nightly phone calls whenever Benjamin had the connectivity. They were a welcome distraction at first, becoming an increasingly important part of her day as she got to know him. He was interesting, charming, and funny all at once, and unlike anyone she had ever met, she could discuss anything on her mind with him.

Victoria caressed Benjamin's picture, remembering how she had been holding and looking at it when he told her he loved her for the first time—a surprise call from a satellite phone just before he went into action at Barbello. The joy was short-lived, crushed when she arrived at work the next morning to learn Benjamin had been grievously wounded and evacuated by helicopter. His survival was in doubt, and Victoria knew nothing she could bring to bear would affect that outcome, but she was determined to be with Benjamin through whatever was to come. She flew down to Miami on the next flight, arriving at the hospital shortly after Benjamin went into surgery. When he revived the following day, the intensity of her relief at finding him awake and able to talk rivaled her joy at finding out he loved her.

A little over a year later, Peter had walked her to the beautiful, flowered altar on Indian Harbour Beach to be joined forever to the love of her life. The thought drew her gaze to their wedding picture. She was in the beautiful white dress her friends Joana Powell and Emilia Hopkins had helped her select, and Benjamin, strikingly handsome in his bemedaled dress white uniform. Having an eidetic memory like Victoria's could sometimes be a curse, but more often it was a gift that allowed her to relive an experience almost as if it was happening again. She smiled as the memory of her wedding ceremony and reception played out before her.

The sound of a key in the front door jolted Victoria out of her remembrance, and she carefully placed the picture on her desk as she stood to go to the door. Benjamin was stepping inside as she came into the room followed by Peter. Benjamin put his backpack down, gathered her in his arms, and they shared a warm kiss, followed by a long hug. Victoria then hugged Peter and kissed him on the cheek. "Sorry to keep you waiting, Peter. It is so wonderful to see you!"

"Victoria, seeing you and Ben together never gets old! And you are even more beautiful than ever. How do you manage that?" Peter said with a warm smile.

Victoria suppressed the urge to answer the question literally, simply smiling and replying, "Oh, that is sweet. Thank you very much, Peter. Will you be staying with us long?"

"No, just for tonight. I have a good deal of business to attend to before I head overseas and might keep odd hours. If I could just get a lift from one of you to a car rental in the morning, I'll be out of your hair."

"I wish you could stay, but I understand. I hope you will still be able to go out to dinner with us tomorrow. I have found an interesting French restaurant in Cocoa."

"Victoria, I wouldn't miss it for all the whiskey in Ireland," Peter replied with an affected Irish accent. After she looked at him in confusion, he added in his normal accent, "Sorry, just getting into character a little for the next job."

"I understand." She nodded, then took him by the arm and led him to the table. "I have prepared a wine service for us. I presume you ate dinner aboard *Kauai*, but if you are hungry, I can prepare some food."

"No, thank you, Victoria," Peter said. "As usual, Chef Hebert provided us with a wonderful meal. All that was missing was a fine wine." He picked up and read the bottle. "Excellent! How about I pour?"

******

Victoria lay with her head on Benjamin's chest, enjoying the rhythm of his deep and slow breathing while he slept. He had just fallen asleep on his back with her tucked between his left arm and his body. She could barely make out his face in the soft glow of the moonlight from the window of their bedroom, the curve of his jaw and his eyes now closed. Victoria traced her fingers over the muscles of Benjamin's right arm, lightly, so as not to wake him. She loved the feel of being with him, the shape of his body, his scent.

They had had a pleasant time visiting with Peter through laughter and stories and two bottles of wine. Benjamin mainly listened as she and Peter reminisced about their times together, touching carefully on their fond memories of Julie, as it was still a painful subject for both of them. After they had said their goodnights and gone to bed, she found she needed to cry over the feelings that had been stirred up in the conversation. Benjamin's ability to sense exactly what she needed was uncanny. He did not try to console or cheer her up, just held her and gently stroked her back in the way he knew made her feel relaxed and safe until her melancholy had passed.

It had been a struggle for Victoria to provide this kind of support for Benjamin in the beginning. Her neurodivergence impeded her ability to read emotions, and he was conditioned by his profession not to share them. As a result, they tended to stumble when confronted with emotional situations. The breakthrough came with the tragedy of his subordinate's death in the Haitian mission when she could console and help him through his profound grief and sense of guilt. The realization that they each not only loved but could lean on the other without restraint removed the last barrier between them.

Victoria gently reached down and pulled the sheets over them, then snuggled into the warm safety of Benjamin's chest. She missed him terribly when he was at sea and always worried about his safety, but these moments together more than made up for it. Victoria yawned and surrendered, finally, to the treasure of falling asleep in her husband's arms.

Chapter 6

Misdirection

***Café Suzette, 332 Brevard Avenue, Cocoa,
Florida
20:47 EDT, 14 June***

Haley

Haley was surprised to admit the evening had been one of the most pleasant she had experienced in a long time. She had dreaded the thought of having to feign friendliness with Pete. However, once they had sat together at the table and began swapping stories, the tension evaporated and she began to enjoy herself.

The food was fantastic, and Haley put aside for now how many additional reps she would have to do at the gym tomorrow to enjoy her last few bites of coq au vin and potatoes au gratin. Through the dinner, she, Ben, and Pete had each shared several amusing stories from the past, while Victoria listened attentively. Haley, worried that she was being left out, finally asked, "Victoria, you are very quiet tonight. I hope we aren't pushing you aside."

Victoria smiled warmly in return. "On the contrary, Haley. I love listening to these stories. You all have had so many interesting adventures."

Haley grinned back. "I imagine you must have some funny stories about settling in with this guy," she said, nodding toward Ben.

"Not really. Although the event of our engagement was somewhat amusing."

"Really?" Haley asked with raised eyebrows and a glance at Ben. "Do tell!"

Ben rolled his eyes and said, "You're going to love this. At the big moment, we were both convinced we'd been given the heave-ho!" He smiled warmly at Victoria and added, "I guess it's safe to reveal our near-miss."

Victoria nodded and began. "Yes, it was just after your change of command ceremony. Benjamin suggested we go out, and he took me to this wonderfully romantic little restaurant in Indialantic. I thought something must be afoot because he asked me to wear the special dress I wore on our first date."

"Oh, yes," Haley said. "The one in the picture in Ben's stateroom. That one is really beautiful!"

"Thank you, Haley," Victoria said. "So, we had a wonderful dinner, and I noticed Benjamin was behaving...well, oddly for him. I was worried that he was upset about how cross I had gotten with him over his last mission and the fight we had about it."

Pete interjected, "You two had a fight? That must have been something to see!"

"Lay off," Haley hushed him with a smile.

"Sorry! Pray continue, Victoria." Pete grinned back.

Victoria nodded and said, "So, when Benjamin said, rather nervously, that he needed something more than our current relationship, I foolishly jumped to the conclusion that he was breaking up with me. I thought the restaurant was his way of breaking it to me gently!"

"I would hardly blame you, Victoria," Haley said with a chuckle and turned to Ben. "*That* was your lead-in?"

Ben shook his head with a smile. "What can I say? At the time, it sounded right in my head. It gets even better from here. Carry on, my dear."

"Yes, so I asked him straight away if he was breaking up with me. He was startled for a moment, then jumped out of his chair, got down on one knee, and immediately asked me to marry him. I was reeling so much from all the emotions I was feeling, I could not speak." She nodded to Ben with a smile.

"I had no idea she was so wound up and thought that I was asking too much of her to answer a surprise question like that on the spot," Ben said. "So I asked if she needed time to think it over." He nodded back.

Victoria said, "Naturally, I did not. I had been dreaming of that moment for months. So I said, 'No,' meaning I did not need to think about it. Of course, the way I said it, Benjamin concluded I was turning down his proposal." She smiled warmly. "When I saw the look on his face was like he had just been struck, I realized the blunder of my reply. I corrected myself as quickly as I could with an emphatic yes!"

Ben reached across the table to take Victoria's hand. "Fortunately for me, we got it sorted out."

"For us both," Victoria corrected him.

Haley smiled, "Aww! What a wonderful story of love overcoming poor communications." She looked across the table at Pete and added, "A lesson for us all."

Pete's right eyebrow raised, and he said, "Quite true. I could not agree more."

The conversation continued into dessert and coffee and finally, Victoria said, "I dislike being the first to say this, but I am rather tired."

Ben looked over in surprise and said, "Yes, I suppose I need to throw in the towel as well. With that professor coming by tomorrow, I need to get things in order. Could you excuse us for calling it a night?"

"No problem," Haley replied. "I would like to stay longer, but I don't want to be a bad influence on my XO!" She looked across the table at Pete and tried to maintain the most neutral expression she could. *Now's your chance, buddy. We can get this train back on the track if you play this right.*

"I'll hang in as well if you don't mind the company," Pete said with a warm smile.

"Glad to have it," Haley replied, concealing her relief as they all stood. After a round of farewells, handshakes, and hugs, Ben and Victoria departed, and Haley and Pete resumed their seats.

"Dare I hope what we have shared this evening might have offered us a chance to get back to where we were?" Pete asked with a tilt of his head.

Haley smiled. "Let's just say I'm keeping my options open. I admit right now I am far less convinced you are a complete asshole than I was when I arrived this evening."

"Definitely trending in a promising direction. I'll take it!"

"Good call. Now are you going to make me sit here and sabotage my diet further with a chocolate ganache tarte or can we adjourn to my place for drinks, *et cetera?*"

"That depends. Who is picking up the check?"

"You, of course. I'm just a poor lieutenant, while you are awash in GS-14 bucks!"

"In that case, away with us! I can ill-afford any more courses in this place!"

3532 Slidergate Drive, Rockledge, Florida 22:13 EDT, 14 June

Ben

Life with someone on the spectrum usually involved certain rituals that needed to be observed, even for those with a condition as mild as Victoria's. For Ben, most of the adjustments were minor, as the Coast Guard Academy had conditioned him to its own rituals of clothes folding and the like. Most of these, like serving different meal items on separate plates to meet her need to keep food items from touching each other, he did now without even thinking. Some he thoroughly enjoyed, like the one in which he was engaged at present: brushing out Victoria's long, auburn-colored hair. It was not just that he loved the soft feel and smell of hair products she used—it was also a prelude to a session of vigorous lovemaking.

They rarely talked while he brushed, but the activity brought with it a question he needed to have answered. As he pulled gently during another pass through the hair down her back, he asked, "Please understand, this is not a complaint, but I thought you were tired. This *is* leading to where I think it is, correct?"

"Most assuredly, my dearest man," Victoria replied. "Besides the obvious benefits to us of calling an early end to the outing, I wanted to allow Haley and Peter the chance to get along with their evening."

"What do you mean?"

"Are you serious, Benjamin? They are lovers."

Ben nearly dropped the brush and gaped down at Victoria. "*What?*"

Victoria turned and took his hand as she looked up at him. "You did not know? I am astounded!"

He sat down heavily next to her. "No! I had no clue! How long has this been going on?"

"Since our wedding, I believe. Despite all the wonderful distractions at the reception, I was able to note they shared a lengthy conversation over several drinks. I thought I might have been mistaken at the beginning of dinner tonight—they were wary of each other at first. However, by the end of the evening, they were sharing very meaningful looks. My sense is that they had some sort of disagreement, which they worked through over the course of the meal."

"That's incredible! That odd exchange after our engagement story makes sense now. Haley was really worked up about something yesterday. Now that I think about it, I bet it is because the first she heard about Pete working with us was from Mercier. Getting news like that from the boss would hack anybody off. Wow, Haley and Pete? Good on them!"

Victoria turned away with a wistful look. "I am not so sure."

"You're worried? Don't be. I know Haley and I had our issues in the beginning, but she's really first-rate. Pete will be lucky to have her."

"It is not Peter's happiness I am concerned about. It is Haley's."

For the second time, Ben was taken aback. "You're not serious. Pete is...well, he's not a Sam Powell, but he's still a guy I'd trust with my life. And I thought you loved him."

"I did, very much. I still do, of course, for all the kindness he has shown me. But Julie's death changed him. He has been very...dark since then. I hope that now the 252 Syndicate has been broken, he can move on and resume his life, but I fear the man I loved is gone."

It was a sobering thought. He genuinely respected and liked Pete, both for his sense of humor and because they had stood facing death together on two tough missions. He was pondering the implications of his CO in a potentially troubled relationship with one of his closest friends when his face broke into a grin with a startling realization. "Whoa, wait a minute! I thought you had trouble reading emotions, you sneak!"

She turned back and smiled warmly. "No, I am quite sensitive to the fact that people are *experiencing* emotions from observation of their movements, muscle contractions in their faces and necks, and verbal and tonal changes. I simply have difficulty identifying what emotion they are experiencing."

"And you have been reading me all this time?"

"Of course! Just like now."

"You can read what my emotion is right now?"

She moved over to sit on his lap and put her arms around his neck. "I certainly hope so!" she said with a mischievous smile.

USCG Cutter Kauai, moored, Trident Wharf, Port Canaveral, Florida
14:37 EDT, 15 June

Ben

Ben stepped up to open the passenger door as *Kauai*'s sedan pulled up to the brow. "Good afternoon, Dr. Hernandez," he said, offering his hand to the middle-aged woman stepping out of the vehicle. "I'm Lieutenant Ben Wyporek, Executive Officer."

"Good afternoon, Lieutenant, and thank you for meeting with me today," she said with a broad smile and a subtle Hispanic accent. Lydia Hernandez was a tall woman, almost Ben's height, full-figured with short, graying brown hair.

"My pleasure, ma'am. Would you care to follow me inside, please?"

"Certainly. Just let me grab my briefcase."

"Of course," Ben said. After she reached in and pulled it from the back seat, he continued. "I'm sorry to make you leave your car outside the gate, but getting a pass for a rental proved to be more than the Space Force could swallow." In fact, Ben had spent most of the morning trying to swing it with the Cape Canaveral Space Force Station's Security Division without success. They had to settle for sending a duty driver to make the pickup for entry to the base. He was actually happy with the result—at one point, it looked like Hernandez would be denied entry, which would have been an embarrassing result for everyone.

"Lieutenant, I'm so grateful to have your support on this expedition, I would gladly have walked here from Orlando."

They passed through the watertight door into the cool fluorescent lighting of the messdeck, where Haley was waiting.

"Dr. Hernandez, may I introduce our captain, Lieutenant Haley Reardon," Ben said.

Haley offered her hand and said, "Welcome aboard, ma'am. I hope you'll forgive the question, but do you prefer to be called doctor or professor?"

Shaking her hand, Hernandez replied with a smile, "You can resolve the dilemma by calling me Lydia."

Haley chuckled. "Maybe over a beer sometime. While we are on the job, you need to be addressed by the proper title or God knows what could happen."

"I wouldn't want to call down the wrath of God on you. 'Doctor' will be fine."

"So be it," Haley replied. She gestured to the mess table, clear except for a tray of pastries, a stack of small plates, and a coffee service. "If you could have a seat here, our culinary specialist has prepared some munchies and hi-test coffee for us. What was it Chef called them, XO?"

"Beignets, Captain."

Culinary Specialist Second Class Thomas "Chef" Hebert was another legacy of the "secret sauce" Haley's predecessor had used to turn *Kauai* into a crack unit. Born and raised in New Orleans, Hebert apprenticed in a small family-owned and run restaurant in the Vieux Carré before enlisting in the Coast Guard. Besides the service's regular commissary support, first Sam, and now Haley contributed funds to provide for his more "exotic" condiment and equipment needs. The result was superb meals for the crew when underway, a significant plus in a patrol boat's otherwise spartan existence. As for Hebert, he loved the work, relished the appreciation he received, and, best of all, got to shoot a fifty-caliber machine gun in his general quarters billet.

"Beignets? How wonderful!" Hernandez said. "Wait, I thought they came with powdered sugar?"

"Too messy for us, ma'am," Ben replied. "So, Chef came up with a glaze that has the same taste."

"Hmm. Let's see," Hernandez said as she sat at the table and took one of the pastries and a plate. After biting into it, she rolled her eyes and said, "Fantastic! I feel like I am back in New Orleans."

"I'm sure Chef will be delighted to hear that," Haley nodded. "When we are done here, Ben can take you on a tour to get a sense of storage space and the like. We are, of course, very interested in your work. I was surprised to learn that St. Ignatius is considered an active volcano, given it hasn't erupted in hundreds of years."

"Yes," Hernandez said after she swallowed a mouthful of pastry. "Four hundred years is a blink of an eye in geologic time. We consider any volcano still associated with a magma chamber that has erupted in the last ten thousand years to be active."

"That puts things in perspective," Haley said. "So, do you think St. Ignatius is going to erupt?"

"Probably not, at least, not in our lifetimes," Hernandez replied. "Eruptions are rarely a surprise—there are usually far more symptoms than what has been reported down there."

"And what would that be?" Ben asked.

"Sporadic tremors and some steam venting. There might be other signs that non-experts can't recognize. That's why USGS wants to take a look, if for no other reason than to rule them out." She finished her last bite and wiped her hands on a napkin. "These really are good."

"I'll have Chef bag up the rest as a care package for you," Haley said. "I need to get them out of here or I'll be in a food coma by the end of the day!"

"Happy to help with that," Hernandez smiled. She reached over and opened her briefcase. "I've prepared some briefing slides, sort of a St. Ignatius Volcanism one-oh-one for you." After handing Ben and Haley a stack of paper, she continued. "St. Ignatius is at the tail end of the Lesser Antilles Volcanic Arc, which is part of a subduction zone where the North American Plate is being pushed under the Caribbean Plate. These conditions tend to produce chains of volcanoes through some complex processes. I'll spare you the explanation unless you really want to dig in for a few hours."

"We'll take it on faith, thank you," Haley said with a smile.

"Good. Anyway, several magma chambers exist along this line, which correspond to most of the islands along the eastern side of the Caribbean. Some have run their course. Others, like La Soufrière on Saint Vincent, have erupted quite recently. St. Ignatius is somewhere in between. As you know, the last eruption took place around four hundred years ago and it was not directly observed. However, the evidence we have suggests it was a violent Peléan eruption similar to the most recent ones on Martinique and Saint Vincent."

"Are Peléan eruptions particularly dangerous?" Ben asked.

"All eruptions are dangerous, Ben," Hernandez said. "Peléan eruptions are characterized by pyroclastic flows and surges at the outset, which are lethal if you are caught in one. They are hot clouds of tephra and eruptive gases that can travel over four hundred miles per hour."

"What is tephra?" Haley asked.

"Tephra is magma that has been erupted into the air rather than flowing along the ground as lava. Depending on the size, it could also be called ash, lapilli, or bombs. In any case, you want to stay out of a pyroclastic flow. If you don't, you're dead, full stop."

"Noted," Haley said. "The ash is bad enough. The Fast Response Cutter I was on got hit with some from the La Soufrière eruption while we were on patrol out of San

Juan. It was the cleanup from hell, but it could have been worse."

"Yes," Hernandez nodded. "The ash is very dangerous. If you breathe enough of it, it will combine with the water in your lungs and you can drown in what is essentially concrete. It can also clog filters, short out electrical equipment and electronics and if enough accumulates and gets wet, collapse a building or capsize a ship."

"Um, now would be a good point to reassure us that an eruption is not imminent," Haley said as her smile vanished.

"No guarantees, but I would not be taking four students with me instead of hard-core USGS types if I thought anything like that was probable."

"You got four students to sign up for field work rather than lounging on the beach all summer?" Ben asked, his smile returning.

"I'd like to say it is because of my inspirational academic leadership, but they'll be getting credit hours tuition-free and enjoying one of the most beautiful islands in the Caribbean. It is a great opportunity for them to actually work with the equipment and see it in action. Still, it comes as a surprise the trip was approved—if not for the Coast Guard pitching in, it would never have gotten off the ground."

Ben shared a meaningful glance with Haley, who said, "Glad to help. Speaking of which, what do you expect from us?"

"Mainly transport of our equipment. I'm sure you have heard that it is devilishly hard to get stuff in there—the harbor is very shallow and the airport is little better than a helicopter pad. There will be a crane to help bring it aboard in Mayagüez, but I'm unsure how we'll manage down there."

"I'll ask Chief Drake to come along on the tour after our meeting," Ben said. "If he doesn't think our boat crane can handle it, he might 'know a guy' who can help us."

Chief Machinery Technician James Drake was the senior enlisted member and the oldest man on the boat at forty-five. Since Hopkins's advancement to the same rank, the crew informally called Drake "COB" for "Chief of the Boat" on *Kauai*, a tradition borrowed from navy submarines. He was the best chief petty officer Ben had ever known because of his mastery of his trade and his leadership among the crew. Six-foot-four and physically imposing, he needed just to lean in to get someone's attention or administer a well-deserved dressing-down. Still, he quickly found an opportunity to work with the individual and give quiet encouragement.

Drake was also a master "wheeler-dealer" who worked an extensive network of connections among fellow chiefs and officers up to Captain's rank to keep *Kauai* well-supplied and running. Somewhat concerned about his "Don't worry, sir, I know a guy..." activities earlier in his tenure, Ben had learned not to ask too many questions, just sit back and enjoy what happened next. If there was any crane service to be had on St. Ignatius, Drake could arrange it.

"That's good news. So, after we get there, I'd ask that you help us with the positioning of the equipment. St. Ignatius is the summit of a volcanic mountain, the base of which extends a couple of miles from shore in every direction. We will use seismic tomography to get a sense of the size and position of the magma chamber, and we need to position some underwater seismometers around the base. You can do that and then retrieve them afterward so that we can process their recorded data."

"Seismic Tomography?" Ben asked.

"Yes. Sound travels more slowly through liquid magma than the surrounding rock. We can generate a sound pulse at regular intervals from a vessel circumnavigating the island. The sensors in the shadow of the magma chamber will experience a delay in receipt of a sound pulse. We have laptop applications that can process the data and present a reasonably accurate picture of the chamber."

"Cool!" Haley said. "Are we going to be the ones making the sounds?"

"No, the generator array is far too large and heavy for *Kauai*. There is a research vessel from Woods Hole transiting the area on the 27th that has agreed to help us with that."

"That's a relief," Haley said. "Once you have the picture, what then?"

Hernandez nodded. "If it's what I expect and hope, a largely solidified chamber with some hydrothermal activity, we can give an all clear, and everyone can go about their business."

"And if it's not?" Ben asked. "What's the worst case here?"

Hernandez's smile disappeared. "If the magma chamber is active and full, we will get USGS to issue an eruption imminent warning, and the local government will evacuate the island. Then we run for it. Any eruption would almost certainly annihilate anything on the island. If the magma chamber is large and full enough, the island may collapse into the space it leaves after it empties, forming what we call a caldera. The island itself would disappear, generating widespread destruction of the nearby islands from tsunamis and ashfall. In the extreme worst case, a structural collapse could open the magma chamber to the sea and generate one of the most powerful explosions we've ever seen."

She paused on seeing Ben and Haley's wide-eyed and slack-jawed expressions. "Hey, the probability of that outcome is very low. And even if it happens, we will have plenty of time to get clear."

Haley blinked and then gave an uncertain smile. "I'll hold you to that, Doctor. One more thing, we've been told we will bring down one of our UAV detachments. What will they do?"

Hernandez's smile returned. "Yes, that is another wonderful service the Coast Guard has provided. We have special sensor pods it will carry to help us perform a topographic survey and sample gas emissions. If there is any displacement of the surface or signs of exsolved magmatic gasses, it will provide another early warning of an eruption. Again, not expected, but just in case. It should not impact your operations—I need first-hand access to their measurements, so they will be operating from the airfield on the island."

Haley nodded. "Good. For planning purposes, we can hang around down there for three days between refuelings in San Juan. The trip up and back should not take more than one day. Also, we have to support a diplomatic event in Guadeloupe, so we will be out of pocket from the 29th through the 3rd of July."

Hernandez made some notes in a small notebook and then said, "That will be fine. We should be wrapped up and ready to depart by the 15th of July."

"Perfect," Haley said. "I have no other questions. XO?"

Ben shook his head. "Good here, Captain."

"Then I'll let Ben conduct the tour." They all stood, and she held out her hand. "It is a pleasure meeting you, Doctor, and I'm looking forward to working with you."

Hernandez shook her hand and said, "Same here, Lieutenant, and thank you."

After Haley left, Ben leaned in and said, "One protocol item, ma'am. When we are on board *Kauai*, Haley's title is 'Captain', not 'Lieutenant'."

"Oh, I'm sorry!" she replied with a pained expression.

"No big deal, ma'am. Just might as well get it right." He held his hand toward the door. "If you will follow me, please.

******

Ben knocked on Haley's cabin door and opened it and stepped in at her "Come in."

"Captain, Dr. Hernandez is safely on her way home with a smile on her face, a song in her heart, and a sack of fresh beignets under her arm," he said with a grin.

Haley smiled in return. "Excellent. Hopefully, she can get them through security without having to pay off all the TSA folks." Her smile faded. "I don't know about you, but I'm still reeling over the eruption scenario she laid out."

Ben nodded and said, "Boy howdy. Who'd have thought the cover story would be more dangerous than the actual mission? Should we ring up Captain Mercier with a 'But, ma'am...'?"

"No, I don't want to go all chicken little. But I do want us covered in case things don't turn out as rosy as she's saying. I can't tell you how scary it was on the FRC when we got caught in that ashfall from the La Soufrière eruption. We had to shut down everything, main diesels, generators, and electronics, and then improvise some shovels to push the ash off the decks. I want to be ready, just in case. Contact the USGS and get a recommendation from them on worst-case personal protective equipment, facemasks, respirators, whatever. I want every member of the crew to have a set plus whatever spare filters, *et cetera,* are appropriate. Have COB call them too and lay on whatever special filters we can get for the engines and ventilation system. Make it an emergency procurement."

"That won't be cheap, skipper. And it's not on our allowance list, so I can't use ship's funds."

"I know. Route the invoices through Captain Mercier. That should get her attention. If not, well, Bridget Morehouse isn't the only one with a rich daddy. I'll tap into *mine* and fund it myself if I have to. The way I figure it, grabbing all this stuff in advance ensures nothing can possibly happen."

"I didn't realize buying a lot of stuff could have so profound an influence on the universe," Ben said with a mock thoughtful expression.

"It's an approach that's worked for us girls since the beginning of time!" Haley said with a twinkle in her eye. "Oh, and include half a dozen snow shovels in that order."

Ben chuckled. "Yeah, a Florida cutter ordering snow shovels in June ought to draw some attention!"

Part II

Chapter 7

Distress

3532 Slidergate Drive, Rockledge, Florida
23:48 EDT, 20 June

Victoria

The eve of a patrol was always a bittersweet time for Victoria. It was the most intimate time they shared, because they both knew there was a chance, however slight, that Benjamin might not come back. When they had first moved in together, he had tried to assuage her fears by appealing to her logical mind and mathematical genius regarding the overwhelming probability in favor of his safe return. However, in this case, mathematics failed her. No imbalance of favorable odds could purge the memory of her sitting beside Benjamin in his ICU hospital bed that night after Barbello, wondering if he would recover or even survive. Eventually, he came to terms with the reality that it was one of those things he could not fix, just accept and be supportive.

Their routine was to dine in so that they could talk freely about whatever was on their minds, having no concerns about being overheard. Benjamin cooked—it was another thing he was much better at than she—usually some fancy new recipe Thomas Hebert had shared with him. After dinner, they would talk, watch a romantic movie, or simply snuggle together listening to music. It was their time, theirs alone, free from their jobs and everything else outside to do as they pleased. The time was the treasure that outweighed the loneliness and worry while he was gone.

This night was noteworthy, as this was the first time she knew in advance that Benjamin was heading out on one of his "special" missions instead of an ordinary patrol. She knew he would be working with Peter, which conveyed its own source of alarm despite assurances from both him and Benjamin that it would be a low-risk mission. However, in her mind, the cover mission supporting the volcano research team was far more worrisome. She accepted the probability of an eruption was low and far less that if one happened, Benjamin and *Kauai* would be caught up in it. Nonetheless, even the contemplation of such a possibility horrified her.

It had been one of their quiet snuggling nights. Over dinner, she shared her fears and Benjamin detailed the steps they had taken to prepare for all the contingencies. By the end of the meal, they had talked through the issues and, after clearing the dishes, settled onto the couch together to listen to a playlist of piano concertos Victoria had prepared for the occasion. It continued to amaze Victoria that a mind as active as hers could find the most satisfying moments in life quietly caressing and being caressed by this man while listening to soft, centuries-old music. After a couple of hours, they went to bed and fell asleep in each other's arms.

They were up before dawn. Since Benjamin would be gone for a month and it was undesirable to leave his car unattended and exposed to the salty air for that long, Victoria drove him to *Kauai*'s berth. After he had taken his travel bag out of the trunk, she gave him a last hug and they kissed passionately. She looked into his eyes, those marvelous eyes as deep azure blue as a clear sky, and said, "Come back to me, Benjamin."

He returned one of his heart-melting sad smiles and replied, "Yes, boss."

She cupped his face in her hands and said, "No. Promise me you will come back."

His smile faded, leaving only the sad look. "I promise, my love."

They hugged once more and then Victoria quickly got into her car and drove off. Her eyes teared up when she glanced into the rearview mirror and saw that Benjamin was still standing there, watching her depart. *No, I cannot be like this every time! I will not be a clingy wife!* She focused her mind intently on driving from that point forward. At this early hour, the traffic was light on the route that took her on A1A across the Banana River and Indian River causeways to Interstate 95 South.

Although Victoria desperately wanted to return home for a good long cry, she drove by their exit on I-95 and continued toward her workplace at Vectorsonds Inc. in Melbourne. She would undoubtedly be the first one into work this morning, which was fortuitous, as she was not in the correct frame of mind to engage in the challenge of making small talk with her coworkers. She had four difficult projects on her plate that would require some effort to get up and running this morning, made easier by the quiet of an empty office.

Benjamin's absences were usually only a week long, a fortunate result of *Kauai* being a relatively short-ranged patrol boat. Victoria hoped the concentration her projects demanded would be enough of a distraction to get her through this first day of a month-long mission, which, besides the danger, would be the longest separation they had experienced since they moved in together. It was all new for her, and not in a good way.

**USCG Cutter Kauai, North Atlantic Ocean, seventy-two nautical miles north-northeast of Acklins Island, Bahamas
11:27 EDT, 22 June**

Marcus

Cadet First Class Marcus Porter sat in the left seat of the FC3 console, listening intently as Williams demonstrated the multifunction displays and controls for the system. Marcus had been astounded by the presence of one of the most modern command-and-control systems he had ever seen on a patrol boat well past the end of its service life. Likewise, the boat's propulsion was amazing: a diesel-electric and battery system more like a modern conventional submarine than the rickety old direct-drive diesels he had expected.

Marcus was coming up on his final year at the Coast Guard Academy in New London, Connecticut. Unlike civilian colleges, academy students, called cadets, were assigned to professional training programs across the summer between academic years to provide hands-on experience and exposure to the Service's many missions. The hardest working and luckiest might be assigned to a special summer-long internship at a single unit for a "deep dive" into a particular mission area. Marcus was one of those very lucky few—his assignment was to the aviation deployment center in Jacksonville, Florida, to work in the unmanned aerial systems program.

Becoming an aviator, the term the Coast Guard used to describe their aircraft pilots, was Marcus's dream from well before he entered the Academy almost three years previously, shortly after his eighteenth birthday. A tall six-foot-two and lean 175 pounds, with the dark hair and complexion of his father and blue-gray eyes of his mother, Marcus lettered in high school baseball and swimming but opted to focus on academics at the Academy rather than competitive sports. He had worked his tail off, setting himself up to compete for one of the twenty slots to Naval Flight Training offered to new Academy graduates each year. Along the way, he completed the Federal Aviation Administration's requirements and was officially rated as a Remote Pilot, certified to operate unmanned aircraft in the national airspace.

His initiative had drawn the attention of the officers in charge of selection for special programs, and his superior performance in academic and military proficiency put him over the top for the assignment. Besides the delight of being assigned to intern in a program he loved, Marcus had the privilege of working with a man he had admired his entire life, his mother's younger brother, Chief Petty Officer Erich Deffler.

As soon as he heard of Marcus's assignment, Deffler called to congratulate him, then sent him copies of the T-20's operating and maintenance manuals and a note that said, "Know these cover-to-cover before you show up!" Marcus was puzzled—he had never heard of the T-20 and wondered what his uncle was up to. His bafflement was resolved on his first day in Jacksonville when he was called into the Assistant Operations Officer's office.

"Chief Deffler is standing up a team for the operational evaluation of the T-20 and he wants you on it," said the lieutenant commander, as Marcus stood at attention. "Ordinarily, I wouldn't even think of putting a cadet on a job like that, but he insists you're one of the Jedis on this system. Is that for real?"

On the inside, Marcus was shaking in his boots. But he had put in the same level of effort studying the manuals as he had the flight regulations while preparing for his FAA pilot's examination and was confident enough to say, "I know the manuals backward and forward, sir. I can do the job."

The officer gave him a long look, then nodded and said, "OK, you're in. Don't make me regret it!"

Marcus quickly worked through the qualification syllabus and was rated as a T-20 pilot, along with his uncle and two petty officers on the team. His excitement was unbounded when Deffler selected him for the T-20's first operational mission—he was the launch and recovery pilot back at the Cape Canaveral Space Force Station during *Kauai*'s operation against the CARE terrorists. That went well enough that when the T-20 was selected for the St. Ignatius expedition, Deffler picked Marcus as one of his two support pilot/mechanics. It would be a tremendous amount of work, but it was the coolest mission he could have imagined in what he had been told was one of the most beautiful places in the world. It did not get any better than that!

Although his stay on *Kauai* was brief, only two days in transit each way, Marcus's duty was to make the most of whatever training opportunities were available. Like all Academy students, Marcus trained first to be a professional mariner, and his interest in the FC3 was not idle. Williams was happy to oblige—he loved showing off "his" system to visitors—and it was clear the good feelings Deffler had accumulated on the boat extended to any on his team.

"And that's all she wrote, Mr. Porter," Williams said. "Do you have any questions?" As an officer-in-training, Marcus was addressed as "Mr. Porter" by the enlisted crew.

"Yes, you said the system has an electronic warfare capability. I have never heard of that on a ship this small. What can you do?"

Williams looked over at Hopkins, who was supervising the training, and got a nod in return. He turned back to the panel and said, "It's strictly passive. We can read the energy level we are receiving from a radar and make a pretty good guess whether it has picked us up. Also, it has a database we can use to identify the ship by the signature of its radar's cavity magnetron, but that only works on conventional radars, not phased arrays."

Holy shit! Marcus thought. *Uncle Erich told me this boat was into some wild stuff, but this is dope!* "Wow. What kind of stuff do you do that needs something like that?"

Williams just smiled and glanced at Hopkins again, who said, "What Petty Officer Williams is not saying is that some of the stuff we get into on board here is 'need to know' only. Now, if you're finished, how about we go down for some lunch?"

"Got it, Chief. And you don't have to ask me twice if I want to eat." He stood and offered his hand to Williams. "Thanks for the tour, Petty Officer Williams."

Williams shook his hand firmly. "My pleasure. See ya around," he said with a warm smile, and then turned back to his panel.

Marcus followed Hopkins down the ladder from the bridge to the short corridor leading to the messdeck. She had been very gracious to take the time to show him around the boat, although he suspected that her affection for his uncle had something to do with it. Marcus was old enough when his uncle got his divorce to understand the pain he was put through and was glad that he found someone so...well, *nice*, in Hopkins. She was attractive, in an older woman kind of way, and just pleasant to be around. He knew Uncle Erich was crazy about her, although he didn't talk about things like that, even to Marcus. As they entered the messdeck, the smell made his mouth water.

"What's on the menu, Chef?" Hopkins called out.

"Chicken and Andouille Gumbo with rice and cornbread, Chief," Hebert responded with a smile.

"Outstanding!" Hopkins said as she grabbed a bowl, a small plate, and silverware.

Marcus grabbed his dishes and food, and the two sat at the mess table. Zuccaro was already sitting there in front of an empty plate, drinking a glass of what looked like lemon-lime Gatorade, and she smiled at him when he sat down. The rules for cadets concerning enlisted were the same as that for officers—"inappropriate" relations would get you busted and, in his case, thrown out of the Academy. But...Marcus had to admit, she was pretty hot, with brown eyes and hair, a nice build, and a pleasant face. He smiled back.

"Hello, Marcus," Zuccaro said, looking at him with a flutter of eyelashes that made him catch his breath.

"I think you meant to say, 'Mr. Porter', Zuccaro," Hopkins interrupted with a frown.

Zuccaro's smile disappeared, and she turned to Hopkins. "Yes, Chief."

"Good. Now that today's lesson in military protocol is complete, shouldn't you be on the bridge relieving the watch?" Hopkins said coldly.

"Yes, Chief," Zuccaro repeated, then stood, smiled again at Marcus, and dropped her dishes in the receiving pan as she left the room and headed for the bridge.

Hopkins sighed, then took a spoonful of gumbo and paused before putting it in her mouth, blowing on it gently. "Care for a word of advice from your friendly neighborhood chief operations specialist?" she said sotto voce.

"Of course," Marcus said, leaning forward.

Hopkins nodded toward the exit through which Zuccaro had just passed. "That is pure trouble. If you run into her when I'm not there, turn around and walk away. Do you feel me?"

"Yes, Chief." Marcus blushed and then quickly took a bite of cornbread. His mortification mercifully ended within a minute when his uncle appeared and, after grabbing some food, came over to the table.

"Em, Mr. Porter, mind if I join you?" At Hopkins's smile and nod, he sat next to Marcus. Even in the close environment of the messdeck, he was careful not to address Marcus by his first name on board ship. "So, what have you guys been up to on this fine day?"

"Oh, I've been showing this young man around, trying to convince him of the error of his ways in becoming an Airedale, and discussing hazards to navigation," she replied, winking at Marcus with the last phrase.

"Not a chance with that. This lad is far too evolved to stay on boats," Uncle Erich said with a grin.

"You watch it, matey!" Hopkins shot back, pointing her spoon at him in mock anger.

Marcus sat contently, listening to their light-hearted banter while he enjoyed the meal. The quality of the food on *Kauai* was another surprise. He had become accustomed to the typical college cafeteria-quality food served at Academy meals and the rarely better, often worse cuisine on the ships he had visited. This food was restaurant-quality and not the restaurants he could afford on his cadet pay. This was mom-and-dad-taking-you-out-to-celebrate-quality food. *Emilia and the chow—no wonder Uncle Erich digs going to sea so much!*

After completing the meal, Marcus went to thank Hebert and then strolled out on the afterdeck. A trip of this length was perfect from Marcus's perspective. Had it been longer, he would have been expected to complete some sort of training syllabus. As it was, since their aircraft and support equipment were sealed in watertight containers tied down on the afterdeck, there was no work for him to do and he could enjoy the gorgeous weather and fresh air in peace. Things would be far more hectic the next day after they picked up the volcano people and went over expectations for flight support on the quick trip from Mayagüez to St. Ignatius.

He glanced off toward the port quarter of the ship. Across the blue sea, barely stirred by swells, a ropy funnel cloud extended from one of the many puffy cumulus clouds to the surface. It was one of the "fair weather" waterspouts common in the tropics in the summer. As many as he had seen in his cadet cruises, Marcus still found them fascinating and sat on a shaded vent head to watch. After a few minutes, it reached its decay stage and disappeared from view.

He stayed for another half hour, but the lack of birds and visible sea life to watch this far offshore left no excuse for him to continue putting off a review of the T-20 manuals. Uncle Erich had only him and Avionics Electrical Technician Second Class Derek Lincoln along to put together their aircraft and ground support equipment once they landed on St. Ignatius. He did not want to be fumbling around and holding things up when they were needed. Marcus took one last long scan of the horizon and then trudged back inside.

Motor Vessel Conch Rounder, anchored,
Turks Island Passage, two nautical miles

southwest of Grand Turk Lighthouse
01:38 EDT, 23 June

Edwards

Cedric Edwards was finishing his third cigarette in the last half hour. It was a dirty, expensive habit that cut down his lung capacity, but on these terrible night security watches, they and caffeinated sodas were the only things keeping him awake. *Smokes and Cokes, can't beat 'em*, he thought as he gazed around the boat from his chair in the wheelhouse.

Edwards was the third deckhand on the *Conch Rounder*, a charter dive boat equipped with compressors and other scuba servicing equipment, and living accommodations to support its crew of six and up to forty passengers for three days. There were twenty-three passengers aboard this night, a dive club from the United Kingdom enjoying a three-day tour of the best of the dozens of dive spots around Grand Turk and East Caicos islands. While the island of Grand Turk was in plain sight less than a mile off their starboard quarter, there were no harbors anywhere nearby, just shallow water leading to beaches. So, rather than waste several hours each day motoring to and from harbors, the boat anchored near a desirable diving spot, and the customers slept on board and used the saved time for more diving.

The *Conch Rounder* was ninety-six feet long, wood and fiberglass construction with two diesel engines, one for propulsion and the other an electrical generator. The latter was running quietly now to provide electricity for the lights and air conditioning for the passengers, asleep in the bunkroom below the wheelhouse where Edwards sat. Behind the bunkroom was a salon area and galley for dining and lounging around between dives. The salon opened to a wide afterdeck, where the divers could don, remove, and store their tanks and other equipment. There was a mechanically raised swim platform on the stern to which the *Conch Rounder*'s skiff was tied.

Besides Edwards, *Conch Rounder*'s crew comprised a captain, a first mate, two deckhands, and a cook. Edwards was the most junior of the crew, hence his being stuck with staying up all night to watch for fire and flooding. In theory, he would sleep during the day on these voyages, to be rested and alert at night. In fact, it was impossible to sleep on a working boat during the day, with the light, noise, and erratic motion. So by the third day of a trip, Edwards was a sleep-deprived wreck, barely able to stay awake on his feet. He had pointed out this fact to the captain some time ago, whose response was to tell him to quit if he couldn't take it—he had plenty of guys lining up to take his place. Edwards was sure this was true—the job paid better than most on Grand Turk. So, having nothing even half as good, much less better to fall back on, he stuck with it, relying on smokes and Cokes to get him through the long nights.

Edwards got up and completed a walk-around of the upper deck, pausing briefly to listen to the generator humming away from the open hatch to the engine space. Most of the boats he had served on would never have left a hatch open at anchor at night with most of the crew asleep. But *Conch Rounder*'s generator had a nasty habit of overheating, leading to shut down, so the hatch was left open for ventilation. The risk of flooding from a sudden-onset storm was low since they had a live roving watch.

After completing his stroll, Edwards returned to his chair, took another swig of coke, and settled in to contemplate the injustice of the world. Soon, his thoughts shifted to how he was to spend his time off at the end of this trip. As his concentration wandered, he lost his grip on the will needed to stay awake and drifted off to sleep in the chair.

"GET UP YOU LAZY PIG!"

Edwards startled awake lying on the deck, his shoulder screaming in pain, to see the chair in which he had been sitting turned over and the wide-eyed first mate leaning over him. "Wha...what happened?" he croaked.

"There's a fire aft!" the mate shouted. "Get your ass down to the main deck and grab a fire extinguisher!"

Edwards jumped up, suddenly aware of the screaming from below and the acrid smell of smoke. He ran to the door in the back of the wheelhouse and threw it open, only to be blown back inside by a blast of searing hot air. Seeing the yellow glow extending from aft to the starboard side door, he ran to the port side door and opened it carefully. No fire here. He stepped through the door, then crawled over the rail and lowered himself to the main deck, grabbed a life vest from the locker, and put it on before turning aft.

There was no one else here on the port side, and Edwards assumed the rest of the crew were on the starboard side, fighting the fire. He turned and trotted aft to grab one of the fire extinguishers kept inside the door of the salon. As he rounded the edge of the superstructure, another blast of burning air blew him backward. The entire afterdeck was in flames, including the entrance to the salon. He turned forward and ran to the bow, rounded the superstructure to find the flames already moving up the starboard side. One crewmember, he could not tell who, was silhouetted by the flames, suddenly turned and jumped overboard.

Cedric, you've done your bit. Nothing more to do here! He took a good fix on the lighthouse on Grand Turk in the distance, climbed over the rail, and fell the eight feet into the cool water alongside. He took one last look at the *Conch Rounder* and was startled to see that someone, probably the first mate, had fired a red distress flare. Yellow flames engulfed the boat from the superstructure aft and were billowing ten feet above the deck. *Those poor people!* Edwards thought, then turned and started swimming toward the lights on the shore.

USCG Cutter Kauai, North Atlantic Ocean, thirteen nautical miles north of Grand Turk

Lighthouse.
02:47 EDT, 23 June

Haley

Haley was startled awake by the ring of the phone above the headboard of her bunk. She grabbed the handset and said, "Captain."

"O.O.D., ma'am," Lee's voice came through the earpiece. "We just picked up a mayday. Vessel on fire with twenty-nine P.O.B. twelve miles south of us. I've just seen a red star fired on the same bearing. I have turned on a direct heading to the reported position at twenty-four knots. Main Control is putting the third engine on line."

As if cued, Haley could hear the whine of an engine starter from aft. "Well done, Petty Officer Lee! Carry on. I'll be up there in a minute. Sound rescue and assistance detail."

"Aye, aye, Captain!"

Haley had already swung her legs out of her bunk and grabbed her trousers. As she pulled them on, Lee's voice boomed over the ship's announcement system known as the One-MC, "Now set the Rescue and Assistance Detail, vessel on fire with twenty-nine people on board. Man all hose teams. Repeat, set the Rescue and Assistance Detail."

By the time Lee had finished, Haley was headed through her door to the bridge ladder, still buttoning her shirt. As she entered the bridge, she could feel *Kauai* coming up on the step of planing mode for her full speed. She trotted over to Lee standing beside Zuccaro, who was sitting in the center seat of FC3.

"Captain on the bridge!" Lee saluted.

"Carry on," Haley said, returning the salute.

"Captain, all three engines on line. COB is in Main Control, bypassing the safeties. We should have thirty knots shortly." She pointed at one of the FC3 screens. It showed a bright glow with little detail. "We are picking up the vessel visually and on infrared. She's the *Conch Rounder*, a dive boat out of Cockburn Town, anchored two miles southwest of Grand Turk light. I've lost radio contact—they had to abandon the bridge because of smoke. But I got they have a fire out of control aft and had evacuated the passengers through the bridge to the foredeck. It sounds as bad as it gets, ma'am."

Haley nodded. "Good job. What's our ETA?"

"Twenty-one minutes if COB can get us thirty knots, ma'am."

Haley turned to see Hopkins and Ben hustling through the door onto the bridge. "I think we can count on that. This is going to be hairy. As soon as Chief Hopkins relieves you, grab your gear and head down to the RHIB. Take Brown and Chen and a P1B with a short hose and nozzle. After we launch you, haul ass, and when you get there, try to keep that fire back from the foredeck. Be careful when you get there. The master will probably try to keep everyone together if he can, but people will be jumping if it's a choice between that or burning to death.

Once we get in contact, stand by in case anybody goes overboard. You clear on that?"

"Understood, Captain!"

"Good. Right. Carry on and good luck!"

"Thank you, ma'am!" Lee said, then turned to Hopkins to carry out the quick relief.

Haley took Ben by the arm, and they walked to her command chair. "What do you think, XO?"

Ben stroked his chin and said, "We have to get those people off, first priority. Recommend we cross the T and bring them over the bow to our foredeck. We use two hose teams to relieve Lee and hold back the fire while we get everyone off. After that, we can decide if we want to make a fight of it or not."

"Over the bow is dicey. Why not side-to-side?"

Ben shook his head. "It sucks, ma'am. But besides the risk of the fire spreading over to us, this is a dive boat. They'll have dozens of scuba tanks under pressure that are getting roasted right now. They have burst disks that should let go before they blow, but we can't take a chance of having a defective one cook off while we are right alongside. Besides mowing down a hose team, the shrapnel could penetrate the hull."

Ben's logic, as usual, was both grim and unassailable. "You're right. I hate it, but we have to play the percentages. Besides the flash gear, everyone on deck should have a ballistic vest and helmet. When you go down, see to it."

Ben nodded. "Yes, ma'am."

"Good. You heard me brief Lee. Make sure we have good comms between us and the boat. In addition to on-scene leader for the fire, you'll have the best perspective to provide conning advice to keep us in position."

"Understood. By your leave, Captain?"

"Yes. Good luck and, for God's sake, be careful."

Ben grinned. "Always. Good luck, Captain!" He then turned and left the bridge.

Haley turned back to the FC3 console. Williams had already arrived and taken the center seat, with Zuccaro shifting to navigation and radar in the right seat. Electronics Technician Third Class Darryl Bunting had arrived and was tending to systems and communications in the left seat. The screen showing the feed from the electro-optical camera now showed the burning vessel clearly, but the details were washed out by the glare from the flames.

She glanced over at the time/position/speed display—13.8 minutes to the vessel at their current speed of 31.2 knots. Haley smiled. *Leave it to COB to under-promise and over-deliver. He must be sweet-talking those electric motors. At this speed, the rotors must be close to melting!* Now came the hard part. She had contributed all she could as captain. The execution was now up to Lee and Ben and his teams on deck. Her predecessor had warned her of this, and she had experienced it herself several times. *Those are your kids down there. They've got the job now and there isn't a damn thing more you can do.* It never got easier.

Chapter 8

Conflagration

USCG Cutter Kauai, North Atlantic Ocean, two nautical miles west of Grand Turk Lighthouse
03:05 EDT, 23 June

Ben

The burning boat was clearly visible from the foredeck as *Kauai* approached at high speed. Hopkins was at the conn on the bridge and was a specialist at the quick stop, the goal being to cut the time to contact as short as possible without overshooting or, God forbid, colliding violently with the other boat. Ben had been with Hopkins for over two years now and was supremely confident in her ability to pull it off. This was his first shipboard fire, and Ben had plenty of fears right now, but the approach maneuver was not among these. He could see the shadow of the boat's foredeck now, silhouetted in the bright yellow flames billowing high from the stern. Although he couldn't make them out yet, Lee had reported there were dozens of people crowded onto the foredeck.

Lee had quickly closed the distance in the speedy RHIB and now held a position twenty feet off the *Conch Rounder*'s port beam. Chen and Machinery Technician Second Class Brown were directing a stream of water from the P1B portable pump to hold back the flames and keep them from spreading forward to where the survivors had gathered. The P1B, designed to pump water out of damaged vessels to keep them from sinking, put out 140 gallons of water per minute and Lee had to use her considerable skill with helm and engine control to keep the boat in position against the thrust from the hose. She and Ben had agreed that as soon as the fire could be reached by the hose teams on *Kauai*, he would call out "clear" three times on the radio. Lee would immediately maneuver the RHIB clear while Brown and Chen shut down the pump.

Ben did another check of his deck crew, all fitted with helmets, ballistic vests, and white anti-flash hoods and gloves, to protect them from the fire. Hebert was the lead on the first hose with two junior seamen backing him up, and Deffler, Marcus, and Lincoln manned the second hose. While they held off the fire from aft, Ben and his rescue party on the foredeck, Bondurant, Boatswain's Mate Third Class Brian Jenkins, and Seaman Mitchell Pickins, would handle lines and help the survivors aboard. *Kauai*'s medical expert, Health Services Technician Second Class Michael "Doc" Bryant, was standing by with oxygen and his medical kit to render first aid.

There was no time to research the *Conch Rounder*'s layout or dimensions, so this rendezvous was a veritable blind date. It would have been too good to be true that the dive boat's foredeck would be the same height as *Kauai*'s and when the spotlight above the bridge came on and illuminated the other boat, Ben was not surprised to see it was about six feet higher. As they slowed down to start the approach, he called his team together. "Boats, I think one guy on the dive boat supervising lines and handing the survivors down to the rest of us," Ben said to Bondurant. "Boats" was a traditional nickname for a boatswain's mate and by *Kauai* tradition was the moniker used for the senior of that rating aboard *Kauai*.

"Roger that, XO. I'm the one for that job," Bondurant said.

"Yes, I had you in mind," Ben replied. With his size and strength, Bondurant was the obvious choice. "Pickins, I need someone on the fender, but it will be tricky. Think you can handle it?" The fender was a large elastomer cylinder that would serve as a bumper, preventing *Conch Rounder*'s bow from contacting and possibly damaging *Kauai*'s hull. It was a difficult and hazardous job, particularly under these circumstances.

"No problem, XO," the big seaman said with a smile.

"Good. Jenkins, you'll handle the line. I don't quite know how this is going to work yet. We're kind of playing it by ear."

"Yes, sir," Jenkins replied.

Ben nodded and then scanned their faces. "OK, guys. It's dark. We don't know exactly what we are dealing with on this boat and we're going to be face-to-face with twenty-nine desperate people. What I'm saying is take nothing for granted and if you see something going wrong, shout it out. Questions?"

"No, sir," they all replied.

"Right," Ben said, then he picked up an electric megaphone and stepped up to the rail. Putting it to his mouth, he broadcasted to the burning vessel, "Ahoy! On the *Conch Rounder*, can you hear me?"

A man stepped from the mass of people on the bow, waved, and shouted back faintly, "Yes! I hear you!"

"Are you the captain?"

"Aye, yes, I am!"

"Sir, we are going to come under your bows and will pass over a line! One of us will follow to help transfer your survivors to our foredeck! Do you understand?"

"Aye!"

"OK! Please tell your passengers to stand away from the bow! We will take them one at a time and it's vital they not try to board until our man calls them over! I know it's scary, but we will hold back the fire until they are all on board! Clear?"

"Yes, clear!"

Kauai was now about one hundred yards away and had already lined up on a perpendicular with the stricken vessel's bow. Ben knew Hopkins was using both differential thrust and rudder to keep their orientation and eventually slow the cutter to a stop. He glanced at the RHIB, where Lee was doing the same to keep the boat in position as the stream of water reached out onto the deck just ahead of the flames. "Hose teams ready?" Ben shouted.

"Team One ready!" Hebert replied.

"Team Two ready!" Deffler followed immediately.

Ben keyed his radio transmit button and said, "*Kauai* One, clear, clear, clear!"

"*Kauai* One, roger!" came Lee's reply. The crewman handling the hose immediately directed it toward the water while the pump ran down and the RHIB sheared off to the right.

"Hose teams engage!" Ben shouted. Within three seconds, two powerful streams of water had converged on the *Conch Rounder*'s deck at the head of the flames. Knowing they required no more attention from him, Ben turned back to the situation on the bow. Bondurant was standing by with a heaving line, a thin rope with a weighted end that tied to the larger and heavier mooring line laid out on the deck. Ben put the megaphone to his mouth again. "On the *Conch Rounder*, stand by to receive the heaving line!"

"We're ready!" the captain shouted back.

Ben turned to Bondurant. "OK, Boats. Show us how it's done!"

Bondurant nodded, swung his arm holding the rope back and forth three times, then hurled it upward toward the other vessel. The end landed there with an audible clang and was immediately seized by two men, who began pulling up the rope and then the mooring line. Ben, Bondurant, and Jenkins tended the line as Pickins rushed forward with the fender, lowering it just slightly over the side. The two vessels pressed together with a shrill squeak from the fender and Ben shouted, "Hold the line!"

With the line acting as a pivot while Hopkins held the two vessels together, Bondurant grabbed hold of *Conch Rounder*'s bow and pulled himself up and over the rail. After disappearing for a few seconds, he reappeared at the rail and shouted over the roar of the flames and the two fire hoses, "Ready, XO!"

Ben nodded and said, "Jenkins and Pickins, tend your lines! Doc, come up here and help me out!"

"Yes, sir!" Bryant said as he trotted alongside.

The first survivor, a young woman in shorts and an oversized tee-shirt, was already sitting on the bow. Bondurant grasped her under the armpits and lowered her until Ben and Bryant had a grip, then released her as they took her down to the deck.

"Are you alright?" Ben asked. The woman did not answer, just nodded furiously. "OK, please stand over there," Ben said, pointing to the empty deck between the superstructure and the gun. After she stumbled off, Ben turned up to see Bondurant was already in position with another woman.

And so it went for the first dozen survivors, with Bondurant passing them down to the other two men. The thirteenth, a shirtless man in shorts, was coughing non-stop and was not able to stand on his own. "Smoke inhalation, sir," Bryant said. "I need to attend to him."

"Right. Take him," Ben said. As Bryant put the man's arm around his shoulders and half-carried him to his medical station, Ben turned to Pickins. "That's good enough, Pickins. Come here and help me out!"

"Yes, sir!" The seaman dropped the rope he was holding and trotted over. Once he was in position, the process resumed with Bondurant handing down survivors to the two men on *Kauai*'s foredeck.

Ben kept a count as the people came aboard. All twenty-three passengers and two of the boat's crew had come aboard when a loud boom sounded from *Conch Rounder*'s aft section. A large fireball shot into the sky and *Kauai*'s foredeck was showered with fragments. Ben ducked instinctively, then gazed in alarm as the boat's bow rose quickly into the air away from *Kauai* as the mooring line started moaning with the heavy strain.

"Ease the line! Ease the line!" Ben shouted, and Jenkins threw off the loop he had on the bit and frantically fed slack overboard. The explosion had blown open *Conch Rounder*'s hull somewhere aft. She was sinking fast by the stern with the rotation lifting the boat's bow. The blast had apparently ruptured the boat's fuel tanks as fire spreading over the water added to the conflagration. The distance was already too great for any further ship-to-ship transfers and there was no way *Kauai*'s hose teams could continue to hold back the fire. Ben shouted at Bondurant,

"Boats! Cast off and abandon ship! We'll have the RHIB pick you up!"

"Already done, sir!" Bondurant said, pitching the eye of the mooring line overboard. He had recognized the danger immediately and untied the line as soon as Jenkins had fed him slack. "There's only three of us left!"

"Roger, that!" Ben replied, then keyed his radio, "Conn, Deck Party, mooring line recovered, breakaway, breakaway, breakaway!"

"Deck Party, Conn, roger out!"

Ben felt *Kauai* lunge backward as Hopkins added a shot of full reverse on the motors and called out, "Hose teams secure!" As the water streams cut off, he keyed his radio again. "*Kauai* One, Deck Party, BM1 and two survivors are going into the water!"

"Deck Party, *Kauai* One, on it!" Lee's voice replied.

The *Conch Rounder*'s bow was almost vertical now and Ben watched with concern as the RHIB darted across *Kauai*'s bow to close on the sinking vessel, then stopped for a good minute and a half near the edge of the burning fuel. It was all Ben could do not to press the transmit button with a query. But he knew Lee's skill and judgment would be up to the task and the last thing she needed was kibbitzing from the boss.

"Deck Party, *Kauai* One, BM1 and two survivors aboard."

"Roger, well done, Lee," Ben replied. "I'm coming up two short. Ask the captain WTF. Over."

"Standby," Lee replied. After another half a minute, she called back. "XO, *Kauai* One. The captain says one was blown overboard and drowned and the other probably deserted. Over."

Damn! He keyed the radio. "Roger, standby." He then stepped over to where Bryant was working. "Doc, what's the score?"

"XO, I've got two on oxygen right now, two with severe burns, and six more that need at least a look in an ER. We need to get them to a hospital NOW, sir!" Bryant replied.

Bryant was an Army Combat Medic before he transferred over to the Coast Guard and was not one to exaggerate. There was no question now about hanging around to look for the missing crewman. Ben keyed his radio again. "Conn, XO, two of the boat's crew are missing, but four of these patients are critical. If we can't get a medevac lined up, we need to get them to a hospital soonest."

"XO, Actual," Haley's voice replied. "Concur. Not a chance at a medevac. We are heading to Cockburn Town now and will haul ass as soon as we recover the RHIB."

"Roger, ma'am." Ben turned to Jenkins and Pickins, who were gathering up the mooring line. "Jenkins, get aft to the crane. Pickins, help out Doc."

"Yes, sir!" the two men replied.

Ben stepped over to the starboard side, where the hose teams were breaking down their hoses for storage. "Chef, take the aviation group and tend to these survivors. Set them up with water on the messdeck, but no chow unless Doc says OK."

"Yes, sir!" Hebert replied, then turned to Deffler and his team. "Come along, gentlemen!"

After they passed by on the way to the tight group of people gathered on the foredeck, Ben turned to look at the *Conch Rounder*, receding in the distance. The fire on the water was still blazing brightly and the tip of the bow was still visible. What was left of the stern had settled onto the bottom, leaving the still buoyant bow above the surface. Ben knew she would soon sink completely, but that event and the intervening hazard to navigation was the problem of the Turks and Caicos government. Ben put his head down, suddenly very exhausted from both the lack of sleep and the exertion of lowering over two dozen people to the deck.

He looked up as the RHIB scooted by to line up and be craned aboard. As usual, the crew had performed superbly, particularly Lee. When Bondurant detached for officer candidate school in a few weeks, they would promote Lee into his billet as a Boatswain's Mate First Class. She was well-deserving and long overdue for the promotion, but she expressed some reluctance to accept it. "I'm not convinced an extra three hundred bucks a month is worth giving up the RHIB for babysitting the deck force, sir," she had told Ben.

He and Hopkins had worked together to persuade her to accept. After listening patiently while Ben outlined the advantages and appealed to teamwork, when her turn came, Hopkins simply said, "Don't be a jackass. Take the damn promotion!" The question of which of them made the most convincing argument would remain unanswered.

Ben strolled aft to meet the crew after the RHIB was craned aboard. A still-dripping Bondurant was shepherding the two survivors forward when Ben arrived. "Nicely done, Boats," Ben said, shaking Bondurant's hand. "We are gathering the walkers on the messdeck. Chef can hook them up with water and I'll see about getting some blankets."

"Thanks, XO," Bondurant replied tiredly and then continued forward.

As *Kauai* kicked up to full speed, Ben stepped over to the crane, where Lee, Brown, and Chen were packing up the P1B pump. "Helluva job, guys," Ben said. "Especially you, Shelley. It was a near-enough thing as it was. Without your quick thinking, we'd have had a lot of dead people on our hands."

"Thank you, sir," Lee replied. "What about the other two? Aren't we going to at least take a stab at looking for them?"

Ben shook his head. "We've got four criticals we need to get to an ER. Can't risk them for one guy who's probably dead and another who abandoned everyone to die. He chose his fate."

"Yes, sir," Lee said, the dissatisfaction apparent on her face.

"Look, it was a job well done. Take the win," Ben said, patting her on the shoulder. "Now, you'll have to excuse me. We should pull in at Government Dock in about twenty minutes and I need to be on the bridge. Well done again, everybody!"

"Thanks, sir," Lee said with a smile.

After climbing the ladder from the deck, Ben entered the bridge from the port rear door and walked straight over to Haley, seated in the command chair. Firing a salute, he said, "Survivors are settled in, Captain."

Haley reached out and gave his upper arm a quick pat. "Nicely done, XO. It looked pretty hairy down there."

"Only when she started going down. When that mooring line hung up, I thought we'd had it. Happy ending though."

"Mostly. Too bad about those two crewmen."

"Too bad about one. Looks like the other one deserted rather than stay and help fight the fire. Either way, it will not end well for him. How are we doing on getting a port clearance? Do I need to do anything?"

Haley grinned. "No, XO. While you were having fun forward, we managed to make contact with the local mounties. They've got ambulances and other transport on the way to meet us. As long as we are just dropping off survivors, they've agreed to forego putting us through the ass pain of a port clearance. We can file our statements later.
"

"No complaints here, ma'am," Ben said with considerable relief. His day was full enough without the additional administrative hell of an unplanned foreign port call. "Bondurant and Lee are pretty wrung out from the operation. I can take the mooring if you like, or relieve Chief so she can jump onto the brief."

Haley cocked her head and said, "Remember, you were in the thick of that operation too, but you can take the mooring if you feel up to it."

"On it, skipper." Ben sat in the unoccupied left-hand seat of the FC3 console, pulled up the PortBrief application, and typed in "Cockburn Town," selecting "Turks and Caicos" and "Government Dock" from succeeding pop-up menus. The application then ran through a series of screens in an electronic version of the standard entering port brief, showing the physical characteristics of the mooring site, winds, sea currents in the area, and known hazards to navigation.

After completing the last screen, he walked over to Hopkins and said, "I'll be taking her in, Chief. I offer my relief."

Hopkins nodded and replied, "I stand relieved, sir. On the bridge, Mr. Wyporek has the deck and conn!"

"Aye!" responded everyone on the bridge.

Ben was tired but looking forward to flexing his mariner muscles. Although the weather was good, clear with light winds, it was still night, with dawn not for another two hours. There was also a strong current just off the end of Government Dock that would disappear when *Kauai* entered the shadow of the mole. Ben would have to anticipate this change of velocity with advance rudder or risk slamming into the mooring. He had made the mistake of not leading a current change once before on his previous ship, slamming the pier hard enough to tear a fender in half. Ben was mortified, but there was no damage to the ship and the captain regarded it as a good teaching moment. The worst part, of course, was that the crew stuck Ben with the nickname "Captain Crunch" for months afterward.

There were no surprises on this occasion as the dock was well lit and it was a straight-in shot with deep water almost to shore. The two ambulances had already arrived, their red emergency lights still flashing, and as they drew closer, he could make out police vehicles and vans. It was a surprisingly quick reaction for the time of night, and Ben suspected they might have been alerted before *Kauai*'s call by someone ashore who had seen the *Conch Rounder* on fire. It only took a few more minutes for Ben to ease the cutter into her mooring and the deck crew to secure the lines. Since they were only making a brief stop to offload the boat's survivors, they kept the engines running. Ben kept the conn on the bridge while Haley went below to meet with the port official.

The situation was quite anticlimactic—Haley shook hands with a tall man in uniform, presumably the senior port official, then waved to Bryant, who supervised the offload of the four patients to the ambulances first, then the six more who trudged to one of the vans. As each patient stepped off, Bryant spoke to another man in white clothing, whom Ben supposed was an ambulanceman, completing a formal medical handoff.

Once those destined for the hospital departed, the other survivors were escorted ashore by *Kauai* personnel and handed off to local police. Ben felt tremendous sympathy for those people who had been jarred awake in the middle of the night, nearly burned to death, and now faced a long fact-finding interrogation in police custody. *Definitely not my choice of a vacation*, Ben thought, shaking his head.

Ben watched Haley finish her discussion with the port official and shake his hand. She then gazed up at Ben and gave him a thumbs up, signaling they were cleared to depart. Ben saluted and then trudged back into the bridge to begin the process of leaving port. Forty-five minutes later, they were rounding Northeast Reef, three miles northeast of the northern most point of Grand Turk to resume their journey to Mayagüez. The remaining three hundred miles of their trip would take about twelve hours, putting them off the dock around 16:30 local time.

Ben handed the O.O.D. watch over to Bondurant and then stepped over to and saluted Haley, who was sitting in her command chair. "I've been relieved of the O.O.D. by Petty Officer Bondurant, Captain."

Haley returned the salute with a smile. "Very well. I'm thinking about calling holiday routine and letting everyone relax until around 14:00. Any objections?"

"I always support my CO, particularly when she is suggesting I can get in some unexpected sack time," Ben replied with a grin.

"Good enough. Everybody did well, of course, but is there anyone in particular I should call out on my report?"

Ben dropped to a whisper. "Yes, ma'am. Lee and Bondurant for sure. If possible, a special mention for the Airedales—I know Chief Deffler would appreciate it and it will give Porter some cred when he gets back to the Academy."

"You read my mind, XO."

"Good, good," Ben said, lowering his head.

"What?" Haley asked.

"I'm not so hot about leaving two guys in the water without at least some search. Lee mentioned it too."

Haley smiled again. "Sorry, I meant to tell you. The police caught the runner swimming ashore about a mile north of Cockburn Town and arrested him. He told them he saw the other man blown overboard without a vest and he never came to the surface. They're satisfied everyone is accounted for."

Ben's grin returned. "That is a relief. Thank you, Captain."

"Backatcha. Now get your ass out of here and down in your rack."

"Aye, aye, Captain."

Chapter 9

Paradise

***USCG Cutter Kauai, Moored, Puerto de
Mayagüez, Mayagüez, Puerto Rico
17:23 AST, 23 June***

Ben

Ben was surprised that Mayagüez was the third busiest port in Puerto Rico given the lack of traffic. They tied up on the wharf next to the Customs and Border Patrol building to take advantage of the additional security it afforded. Although *Kauai* maintained a live watch, between the crated unmanned aircraft system and the geological equipment arrayed for loading on the wharf, there were tens of millions of dollars' worth of equipment that needed to be protected. That equipment was being re-arranged at the moment at Ben's direction, with the UAV crates coming ashore to make room for the ocean-bottom seismometer units. The practice, known as combat loading during wartime, placed cargo to be unloaded first toward the outside to improve off-loading efficiency.

The ten ocean bottom seismometers would remain on board *Kauai* until they were dropped into position off St. Ignatius's coast, so these came on first. Yellow-colored to make them easy to find during recovery, they stood roughly three-and-a-half feet tall and were made of two conjoined spheres. The top one contained the instruments and recording equipment and was around one-and-a-half feet wide, and the slightly smaller one below contained the battery pack. At the bottom of the device was a fifty-pound anchor to help the unit descend through the water after release and hold it in place on the bottom after it was dropped. Each unit with anchor weighed around two hundred pounds and was loaded aboard by the light crane Dr. Hernandez had arranged, after which one of *Kauai*'s crewmen carted it to its storage spot using a hand truck.

The geologists' land seismometers came aboard next, twelve cases holding eight units each. Hernandez and her student aides would position them around the island after their arrival. Last, the UAV crates were reloaded, with Deffler standing beside Ben, watching nervously as Bondurant directed the operation from the afterdeck.

When the last crate had been loaded into position and Lincoln started tying it down to the deck fittings, Deffler turned to Ben with a smile. "Not that I was worried, you understand, sir," he said. "It just would be my ass if anything happened to those babies."

"I don't think your ass would be alone in that sling," Ben replied. "Now why don't you run along and join Hoppy for dinner?"

"WILCO, sir," Deffler said, then turned and went inside.

Ben stayed on the afterdeck, watching the crane move off to be replaced by a waiting tanker truck. Chief Drake, accompanied by two junior enlisted from the engineering division, met the driver to coordinate the topping off of *Kauai*'s diesel fuel tanks. They had consumed about a third of their fuel on the trip down. *Kauai* could probably make it to their first port call in San Juan with what they had, but with no fuel for them in St. Ignatius, they were not taking any chances. *The only time you have too much fuel is when you're on fire,* Ben recalled the frequent murmur of his airline pilot father.

Food was another matter. There were no grocery stores anywhere nearby, and he was sure any that had been available would break his budget. They left Port Canaveral with enough food and drink to last for six days, sufficient to get them through the first leg of the mission. They could replenish food stores far easier in San Juan, which had a large logistics facility to support the seven patrol boats stationed there.

With the short port stay—they would depart at 08:00 tomorrow—lack of available vehicles, and no entertainment within walking distance, Haley and Ben had decided against letting the crew go on liberty that night. The crew was content to wait until St. Ignatius, by all accounts a beautiful place with pleasant restaurants and bars a short walk from the harbor. It would be far more pleasant than a dingy harbor, miles from anything interesting.

As Ben watched, Drake turned and gave him a thumbs up—the truck had sufficient quantity and quality fuel to meet their needs. Ben returned a wave and then turned to go back inside *Kauai*. Whether underway or in port, Hebert would have a quality meal available, and Ben was suddenly starving. After a quick meal, he would clear up whatever paperwork had accumulated during the day and then, finally, would be free to put in a call to Victoria.

******

"Hello, Benjamin!"

"Hello, Victoria. How was your day?" Ben smiled, as he always did when going through their phone call ritual. They had been opening phone calls with this same greeting almost from the beginning of their relationship a year and a half ago. It was one of those special things between them they held on to after Victoria moved in and even into their marriage.

"Oh, it has been a splendid day in terms of progress in the two Defense Department projects I am working on. However, I would much rather talk about the rescue you were involved in this morning."

Ben blinked. "How did you know about that?"

Victoria laughed. "Have you forgotten that I am a data scientist? I have bots crawling throughout the Internet searching for information on several subjects. They send me alerts whenever they encounter the word 'Kauai' or the phrase 'Coast Guard' among recently posted data. If it looks like it is important, I can start a deep search for more information."

He frowned. "Oh. I'm a little disappointed. I was looking forward to telling you about it."

"Oh, no! No, no, no! I only know that you were involved and that you rescued several people. I am extremely interested in learning the details. Please, Benjamin, tell me what happened!"

Ben smiled again. Even now, a year-and-a-half into their relationship and a month into their marriage, Victoria's curiosity about Ben's life aboard *Kauai* never diminished. He and the rest of the crew were her family, and she had an intense need to know about their experiences. Victoria's job at Vectorsonds involved some of the most vital work being done for the government and her salary was several times what Ben earned as a Coast Guard junior officer. Yet, she never failed to make him feel like he and his shipmates were the most important people in the world. Ben knew it was one of the aspects of her condition, admittedly a positive one, but he was still gratified by the attention.

"Of course. It was another one of those 'dragged out of bed at oh-dark-30' deals..."

******

"Benjamin, I am so proud of you, particularly your anticipation of the explosion of the scuba tanks. What a disaster that would have been!"

"Thank you, Victoria, but I am pretty sure that wasn't from scuba tanks. The investigation will probably tell the tale, but I think it might have been a mostly empty fuel tank or some pressure vessel associated with servicing the scuba equipment. I'm embarrassed I didn't think of either of those as a possibility. I guess we got lucky."

After a long pause, he continued. "I know you worry about this stuff, Victoria, and sometimes wonder if I should hold back some of the more lurid details. I mean, it can't do you any good to know how scared I was."

"Benjamin, you must never feel that way. I appreciate you want to spare me, but not hearing the details from you would lead me to speculate, and with my vivid imagination, the pictures in my head would be far worse. Please promise me you will hold nothing back."

"I promise, my love. That is, I won't hold back anything I'm *allowed* to tell you about."

"I understand," Victoria said, followed by a deep breath. "I have been looking at pictures of St. Ignatius on the Internet. It looks quite beautiful."

"So I have heard. I don't think we will have time to see much, as we will have a great deal to do. I would rather wait to enjoy it with you, anyway. Maybe, if it checks out, we can go there for a vacation."

"Oh, that sounds wonderful!" After another pregnant pause, she said, "Benjamin, I know you are tired and have another long day ahead of you. I miss you so much and wish I could talk to you all night, but you need your rest. Do you think you will have time to call tomorrow?"

"Same as always, love. If we are in port, I'll call. Maybe I'll have a picture or two to share. I miss you and love you without end."

"I love you, my dearest man. Please get some rest and I hope to speak to you tomorrow. Good night."

"Good night, Victoria." After the call ended, he sighed, then reached across his desk to touch the portrait of Victoria in her wedding dress. *Two days done. Sleep well, my love.*

USCG Cutter Kauai, Caribbean Sea, thirty-eight nautical miles west-by-north of Jamestown, St. Ignatius, U.S. Virgin Islands
15:07 AST, 24 June

Marcus

Marcus sat on the capstan just aft of *Kauai*'s bow, taking advantage of what was likely to be his last idle daytime moments to enjoy the beauty of the Caribbean. They had left Puerto Rico behind, the mountains of the Cordillera Central sinking below the horizon just a few hours ago. They would catch their first sight of St. Ignatius within an hour when the peak of Mount Acadia came over the horizon and would moor in the harbor at Jamestown by 16:30. In the meantime, *Kauai* had the Caribbean Sea to herself.

It was a hot day, over ninety degrees. But the combined effects of the light easterly trade winds and *Kauai's* twenty-knot speed through the water produced a stiff breeze that made the temperature comfortable, even with the sun almost directly overhead. The sky was dotted with the usual cumulus clouds and the water was the bluest Marcus had ever seen, scarcely folded into waves by the wind and marked only occasionally by the wakes of flying fish, leaping from the water and gliding for surprising distances on their outstretched wing-like fins. It was his first encounter with the remarkable creatures, and he took them for small birds at first sight.

After *Kauai* sailed from Mayagüez, they had spent the rest of the morning on the messdeck in discussions led by Dr. Hernandez about roles and responsibilities for the upcoming expedition. Marcus was surprised by how outgoing and friendly she was and took an instant liking to her. Unfortunately, he could not say the same for her entourage: three snotty graduate students and a sullen technician from the Woods Hole Oceanographic Institution, the latter along to operate the ocean bottom seismometers.

Marcus was delighted to hear they would get plenty of flight time. Their first task would be a detailed survey of the island with the new digital cartography camera pod, whose data would reveal any deformation of the surface.

Once that was complete, they would make daily sorties with the hyperspectral imaging pod, looking for what Dr. Hernandez called "exsolved gasses." They would be operating from the tiny airfield on the opposite side of the island from Jamestown, where hangar space, as well as fuel and a short runway were available. The university crowd would also be based at the airport, in a little-used office space in the administration building.

Kauai would spend tomorrow dropping the ocean bottom seismometers around the base of the volcano that formed the island. Dr. Hernandez would use these and the ninety-plus land-based sensors her students would place at various locations on the island to develop a picture of the interior of the volcanic system. In a few days, a research vessel from Woods Hole would circle the island at a distance, generating sound pulses at regular intervals with large air guns mounted on a sled towed behind the vessel. After that operation was complete, *Kauai* would retrieve the ocean bottom seismometers and Dr. Hernandez would feed their recorded data into a program that would generate the picture. Marcus could barely follow the concept and was clueless about the math they were discussing, but still found the idea fascinating.

The good news was that their logistical needs were squared away. Chief Drake had arranged for a small crane and flatbed truck to unload their gear and transport it to the airport. Dr. Hernandez had coordinated hotel rooms for everyone and two SUVs for their use. Marcus was happy to hear this—as much as he liked the crew and chow aboard *Kauai*, the ability to spread out in a spacious room and take long showers not limited by water restrictions would be awesome.

The government of the U.S. Virgin Islands, of which St. Ignatius was one, was in the city of Charlotte Amalie on the island of St. Thomas, sixty miles to the north. The local government was run by two officials elected by the island's six hundred fifty-odd permanent residents, the island administrator and his deputy. According to Dr. Hernandez, the administrator was off-island today, so they would be met at the wharf by Deputy Administrator Isabelle Jones, who would greet them and pass any last-minute instructions.

Marcus had dug into whatever details he could find about St. Ignatius on the Internet to develop a plan for whatever free time he had. From what he could work out, the island was largely unspoiled by either industry or tourism. Blessed by a lack of any resources worth the trouble of mining, the terrain on St. Ignatius was a verdant mixture of vegetable agriculture, grassy meadow, and submontane forest, with a small area of cloud forest surrounding the peak of Mount Acadia. Even the animal life was unremarkable—the usual collection of insects, small lizards, and tropical birds found throughout the region, except for a unique species of iguana unsurprisingly named the Ignatius Iguana but known locally as the Iggy-Iggy.

St. Ignatius's small, shallow harbor and airport, so tiny that only short takeoff and landing aircraft and helicopters could safely operate, kept tourist traffic at a small fraction of what other islands in the area experienced. There was a single scheduled ferry to Charlotte Amalie and Frederiksted on St. Croix, but the reviews Marcus could find ranged from scathing to worse on the quality and reliability of service. In the absence of tourists, there were just a few restaurants and hotels, and nightlife was practically non-existent. These realities made Marcus doubly glad of the expected high tempo of flight operations, as St. Ignatius was shaping up to be the most boring place he had ever visited.

Marcus had just finished following a flying fish on a long flight from takeoff to splashdown when a small dark shape on the horizon just left of the bow caught his eye. While he fixated on it, it seemed to rise ever so slowly from the blue sea and resolved into a dark mound with an elongated cloud around the top. Eventually, a pair of shorter summits appeared, one on each side of the tall peak. He recognized the profile from the various pictures on the Internet as the view of St. Ignatius from the west.

It took the better part of an hour for *Kauai* to make her approach along the southern coast of the island. As they closed on the island, Marcus could make out more details. The western side of the island appeared to be steeper, a mixture of dark brown and green leading to sheer cliffs at the water's edge. The southern and south-eastern sides were different—gentle slopes of green dotted with the pink and white shapes of houses. Although he knew the geography, Marcus had difficulty picking out the harbor from the background of the island. It was a two-hundred-fifty-foot mole stretching from a slight indentation in the coastline to the right of the major settlement of Jamestown.

"Now, set the Special Sea Detail. RHIB crew man up!" The announcement jolted Marcus into action. *Kauai* would provide her own line handlers, transported in advance via the patrol boat's RHIB. Marcus had volunteered for the duty, partially out of courtesy to his hosts, but mainly because he thought he would be bored just standing around the deck. He grabbed the boat helmet and life vest he was issued and made his way back to the boat deck where Lee, Chen, and Seaman Smith had gathered. Lee would be the RHIB's coxswain for the sortie, Chen the boat crewman, and Smith would be landed ashore with Marcus as the other line handler.

"Hello, Mr. Porter. Ready for some boat ops?" Lee asked with a smile.

"Of course, Petty Officer Lee," Marcus answered. His uncle had briefed him on each member of the crew before they reported aboard *Kauai*—Lee's chapter was delivered almost with a sense of awe. In the two years she had been aboard *Kauai*, Lee had earned the Coast Guard Medal for saving a young family during a hurricane and the Silver Star for an action so classified his uncle did not even have a hint of the details. This was his first face-to-face encounter with her, and he was careful to suppress his admiration behind a veneer of nonchalance.

"Good. Just do as you're told and if you have any questions, don't be afraid to ask. You copy?" she asked with a warm smile.

"Roger that," Marcus answered and put on his vest.

Bondurant was operating the boat crane and lifted the RHIB out of its cradle and over the side. When it had been lowered even with the main deck, Bondurant paused so that Lee and her crew could jump in, then dropped it slowly into the water.

After starting the RHIB's engine, Lee activated the quick-disconnect on the hoist block. With the crane now free of the boat's weight, the arm swung upward, taking the hoist block with it. Lee goosed the engine and veered off to the left, accelerating to move ahead from *Kauai*.

As he sat on one side of the boat holding the lifeline, Marcus glanced out ahead of the speeding RHIB to see that Lee was heading toward a ladder about three-quarters of the way down the mole. She would pull up next to the ladder and, after Marcus and Smith had safely climbed it, return to *Kauai*. They approached the ladder at what Marcus thought was rather a high speed and was about to comment when Lee threw the engine into reverse and slowed the speed to a crawl a few feet before the ladder. As they drifted into it, Lee turned to Marcus and said, "Up you go, Mr. Porter."

"Right," Marcus said, grabbing the ladder and heaving himself up and out of the RHIB. The ladder was a little slick from wetness and marine growth, and Marcus's foot slipped on the first rung he stepped on. Fortunately, he was able to steady himself without falling off and swiftly climbed the six feet up to the mole with Smith on his heels.

Once they were both safely up and off the ladder, Lee pivoted the RHIB and headed back to *Kauai* at top speed. Marcus took a cloth out of his pocket to wipe the rust and ladder slime off his hands and glanced down the mole toward the town. There were two small buildings at the foot of the mole that he supposed were associated with customs or harbor administration. As he glanced at one of them, a woman stepped out the door and began walking toward them.

Marcus could not stop himself from staring as the woman approached. She was very tall, just under six feet, wearing a white and pink flower print dress that stressed her curvy figure. Her long chestnut-colored hair pulled back into a messy ponytail framing her face, round with large dark brown eyes and full red lips. She was, in short, one of the most beautiful women he had ever seen. As she approached effortlessly across the rough pavement on high-heeled sandals, Marcus could see she was very young, perhaps only a year or two older than he was. *Could* this *be Isabelle Jones? No way!*

The woman stepped up, flashed a smile that made Marcus's heart skip a beat, and then offered her hand. "Hello! I'm Isabelle Jones."

Marcus reflexively reached for her hand, then remembered he had just climbed a slimy ladder and yanked it back. "Excuse me, ma'am. The ladder I just climbed was filthy."

"*Ma'am*? Really?" she said with a tilt of her head. "Please call me Isabelle, or Izzy, if you like. My grandmother is the only one who gets called ma'am around here. Now, what should I call you?"

Even her voice was wonderful, husky, her accent a delightful mix of General American with a melodic touch of the West Indies. "Um, Cadet First Class Marcus Porter," he managed to say.

"That's quite a mouthful. Do you mind if I call you Marcus?" she said, with a twinkle in her eye.

Marcus could feel his face growing red in embarrassment. "Yes, that would be fine, mm...Isabelle. This is Seaman Phillip Smith."

"Miss," Smith said with a nod.

"A little better. The Isabelle-Izzy thing goes for everybody," Isabelle said. "Do you go by Phillip or Phil?"

"Phil, Miss...Isabelle."

"Sweet. So, welcome, both of you, to St. Ignatius. I would like very much to talk more, but I don't want to make you miss your boat," she said, nodding over Marcus's shoulder.

He spun around to see *Kauai* approaching the end of the mole, turned to Smith and said, "Let's go!" then glanced at Isabelle and said, "Excuse us, please." He trotted down the mole after Smith and could almost feel her eyes on his back. *Brilliant, Marcus! Cadet First Class? More like Doofus First Class!*

******

Marcus was standing on the mole in a group including *Kauai*'s two officers, Chief Hopkins, Dr. Hernandez, and Isabelle, discussing the upcoming operations. The crane and flatbed truck had arrived and Chief Drake and his uncle were closely supervising the offload of their equipment. Marcus thought his place was helping with the shifting of aviation equipment, but Uncle Erich had set him straight—he needed to think and act like an officer. Besides, his uncle needed an ear in the meeting so he knew what was being planned.

"I have the positions of all the drop points entered in the FC3, Captain," Hopkins said. "I think we can expect nine to ten hours from start to finish."

"Good," Captain Reardon said. "We'll plan to get underway at zero-eight-hundred tomorrow morning. That should give us time to deal with any hiccups and still return by sunset. How are we looking for fuel?"

"We're down to about eighty-two percent, Captain."

"Assuming we stay down here through that research vessel's run, pick up the OBSs the next day, and generate our own power while we are here, what will we have when we pull into San Juan on the 28th?"

"If we keep the underway portions under twenty knots, we should still be over fifty percent, ma'am."

The captain turned to Isabelle and said, "Miss Jones, if you can stand us tying up your wharf space until Monday, we would like to hang around."

"Absolutely no problem," Isabelle said with a grin. "In fact, if you can shake your crew loose, I think we can promise them an interesting time. Our annual carnival is on Saturday and Sunday."

"That *is* a lucky break," the captain returned the smile. She turned to Hernandez. "I hope your kids will be able to partake."

"We should be done placing the sensors by then," Hernandez said. "Although I can't promise I can pry them off TikTok and their video games when they're not working!"

"Their loss, if that's the case," the captain said. "Well Miss Jones, if there is anything the crew of *Kauai* can contribute to the festivities besides more spectators, please let Ben or me know."

"Thank you, Captain." Isabelle nodded. "I think..."

She was interrupted in mid-sentence by a low-level rumble, like distant, continuous thunder, accompanied by a vibration that seemed to creep up Marcus's legs. He was born and raised in Port Huron, Michigan, one of the most geologically stable areas in the U.S., hundreds of miles from the nearest fault line. He had never experienced an earthquake before, and the experience was unnerving, requiring a concentrated effort to appear unconcerned. The tremor began fading away after about fifteen seconds and disappeared completely after another five.

Hernandez's smile vanished. "That was interesting. Are they always that long?"

Isabelle's smile appeared strained. "They have been getting longer and more frequent lately."

"How frequent?" Hernandez pressed.

"We are getting two or three a day."

"I see," Hernandez said, then turned to Marcus. "How soon can you get into the air?"

Marcus was startled, as he had not expected to be answering questions. He glanced at his uncle, still occupied with the unloading, and then replied. "Definitely not today. It will take three or four hours minimum to assemble the bird and check it. We can't fly at night, not that there would be any point to it. If we hit it hard tonight, we should be able to launch at dawn."

"If any of our guys can help, just say the word, Mr. Porter," the XO said.

"Yes, sir. If we could get a couple of guys to help set up the catapult, that would put two of us on the bird instead of just one."

"Consider it done. Take Chen and Jenkins with you." The XO nodded.

"Thank you, sir."

"Alright, Doctor, I'll say it," the captain said. "Should I be getting worried right now?"

"No, Captain. Things are just a little different from what I expected. It's probably that we are further along in the hydrothermal cycle than I thought. However, you can't be too careful."

"Agree one hundred percent. By that, I mean if you have even the slightest inkling that things are heading downhill, I need to know soonest. Am I clear?"

"Very clear, Captain. Believe me," Hernandez said with a smile while pointing at herself. "This is not the stuff of heroes."

"Right. I'll hold you to that," the captain said, then turned to Isabelle. "Miss Jones, I hope you still have some vehicles for us."

"Yes, Captain," Isabelle said, recovering her beautiful smile. "Two SUVs and a sedan are parked over by the Customs building, if you would care to send someone to collect the keys."

"Certainly. Mr. Porter, could you handle that, please?"

"My pleasure, ma'am," Marcus replied.

"I thought as much. Make it so."

"Aye, aye, ma'am," Marcus said, then smiled and bowed slightly to Isabelle. "At your service, Miss Jones."

"Indeed. Follow me please." After they had walked out of earshot, she turned her head and said, "My, My. *Mister* Porter. And a flier too. You are just full of surprises!"

"I'm not a flier. Not yet, anyway. I *am* a UAV pilot, which is pretty cool."

"I should say so." After a brief pause, she continued. "I owe you an apology."

"For what?"

"For teasing you when we first met. That was shitty of me when all you were doing was showing respect."

Marcus grinned. "That's OK. I've had a lot worse."

"Still, I would like to make it up to you. Will you have any time to attend the carnival?"

He winced and said, "I don't know. Dr. H seems pretty worked up about things. I expect we'll be hard at it for a while, at least during the daytime." For the first time in his life, Marcus had a pang of regret about being a pilot, particularly when he saw the look of disappointment on Isabelle's face.

"Oh. Well, if that doesn't work, maybe you can come over for dinner with Gran and me."

"Really? I mean, sure, I'll make that work somehow."

"Done. Once you get settled into your...what do you call your work?"

"Op tempo, for Operations Tempo."

She smiled again. "Yes, Op tempo. I'm learning all sorts of things today." They had reached the office building, a single-story white stucco façade with a red metal roof. She briefly fumbled with a set of keys, then unlocked the front door and led him inside. The office was brightly lit and comfortably air-conditioned, with several pictures and decorations on the walls, conspicuous among which was a diploma from the University of Florida. It was obviously Isabelle's office, and the diploma explained her accent. "There you are," she said, pointing to three sets of keys sitting on the desk. "Please tell your guys to be careful—that is three-quarters of our rental fleet."

"Noted. Cancel the drag races on this trip," Marcus deadpanned. For a moment, long enough for him to think *Uh oh*, she had a startled look. Then she almost doubled over laughing. *Man, even her laugh is beautiful!*

"Alright, alright, you got me." She grabbed a sticky note pad from the desk and scribbled on it. "Here's my number. Call me once you're settled in, flyboy. Now, if you'll excuse me, I have to take care of some government stuff."

"Yes, ma'am!" Marcus answered, grabbing the keys and heading out the door toward the cars. *Revised assessment: St. Ignatius is looking pretty awesome.*

Chapter 10

OpTempo

USCG Cutter Kauai, underway in the Caribbean Sea, 8.6 nautical miles east of Jamestown, St. Ignatius, U.S. Virgin Islands 08:37 AST, 25 June

Ben

They were approaching the position for the drop of the first OBS, and Ben was on the afterdeck to observe the operation. There was no need for him to be there to provide guidance or supervision—Bondurant and his assistants knew their jobs—it was just beneficial to have an extra set of eyes when dealing with visiting technicians. Besides, Ben was fascinated by the process and wanted to watch. He had his cell phone to record pictures and video he would send to Victoria after they returned to port this evening.

Kevin Ryan, the technician from Woods Hole, was running through the final checks of the unit before it was attached to *Kauai*'s boat crane and lowered over the side. The unit was sturdy—required for it to withstand the pressure of the water at the depth it would be deployed—and the sensors and recorders were the most robust available. However, it was still important to check and recheck to ensure settings were correct and the components were operating correctly, as there were no "do-overs" in an operation like this.

The last check was on the anchor release. The OBS had a fifty-pound flat square of concrete attached to the bottom by a quick-release hook operated by a solenoid. It was triggered by a coded sonic signal sent by the recovery vessel. When the sensors in the unit received and verified the signal, the anchor was released and the unit floated up to the surface. Ryan stepped back from the unit and pressed a button on the hand-held device he was holding, triggering a metallic "snap" from the unit. He bent over and reset the hook, then stood and gave Bondurant at the crane controller a thumbs-up. "Good to go, John!"

Bondurant brought the crane arm over the OBS and lowered the hoist block to Ryan, who attached it to the lift ring atop the unit and gave another thumbs-up. The unit slowly lifted off the deck and when the bottom was four feet high, Bondurant swung it over the side and slowly lowered it into the water. Ryan held a line attached to the hoist block's quick disconnect and was awaiting a signal from the bridge that their position had been precisely marked using the Global Positioning System. Hernandez had told them the exact placement of the sensor was unnecessary, but the exact knowledge of where it ultimately ended up was vital. Ben heard the signal to Ryan over his headset. "Deck party, Conn, good fix, drop now, now, now."

At the third "now", Ryan tugged the line, the hoist block popped from the OBS's lift ring, and the unit quickly sank from sight. After following the OBS down with his cellphone camera on video, he turned it on Ryan and said, "Nice work, Kevin! How about a shot of you on the Caribbean for the folks back home?"

Ryan turned, struck a "Captain Morgan" pose, grinned, and said, "Arrrrrgh!"

After turning off the camera, Ben gave him an OK sign and said, "That was perfect! I'll send you a copy!"

Ryan returned a thumbs-up and then turned to the next OBS in the queue as Ben stepped forward next to Bondurant. "Any issues with this, Boats?"

"No sir. It's a lot easier than working the RHIB."

"Good. In that case, be sure to rotate Lee and Jenkins through for at least a couple each. We have to work them into this stuff more so they can take over after you move on."

"Roger that, XO."

Ben nodded and continued up to the bridge. Lee had the OOD watch and was conning *Kauai* to the next drop point, six miles distant, while Haley lounged in the command chair. Ben stepped up to her and saluted. "The first one went without a hitch, Captain. Ryan knows his business."

Haley returned the salute. "Good to hear. I'll step down for a look myself once we get into a rhythm." She looked down and spoke in a whisper. "Amazing how this 'decoy' mission seems to throw shade on the main event. I think when we pull in tonight, I will give Mercier a buzz unless Hernandez comes back with a big 'never mind' after the flights today."

"What can she do?"

"Get her staff to make some calls to the French, Limeys, and Dutch to line up some transport in case we have to evacuate these people. She'll probably rip me a new one for being a drama queen, but I'd prefer that to being responsible for a lot of people getting burned up." She looked up at Ben's quizzical expression and said, "I know, I know. But after seeing the good doctor's reaction to that quake yesterday, I'm coming down quick from the 'best case' assumption."

"Very good, skipper. Is there anything I can do to help?"

Haley reached out and squeezed his shoulder. "Nope. Let's just keep playing through for now."

"Roger that!"

William F. Baker Airport, St. Ignatius, U.S. Virgin Islands
10:02 AST, 25 June

Marcus

Marcus was getting the droops, the micro-sleeps that crept up on you when you had not gotten enough good sleep the night before and you were stuck in a sedentary job. He was currently standing his shift as the observer for the T-20 UAV, watching the display from the electro-optical camera on the aircraft as it scanned the area around it for flight hazards. Uncle Erich was in the other chair, taking a turn as pilot-at-the-controls—not that there was much to do in that role right now as the aircraft was automatically flying a preset pattern.

The flight began at six o'clock that morning when they had launched the T-20 into the dawn sky from the catapult positioned next to the runway, its small gasoline engine buzzing as it climbed to an altitude of two thousand feet above sea level. The aircraft would perform a parallel search—flying north over the island at minimum speed until passing the shore, turning left one-hundred-eighty degrees, and flying south in a track one-eighth mile offset to the west. Upon reaching the opposite shore, it would turn right one-hundred-eighty degrees for another eighth-mile offset. This pattern would repeat until the entire surface of St. Ignatius had been mapped by the aircraft's topographical camera pod.

When the mission was complete, the aircraft would return for a soft belly landing in the grass next to the runway. The flight crew would service the aircraft, download the data from the pod, and replace it with the hyperspectral imaging camera for the next day's operations. They would then mount the aircraft on its catapult and call it a day. The aircraft could fly at night every bit as well as during the day. However, with no radar, the risks of a mid-air collision jumped higher at night. Besides that, there were only three men on the team, and with two required to control and observe whenever the UAV was airborne—they would quickly be exhausted by round-the-clock operations.

Although the launch occurred at dawn, their day began much earlier at four-thirty when they arrived from the hotel. Marcus and Lincoln began preparing the aircraft for flight and Uncle Erich called up to Coast Guard Air Station Borinquen in Western Puerto Rico to coordinate a temporary flight restriction over St. Ignatius while the UAV would be operating. After the launch, Lincoln had retired to the cot in one of the offices to rest during the first six-hour shift. He would rotate into the pilot's position at noon, with Uncle Erich shifting over to the observer, while Marcus took a turn to rest.

Marcus's sleep deficit stemmed from a combination of a late night assembling and testing the aircraft, the general first-night acclimation challenge, and a late-onset bout of claustrophobia triggered by the second earthquake they had experienced that day, shortly after they arrived at the hotel. His mind had raced at the possibilities when the ground could not be relied upon to stay still, settling on the thought of the building collapsing on top of them while they slept. The horror of being buried alive haunted his dreams during the brief periods he got some sleep.

"Stand up and walk around," Uncle Erich said, startling him out of one of his inadvertent mini-naps. "It's OK, I'll cover you. Hit the head and bring us both back a cup of coffee."

"Roger that, Chief," Marcus replied tiredly as he stood. He dutifully headed for the restroom, referred to as "the head" in the nautical services. On his way back, he stopped by the table and poured two cups of coffee from the large thermos Isabelle had brought for them an hour before the launch. It had been a wonderful surprise to see her, dressed down in simple jeans, a loose T-shirt, and tennis shoes, but every bit as beautiful as the evening before. Along with the coffee, she brought a sack of pastries from the town bakery, knowing they would be hungry, an immensely thoughtful gesture that moved them all.

"You look like you had a rough night, flyboy," she said on her arrival.

"Yeah. A lot of work and this mobile ground you have here is going to take some getting used to," he replied.

"Yes, for us too." Her smile became sad. "It is a very recent development." She looked over at Uncle Erich, who smiled and raised his coffee cup to her. She nodded and turned back to Marcus. "I hope you like the coffee. We grow it locally and take some pride in it."

"Any caffeine would be great right now, but I'm sure this will be heaven. It was awesome of you to think of us and take the trouble to haul it down here so early."

She grinned again. "My contribution to the team. I know you are very busy, so I'll let you get to it. Remember, I expect to hear from you about dinner soon."

"Count on it," Marcus replied.

She nodded and said, "Take care, Marcus." Then she turned to return to her car.

He was still thinking about her when he reached the control station and handed his uncle the coffee before resuming his seat.

After taking a sip of his coffee, his uncle said, "She's quite the lady."

"Are you reading minds now?"

"Naturally, I'm a chief!" he quipped. "Of course, yours isn't exactly *War and Peace*." After another sip, he continued. "You need to be careful, Marcus."

His use of the first name, even in this situation where they were alone together, reflected a level of concern that got Marcus's attention. "About what?"

He took a deep breath. "I can see you've got the hots for Isabelle, and why not? She's smart, sweet, and drop-dead gorgeous. You are a fine young man and you are going to make an outstanding officer if you stick to it. But you are still a college student—remember that. She's a successful woman on the move and a politician to boot. It's a different world from you and me."

Marcus was shocked and could feel anger welling up inside him. "So, you're suggesting I ghost her?" he snapped.

"Not at all. Just be realistic. We'll be moving on in a couple of weeks and whatever there is then will end." He turned to look at him. "I don't want you to get hurt."

Marcus turned back to his screen, trying to mask his irritation. "Thanks. I think my personal life is my business, *Chief*," he said huffily.

"I beg to differ, *Mister*. While we're here, you're part of *my* crew. I need you with your head in the game, not mooning around after someone who's out of your league."

Marcus's jaw clenched and then eased and he took another sip of the coffee. Isabelle wasn't exaggerating—it was delicious, with a unique nutty flavor and quite potent. He could feel his anger fading into resignation. His uncle was right. Isabelle's first reaction to Marcus had been amusement at his awkwardness. She turned around quickly into someone very charming, and he was sure that was not just for show. But the fact remained, she clearly did not see him as an equal. It hurt, but it also took some of the pressure off him. He had been worried about making another embarrassing blunder when they were together. Now he could relax around her.

OK, time for a slice of humble pie. "You're right, Chief. Sorry. You've got nothing to worry about."

"I know that, son," he replied, giving Marcus a pat on the back and then turning back to his control panel.

USCG Cutter Kauai, Moored, Jamestown, St. Ignatius, U.S. Virgin Islands
19:08 AST, 25 June

Ben

They had gathered on *Kauai*'s mess deck to report on the day's activities and plan for tomorrow. Besides Ben, Haley, and Hopkins of *Kauai*, Hernandez and Deffler were all seated at the table. Ben felt some compassion for their guests. They had been hard at work hours before *Kauai* got underway this morning, Deffler with his aviation crew, prepping his UAV for launch and Hernandez driving to dozens of points around the island to position their seismographic sensors. All of them were enjoying freshly brewed cups of St. Ignatius's finest, a treat that brought even the above-average brand Hebert stocked to shame.

"So, no problems on the sortie this morning," Deffler said. "We have offloaded the pod and provided the extracted data to Dr. Hernandez. The hyperspectral camera is installed and tested and the bird is full up on the catapult and ready for launch."

"Good job, Chief," Haley said. "We have placed all the OBSs more-or-less where you wanted, doctor. Ryan says all the drops were right on and he expects good results when we do the pickup in a few days. So, how did you and your people do?"

Hernandez managed a tired smile. "Excellent. All the sensors are in place and we've started continuous recording. As for my kids, let's just say after kicking them out of bed at four a.m. and pushing them hither and yon for over fifteen hours, I've lost the title 'Best Prof Ever!'."

Hopkins nodded and said, "Tell me about it. I've got a boy at home just getting into the terrible teens and another hot on his trail."

"Aw, MOM!" Ben said with a grin, drawing a smile and finger wag from Hopkins as the rest of the gathering chuckled.

Haley's smile faded as she turned from Ben to Hernandez. "On to a less comic subject, doctor. I appreciate you have just laid your sensor grid and don't have a lot of firm data yet. But my sense is that we may no longer be looking at the 'best case' here. Am I wrong?"

Hernandez's smile also disappeared, and she replied, "I wish I could say that you were. It is early days for the sensors and my two laptops will crunch the UAV data through the night." She smiled slightly. "Another downer for my students who had been using them for high-end gaming. Anyway, you're right, captain. I'm not pleased about what I've seen so far.

"We've had three tremors that we could actually feel today. My 'seat-of-the-pants' read was that they ranged between 3.5 and five on the Richter scale. I'm sure there were many more that were too mild to detect without instruments. I'll know more tomorrow once the topographical analysis is complete and we get data off the terrestrial net."

Haley sat up. "So you *do* think there will be an eruption?"

Hernandez leaned back and crossed her arms. "I need to be careful here. From my experience and what I know about these islands, I am more inclined than not to believe there will be an eruption. But this is another 'seat-of-the-pants' assessment, almost totally unsupported by reliable data. Even if I was sure of an eruption, whether it would be in days, weeks, or months and whether it would just be a minor annoyance or a global catastrophe, I don't know...yet."

Ben could feel that nagging fear building, like a large block of ice in his stomach, and chimed in, saying, "Given the risks, wouldn't it be prudent to call an alert, maybe even start an evacuation?"

Hernandez shook her head. "Too early. For one thing, it's not my decision to make, it's USGS's. And no point in calling them yet—they'd just tell me to call back when I had some data. I certainly would if I were in their position. Before you give an order that will rip people out of their homes, you need to be damn sure there's clear and convincing evidence behind it. It's a big deal, even for just a few hundred people."

"I see," Ben said. As he thought more about it, he appreciated the dilemma and the danger of crying wolf. It did not melt the ice block in his gut, but at least he understood the decision.

Haley turned from Ben to Hernandez and said, "Alright, what should we plan on for tomorrow?"

"Captain, there is not much you and *Kauai* can do for me over the next couple of days, but please remain nearby in case something comes up."

"That we will." She turned to Ben and said, "Good news, XO. We turn people loose for carnival."

"Good deal, Captain. I'll see to it."

"So, doctor, will you be granting liberty for your crew?"

Hernandez shook her head. "No. Not tomorrow, anyway. We'll all be crunching data and I'm sure that with eighty sensors in the field, we'll find some that went bad and have to be replaced. Same bad news for you, Chief. I need you doing gas surveys around the summit and the vents we know about."

"I thought as much," Deffler said. "And the boys were expecting it, so no worries here."

"Chief, if it will help, you can have Chen or Jenkins again," Ben offered.

"Thanks, sir, but I think we'll be OK. They were a huge help putting the catapult together, but there isn't much they can help with during the flights."

After a brief pause, Haley scanned the table and said, "Anybody have anything else? No? Then I guess we are done here. Oh, doctor, Chef wanted me to give you this." She handed Hernandez a sack.

"Beignets! Well, I've certainly been running my ass off enough to not worry about the calories. Please thank him for me." She stood from the table and said, "Now, I just have to figure out a way to hide them from my students!"

As the group stood and made their separate ways out, Haley stepped next to Ben and whispered, "Meet me in five in the cabin?"

"Yes, ma'am."

✶ ✶ ✶ ✶ ✶ ✶

"Mercier here," came the captain's voice from the speakerphone in Haley's cabin.

"Good evening, ma'am," Haley said. "It's Haley Reardon, and I'm on speaker with Ben Wyporek in the room."

"Hello, guys! How's paradise?"

"We are hoping to get a look at it tomorrow, ma'am," Haley replied. "Sorry to bother you so late, but I wanted to give you a heads-up. It's not something to sound general quarters over, but I thought the more notice, the better."

They could hear an audible sigh. "Oh, boy. What's going on?"

"Ma'am, Dr. Hernandez is leaning toward an eruption happening down here rather than just the hydrothermal event she was talking about before."

"Oh, crap! When?"

"We just placed the sensors today and don't have any data yet, ma'am. It could be anywhere from days to weeks."

"OK. Is USGS about to call us?"

"No, ma'am. Dr. Hernandez says there's no point calling them without data. So, they don't even know yet."

"If there isn't enough data to get them on the phone, what do you expect me to do?" Ben could detect Mercier's irritation, even through the speakerphone.

"Ma'am, Dr. Hernandez and the USGS bigwigs think about time in terms of phone calls. We have to think in terms of logistics. The port here is tiny and shallow, as you know, and the airport isn't much more than a helipad. If the ball drops, we'll need to figure out how to evacuate six hundred and fifty civilians. The regular ferry service between here and the other Saints is a joke—it will be practically useless for a mass evacuation. I think it would be prudent to have the staff look into some options in case we have to pull everyone out in a hurry."

There was a long pause, then Mercier said, "You know, it's a good thing you two are among my favorite people because sometimes you sure can be a pain in the ass. Leave it to you to turn a decoy mission into a major op."

"Sorry, ma'am. Couldn't think of another option."

"No, that's OK. What good is it being a captain if you can't create hardship for staff officers? I'll get a couple of them on this first thing tomorrow. Now, anything else? There's a glass of cabernet urgently awaiting my attention."

"Nothing from me, ma'am." Haley glanced at him. "Ben?" When he shook his head, she continued. "That's all the love we can share tonight, ma'am."

"Good enough. As soon as you know something, call me. Doesn't matter what time."

"Yes, ma'am. Thanks for your patience."

"No problem. Take care and good luck." Then the call abruptly ended.

Haley turned off the speakerphone and said, "That went better than I feared." She rubbed her eyes. "I don't know about you, but I'm going to try to get some sleep. Maybe I can get ashore and look around tomorrow."

"Sounds like a plan. I'll just check in with Victoria and then see if I can get head down for a change."

"Good on you. Tell her I said hello."

"WILCO. Goodnight, boss."

"Goodnight, Ben."

Ben stepped next door to his stateroom and shut the door. After settling in at his desk, he pulled out his cell phone and dialed Victoria.

"Hello, Benjamin!" she answered after the usual two rings.

"Hello, Victoria. How was your day?"

"Oh, it was a typical day for me. I made some progress on the Handley project, I am happy to say. I was delighted to receive your texts with the pictures and video—that was the highlight of my day. Now you must tell me about the operation in detail. Yours are the only pictures and video I could find of the latest ocean bottom seismometer."

Their conversation was the usual exchange of highly technical information and playful banter, but Ben noticed a slight change in the tenor of her voice. He thought he had recognized it last night but wasn't sure. "Victoria, do you remember after Juan died when you said we were formal partners and I should not hold back when something was wrong?"

"Yes," she said in a subdued tone.

"Victoria, something is wrong. I can tell from your voice. This has to go both ways. Please tell me."

"Benjamin, I am just so worried about you that I find it difficult to think of anything else. I know I should not obsess over this, but you know how I am. I am reluctant to add to your concerns, but I do not know what to do."

He swallowed hard, frustrated by the fact that Victoria needed help and he wasn't there for her. This was one of the challenges of her condition. She had no friends at work. Being a childless twenty-four-year-old made it difficult for her to connect with the wives of the other married crew, all of whom had children and were in their thirties and forties. Her only deep friendships were with Hopkins and Joana Powell, wife of Sam Powell, Ben's close friend and former captain of *Kauai*. But Joana and Sam had moved away six months ago with Sam's transfer to the Naval War College in Newport, Rhode Island. Suddenly, the name jumped out at him. *Joana. That might work.*

"Victoria, I have an idea I would like you to think about. Why don't you call Jo and see if you can visit up there for a week or so?"

"Oh, no. No, no, no. I could not just leave on the spur of the moment."

"Victoria, you haven't taken any vacation from work, other than the week of our honeymoon, in the year-plus you've been there. They could hardly object to some R&R for their most productive employee. Nothing is going on at the house that needs your attention. You always wanted to see New England. Here's your chance."

"It is the Independence Day holiday, Benjamin. Joana might have plans. What if I call and she says no?"

"Then you are no worse off than you are now. But I think Jo will jump at the chance to be with you. When I talked to Sam a few weeks ago, he said Jo's parents were getting on her nerves—I think she needs a break with a friend as much as you do."

"I do not know, Benjamin. Even if she says yes, I will have to fly. You know how I am with airports and crowded airplanes."

"There are non-stop flights from Orlando to Providence and you could fly first class, where they take good care of you. We have plenty of money. Might as well use it to do some good. Please do this, Victoria. It would be a great help to me, knowing you are safe and happy with Jo while I'm gone."

"Very well, I will ask Joana." He could hear a slight change in her voice, which gave him hope.

"Thank you. Why don't you call her right now? I'd sleep better knowing this is settled, even though I'm confident it will be yes."

"Yes, that is a good idea. I will call you back shortly."

"I'll be here. Good luck, my love!"

"Goodbye, Benjamin."

After the call ended, Ben logged on to his laptop to knock out a few administrative chores. Fifteen minutes later, his cell phone rang with Victoria's callback number. Smiling, he pressed the answer button and said, "Coast Guard. You sink 'em, we save 'em."

There were three seconds of startled silence, followed by Victoria's wonderful laugh. "That was funny, Benjamin! I did not expect you to say that!"

"What can I say? I'm in a puckish mood tonight. So, don't keep me in suspense. How did your call go with Jo?"

"Oh, she said yes, after she squealed with delight. I will fly up there the day after tomorrow. You were correct, Benjamin. I am so glad I took your suggestion!"

The excitement in her voice was contagious. "That's wonderful! How long will you stay?"

"I am planning to stay for one week, but I can change it if I want to. Oh, Benjamin, I am so excited! I have so much to do!"

"Then I'll let you get to it. I am relieved to hear you so happy, my love. I'll talk to you tomorrow night."

"Goodbye, my dearest man!"

"Goodbye, Victoria." After hanging up the phone and putting it inside his desk, he reached over to touch Victoria's wedding portrait. He could sleep well now, even with his unease after the somber meeting on the messdeck. It was a tremendous relief to know she would be with their closest friends while he was down here.

In case something happened.

Chapter 11

The Silence of Death

**William F. Baker Airport, St. Ignatius, U.S. Virgin Islands
11:37 AST, 26 June**

Marcus

Marcus was in his element. He was not just sitting there monitoring the instruments as the UAV flew a pre-set pattern, but actually flying the aircraft using joystick and throttle controls. Unlike the previous day's flight, they were flying point-to-point on the island to scout potential points of volcanic gas emissions. Once they reached a targeted point, Marcus would keep the aircraft in orbit around the position, compensating for wind drift, and holding the aircraft about five hundred feet above the ground while the hyperspectral camera scanned the scene.

Uncle Erich sat to his left, controlling the camera operation and interpreting the readout on the screens before him. Lincoln was off today for crew rest, enjoying the first day of Carnival in Jamestown. Marcus's turn would come tomorrow and, being free to carouse this evening, had made a date for dinner with Isabelle at her grandmother's home.

Dr. Hernandez sat behind them on this flight in the consultant role, as the real-time interpretations of the readouts were important and could induce changes in their flight plan. The woman's presence with them was an ominous sign that trouble was brewing in the earth below them. She had dark circles under her eyes and her demeanor was far more restrained than in the previous encounters Marcus had had with her.

Their day had begun at six-thirty that morning when she laid out a marked-up topographic chart of the island on the table before them. "We will start at the summit of Mount Acadia," she said, pointing to the elevated area at the approximate center of the island. "It is vital to check each of these crevices thoroughly. Sulfur dioxide and carbon dioxide emissions are heavier than air and will pool in low-lying areas if not dispersed by the winds. We will also check the areas around the known vents, here, here, here, and here," she continued, pointing in turn at four red Xs on the chart. "Finally, I would like a thorough survey of this area here," she said, tracing her finger along a half-mile wide dark blue semicircle anchored on the island's northwest shore. "The topographic data showed a two- to four-meter uplift in this area that might be the emergence of a new vent."

As if to punctuate her remarks, the ground trembled again, rattling the windows and cups on the table by the coffee thermos they had brought with them. Hernandez ducked out of the room for a couple of minutes and then returned. "Four-point-three, centered here," she said, pointing toward the center of the uplift area.

"Second one today," his uncle said, shaking his head.

"Twenty-third, actually," Dr. Hernandez replied. "The others were too mild to be felt by us. Our ground instruments picked them up.

There had been no other tremors strong enough to be felt since the early morning event and their investigation of the terrain around Mount Acadia's summit and the first two known vent locations revealed nothing out of the ordinary. They were approaching the third now as Marcus flexed his wrists, hands, and fingers, preparing to take manual control. When the distance readout at the top right corner of his screen read 1.0, he grasped the throttle lever and joystick and punched the button to disengage the autopilot. "On manual control," he announced.

"Roger, manual. Zero point eight to go, initiating scan," his uncle said.

On reaching the orbit point, Marcus pushed the stick to the left, putting the UAV in a left bank, performing a pylon turn around the target point, and making slight adjustments to the pitch and throttle to keep the aircraft at the correct altitude. His world was now the center screen of the control panel, displaying aircraft attitude, airspeed, altitude, and turn rate. He had held the orbit for around twenty minutes when his uncle said, "Scan complete. Negative on target gasses. Course to point four is two-zero-two."

"Roger, coming to two-zero-two," Marcus said.

His uncle switched the scan off and then turned to look at Dr. Hernandez. "Three down without a trace, doctor."

She was gazing at the hyperspectral imaging screen, watching the flashing green "NEGATIVE" annunciation. She sat back with folded arms, lightly tapping the end of a ballpoint pen on her lips, and gazed at the ceiling for half a minute before replying. "Well, good news so far. I'm at a loss to understand it, though. With all these tremors, we should see some signs of out-gassing."

"We still have one more vent and the uplift area," his uncle replied.

"Yes. Let's see if our luck holds."

When the aircraft reached the desired south-southwest heading, Marcus leveled the wings and punched on the autopilot. "Steady on two-zero-two, three minutes to point four." He began his flexing exercises for the next orbit, an old trick he learned during his video gaming days in high school. It almost certainly wasn't needed with the short periods he held direct control, but he wasn't taking any chances—the last thing he needed while piloting was a hand cramp.

The fourth vent location proved to be another dry hole. The remaining survey would be flown much like the topographical survey of the previous day, a narrow-off-set parallel search pattern controlled by the autopilot. He steadied the aircraft on the new course toward the uplift area and punched on the autopilot, then sat back in his seat and tried to relax while concentrating on the panel. In the unlikely event the autopilot failed, he would have to assume control immediately at that low altitude to prevent a crash. There was no time to play catch up with the operating situation.

After the aircraft arrived and automatically turned onto the first leg of its survey pattern, Marcus asked, while keeping his eyes on the screen, "Doctor, assuming we don't find anything today, will we be doing the same thing tomorrow?

"No, Marcus. I see no point in that. I would like the air-craft available in case we have to investigate any activity, though."

His uncle nodded, also without looking from his screen. "We'll keep what we call a 'Bravo Zero' manned up from dawn until sunset. The aircraft won't be flying, but it will be ready for launch on the catapult and we can have it in the air within ten minutes of a call."

"That will be excellent," Dr. Hernandez said. "We won't make that call unless something changes significantly."

"Fair enough."

The survey of the uplift area also proved to be a bust, and Marcus commanded the UAV to return to base. As it approached the airfield, he retracted the hyperspectral camera into the aircraft to protect it and brought the aircraft down for a smooth landing in the grass alongside the runway. After securing the ground control station, Marcus and his uncle walked out to the runway, picked the aircraft up onto a wheeled trolley used for ground transport, and tugged it into the hangar for the through-flight servicing. An hour and a half later, it was back on its catapult and ready for launch, freeing the team for the day. About halfway through the drive back to the hotel, Marcus glanced at his uncle and asked, "Are you sure you don't need me tomorrow?"

"No, Marcus. You have a good time tonight. If you want to get lit, you're cleared hot. Just don't drink and drive and, for God's sake, don't do anything to get us kicked off the island!"

Marcus feigned a disappointed look and said, "Aw, gee, Uncle Erich! You're as bad as Mom!"

"Son, I grew up in the shadow of that woman. Believe me, I'm not even close!"

******

Isabelle picked Marcus up at the hotel about an hour later, after he had showered and changed into khakis and his dark blue academy polo shirt. "You look quite handsome, Mr. Porter," she said with an alluring smile when he met her at the door of the hotel. She, of course, looked fabulous, her chestnut hair down over her shoulders in cream-colored slacks and a loose green top, creating a challenge for him not to stare at her during the short drive up to her home.

Isabelle's grandmother's house was fascinating, even for a young man whose interests narrowly focused on aviation, sports, and the female of the species. Nestled in a narrow valley halfway up the side of Mount Acadia, it had been in Isabelle's family for generations. It was larger than most of the homes he had seen on the island, although smaller than the typical American suburban house, two-storied, timber-framed in the style found in Denmark and the rest of northwest Europe, with a yellow stucco exterior. The unexpected combination of a beautiful, nineteenth-century, western European house set among orchids, bougainvillea, and palm trees was captivating and Marcus was frozen in wonder, looking at it until a smiling Isabelle gently tugged his arm and led him inside.

The interior of the home was another fascinating blend of architecture and décor. It featured an open floor plan with half-paneled walls, beautifully carved wooden archways, and antique furniture combined with a mixture of old and new, European and Caribbean wall and table decorations. What could easily have been an eclectic mish-mash was a seamless blend that bridged the centuries and led Marcus to imagine what it must have been like on St. Ignatius back when it was a Danish colony but without the feeling of being in a stuffy museum.

Marcus stopped to gaze at a large wedding portrait from what he guessed was the early seventies, featuring a handsome, swarthy young man with a pencil-thin mustache in a white tuxedo and a stunningly beautiful young woman in a white wedding dress, her long dark hair swept into a braided updo. As Isabelle stepped next to him, Marcus said, "Wow. Would I get myself into trouble saying she is wicked hot?"

Isabelle chuckled and said, "Not at all. Would you like to meet her?"

"*What*?"

"Those are my grandparents. The wicked hot lady in that picture is in the kitchen putting the finishing touches on our dinner."

Marcus grinned back. "Rowrr," he mock-growled. "Lead on!" He was seriously hungry and the wonderful fragrance of home cooking permeating the house had had him salivating since they came inside. A short walk and a couple of turns later put them in a medium-sized kitchen, where a woman stood at the stove, stirring a pot. She had her back to them, but Marcus could see she was slim and tall like Isabelle, with an erect posture and graying dark hair gathered into a bun.

"Gran, this is Marcus Porter. Marcus, my grandmother, Adelaide Jones," Isabelle said.

The woman turned and Marcus could clearly see she was the woman in the portrait, obviously many years on, but still striking, with a lovely face and sparkling eyes. She briskly stepped over with a broad smile and hand outstretched. "So, you are the handsome flier. I am pleased to meet you, Marcus."

Handsome flier? Hmm. "Thank you, ma'am. Same here."

"Better be careful, Gran. Marcus thinks you are pretty hot."

"*Really?*" Adelaide said with a cock of her head. "You trying to bag yourself a rich widow, young man?"

Marcus smiled and waded in. "If she looks like you, I think I could be persuaded."

Both women chuckled, and Adelaide replied. "Handsome and charming too—I'll take him! Wrap him up for me, Izzy!"

Marcus laughed. "Sorry, ma'am. Can't jump ship with obligated service hanging over my head."

"Damn! Isn't that always the way? Well, it's nice to have you for a while, anyway."

"Thank you, ma'am. Is there anything I can do to help?"

"Sure. If you and Izzy can get those salad bowls into the dining room for me, I'll have room to finish this chicken.

Marcus looked down at the small table holding six bowls of salad. "I hope these aren't all for us. I need to save room for the chicken."

"No, no," Adelaide said. "The neighbors will eat with us, too. I couldn't keep a visitor all to myself. It wouldn't be neighborly."

As if on cue, there was a knock at the front door and Isabelle said, "Excuse me." She returned with a couple Marcus estimated to be in their early thirties, dressed similarly to Marcus and Isabelle, accompanied by a pretty young girl who looked to be about six in a red polka-dot dress and sandals. "Marcus Porter, these are our neighbors, Nathan and Laetitia Evans and their daughter Persephone, but we call her Percy, right?" Isabelle said, looking down with a smile.

"Yes," the girl replied shyly.

Nathan held out his hand and said, "Call me Nate, please."

"Pleased to meet you," Marcus said, shaking his hand.

After the greetings, everyone sat for one of the finest home-cooked meals Marcus could remember. He was astonished at how relaxed he felt among a diverse group of people he had just met, discussing his mission on St. Ignatius, his family, and the academy. They all listened intently to his tale of fighting the fire and rescuing the survivors. He guessed all visitors were intensely interesting to the residents, one of the downsides of living in such an insular environment.

Persephone, who had been listening in silence, spoke up after the rescue story. "Marcus, are you married?"

Marcus smiled at the question. "No, sweetie. You can't be married when you are a cadet."

"Oh. Will you always be a cadet?"

"No. By this time next year, I'll be an officer. Officers can be married."

"Oh," she said. After thinking for a few seconds, she asked, "Are you going to marry Izzy?"

Marcus was startled and glanced across the table at Isabelle, who was putting a napkin to her mouth to conceal an amused smile. He quickly recovered, leaned down to Persephone, and said, "Uh uh. She's waaaay too old for me!"

"Well!" Isabelle exclaimed in a mock huff as the other adults exploded in laughter.

"Marcus, Percy is a bit too forward, sorry about that," Laetitia said. "And I'll head her off before she proposes marriage to you, now that she knows you're unattached."

"I'm flattered," Marcus said and smiled at Persephone again. "Tell you what. If you are still interested in twelve or thirteen years, give me a call. I should be a lieutenant commander by then."

"Does a lieutenant commander make a lot of money?" Persephone asked.

"Tons more than a cadet, that's for sure," Marcus replied.

"Oh." Persephone nodded. "Then I'll wait until you are a lieutenant commander."

"Smart girl," Marcus said, to more laughter around the table.

"If you'll excuse us, Adelaide, I think it's time to get our young debutante home to bed," Nathan said.

As they all stood, Marcus shook hands with Evans and then kneeled to hug Persephone. "Good night, sweetie."

"Good night, Marcus. Will I see you again?"

"I hope so."

After the three had departed, Marcus turned back to help clear the table. Isabelle met him with hands on her hips and a raised eyebrow. "*Too old*? That was the best you could come up with, *Mister* Porter?" She playfully slapped his arm. "Now, if you want to salvage the picnic I have planned for us tomorrow, you'd better jump on clearing this table!"

At that moment, another tremor began, the rumble building slowly until the dishes in the china cabinet were rattling and the lights flickered. After about half a minute, the tremor faded out, and they all stood frozen in shock. Marcus swallowed hard to overcome his dread and said, "Clear the table—on it! Jeez, take it easy, Isabelle!"

The two women both looked in surprise at Marcus and almost simultaneously burst into nervous laughter. Isabelle then gave him one of her sweet smiles. "Nice save, flyboy. There's hope for you yet."

"Hope has always been my first strategy," Marcus said as he gathered plates from the table.

Acadia Forest Reserve, St. Ignatius, U.S. Virgin Islands
10:23 AST, 27 June

Marcus

He had had a delightful time at Isabelle's home. Once the dishes were cleared, Adelaide led him through the house, stopping to tell the story behind each picture and collectible. Unlike Isabelle, she had spent her entire life here, leaving only for short visits to the other islands or the mainland U.S. The concept of living in a single house for one's entire life was alien to most Americans like Marcus, and he wondered at how it and its history were so entwined in Adelaide's essence.

The three sat down for coffee and an hour more of light conversation upon completion of the tour, after which Isabelle drove Marcus back to his hotel and left him with a kiss on the cheek. He was a little disappointed, but not surprised, as things seemed to be playing out more or less as his uncle had predicted. The follow-up date this morning was definitely a positive sign, however.

Marcus learned that Isabelle's was among the first families on the island, relatively wealthy and generally well-liked. Adelaide had helped her late husband build a successful coffee export business and then ran it after he died until retiring a few years ago. Her son and only child had left the island for college in the States, where he married a classmate and decided to stay. Isabelle was also an only child, and, tragically, her parents had died in a house fire when she was away at summer camp at age nine. Naturally, she came to St. Ignatius to live with her grandparents.

Despite the risk of losing her to the mainland as she had her son, Adelaide insisted Isabelle attend college like her parents. She picked the University of Florida for the climate and easy lifestyle, but after graduating with a BA in Business Administration and a minor in Public Relations, she returned home to St. Ignatius to a job in the coffee business. When the deputy administrator post came up in the election the previous year, she entered the contest and prevailed over three other candidates to become, at twenty-two, the youngest elected official in the island's history. She attributed her win to name recognition, although Marcus was sure her education, charm, and beauty were the more significant factors.

Their day together began with a quiet cup of coffee in a shop near the hotel. Isabelle was back in casual clothes: jeans, a loose, sheer dark blue blouse over a light blue top with gray walking shoes. Marcus was in his normal liberty uniform, a variation of last night's polo shirt and khakis. On the way out of the shop, they bought a bottle of wine, some fruit, and cheese and headed in Isabelle's car for Acadia Forest Reserve, a park that included the summit of Mount Acadia down to the lower reaches of the cloud forest surrounding the peak. Just past the sign marking the entrance to the park, Isabelle pulled off the road onto a small, flat area of hard ground and parked. The area was surrounded by trees, mainly the small-leaved mahogany that dominated the island, mixed with short palms and scrub bushes.

"Here?" Marcus said, decidedly unimpressed with the scenery.

"Oh, no," Isabelle replied with a shake of her head. "It's about a quarter-mile further up. This is the last place that has space to park."

"Got it," Marcus said, pulling the backpack holding the wine and food out of the back seat. He looked up to see Isabelle holding out her right hand with an inviting smile.

For a brief instant, he was locked in conflict between the excitement of anticipation and the fear of a blunder. *Is this really happening?* He bought himself time to take a breath by slinging the backpack over his right shoulder, then smiled and took her hand. It was exactly as he expected it to be, soft and warm, with a light, but firm grip.

It was perfect.

He stepped up beside her and they began walking up the road, under the canopy of trees that cut off the sunlight and created a cool haven from the summer heat. The further they walked up the slope, the darker it became, with the fierce sunlight giving way to a soft continuum of green with wisps of fog drifting between the trees. Despite his excitement at walking hand-in-hand with this beautiful woman, he found himself gazing around in fascination. It was like stepping into another world.

After a brief walk up the road, Isabelle said, "There's the path over to the right." She turned and led Marcus through an opening in the trees that was less a worn path than a continuous gap between the ferns and bromeliads and the thick trunks of the mountain mahogany trees. The fallen leaves muffled their steps. The only sound in the wood was their rustling, blending with those in the canopy stirred by the light breeze. When they had walked a few dozen yards down the path, they reached an open area crossed by a wide stone ledge and stopped. "Behold—my sitting room!" Isabelle said.

"It's unreal," Marcus shook his head in wonder and voiced aloud what he had been thinking. "Like being on another planet."

"Exactly why I like it," she said. "Come over here. The ledge is the perfect height for sitting and vibing." Isabelle took the backpack from him and they stepped over and sat down on the ledge on either side of a round protrusion in the wall. "You like my nice bistro table?" she said with a grin as she patted the surface.

"It's just about right," Marcus replied.

"Yes, yes," she said, pulling out paper plates, some plastic ware, and the cheese, crackers, and fruit. Last, she pulled out the wine bottle with two plastic cups on top. When she took the cups off to open the wine, her hand froze. "Oh, shit!"

Marcus, who had been gazing up at the surrounding trees, swung back around. "What?"

"It's got a cork and I don't have an opener. Dammit! Everything was going so well..."

"Hold on," Marcus said with a grin.

"Don't tell me you have a corkscrew on you!"

Marcus reached back and withdrew his Victorinox Climber knife from the pocket on his belt. His older sister, who was probably the biggest Richard Dean Anderson fan ever, had given it to him as a high school graduation present. "Every boy should have a MacGyver knife," she told him. Marcus just decided he was going to give her an extra big kiss and hug the next time he saw her.

"*Semper Paratus*, my lady. Tool eleven," he said, handing her the pocket knife after pulling out the corkscrew.

She gave him the warmest smile he had ever seen. "I should have known. *Semper Paratus*—always...what?"

"Ready."

Her eyes grew wide for a second, and then she put her head back and laughed. "How long have you been waiting to use that line?"

Marcus smiled and said, "It's not a line, it's the Coast Guard motto."

"No way!"

"Way."

She laughed that lovely laugh and then attacked the bottle. "Again, I should have known."

They spent the next hour and a half talking, munching the fruit and cheese, and sipping wine. Marcus was as-tounded at his good fortune to be with this beautiful, charming, intelligent woman in this wondrous place. It was fascinating, fun, and...honest—no posturing or pre-tenses, just two young people sharing a moment together. He felt a distinct pang of regret when Isabelle suddenly stood up.

"I love this place," she said. "But after an hour or so, my ass doesn't. There is one more thing I'd like you to see while we're here."

"What's that?"

"A waterfall. The only one on St. Ignatius. It's in a cut about a quarter mile further in."

"I'm in," Marcus said. After packing the trash and remaining food and wine in the backpack, they set out along the trail again, with Isabelle in the lead. They had been walking for five minutes when Isabelle suddenly stopped in her tracks. Marcus, barely missing colliding with her, said, "What's up?"

"Something's wrong. We should be able to hear it by now," she said with a frown.

"Do you want to go back?"

She briefly hesitated, then replied, "No. I need to see."

Marcus stepped up, and she took his arm and they continued to walk forward. Marcus could sense her apprehension. That and the eerie lack of noise—no water, no birds, not even the hum of insects that you would normally expect to hear—conjured a deep fear inside that he struggled to suppress. They turned a corner on the path and stepped into a very large open area, with moss-covered stone cliffs on three sides and a still pond in the center.

"It's gone," she said in disbelief. "It used to be there, coming through that cleft." She pointed to the center of the opposing wall. Her hand dropped, and she started looking around the sides of the tiny valley. Suddenly, she screamed, turned, and buried her face in Marcus's chest.

"What is it?" he shouted. She didn't look up, just pointed off to the side. Marcus looked in that direction and saw a large lizard lying motionless on its side. He held her tight, letting her catch her breath.

Eventually, she pulled away slightly, put her hand on his chest, looked up at him with a sad smile, and said, "Sorry about that."

"I'm not," Marcus replied. "Are you going to be alright?"

"Yes. Just a girlie thing. Let's get out of here."

Marcus was about to move, then paused. "I know you're shook, and if you want to go, I'll go, no argument. But it might be helpful to know what happened and if it has to do with the volcano."

Her smile vanished. "What are you suggesting?"

"I should get a sample of the water."

She took a step back, her eyes locked on his face. After a second or two, she dropped her gaze. "You're right. There are a couple of water bottles in the backpack that should do."

Marcus dropped the backpack and pulled the bottles out. He was stepping forward when she reached out and gripped his arm, stopping him in his tracks. "We should bring the Iggy-Iggy too," she said, looking up into his face.

Marcus nodded and continued to the side of the pond. He couldn't smell anything, but he knew from his hazardous materials training that meant little. He opened both bottles and emptied one. *Hopefully, if my hand starts to burn, I can wash it off.* He slowly inserted the opening into the water, rolling it slightly as the bottle filled, then tipping it upright and screwing the cap back on with minimum contact of his fingers with the water. To his great relief, there was no burning of his skin, but he still rinsed his fingers and the bottle with the clean water from the other bottle. *Now for the lizard.*

Marcus stood from the pond and stepped back to where Isabelle was standing dejectedly. He put the sample bottle in the backpack, then carried it over and set it down beside the iguana. It was definitely dead, not in a torpor, its eyes wide open and legs stretched out. He swallowed hard, took a deep breath to overcome his revulsion, and reached out to pick up the dead lizard. *At least it hasn't started rotting.* It was not heavy, perhaps five pounds, and the body fit easily in the backpack, two-thirds of its three-foot length being the tail which Marcus coiled into the bag. After zipping it shut, he rinsed his hands again with the clean water, stood and slung the backpack, and then stepped back to where Isabelle was standing.

She said nothing, just briefly gave him a sad look, then took his arm. They walked in silence, back through the forest and down the road to the car. Marcus was conflicted, thinking he should say something to comfort her. Every idea he could come up with was stillborn in his head, either being too stupid for further consideration, or too risky.

They reached the car and Marcus was putting the backpack in the rear seat when Isabelle finally spoke. "Could you drive, please?"

"Natch. I'll take you home."

"No. We need to get to Dr. Hernandez with this." She looked up at him, and seeing his concern, managed another sad smile. "It's OK. I've come this far. Is she at the hotel?"

"No, that Woods Hole ship is doing its run today. She wanted to be in the office for that."

"OK, to the airport, then." He stepped over to open the passenger door for her and she suddenly threw her arms around his neck and buried her face in his chest. "I'm sorry it got ruined."

"What?"

"Our day together."

Marcus reached down and gently lifted her face to him. "Are you kidding? It was *fire*! Best day ever!" he said with a grin.

She smiled back and then pulled him into a long, sweet kiss that made his heart pound in his chest. When it was done, she cupped his face with her right hand and said, "OK, let's roll, flyboy." She then handed him the key fob and climbed into the passenger seat.

Marcus closed the door and started around the back of the car. He was in deep trouble now. Despite his best efforts, he was falling in love with Isabelle Jones.

Chapter 12

Alarm

USCG Cutter Kauai, underway in the Caribbean Sea, 8.8 nautical miles northeast of Jamestown, St. Ignatius, U.S. Virgin Islands
10:03 AST, 28 June

Ben

The process of picking up the OBSs was far slower than the one dropping them. *Kauai* cruised to the position they had marked on their electronic charts for a sensor and then sat at all stop while Ryan played his "wake up tune" through a sound transducer hung over the side. The sound signal took only a fraction of a second to reach the bottom of the Caribbean, around fifteen hundred feet down in this location. But after releasing its anchor, the unit would only ascend at five feet per second, leaving several minutes of waiting and scanning. Since there was no way to tell how much or in what direction a unit might

220

drift in either its descent or ascent, they had to scan in all directions, awaiting the appearance of a red triangular flag above the surface of the water.

The RHIB idled alongside, with Jenkins as coxswain and Chen as his crewman. Once an OBS popped up, they would move over to it and stay in a position to attach the hoist block of *Kauai*'s crane for the lift back aboard. Lee was operating the crane this morning and Bondurant was standing watch as OOD. Not knowing exactly where the unit would surface was a little worrisome, and Ben asked Ryan what would happen if it came up directly under *Kauai*'s hull.

"As long as your props aren't turning, you've got nothing to worry about. A couple thuds and it pops up on one side or the other," Ryan said.

"And if it comes up under the RHIB?" Ben asked.

Ryan shrugged and glanced at the RHIB. "Not sure. We never had that happen."

By the time Ryan had turned around, Ben was already on the radio to the RHIB, telling them to close up on *Kauai* in case the crew needed to be picked up. His next call was to the bridge to ensure Bondurant was bringing the motors to a complete stop and not keeping them turning for minor adjustments in position. Another on the lengthy list of things he had to worry about as XO.

They already had recovered two of the units. Ryan had stood by on the afterdeck as each was brought aboard, guiding them gently into the bottom half of the container in which they would eventually be shipped back to

Woods Hole. He would then plug his laptop computer into a USB port in a previously sealed compartment atop the unit and download its data. Once accomplished, he installed the top half of the container and moved the unit to the storage area using a hand truck.

Ben's radio crackled. "Target in sight, three-zero-eight relative, four hundred yards."

"Roger, I have the target," Jenkins's voice replied. Seconds later, the RHIB roared off on a bearing off *Kauai*'s port bow. Ben felt the patrol boat's motors kick on, and she ponderously pivoted left to follow. It took a little over a minute for *Kauai* to pull to a stop alongside the floating OBS and the RHIB. Lee moved the hoist block into reach and Chen attached it to the lift ring on the OBS. The process took time, but even without its concrete anchor, the unit weighed over one-hundred-fifty pounds and was too ungainly to be retrieved by hand. The unit was lifted from the water and craned onto the afterdeck, where Ryan was waiting to do the download. Another OBS was sealed and ready for shipment and being moved to its storage location. Wash, rinse, repeat.

At this pace, they would finish in about four hours. Once the last unit was recovered, *Kauai* would jog back to Jamestown for a brief stop to deliver a portable hard drive containing all the data to Dr. Hernandez's team. The patrol boat would then head out on the six-hour trip through the Virgin Passage east of Vieques and Culebra and hook west to San Juan. With any luck, they would be snugged in at the wharf on the Coast Guard base by midnight, as Ben knew he needed the sleep. The next few days, first restocking after offloading Ryan and his gear, then the journey to Guadeloupe and back with that killer Lamonde on board would be another ordeal.

Ben had made plans to keep Lamonde, Pete, and the defector isolated while they were on board. He was shuffling the crew to temporary quarters to create a vacant four-man room for their guests. He didn't mind sharing his stateroom with Pete as he had on missions in the past, but he would be damned if he was going to expose any crewmembers to Lamonde or a scumbag who would sacrifice his family's lives for money. Once they were shed of their passengers after the pickup, they could get back to normal.

Ben smiled and shook his head. *Yeah, normal. Head back down to an island with a volcano getting ready to blow its top. Just another day at the office!*

He looked over toward the island five miles in the distance. *Kauai*'s mission today had gained more urgency in the wake of the discovery of the dead animals near the summit of the mountain. They had held a debriefing yesterday evening after field tests of the pond water Marcus Porter had collected showed sulfuric acid in much higher concentrations than would normally be expected. Between the dead lizard he had found and several others an expedition to the site had gathered, Dr. Hernandez was convinced the mountain had recently spewed a lethal cloud of sulfur dioxide that had killed the animals en masse and poisoned the pond. It was another bad sign pointing to an imminent eruption.

Dr. Hernandez had already processed the signal data from the research ship picked up by her land sensor net—the complementary data from the OBSs would complete the picture of the magma chamber under St. Ignatius. Once the "volume of melt", as Dr. Hernandez called it, was known, the decisions regarding issuing alerts and evacuating the populace would follow.

The UAV was now in the air almost continuously in orbit over the island, single-pilot manned with Deffler, Porter, and Lincoln running six-hour shifts. The normal safety-of-flight restrictions on single pilot and night flying were suspended in the emergency. If any significant tremors were detected by one or more of the sensors, the aircraft would immediately vector to the site to check for out-gassing.

There was a meeting scheduled for 13:00 this afternoon between the local administration, the governor's office, the USGS, and the Coast Guard to discuss evacuation options for the island's residents. Dr. Hernandez was convinced that an eruption of Mount Acadia was imminent, but the USGS needed more evidence before pushing the go button on an operation that would, at best, upend the lives of hundreds of people. Hence the urgency of the OBS recovery operation.

Ordinarily, *Kauai* would have remained in the area to provide an additional means of escape should the worst happen. However, the operation at Île Oiseaux was already underway, with Pete arriving down there today and pickup continuing as scheduled on the 1ˢᵗ of July. Barring a full volcanic eruption with certain loss of life, *Kauai* was committed to completing the DIA mission. It was the correct decision as far as Ben was concerned—even Dr. Hernandez admitted it could be weeks before the danger fully manifested and *Kauai* would just be a backup for whatever ferries or other vessels the authorities would muster. Still, the thought of being hundreds of miles away while people, particularly Coasties, were at risk did not sit well with either Haley or him.

With about ten minutes to go before the next pickup, Ben strolled inside to hit the head and grab some chips and sodas for the crew stuck on the operation. The winds were very light today, almost calm, and other than brief periods in between pickup points when *Kauai*'s speed could generate some wind, the heat and sun beating down from almost directly overhead were oppressive.

His first stop was the crane control station where Lee sat awaiting the next operation. Ben knew she would have much rather be driving the RHIB right now, but she would get her turn in a couple of hours when she and Jenkins swapped places. As Ben came up to her, she started to stand, and he waved her back down. "Petty Officer Lee, I've got Coke, water, and chips. What's your pleasure?"

"I'll take one of each. Thank you, XO," she said gratefully.

"Done," Ben said and handed them over.

Lee immediately popped open the Coke and took a long gulp. "I don't know what's worse, the heat or the boredom," she said distractedly as she gazed at the RHIB cruising alongside.

"Time for a new outlook," Ben said. "Now that you're moving into upper management as the new Boats, you'll need to get used to a lot more watching than doing."

"Tell me about it!" she said sadly.

Ben chuckled and said, "Hang in there. Let me know if you need anything."

She gave him a warm smile in return. "Thanks, sir."

Ryan was his next stop. The young man was sitting in a shady spot next to the OBS storage area, smoking a cigarette and, like Lee, watching as the RHIB cruised alongside.

"Kevin, I've got icy Cokes, water, and chips," Ben said, careful to stay upwind.

"I'll take a Coke. Thanks, man," he said, taking one out of Ben's hand.

"Hot one today," Ben said.

"Yeah. It figures. When I get a job down in the Caribbean, it would be in the damn summer. I'll bet come December they'll have me off of Cape Race freezing my nuts off and puking my guts out."

"Hey, in a few days, you'll be back home spending all those overtime bucks."

"Here, here," he said, raising the Coke to his lips.

Ben's headset crackled again. "Approaching point four, deck crew stand-to."

"OK guys, here we go again!" Ben said. He stepped aside as Ryan stood and picked up his sound gear. It comprised a frame about as large as a fishing tackle box with a twenty-foot cable having a three-inch ball-looking device on the end holding the sound transducer. Ben could feel and see *Kauai* slowing as they neared the next reference position, eventually coming to a stop in the water.

"Deck crew, Conn. At all stop," chirped Ben's headset.

"Conn, deck crew. Roger, hold," Ben responded, then gave Ryan a thumbs up. As the technician carefully lowered the transducer into the water, Ben turned to see the RHIB coming to a stop alongside. He leaned over and said, "I've got Cokes, water, and chips, guys! Anyone interested?"

"Hell yes, XO! Hand those bad boys down!" Chen shouted up with a smile. Ben had been carrying everything in a couple of plastic supermarket shopping bags. He leaned over and handed both to Chen as soon as they came within reach. "Thank you, sir!" the young petty officer said after pulling down the bags.

"No problem," Ben replied and stood up. Ben resumed his watch, scanning the sea out to the horizon off the starboard quarter in sectors of about forty-five degrees, looking for the telltale red flag of a surfaced OBS. It was still pretty early in the process and the unit likely would have two or more minutes of ascent left before breaking the surface, but he wanted to have a scanning rhythm going before that happened. As luck would have it, his sector was the lucky one, and he caught sight of the tiny red flag about three boat lengths away.

"Conn, deck party. Target in sight, one-five-zero relative, one hundred yards."

"Conn, roger."

He leaned over and shouted to the RHIB crew, "Starboard quarter, fellas. One hundred yards."

"Roger that, sir," Jenkins replied and goosed the RHIB's engine while cranking the wheel to the left. After arcing through a left turn that cleared *Kauai*'s stern, he reported further by radio, "*Kauai*-One, target in sight."

Ben nodded in satisfaction and then stepped back to watch another recovery operation in progress. As *Kauai*'s motors kicked in and she began a pivot to the right, he glanced over at the island again, just a dark purple shape in the distance, and wondered how the efforts ashore were going.

Office of the Administrator, 63 Haabets Gade, Jamestown, St. Ignatius, U.S. Virgin Islands
12:57 AST, 28 June

Marcus

Marcus was tired. He had enormous trouble finding sleep last night, his mind a battleground of emotions. The adrenaline accompanying their discovery of the valley of death had worn off by the time he returned to his hotel room and he was left with the realization of how close he and Isabelle had come to being killed.

The debriefing that night, after the recon team had returned, had been both somber and alarming. Dr. Hernandez had seen this sort of thing before in her earlier expeditions—the diversion of water features like Isabelle's waterfall and the mountain belching large clouds of ex-solved magmatic gas, either carbon dioxide or sulfur dioxide, which, being heavier than normal air, settle into a canyon or other depression in the ground and suffocate any animals there. The iggy-iggy and the other lizards the recon team had found near the former waterfall had been felled in their tracks and suffocated while the water in their lungs changed to highly corrosive sulfuric acid. Trade winds eventually recirculated and dispersed the toxic gasses, leaving no evidence behind but the sudden silence of death. The idea of going through an experience like that himself was a horror that led Marcus to fear the dreams that sleep would bring.

Marcus's salvation proved to be his recollection of the moments he and Isabelle spent together in the paradisiacal cloud forest, particularly the heart-stopping kiss at the very end. The warm, sweet memories broke the grip on his mind of the what-if terrors, bringing a few hours of sleep before he had to rise at 04:30 to relieve his uncle as the UAV pilot.

Using the excuse that he was busy as the lead pilot, Uncle Erich had sent Marcus to attend the meeting as the representative of the team. Tired as he was, Marcus jumped at the chance to be with Isabelle again, even if it was only to share glances during the meeting. She and the island's Administrator, Robert Thomas, had not yet arrived in the small conference room. Besides Marcus, Dr. Hernandez was present, along with Sergeant Edmond Platt, head of St. Ignatius's four-man detachment of the U.S. Virgin Islands Police Department. Dr. Hernandez looked even more tired than Marcus felt, not surprising, given the stress of the responsibility she had borne since her arrival. She was scanning her notebook to prepare for the meeting, while Platt was just staring at the ceiling, tapping his fingertips together.

The door flew open and a portly, middle-aged man strode purposefully in, closely followed by Isabelle, who was wearing the same "official" look she had had in their first meeting. As the man, balding with graying black hair and about Isabelle's height, moved quickly to the head of the table and sat, Isabelle said, "Administrator Robert Thomas, I'd like to introduce Dr. Lydia Hernandez representing USGS, Cadet Marcus Porter of the U.S. Coast Guard, and you know Sergeant Platt, of course."

Thomas looked at Marcus like he was some sort of slimy bug and said, "What on Earth is a cadet doing here?"

"Mr. Porter is one of the pilots in the Coast Guard aviation detachment," Isabelle responded. "His aviation expertise could be needed."

Thomas glanced at her and said, "Alright. Make the call."

Isabelle reached over to the speakerphone in the center of the table, dialed in a phone number and PIN, and then sat in a chair beside the balding man. She glanced for a second in Marcus's direction and, given the tense atmosphere in the room, he was careful not to show any response.

There was a beep from the speakerphone and a mechanical voice said, "You are now joining your conference." There was another beep and then a conversation underway came through the phone, suddenly stopped when a richly melodious voice with a West Indies accent said, "Hold up. Who just joined, please?"

"It's Administrator Robert Thomas on St. Ignatius, governor."

"Bob! Glad you could join us! I've got Danny Witchell from Homeland Security, Vic Norbert from USGS, and Admiral Harry Pennington from Coast Guard on the line. Who else do you have down there?"

Thomas, who was clearly irritated by being addressed as "Bob", nodded at Isabelle, who said, "Deputy Administrator Isabelle Jones, governor."

"Izzy! It's good to hear your voice. How's Adelaide?"

"She's fine, sir, thank you," Isabelle said, then nodded at Dr. Hernandez.

"Dr. Lydia Hernandez, University of Puerto Rico, governor."

"A pleasure, doctor. Looking forward to your presentation."

They all turned toward Marcus and he suddenly felt a tightness in his chest and difficulty breathing. "C-Cadet First Class Marcus Porter, Coast Guard Academy, sir!"

"Coast Guard Academy? My goodness, Marcus. How did you get caught up in this?"

"Summer program, sir. I am a member of the aviation detachment."

The voice laughed. "Talk about luck. OK, anyone else?"

Platt leaned forward. "Just me, sir. Sergeant Ed Platt, V.I.P.D."

"Thanks, Sarge. Alright, everybody, we are here because the rumors I'm getting from down there combined with conversations I've been having with USGS have scared the pants off me. Now, Vic is telling me they are on the verge of skipping the 'Watch' alert stage and going straight from 'Advisory' to 'Warning' for St. Ignatius. I think you all know what kind of mayhem that will cause with airlines, cruise ships, *et cetera*. Before I get one of those 'What the hell are you doing down there, Steve?' calls from the president, I'd like to get the straight story. Now, what have you got for me, Bob?"

Thomas turned to Dr. Hernandez and said, "I'll defer to Dr. Hernandez, governor."

Dr. Hernandez nodded and then launched into a brief history of the expedition up to then, sticking to layman's terms and avoiding much of the complicated jargon and mathematics that had made Marcus's eyes glaze over in previous meetings. She rounded off the presentation by stating, in her opinion, the evacuation of the population needed to begin as soon as possible.

"Doctor, you mentioned the Coast Guard cutter is picking up the ocean sensors as we speak. Is it possible they might tell us a different story, that an alert and evacuation might not be necessary?"

"No, sir," she replied with conviction. "There is no doubt that a major eruption is imminent. We have had steadily increasing earthquake swarms and magmatic gas emissions, and our ground sensors are now picking up what can only be interpreted as harmonic tremor—magma rapidly moving into the shallow chamber just under the mountain. At this point, the data we are awaiting will only help us forecast the scale of the eruption, that is, how far the effects will extend beyond St. Ignatius."

"What effects are we talking about here?"

"Certainly ashfall across the Virgin Islands, Puerto Rico, and anything in the Lesser Antilles north of Guadeloupe. Depending on the volume of eruptible magma, the deposits could be significant. But that's not the worst of it."

"I know I'm going to regret asking this, but what is the worst?"

"It's important to remember that St. Ignatius is not an island with a volcano. The island *is* the summit of a volcano. We have measured deformation in the surface through our overflights. If this or the earthquakes have disrupted the interior structure of the mountain, it could collapse into a caldera as the magma chamber empties, triggering large tsunamis. Also, keep in mind this volcano is two-thirds underwater. If some structural collapse opens the magma chamber to the sea, we could have the largest explosion ever seen."

"Jesus, Mary, and Joseph! If that does occur, how much warning will we have before the tsunamis hit?"

"In the Virgin Islands, sir? Two to three minutes after initiation for St. Croix, maybe ten to fifteen for St. Thomas and St. Johns." After about five seconds of dead silence on the phone, Dr. Hernandez asked, "Are you still there, sir?"

"Unfortunately, yes. So what you're saying is that there will be practically no warning. Is that how you see it, Vic?"

"Yes, governor," an unfamiliar voice said. "I would like to emphasize that we won't have a very good estimate until we can get a firm picture of the magma chamber, and Lydia is portraying the absolute worst case. But if there are tsunamis, they will propagate at around five hundred miles per hour. You should plan to evacuate any low-lying areas facing south as soon as the eruption begins rather than wait for the bang."

"Define 'low-lying' for me, please."

"On St. Croix, I would clear out any place lower than sixty feet above sea level. Maybe half that for the others."

After another long pause, the governor said, "Right. We'll hold and pray on the distant effects until we get a better idea of how bad it's likely to be. Do you have a timeline for when that analysis might be complete, doctor?"

"*Kauai* should be back within a few hours, but I have to parse and load the data and the runs involve some complicated calculations and post-processing. I should have something by eight a.m. tomorrow."

"Good. I wish it would be earlier, but I get it. Back to the immediate problem. I think we all concur that St. Ignatius should be evacuated. Does anyone disagree?"

Marcus looked at Thomas, expecting some pushback, but the man just stared at the phone. He made brief eye contact with Isabelle, who returned a deeply sad look, the sight bringing home the reality of the situation to him. They were talking about all the residents of St. Ignatius abandoning their homes, probably forever. Marcus had not contemplated such a thing before and found the thought of Isabelle's beautiful family home being destroyed immensely sad. He couldn't imagine what it must be like for Isabelle and her grandmother.

"I'll take silence as no disagreement," the governor continued. "Now we need to figure out how to get it done. Admiral, do you have anything that can help us?"

"The President has authorized me to set up a National Incident Command," said a third voice Marcus took to be Admiral Pennington. It was a firm, no-nonsense voice, but also had a timber that generated trust. Pennington had a reputation in the organization for being an outstanding leader, demanding excellence, but also ready to go to the mat for his people. "I was going to locate the Emergency Operations Center in San Juan, but with Puerto Rico in the crosshairs, we'd better keep it on the mainland. I'll see if I can sweet-talk General Miller out of some space at Southern Command Headquarters over in Doral. Regardless of where it is, we should be up and running within a few days.

"That leaves us with the operational challenges. The harbor at Jamestown is the problem. It is far too shallow for anything but our smallest short-range boats. There is one company with the right kind of vessel in St. Croix, but we have suspended their operating license for safety non-compliance. We are looking into the legalities of temporarily leasing it, patching it up, and manning it with coastguardsmen during the emergency. I'm sure you can imagine what a legal nightmare that is, but a declared state of emergency could definitely help that along. We are also talking to the British about a loan of one of their passenger vessels in the U.K. Virgin Islands and the Dutch have a perfect vessel for the job they run between Saint-Martin and Saba. We need help from State to clear the wickets on those."

"This is Danny," said a fourth voice. "I'll start on that, but Admiral, can't you park a large cutter offshore and ferry people out to it?"

"No," replied Pennington's voice. "It's too dangerous. The cutters' freeboard is such that they would have to climb ladders to make it on board. Going from a boat to a ship at sea is a lot harder than it looks, and most civilians couldn't hack it. We'll do it if the alternative is certain death ashore, but not otherwise. I think with the ferries we can lay our hands on, we should be able to get every-one off in a few days."

"How about a call to arms like Dunkirk?" an unknown voice said. "There are hundreds of boats and yachts around the islands."

"You must be joking," Pennington said disdainfully. "Even if we had a prayer of organizing anything in time, it would be a complete circus. We'd kill a lot more people than we saved. No, the ferries are our best bet. We should be able to pull it off if that damned volcano can wait a week."

"What do you think, doctor?" Norbert asked.

"It's possible," Hernandez answered. "No vents are currently active, although that could change quickly. As long as we get moving as soon as possible, it should be alright. But there's no margin for error."

"I understand, thank you."

"One more thing, Mr. Norbert," Dr. Hernandez said. "I need to get my students out of here. They've gone well above and beyond already, and frankly, this is a job for professionals. I'm going to send them out to San Juan this afternoon on *Kauai*, but that leaves just me on the instruments down here."

"Way ahead of you, Lydia. I have a crisis team gearing up right now for a flight into San Juan and I'm chartering a Twin Otter to get them down to the island by tomorrow afternoon."

"That's a relief!"

"What about you? You've gone well above and beyond yourself. The plane can bring you out on the return flight."

"Not a chance in Hell! Do you think I would pass up an opportunity to be on the ground for this?"

Marcus could almost hear a smile on the other end of the phone when Norbert replied, "OK, OK. But our team lead calls the plays. When he says bug-out, you bug-out. Clear?"

"Clear, thank you."

The governor came back on and said, "Well, I think we have a good plan. Does anyone else have anything to add?"

"Excuse me, sir, Cadet Porter here," Marcus said, drawing a glare from Thomas.

"Yes, go ahead, Marcus."

Marcus swallowed hard, then said, "Yes, sir. It's that we have the UAV more-or-less in the air twenty-four-seven. We'll need a heads-up about ten minutes before the Twin Otter or any other aircraft arrives so that we can deconflict the airspace. If whoever is doing their flight planning can call Air Station Borinquen, we can work something out."

"Thank you, Mr. Porter," Norbert said. "I'll pass that along."

"OK, I'll ask again," the governor continued. "Does anyone else have anything to add? No? Right. Bob, you and Izzy get everyone down there ready to evacuate. If you or Sergeant Platt feel you'll need reinforcements, either more V.I.P.D. or even National Guard, pick up the phone. I'm telling my staff your calls come straight through whatever else I have going on. Let's all plan to reconvene at eight a.m. tomorrow. God willing, we'll all get through this. Goodbye and good luck, everybody!"

The speakerphone emitted an irregular series of beeps as the participants disconnected and Isabelle reached over and pressed the hangup button. Thomas looked impassively around the table, then said. "You all know what to do. If anything changes, you are to call me at once. We'll meet here at seven-thirty tomorrow to pre-brief for the eight o'clock meeting. Any questions?" After scanning around the table, he abruptly stood and walked out of the room, followed by Dr. Hernandez.

Marcus stood and walked around the table to stand before Isabelle. Her face was a shroud of despair, and her eyes were welling with tears as she gathered up the papers on the table into a folder. "Isabelle, I'm so sorry," he said. "Is there anything I can do to help?"

Isabelle said nothing, just looked up at him with heartbreaking sadness and hugged him. She jumped when Thomas shouted from outside the room, "Miss Jones!" Isabelle took a step back, touched Marcus's cheek with her free hand, and managed a sad smile as she rolled her eyes. She then turned and walked from the room.

Platt stood and gave him a pat on the shoulder. "Nice catch, son."

As they turned to walk out of the room, Marcus asked, "I get that this is as bad a situation as it gets, but what is that guy's issue with us?"

Platt smiled and said, "Same one today as every other day. He's an asshole."

"Right," Marcus said, closing the door behind them.

Chapter 13

Grim Prognosis

USCG Cutter Kauai, Moored, Jamestown, St. Ignatius, U.S. Virgin Islands
17:18 AST, 28 June

Haley

Haley watched the activity on the mole while standing beside the canvas-covered fifty-caliber machine gun on the starboard bridge wing. Unlike their previous visits, *Kauai* remained at special sea detail, with all three diesel generators running. They would remain moored just long enough to hand off the portable hard drive to Dr. Hernandez and load her three students and their baggage for the trip to San Juan. That her team was bugging out had come as a very unwelcome surprise, indicative that the situation on St. Ignatius was far more serious than anyone expected.

Ben was hard at work as usual, talking to Dr. Hernandez while her students stepped gingerly across the brow to the afterdeck, loaded with their baggage. *Thank God this is all officially within U.S. territory. Who knows what those kids have picked up and packed for the trip back?* Haley and Ben had agreed they would keep those bags under lock and key during the trip up to San Juan so that the crew would not get drawn into anything that would delay their next leg down to Guadeloupe or call attention to their mission.

Regarding the mission, Haley was thoroughly conflicted at this point. *Kauai* was invaluable here, where her shallow draft could facilitate quick loading and evacuation of the residents. Ben had told her after the Pan-Commonwealth airliner went down a year ago in March, they had been able to squeeze all one hundred twenty-six survivors into *Kauai*'s hull for the six-hour trip from the crash site to Nassau. They couldn't hold that many of the islanders with their belongings, of course, but they could certainly hold more than any of the island ferries Haley had seen.

She hated the idea of sailing away from the scene of the action, even if it were only for a few days and the chances of the volcano popping in that time were vanishingly small. In fact, the only thing she hated worse was the alternative of disregarding her orders. There was no question that decision would result in her relief of command, court-martial, and dismissal from the Service—a terrible fate, to be sure, but not even remotely as bad as the one Pete faced if he were burned and left on Île Oiseaux. The orders had spared her that choice, and she was relieved. Had they gone the other way, she did not know if she could obey them. This was the real problem.

Haley was in love with Peter Simmons, and the reality of it weighed heavily on her.

The last few days they had together had clinched it. Everything argued against it: the brevity of their relationship, her fury at him over the surprise of his assignment, that she was far better off professionally with no personal attachments, and the intrinsic worry incumbent on loving someone who works outside all the normal rules of civilization. Yet, she could not go back to the way it was before she had met him. The memory of how she had felt when she thought they were breaking up, the soul-crushing, near grief that they had come to the end, was burned into her mind.

The dinner with Ben and Victoria provided the opportunity to meet on neutral ground and fix the issue between them. Haley realized it was not simply a matter of the potential for embarrassment in front of her boss. It was that this life of his spent in the darkness was not compatible with their happiness as a couple. If they were to be together, she *needed* to know what he was doing and facing. She was prepared to accept that it could never be and resume the friends-with-benefits association. But during their second sojourn, he made the startling confession that he was thinking about leaving the agency.

Pete had shared the story of how he came to be in the DIA and the single-minded focus he had had on annihilating the 252 Syndicate. That aim had been achieved as a result of a forgotten laptop computer Ben had retrieved from a sinking smuggling vessel. U.S. law enforcement and Europol had penetrated the organization's databases and systematically unwound the network of illicit real estate, front companies, and corrupt politicians and police. The 252 Syndicate had been reduced to a shadow of its former self, its power and wealth destroyed. Its few survivors who had escaped incarceration were scattered among the lower-tier crime organizations endemic in the former Soviet republics.

The rapid collapse of the 252s had come as a surprise to everyone, especially Pete, who had not expected it to occur within his lifetime. He was confronted with the fact that his *raison d'être* within the DIA was gone, and he was left with increasingly grubby tasks like the one he was engaged in today. These could not be sustained without commitment, and after Barbello and the Haitian operation, Pete had lost the faith.

The depth of the animus between Pete and Jennifer Irving that led to his reassignment to the DNI staff was mind-boggling, almost like something you would find in a tawdry spy thriller story. Haley had dealt with difficult, sometimes outright bullying superiors in her career, but simply couldn't conceive that anyone as evil as Irving seemed to be could rise to the top of her profession. When she said as much to Pete, his reply was a shrug and words to the effect of "perhaps not in the Coast Guard, but in the intelligence community, it happens sometimes."

Kevin Welles, the current DNI, was aware of the situation and did his best to protect Pete, for whom he had tremendous personal and professional regard. But they both knew that Irving coveted the DNI position and, given the politics of the times, stood a good chance at getting it once Welles retired. They also knew that her ascension would be a disaster for the IC and Pete personally, but there was little either could do about it. Facing this on top of the loss of his primary motivation for staying in the game, Pete was looking for an off-ramp.

If anything, this argued even more against Haley committing to a relationship. She feared becoming an emotional crutch for a man who was leaving a career behind without a firm prospect of a future. Still, Pete was brilliant, a survivor who had pivoted successfully from an almost comically civilian lifestyle to one of the utmost deprivation and danger. If anyone could pull off another life change, it was him, and if she could help make that happen, she was all in.

The onload was complete, and as Haley watched, Dr. Hernandez gave Ben a warm hug and then waved up at her. Haley returned the wave and the thumbs-up she got from Ben before he stepped aboard. This was another tricky path ahead. She knew Pete and Ben were friends and that Victoria was practically a little sister to him. The last thing Haley needed was for her second in command to get caught up in any of her private emotional issues. She had faith Pete would live up to their agreement on discretion, and only hoped she could as well. After taking a deep breath, she turned and walked through the open bridge door. As she climbed into her command chair, she called to Hopkins across the bridge, "OK, Chief. Let's get going."

"Aye, aye, Captain."

Aérodrome de Pointe-à-Pitre Le Raizet, Les Abymes, Grande-Terre, Guadeloupe, France 18:37 AST, 28 June

Peter

It had been almost thirty hours since he left Dublin on the Aer Lingus flight to Paris on the first leg of his journey. After an eighteen-hour layover, spent entirely in the high-end lounge catering to first-class passengers, he had boarded an Air France Boeing 777 for the eight-and-a-half-hour flight to Pointe-à-Pitre, the main international airport in Guadeloupe. He had had some excellent wine in the lounge and dozed fitfully in one of the more comfortable recliners. There had been plenty of time to go off-airport and get a good night's sleep at one of the local hotels. But long experience had taught him that every encounter with security was risky to downright dangerous when traveling under an alias, even within a nominally friendly country like France, and was to be avoided if practicable.

The flight from Paris had been uneventful and the service in first class was as good as ever. Peter had had just a couple of glasses of wine and no liquor. He would have preferred not drinking alcohol at all, but a certain amount of consumption was needed to maintain his alias as an important Irish businessman. He nursed these through the flight as he pretended to read the government economic and commerce reports his friends in the Garda had provided. They were absolutely genuine, if dated, in case any customs official or one of Laurent's security thugs checked on them. These were now carefully stored in the folio under his arm while he awaited his suitcases at the Air France baggage claim.

"*Monsieur* Shea?" a low-toned voice said from behind him after he had pulled both his bags off the carousel.

Peter turned to find two men, one tall and muscular, the other his size and build, both clean-shaven with short, military-style haircuts and wearing dark suits with open-collar shirts. "*Oui*?" Peter replied.

"*Monsieur*, we are here to take you to the island," the shorter man said in English with a heavy French accent. "Are these all your bags?"

"Yes, that's the lot," Peter said, switching to Wexford/Irish-accented English.

"*Bon*, Anton will take them. Follow me, please."

"Right-o," Peter said, following behind the smaller man. Not surprisingly, they did not walk toward the terminal exit, but toward an unlabeled door away from the carousels. On reaching the door, the man knocked twice, and it was opened from inside a few seconds later by a third, similarly dressed and groomed man. *All former legionnaires, no doubt.*

"Do you know why we are here, *monsieur*?" the first man asked.

"I assume you are not customs officials, so this must be a search for bugs," Peter said.

"Correct. We will need you to disrobe so that we can inspect your clothing." He pointed to a white terrycloth robe hanging from a hook on the wall. "You may use that robe while you wait."

"It's fine, boyo. They tol' me to expect such," Peter/ Shea said and started taking off his tie. He was able to maintain an affect of nonchalance simply because he was sure there was nothing for the security men to find. He was going in cold—no special gear of any kind. In terms of technology, all he had was an iPhone and a pricy tablet, each tricked up with the usual apps, email, file history, and sets of files whose properties all showed D. Shea as the author.

The first man turned toward him with a tray holding his phone, tablet, and wallet and said, "No watch?"

"I left it in the safe back in Dublin. It's a Rolex and I don't need it growin' legs, if you get my meanin'."

"*Bon*," the man said, then turned and walked through the door.

Peter sat in a metal chair under the clothes hook and glanced at the tall security man who had remained behind. "You speak English, fella?" After a few seconds of no reaction, he tried again. "*Parlez-vous anglais?*" After a few more seconds of a blank stare from the other man, Peter said, "Grand," then pretended to concentrate on the door.

After ten or fifteen minutes, the two men returned with his clothing. "Where's my suitcases?" Peter said, taking his clothing from the first man.

"We have taken them to the van. Know that we have extracted your toilet case. We will provide any toiletries you require."

"Grand." Peter knew they would remove anything that might conceal a recording or communications device, but included it to reduce the suspicion that he might be something besides a rich, horny pedophile. He donned his clothes, neither too fast nor slow for the same reason, all under the unblinking gaze of the three men.

When he had finished tightening his tie, the first man said, "Follow me please." Peter complied, walking a stride behind him, with the tall second man trailing him by the same distance.

During the walk through the terminal, he noted a couple of uniformed police and airport security officials glance in their direction, then quickly look away when they seemed to recognize the men. *OK, the cops are bought. That's good to know in the event this thing blows up.* The observation was consistent with the intelligence they had on the operation here and *Le Milieu*'s normal procedure. The payoff was probably small, particularly by American or European standards, just enough to guarantee that no one saw anything.

They stepped out of the main terminal and climbed into a white van. It was half an hour after sunset by this time and the streetlights around the airport were just coming on as they turned into the general aviation terminal and drove through the security post and onto the ramp toward a waiting helicopter. Peter could see it was one of the newer Airbus H160s.

They pulled up next to the helicopter and Peter and his two companions stepped out of the minivan into the warm and humid night and climbed into the rear as one of the crewmen loaded his bags into a compartment behind the cabin. He swallowed hard, then worked into the seat on the right side of the cabin and fastened his seat belt. He did not like helicopters—there were far too many spinning components, the failure of any of which would cause a fatal crash.

The pilot climbed aboard and started the helicopter's two engines and, after a short runup and taxi, pulled to a stop at the edge of the ramp. There was another brief pause, and then the aircraft suddenly shuddered and sprang into the air. Peter closed his eyes tightly and willed his dancing stomach to settle down. *Relax. If you puke your guts out, it will only reinforce the assumption of these thugs that you're some rich paedo-pussy.*

After a brief climb, Peter felt safe enough to open his eyes and look out. They were skirting the eastern shoreline of Basse-Terre, the lights showing the small villages and larger Capesterre-Belle-Eau, with La Grande Soufrière silhouetted in the red and purple to the west. It was a short flight, only fifteen minutes, and he could see a few lights on the ground as they overflew the Îles des Saintes. The hotel and helipad on Île Oiseaux were well-lit and as they wallowed down on the final approach, Peter again squeezed his eyes shut until they were safely on the ground.

While the engines and main rotor ran down to a stop, Peter unbuckled his seatbelt and climbed out. Like Pointe-à-Pitre, Île Oiseaux was warm and humid, but a light breeze from the east brought a cool freshness to the scene. He watched as a young man in a bellman's uniform made his way toward the baggage compartment of the helicopter, then turned back to look at the hotel. The helipad was atop a small hill about a thousand feet from the main building, with a lighted flagstone path leading down to what appeared to be the main entrance. Peter could barely make out the outline of the island against the sea in the deepening darkness.

The first man broke into his quick survey. "If you will follow me, *monsieur*, we will get you settled into your suite."

"Grand. Crack on, friend!" Peter/Shea smiled back. He would have preferred landing in daylight when he could have gotten a close-up aerial view of the hotel and grounds. Peter had excellent knowledge of the general layout of the buildings and a sense of the pattern of life, thanks to a couple of Global Hawk sorties from a few days ago. He would need much more before they could attempt an exfil of the defector.

Fortunately, Declan Shea's biography included an almost rabid interest in tropical birds, found in abundance on Île Oiseaux, hence the name. Peter intended to borrow an electronic camera from the concierge the next morning for a nature walk of the island. The rules were that guests could photograph whatever they liked with a staff-provided camera, but the house had the absolute right to review and withhold any photos for any reason. Peter was certain there would be many feathered friends presenting themselves for pictures with interesting island features discreetly in the background.

They walked down the flagstone path at a brisk pace. Even in the muted light provided by the hanging yellow lanterns, Peter could see that the landscaping was magnificent, with carefully trimmed trees and bushes and the lingering scent of gardenia, despite the breeze. He was looking forward to seeing it in the daylight, one of the guilty pleasures he could actually indulge in on this assignment.

The heavy wooden doors of the hotel swung inward as they approached and the first man said, "Enjoy your stay, *monsieur*."

"Thanks, friend," Peter/Shea said and stepped inside. The lobby was impressive—a masterpiece of interior design, both welcoming and awe-inspiring, with soft, warm lighting bathing the marble floors and tasteful furnishings in a gentle glow. A single, impeccably dressed man stood behind a gleaming wooden reception desk and flashed a brilliant white smile when Peter walked over.

"*Bonsoir, Monsieur* Shea. Your room is ready, of course. Here is your key," the man said, handing Peter a card key. "Phillipe here will carry your bags and show you to your room. If you need anything, simply call me and I will see to it."

"Grand. Any chance of a meal and drink?"

"*Bien entendu*! There is a fully stocked bar and room service menu in your room, *monsieur*."

"*Quare*!" Peter/Shea turned to the bellman. "Lead on, Phillipe!"

The hotel was a single story, and the walk to his room was a short one. Like the lobby, the hallways were tastefully decorated and warmly lit. His room was spacious, with a high ceiling and separate sitting and sleeping areas. He crossed over to an armoire in the sitting room and opened it to find a fully stocked wine and liquor bar. *Sheesh, that guy wasn't kidding*, Peter thought, picking up and examining a bottle of Jameson Special Reserve. "Come to da, *mo gra*!"

"*Pardon, monsieur*?" Phillipe said.

"Oh, ah, just put those on the bed, mate," Peter said, nodding to the bedroom.

"*Oui, monsieur.*"

Peter pulled a twenty euro note from his billfold and handed it to Phillipe as he passed, heading toward the door.

"*Merci beau coups, monsieur*!"

"*De rien.*"

After the bellman had left, Peter picked up the bottle of Jameson again. *What the hell? The taxpayers have already shelled out twenty-five grand for this room, might as well get something for it.* He opened the bottle, poured two fingers into a glass, and took an easy swallow, savoring the smooth malt flavor with hints of vanilla and citrus. *I could definitely get used to this. Pity it will be the last time.*

He took another swallow, then picked up the menu to browse for a meal. He was suddenly exhausted, the thirty-six hours without good sleep catching up to him. His orderly mind was still able to spit out an efficient plan: order the meal, take a quick shower, chow down, and hit the sack. He was looking forward to a good night's sleep, lightly lubricated with some Jameson-induced Irish dreams. He would need it for what was to come.

Office of the Administrator, 63 Haabets Gade, Jamestown, St. Ignatius, U.S. Virgin Islands
07:51 AST, 29 June

Marcus

They were gathered again in the same conference room, where the atmosphere, if anything, was even more somber. Marcus was feeling the effects of the grueling duty schedule on top of having to attend these meetings. The nominal six hours on/twelve hours off was deceptive, as there were always things like servicing the aircraft and attending planning meetings that needed his attention during the twelve-hour periods he was not piloting. The underlying tension of the situation, punctuated by the ever more frequent and violent Earth tremors, amplified the stress.

Marcus glanced across the table at Dr. Hernandez and noted that, as rundown and anxious as he felt, she looked worse. He knew she had been working on the data delivered by *Kauai* for most of the night, and she was clearly exhausted. She had readily accepted when Marcus offered to drive her over from the airport to the meeting, and largely rode in silence, staring out the window the entire trip. It wasn't just fatigue—she had the look of someone who had to tell a parent their child had just died.

The other occupant of the room, Sergeant Platt, looked as unconcerned as he had at the earlier meeting. Marcus envied the man's coolness in the situation and wondered if it was a cop thing or if it came naturally to him. When Marcus glanced at him, Platt nodded, as if to say, "Don't worry, son. It will be OK." Inspired by the quiet confidence, Marcus smiled back in return.

Even the entry of Isabelle and Thomas was more subdued than the last meeting. Thomas's arrogant look was gone, his face drawn, eyes staring straight ahead as he walked slowly to the head of the table and sat. Isabelle was beautiful, of course, dressed up in her "official" clothes with her hair drawn back as usual when she was on the job. As she walked around to her place at the table, she had a haunted look, grim-faced with eyes red-rimmed from crying. She gave Marcus a brief look with a slight, sad smile that made his heart ache. She was carrying a terrible load and there was nothing he could say or do that could help. He hated it.

Isabelle dialed the speakerphone in the center of the table and after the usual phone conference kabuki, the governor's voice came on the phone. "Hello, everyone. I wish I could say I am glad to hear from you. Who do we have down there, Robert?"

Robert, not Bob, Marcus thought. *The game-playing is definitely behind us.*

"Same as before, sir. Isabelle Jones, Dr. Hernandez, Mr. Porter, and Sergeant Platt."

"Right. What can you tell me?"

"I'll start, sir," Thomas said. "Miss Jones, Sergeant Platt, and I have worked up a roster of everyone currently on the island and a prioritized list for evacuation. We have been on the phones most of the night and Sergeant Platt's officers have been going door to door for those we couldn't confirm by phone. We can begin the evacuation at any time."

"Are you getting any pushback?"

"No, sir. They're good people. They're also frightened enough by the earthquakes that they do not need any convincing."

"There's that, I suppose. Anything else?"

"No, sir. Just waiting on a schedule for the ferries."

"OK. I'll defer that one to Admiral Pennington in a minute. I think now we need to get a sense of what we're facing. Do you have something for us, doctor?"

Dr. Hernandez leaned forward. "Yes, governor. We have a pretty good model of the volcano's system from the seismic tomography data and it's not good news, I'm afraid. The shallow magma chamber that feeds the mountain is about forty-five cubic kilometers in size and it is full. I estimate about three cubic kilometers of melt and maybe another fifteen of mush, which is what we call rock that is not completely melted but is still eruptible. There is no question here that St. Ignatius as we know it is finished—nothing will be left alive on the island after the eruption, assuming the island is still here. The issue we have now is what measures need to be taken for the other islands. Based on what we have seen historically and the model we have of the chamber, I expect an eruption of somewhere between one and ten cubic kilometers of ejecta. Vic, is that what your USGS people are seeing?"

"Yes, we concur with that estimate," Norbert replied.

"Yes. Well, I have used a USGS computer tool for modeling ash dispersion to estimate the likely range of ashfall, and the predictions are disturbing. I think St. Croix is looking at somewhere between four and thirty inches of ashfall and the northern islands between two and twelve inches. You should definitely prepare for a major disaster throughout the territory, particularly on St. Croix. Do you agree, Vic?"

"Definitely. We are putting out a Volcano Alert Notice upgrading St. Ignatius to 'Warning' and bumping up to 'Orange' for aviation. Danny, you need to contact Governor Rincon, since Puerto Rico is looking at a serious ash deposit as well. What is your estimate, Lydia?"

"Heavy on the eastern side of the island, between one and twelve inches. Could be as much as five inches as far west as Aguadilla."

"My God!," Danny Witchell, the Homeland Security official, exclaimed. "Yes, I'll get on to him as soon as we break."

After a brief pause, the governor's voice came on again, "Do we know when it will begin, doctor?"

"No vents have opened as of yet, sir, but it can happen at any time. I'm sorry I can't be more specific. However, once a major vent opens, I expect things will proceed quickly. By that point, evacuation would be impracticable."

There was an audible sigh from the phone, then the governor continued. "Admiral, I hope you have some good news for us."

"I think so," Pennington said. "General Miller has stepped up and we are setting up the Emergency Operations Center at SOUTHCOM. On my order, Sector San Juan personnel have seized the two ferries we were discussing in St. Croix and expect to have them operational within a few hours. The owners can take us to court later if they want. The Dutch are sending one of their fifty-passenger inter-island ferries from St. Martin and it will arrive in Jamestown in a couple of hours. We should be in good shape to get everyone off to St. Croix by the end of the day tomorrow."

"Admiral, that won't do. You need to take them to St. Thomas," Norbert interrupted.

"That's three times further! We'd be looking at two days to complete the evacuation instead of one. Are you serious?"

"Admiral, St. Croix could be smothered by several feet of ash, not to mention being hit by tsunamis. The residents there will be fighting for their lives as it is. You can't expect them to cope with another seven hundred refugees."

There was another long pause, and then Pennington came back on with a resigned tone. "Very well. We'll plan on taking them up to Charlotte Amalie. God help us! Anyway, we are dispatching two fast response cutters from San Juan to picket positions along the evacuation route. If any ferry runs into any trouble, they'll be on hand to assist. We are evacuating anything else that can move to Guantanamo Bay. That will be the rallying point for the relief effort—everything coming in for help and relief will stage out of there. Danny, you need to work your magic up in D.C. Get the president to declare and light a fire under the DoD to get some logistical support down there. Nothing is too much or too soon."

"Roger that," Witchell said. "That will be my second call, assuming Governor Rincon doesn't reach through the phone and strangle me!"

"Good, good. That's all I have except to pass on a well done to you and your team, Mr. Porter. You've done us proud and I'll pass that on to Dawn Sanders and Keith Rooney."

Marcus nearly fell out of his chair. *He's going to call Captain Rooney, the CO of Air Station Jacksonville, and Admiral Sanders, the Superintendent of the Academy? Holy shit!* "Um, thank you, Admiral!"

"Not at all. You guys keep up the good work and stay safe."

"Thank you, sir!" Marcus said. *It's true what they say about him. All this going on and he still takes the time to reach out for us.* He glanced at Isabelle and got a warm smile in return.

"I'll second that," the governor said. "Now, Vic, what's the status of your advance team?"

"They're on the ground at Luis Muñoz Marín as we speak and should take off for St. Ignatius in an hour or so. Lydia, that offer to take you off still stands. Care to reconsider?"

For the first time this morning, Marcus saw Dr. Hernandez smile. "Thanks, Vic, but no thanks. I'm in on this one till the end."

"OK. But please, for me, be careful, will you?"

"Always."

"I guess that's about all we can do for now," the governor said. "Robert and Isabelle, I know this is hell on earth for you. You've done a magnificent job. If you need anything, any time, you call me. The orders are still on that any call from you gets put through immediately, even if I'm on the phone with the president."

"Thank you, sir," Thomas said. "As the admiral said, God help us all."

"I could not have said it better. Good luck and I'll see you when you get up here. Goodbye, everyone."

The phone beeped, and when the dial tone came on, Isabelle reached over and pressed the hang-up button. They all sat in silence for about five seconds, then Thomas said in a flat tone, "Anyone have any questions or anything to say?" After another few seconds, he continued. "Alright, you know what needs to be done. Good luck to you." He stood and walked out the door without looking at any of them.

Dr. Hernandez looked at Marcus and said, "I need to get back on the instruments as soon as I can, Marcus."

"Right. Let's roll, ma'am. I'll meet you at the ride."

She stood, followed by Platt, and the two walked out the door. Marcus got up, walked around the table, and stood before Isabelle. "I can't even imagine what you are going through. I'm ashamed I can't think of anything to say or do that would help. Is there anything I can do?" he asked pleadingly.

She put her arms around his neck, briefly leaned her forehead against his, and then kissed him firmly on the lips. She pulled back and said, "This. Keep doing your job. Stay safe for me." She then brushed away a tear and lightly squeezed his shoulder as she passed him on the way out the door.

Part III

Chapter 14

Sortie

USCG Cutter Kauai, Moored, U.S. Coast Guard Sector, San Juan, Puerto Rico
15:03 AST, 29 June

Ben

Ben was on the wharf, watching as the last of their replacement stores were brought aboard. They had refueled early that morning, shortly before offloading the OBS containers. Of their passengers, the students departed just after midnight and were probably safe at home by now. Ryan was still in the area, of course, remaining with the instruments until they were transferred to FedEx for shipment back to Woods Hole.

They would depart at 18:00 this evening for the fifteen-hour journey down to Basse-Terre, the capital city of Guadeloupe. The trip was timed to put *Kauai* into the city's Port De Basse-Terre promptly at 09:30 the following day. Its wharf was relatively small by commercial port standards, barely long enough to accommodate a single cruise ship, and most traffic used the large cruise terminal at Pointe-à-Pitre. However, the location was ideal for the mission, a little under a mile from the Palais d'Orléans, the Préfecture building where the reception they were attending would be held.

Like Haley, Ben had mixed feelings about the mission. He knew there was no choice of their going if Pete was to come out of this alive, but wasn't happy about being out of contact with their UAV team on St. Ignatius while they were at risk from a volcano. He couldn't see why the Île Oiseaux operation wasn't aborted, given the reality of the situation in St. Ignatius he and Haley had reported up the chain days ago. It was another case of the higher-ups in the I.C. shoving his crew and other good people into a damned-if-you-do-damned-if-you-don't situation with limited justification, and Ben, for one, was tiring of it.

Haley was over at the Sector Headquarters to complete the normal port visit administrivia and try to get some official information on what was happening back on the island. Drake had already pulsed the local chief's network, and the news was frightening. Word going around was that St. Ignatius was about to blow and that San Juan and most of the rest of Puerto Rico were going to be clobbered by tsunamis and ashfall.

The frantic activity around the Sector stoked this apprehension—six fast response cutters were based here and of the four that were normally in port at any time, two had departed that morning and the other two were hurriedly reassembling components broken down for maintenance so that they too could bug out. All the patrol boats of San Juan and the aircraft stationed across the island at Air Station Borinquen were headed west to the U.S. Naval Station at Guantanamo Bay on Cuba's southeast coast. It was a case of discretion being the better part of valor—they could not operate in the ash, which, besides being a health hazard, wreaked havoc on engines and electrical components. They would return to assist once the air was clear.

The prospect of the loss of San Juan as a logistical base presented a tremendous headache for Ben. There was no fuel available in Basse-Terre, as commercial traffic was required to use Pointe-à-Pitre, and hauling the thousands of gallons required to top off via truck would be expensive and risk exposing their covert mission. This had not been a problem when the mission was planned, as the round trip from San Juan to Basse-Terre and back was well within *Kauai*'s range. But by the time they cleared Île Oiseaux, they would be far short of the fuel needed to make it to Guantanamo Bay. They could make it back to Mayagüez, but it would be very tight. *They should have called off this dumbass mission!* Ben thought for the umpteenth time today.

Ben's ruminations were cut short by the sight of a soldier in Army Combat Uniform carrying a rucksack and walking straight for his location. As the man neared, he could see it was the DIA man Lamonde, wearing the insignia of a captain and wearing a fictitious nametag that read "Tucker."

Lamonde stopped a few feet from Ben and dropped the sack. "Good afternoon, Lieutenant."

"Good afternoon, Captain...Tucker," Ben replied. "We have your quarters available if you care to follow me."

"Excellent," Lamonde said, shouldering the rucksack.

After leading the agent inside and down to the vacated berthing area, Ben turned and said, "These will be your quarters for the mission. The head is at the end of the passageway on the left. I have to insist that you interact with the crew as little as possible. If there is anything you require, contact me on that phone," he said, pointing to the wall phone in the corner.

"Mighty neighborly of you," the agent replied with a cold smile. "Can I ask what the timetable for this trip will be?"

"We will get underway at eighteen hundred and should arrive at Basse-Terre at oh-nine-thirty tomorrow. Plan on an initial planning meeting around twenty hundred tonight. The details of the rendezvous with Agent Simmons haven't been finalized as far as I know, but one way or another, we'll be returning here no later than noon on the third."

Lamonde's smile faded. "We'll do our best, but you should remember who is working for whom here. The mission will take us where it takes us."

Ben turned to look him in the eye. "*You* should remember that this boat runs on diesel fuel and that commodity will be exhausted by noon on the third, regardless of the state of the mission. And while we are on the subject of who works for whom, I would like to clarify something for you. *We* work for the Seventh Coast Guard District, not *you*. Our assigned mission here is to support you, if practicable. We will do our best to provide that support, but the safety of the crew and the boat remain the captain's and my priority. Keep that in mind."

Lamonde flashed that cold smile again. "Thanks for the clarification, Lieutenant. I will keep that in mind."

"Fine. Is it your intention to continue your masquerade as Army Captain Tucker?

"Why not? You got a problem with me wearing the uniform or something? An alias like this is ideal. A civilian screams IC, whereas a soldier leaves some doubt. If I don't use the right term or say something unusual, they'll just think I'm a dumb grunt."

"No problem here. I just need to know what I should tell the crew. And while we're at it, what first name goes with this alias?"

"Greg. I use my own first name in low-risk situations like this. One less thing to keep track of."

"Fine. Unless you have any questions, I'll need to leave you to attend to my other responsibilities."

"No, Lieutenant. I am good to go. Thank you for your support," Lamonde finished with a smirk.

Ben turned without another word and returned to the wharf where Hebert and Drake needed his signature on some receipts for foodstuffs and engineering supplies.

God, that guy gives me the creeps. Can't let him bait me like that. After Hebert handed him a clipboard, he had to do a double take on reading the invoice it was holding. "Twenty cases of bottled water? Not that I'm unhappy, Chef, but where the Hell did you score that with everyone stocking up for the bug-out?"

Hebert didn't reply, just glanced at Drake, who smiled and said, "XO, I know a guy."

"I might have known. Disregard the question." He was happy for some good news—unlike larger ships, *Kauai* could not replenish its potable water by distilling seawater. If they were called upon to carry evacuees, their limited supply would run out quickly. After signing, he looked up to see Haley approaching from the direction of the headquarters building. When she reached them, all three men saluted. "Good news, Captain?" Ben asked.

"About the same, I'm afraid," Haley replied, returning the salute. "How are things going here?"

"Just finished the on-loading, ma'am," Ben said. "Our passenger is onboard and tucked away in his quarters."

"Good, good," Haley said. "XO, let's you and I have a chat in the cabin. Chef and COB, I'll see you later."

"Ma'am," the two men said as Ben turned to follow Haley aboard.

After following Haley into her cabin, Ben said, "Door closed?"

"Oh, yes." After he had complied and sat in the spare chair, Haley continued. "Pete is on Île Oiseaux. One of our guys on the ground in Guadeloupe saw him being picked up by Laurent's men. Nothing else so far."

Ben was rubbing his temples with both hands. "I was hoping you were going to say the damn thing had been called off. I'd have loved going down and showing Lamonde, alias Captain Greg Tucker, the door."

"Unpleasant?"

"Creepy as hell. I don't know if it's the knowledge that he's a contract killer with a CAC card or just something about his personality. All I know is that I'd rather not be in the room with him without a loaded gun in my hand." He looked up, and seeing her look of concern, said, "Hey, it will be OK. I had to explain to him the difference between being supported and being in command."

"Think it took?"

"I doubt it, but it hardly matters. He can order and holler or howl at the moon. It will have the same result in the end. On another subject, what's the word on the volcano?"

"No eruption yet, but they're evacuating the island. That was in the works before we left yesterday. The big news is that our data has Dr. Hernandez and the USGS guys rattled and they are pretty sure the effects are going to reach here."

"So I gathered from the bugout. Skipper, if we lose San Juan, things will get dicey pretty quick. I mean, if this place gets closed down, assume the Virgin Islands are off the table too. COB's and my back-of-the-envelope calculations say that if we're frugal down south, we can make

Mayagüez with about fifteen percent fuel left. I'd feel a lot easier if we could top off while we're down there. Surely, with what's going on, the French wouldn't get tipped off to the op by us doing what any prudent mariner would do."

"I pointed all that out to Captain Mercier, Ben, believe me. The answer was a flat-out no. My sense is her hands are tied just like ours."

"And what happens if we lose access to any ports in range and run out of gas?"

"Call for help," Haley answered, shaking her head. "We have the equipment and procedures for refueling from the medium endurance cutters."

"Dumb," Ben replied. "Do they think the other ships won't have anything else going on with all hell breaking loose? Dumb, Dumb, DUMB!"

Haley grinned at him. "Feel better now you've got that off your chest?"

He smiled back. "Strangely, no, but I'm ready to move on. Back to down south. We seem remarkably planless for an operation this far along. Do we even have a landing site selected?"

"I'm told it's down to three. Pete will do recons on the ground today and tomorrow and will provide recommendations hidden in 'business' emails from Declan Shea to his firm in Ireland. We'll need to go over them with your favorite DIA guy this evening, then tomorrow we can kluge all the intel together into a coherent plan."

"Oh goodie," Ben said with a grimace. "We should be through the Virgin Passage by about twenty hundred. You OK to meet on the messdeck then with Lamonde...sorry, I mean Tucker, and Chief Hopkins?"

"Yes. We need to get any open discussions done before we pull into port tomorrow. Also, excuse me for saying this, but have you done the security briefing with the crew yet? I don't want anyone letting it slip we have a special passenger while they're on liberty in Basse-Terre."

Ben nodded. "They know better, but a reminder wouldn't hurt that we keep stuff inside the family. I'll pass the word at quarters before going to special sea detail."

"That will work."

"Anything else, Captain? I would like to try to get a call through to Victoria if I can. No telling what things may be like over the next couple of days."

"Good call. Tell her I said 'Hi'. I'm going to drop a line to my dad myself."

"Good plan," Ben said, then stood and turned for the door. "Best one I've seen so far today."

* * * * * *

Ben was staring at the picture of Victoria in her green dress when a knock sounded on his door. "Come in!"

Bryant cracked open the door and stuck his head in. "Got a minute, XO?"

"Sure, Doc. Five of them, actually, before I have to head to a meeting. Come in and have a seat." After the young petty officer sat in Ben's spare chair, Ben said, "What's on your mind?"

"Just wanted to give you a heads-up, sir. I distributed the initial issue of the respirators and eye protection for the crew and went over how to use them. Also, I finally replaced the oxygen we used up on the boat fire and I scored an extra couple of loaner tanks, just in case."

Ben nodded and smiled. "Good job! Did COB wrangle that for you?"

"No, sir. Most people don't know what we know yet."

"Ah, brilliant."

"Yes, sir. Do you want me to issue gear to the spook?"

The question was jarring, and Ben did his best to control his reaction. "What makes you think he's a spook?" he temporized.

"He sure as hell ain't an Army captain, sir," Bryant said with his usual impassive expression. "What else would he be?"

Bryant was an excellent medic with an eye for details that rivaled Victoria's. Fortunately, he also had a disdain for small talk. Ben didn't know what minutiae gave Lamonde away to Bryant, but it was unlikely that anyone else aboard was on to him yet. Ben leaned forward and whispered, "OK, Doc. He's with Dr. Simmons's outfit. That's a lot more than you should know, so you need to keep it quiet. Clear?"

"No problem, sir. As I was saying, should I issue a set of gear to Captain Tucker?"

Ben sat back and smiled. "Sure. I hope he'll be gone before he puts it to any use but go ahead and give him the training as well."

"Understood, sir."

"Was there anything else?"

"No, sir. That's it."

"Good," Ben said as he and Bryant both stood. "Thanks for the update, Doc."

"No problem, sir," Bryant said, then turned and walked out the door.

Ben gritted his teeth and took a breath, then headed out the door to pick up Lamonde. On reaching the closed berthing area door, Ben knocked and then stepped inside and closed the door at Lamonde's "Come in."

Ben cringed at the cold smile the agent flashed and then said, "That ACU jacket, take it off."

"What?"

"You heard me. Our health services tech is on to you. He was an Army combat medic and has a pretty good eye. When he steps in later to issue you your volcano gear, you can ask him how you screwed up. In the meantime, we'll assume it has something to do with how you rigged the jacket. Now, follow me, please."

"Right," Lamonde unzipped and peeled off the jacket, tossing it on a bunk and picking up a tablet PC on his way out of the door.

A short walk put them on the mess deck. Hopkins was already there and stood when Ben and Lamonde came in. Hopkins had a haunted look, quite unlike her normal good humor, and Ben knew exactly what it was about. She and Deffler were in a very close relationship, on the verge of getting engaged, and she was worried about his being left behind on St. Ignatius. Ben felt the same, and when his and Hopkins's eyes met, they nodded, passing the message "I understand" between them without words. "Captain Tucker, this is Chief Operations Specialist Emilia Hopkins. I asked her here as she is our navigation expert and can provide insight into the alternative approaches to the island."

"It's a pleasure to meet you, Chief," Lamonde said and extended his hand.

"Same here, sir," Hopkins said as she shook his hand.

Ben turned as Haley came into the room, waving her hand to forestall any calls to attention. "Captain Greg Tucker, this is the Captain, Haley Reardon."

"Pleased to meet you, ma'am," Lamonde said, shaking her hand.

"Likewise," Haley said, wearing a tight smile. "You getting everything you need?"

"Yes, indeed. All set."

"Good. We're understandably quite interested in what you have to tell us. I've asked Chief to bring down a nautical chart for reference," Haley said, nodding at the chart spread across one of the tables.

"Excellent. As you know, Agent Simmons flew to the island last night. He has used this first day ostensibly for a nature walk to satisfy his bird-watching fetish. Actually, he has been doing a detailed reconnaissance on the three potential egress routes and gathering some equipment we have covertly inserted onto the island."

"How did you manage that?" Ben interrupted. "I thought their security is super tight."

"It is. We used a special multi-rotor UAV, similar to what Amazon and other companies are using for drone deliveries, with a few mods that make it virtually silent and invisible to anything but the most powerful fire control radars. The UAV was launched and recovered by one of our boats as it sailed through the Dominica Passage a few nights ago. Simmons confirmed he has found the container and secured the contents via a code he inserted into one of his normal emails."

"What was in the package?" Haley asked.

"The usual kit," Lamonde replied. "A suppressed pistol, ammo, combat knife, knock-out syrettes, electronics, *et cetera*."

"I see," Haley said. "So, what now?"

"He'll conduct another walkabout tomorrow to confirm his alias and make sure they have made no changes to the guard postings or anything else. The exfil operation is a go for the night of the first. He will duck out in the middle of his sexual tryst to link up with the defector and bring him to the rendezvous point."

With the mention of the phrase "sexual tryst", Ben reflexively glanced at Haley's face. Other than a slight twitch in the corners of her mouth, she showed no reaction. He turned back to Lamonde and asked, "Where is the rendezvous point?"

"That depends. Our boat was also equipped with electronic warfare support equipment to chart the island's maritime radar emissions. We think we have identified three lanes of signal attenuation that provide the best options for a stealthy approach. They lead to two areas that have a suitable landing site. Let me pull up the map on my tablet and we can reconcile them with your nautical chart."

They all gathered around the chart as Lamonde made some selections and then placed the tablet on the table. Hopkins gazed intently at the tablet and then traced what Ben assumed were the routes across the chart on the table. After a couple of minutes, she stood and said, "This one furthest west is no good. We'd have to turn twice to clear this shoal here, which might present enough radar cross-section for them to pick us up." She pointed at a marked shallow area on the chart. "The other two are both doable, but I think the center one is the best in terms of approach and departure angles, given the currents through the passage."

Haley looked up from the chart and said, "What do you think, XO?"

Ben nodded and replied, "Looks good to me, Captain." He turned to Lamonde. "OK, we make the approach. Then what?"

"We launch your boat to take me ashore. I cross to the rendezvous point to link up with Simmons and the defector and then we come back by the same route."

"I think we should launch a mile or so offshore like we did in Haiti, Captain," Ben said. "No sense coming in on batteries and blowing it with the sound of the crane."

"Agreed," Haley said with a nod. She looked at Lamonde. "We are nearly silent on batteries, and the RHIB's engine is muffled and quiet at low speed, but the hydraulics operating the crane could make enough noise to be an issue. We can launch far enough offshore not to be heard and tether the boat until we get to a good launch point."

"Whatever you think, Captain," Lamonde nodded. "Not sure if it will be a problem, but I'm always interested in cutting back on the risk."

"We'll plan on that then," Haley said. "Chief, can you set up that approach in the FC3, please? Also, put the eastern track in as an alternate, just in case."

"No problem, Captain," Hopkins said.

"Speaking of risk, what will the opposition have? Do they run boat patrols?" Haley asked.

"No. Laurent is an old hand at garrison work. He knows active patrolling uses up your manpower and tells the enemy where you are, and more importantly, where you aren't. They have a roving watch ashore and a rapid response boat capability for anything their radar picks up. If we can get in and out without being detected on radar, we shouldn't have a problem. Simmons and I can handle any rovers we run into ashore."

"Good to hear," Haley said. "We will be at General Quarters, just to be safe."

"That would be prudent."

"And what about the French? Do they have any active presence in the area?"

"The French Navy has a base at Fort-de-France in Martinique with two surveillance frigates and some lighter patrol and support vessels, but nothing up here. As far as we know, they just run counter-smuggling patrols down south. We haven't seen them doing any security operations around here. They won't be a factor. We believe Laurent pays the local police to look the other way in terms of his business. If anything, that would keep them away from the island. Bottom line, we don't see an outside threat to the mission."

"You better be right, Captain. Our asses will really be in a sling if one of those frigates catches us off the beach at Île Oiseaux.

"As I said, no worries, Captain. Now, what is your overall plan?" Lamonde asked.

"We will sail as planned at eighteen hundred, cruise east through the Dominica Passage and thirty miles beyond, then shut down the emitters and double back. That will be a good two to three hours after twilight. If that's too early, let us know and we'll adjust. When we get within two miles of the landing point, we'll launch the RHIB and go on batteries."

"How long can you run on batteries?" Lamonde asked.

"Eight to ten hours at the low speeds we'll be doing," Haley answered. "Ben, I want you in the RHIB. Who's your crew?"

"Lee on coxswain and Chen as the boat crewman, ma'am. Lee and I will carry M4s and pistols, Chen with a pistol and the shotgun."

"Good call," Haley said. "Anybody got anything else?" After receiving a unanimous response of shaking heads, she continued. "In that case, good night, everyone. XO, can I see you in the cabin, please?"

"Yes, ma'am," Ben said. "Goodnight, Chief, Captain."

"Good night, sir," Hopkins replied while Lamonde nodded.

It was a short walk back to Haley's cabin. After her door was shut and both were seated, Haley asked, "What do you think, Ben?"

"Everything seems to make sense, skipper. You worried about what Pete said?"

"A little. I was tempted to send someone ashore with Lamonde, but there's too much chance of screwing up the mission."

Ben looked her in the eye and said, "Agreed. Don't worry. I'll take care of it."

Haley raised her right eyebrow. "How do you intend to do that?"

Ben looked down and shook his head. "I don't know yet, but I'll think of something."

USCG Cutter Kauai, underway in the Caribbean Sea, 6.8 nautical miles west-northwest of Port De Basse-Terre,

Guadeloupe, France
08:13 AST, 30 June

Ben

They would go to Special Sea Detail for the entry into Port De Basse Terre in a little under an hour. Ben was standing the morning O.O.D. watch, having relieved Lee half an hour earlier. The bridge was uncrowded for the time being, with just Ben, Smith at the helm, and Bunting at the FC3 console. Ben raised his binoculars again to look at the looming green bulk of La Grande Soufrière, another volcano among many in the area, and, at nearly five thousand feet, the tallest mountain in the Lesser Antilles.

Ben had already changed from the normal working uniform to the more formal tropical blue before he relieved the watch, anticipating he would not have time to change later. He did another sweep of the horizon for three-hundred-sixty degrees, and then, satisfied that *Kauai* was safe from collision for another few minutes, stepped over to the FC3 console. "Fire up the camera, Bunting. We should be able to see the port by now."

"Aye, aye, sir," the young petty officer said, then pressed several buttons to activate the electro-optical camera on the mast. A few seconds later, the camera was up and running and one of the screens showed a video picture of the island ahead.

Ben said, "Thanks, I've got it," and used one of the console joysticks to trace the camera view along the shoreline of the island of Basse-Terre, dark green hills sloping steeply down to bright white beaches, the pale blue of shallow water leading to the deep blue of the Caribbean Sea. He could see hundreds of houses now, white with red roofs, typical of the Caribbean islands, growing denser as the city of Basse-Terre came into view.

He was about to step away from the console when a flash of gray passed through the screen as the camera panned across Port De Basse Terre. Ben pushed the joystick back to the left, slowly panning back to the wharf, and then froze in shock when the gray shape reappeared. There was no mistaking the shape and color of the vessel moored at the southern end of the wharf.

It was a warship.

Ben stared for a few seconds at the image, then said, "Bunting, take over. Get me an I.D. on that ship."

"Yes, sir!"

Ben stepped over to the ship's telephone and dialed Haley's number. She picked up after one ring.

"Captain."

"OOD, ma'am. Could you come to the bridge, please?"

"On the way," Haley said, hanging up without waiting for a reply. A few seconds later, she was bounding into the bridge, pre-empting Ben's call to attention with a wave of her hand. "What's up, XO?"

Ben noticed she had also changed into tropical blue in anticipation of the port arrival. "Look, ma'am," Ben said, nodding at the FC3 screen. "Bunting's checking the ID now."

Haley stared at the screen and then looked up at Ben. "Shit!"

"Captain, I have an ID," Bunting said.

"Go ahead."

"*Frimaire*, *Floréal* class surveillance frigate, ma'am. Homeport Fort-de-France, Martinique."

"Thank you," Haley said, then looked at Ben and nodded toward the starboard bridge door. Ben followed her out onto the bridge wing and they came to a stop beside the starboard machine gun. "So much for our so-called intelligence!" she whispered. "What the hell is she doing here?"

"Same as us, I suppose," Ben whispered back. "Showing the flag for the big ceremony tomorrow."

"Great. That's all we need! Send a message over secure chat, personal to Captain Mercier. 'French frigate in Port de Basse-Terre. Request advise.' Do it yourself and get it off right now."

"Yes, ma'am," Ben said, then turned and stepped back into the bridge. "Any contacts within five miles, Bunting?"

"Negative, sir."

"Very well." Ben sat in the right seat of the console and used the trackball to select "Secure Chat" on the screen before him, then clicked on the "New Message" icon. When the new window popped up, he selected "Immediate" under the precedence pull-down, typed, "CCGD7(DCS)" in the "To:" box, then in the message box below, typed, "French SURVEILLANCE Frigate Frimaire moored Port de Basse-Terre. Request advise." After checking it, he pressed the "send" button, and the window disappeared.

It would take several minutes for the message to be received, logged in, printed, and delivered to Captain Mercier. Ben stood and stepped to the door. "It's on the way, ma'am."

"Thanks, XO."

Ben nodded and resumed his OOD watch. A little over fifteen minutes later, Bunting called across the bridge, "Incoming immediate message, sir."

Ben stepped over to the screen and as Haley stepped up behind him, he clicked on the "Message Received" icon. A small window popped onto the screen.

FM: CCGD7(DCS), TO: CGC KAUAI.

CONTINUE MISSION.

Chapter 15

Undercover

***USCG Cutter Kauai, Moored, Port de
Basse-Terre, Basse-Terre, Guadeloupe,
France
10:03 AST, 30 June***

Haley

The arrival was uneventful, and Haley was proud of the effort the deck crew put out to shine in front of the French warship. Bondurant took the OOD for the mooring, allowing Hopkins to instruct and dispatch crewmembers to positions at the bow, stern, and mast to transfer the colors as soon as their first mooring line went over. Ben handled the salute and rendering of honors as they slowly passed down *Frimaire*'s starboard side on the way to their berth at the north end of the quay.

Haley had to admit *Frimaire* was a beautiful ship, sleek, with gleaming, spotless light gray paint throughout and her hull number F736 in large black characters on the hull just aft of the anchor. She was almost three times *Kauai*'s length, twice as tall, and carried a one-hundred-millimeter gun in a turret on her foredeck. *Frimaire* outclassed them in every respect but speed, where *Kauai* had the edge at thirty to twenty knots. *Not that that would do us much good with a radar-controlled gun lobbing thirty-pound shells at us at a rate of seventy-five per minute. Kauai would last about two minutes in that fight!* Haley shuddered slightly at the realization that their mission had made the possibility of the two ships being locked in a fight far less unthinkable.

They were still securing the bridge, with Haley standing on the starboard bridge wing, when she saw a young male officer in an all-white tropical uniform strolling along the quay toward their quarterdeck. "Looks like we have company, XO," she said, turning her head slightly toward the door.

"Customs?" Ben said, poking his head out.

"From *Frimaire*, I think," she replied. "We'd better head down."

"XO, Williams and I have got this," Hopkins said from across the bridge.

"Thanks, Chief," Ben said, then turned to follow Haley while adjusting his dark blue garrison cap.

They stepped down the ladder at the rear of the bridge to the boat deck, then hopped down to the main deck and turned aft to where the quarterdeck was being set up. The officer was waiting on the quay as they stepped over and snapped to attention and rendered a crisp salute as they approached. "*Enseigne de vaisseau de 1re classe* Henri LeClerc, *Marine nationale, frégate de surveillance Frimaire*, at your service, *madame et monsieur*!"

They both saluted in return, and then Haley said, "Enchanté, *Enseigne* LeClerc. I am..." She paused, trying to remember the French term for a naval lieutenant. "*Lieutenant de vaisseau* Haley Reardon, *le commandant* of *Kauai*, and this is le *commandant en second, Lieutenant de vaisseau* Benjamin Wyporek." As they shook hands, she continued. "Now I hope you don't mind continuing in English, as my French is not up to it."

"Of course," LeClerc said with a grin. "My commandant offers his compliments and welcome to France and hopes you will accept his invitation to join him for refreshments and dinner aboard *Frimaire*. Would fifteen hours be at your convenience?"

"We are honored by the invitation," Haley replied with a warm smile. "Fifteen hours would be most convenient."

"*Parfait, madame*" LeClerc replied.

"May we presume that our tropical blue uniforms will be adequate dress for the visit?"

"Yes, in fact, it is preferred."

"Very well, then. Please pass him our respects and we look forward to meeting him this afternoon."

"*Très bien!*" They shook hands again, then LeClerc snapped off another salute and, after it was returned, pivoted and walked briskly toward *Frimaire*.

"Let's go!" Haley whispered, and they both strode back aboard and then forward to the messdeck, where Hebert was putting up breakfast dishes. "Chef! I have an emergency for you."

"Yes, ma'am," Hebert said, turning to them.

"I need to get some booze for a gift for the wardroom on the French frigate. What do you think, wine? Champagne?"

Hebert shook his head. "Only if you want them to think we're wussies, beggin' your pardon, ma'am. You need an excellent brandy, or better still, cognac."

"Think you can find some in town right away?"

Hebert shrugged. "If I can, ma'am, it will be expensive as hell!"

"Will two hundred cover it?"

His eyes widened. "Probably, ma'am."

"OK, go grab Bondurant. I don't want you walking around alone with that much money. See what you can find online and call around while I dig up the cash."

"Yes, ma'am!" Hebert said, then turned and trotted toward the berthing area.

Haley turned to see Ben looking at her with his right eyebrow raised. "Don't worry, Ben. I'm doing this out of pocket. Even if Mercier doesn't make it right later, it will be worth it to buy some goodwill over there."

Ben smiled and said, "I am sure you know what you're doing, *mon commandant*!"

Haley rolled her eyes and said, "Oh, give me a break!"

******

Haley strolled briskly down the quay with Ben from *Kauai* to the much larger warship, decorative bag in hand. Hebert and Bondurant had come through, finding a high-end bottle of cognac in a small wine shop in a side street off the main esplanade of Basse-Terre. It took a substantial part of the money she had allotted and, hopefully, it was worth it.

The language could be a challenge depending on the French captain's command of English. Haley was a competent Spanish speaker and knew a little French, and Ben was competent in German, but knew almost no French. She had drilled him on the correct line to use when requesting permission to come aboard. Hopefully, a translator would be available beyond that point.

As the senior, Haley led the way up the brow, as the boarding ramp to the ship's quarterdeck was called. As they approached the top, a French officer she recognized as LeClerc stepped forward. *Someone who can speak English, Thank God!* Just short of the ship's side, she stopped, crisply saluted the French flag flapping lazily from the flagstaff on the stern, then turned and held the salute to LeClerc and said, "*Voulez-vous me permettre de monter á votre bord, monsieur?*"

LeClerc returned the salute and said, "*C'est un plaisir pou moi vous recevoir á bord, madame.*"

Haley stepped aboard and stood to one side as the protocol was repeated with Ben. The grinning LeClerc then continued, "It is my honor to welcome you aboard *madame et monsieur.* Would you follow me please to the officers' mess? The commandant awaits you there."

"With pleasure," Haley said. They followed the young officer forward along the main deck, through a hatch, and then through several passageways before arriving at an ornate wooden door bearing the ship's crest and a large teak plaque with *FRIMAIRE* carved in and accented with gold leaf. LeClerc opened the door, stepped through, and held the door for Haley and Ben.

The room was spacious and well-decorated with wood paneling and a variety of plaques. There was a large metal dining table in the center surrounded by ten metal chairs and a separate sitting area with a leather-upholstered wrap-around couch and matching easy chairs. A tall, broad-shouldered man with graying black hair, whose deep tan complemented his white tropical uniform displaying the shoulder boards of a *Capitaine de frégate,* equivalent to a commander in the Coast Guard, stepped forward with a wide, warm smile. "Welcome, welcome! Louis Moreau, at your service, *Capitaine* Reardon," he said with a low, booming voice while shaking her hand. He turned to shake Ben's hand. "Pleased to meet you, Lieutenant Wyporek. Did I pronounce that correctly?"

"Yes, sir. Thank you," Ben replied.

"Commandant, I hope you and your officers will accept this gift from the crew of *Kauai,*" Haley said, offering the gift bag.

"Oh, you are too kind," Moreau said as he took the bag. "*Mon Dieu!*" he exclaimed after extracting the bottle. "What an extraordinarily thoughtful gift! We shall relish it. I would love to offer a similar gift in return. Or is the Coast Guard as allergic to spirits as your Navy?"

"We have the same allergy, I fear, sir," Haley replied.

Moreau chuckled. "*C'est tellement dommage!* We will have to think of something. In the meantime, this is my executive officer, *Capitaine de corvette* Marcel Dumas, and my operations officer, *Lieutenant de vaisseau* Andre Durand." After handshakes all around, Moreau took Haley and Ben on a tour of *Frimaire*, ending an hour later back in the officers' mess, where they sat at the mess table for cocktails.

"Your ship is magnificent, Commandant," Haley said.

"*Merci*, madame," Moreau replied. "If I may compliment you, I was very impressed with the handling of your vessel this morning. I was somewhat surprised to see an Island Class patrol boat. I had thought they were being superseded by your Fast Response Cutters."

"You are correct, Commandant. *Kauai* is one of the last of her class," Haley said. "It was decided that she could still be useful as a patrol vessel for rocket launch range safety and as a test platform for new systems. So, her electronics and powerplant were replaced, and she was moved to Port Canaveral."

"Ah, yes. Old, but still in the fight. No? Like *Frimaire*," he said, patting the wall. "You speak of materiel improvements. I am a former engineer myself and am curious to see what you have. May I call upon you for a tour tomor-row morning before the ceremony?"

"We would be honored to have you or any of your of-ficers aboard for a tour. You may not want to all show up at once—we do not have much space," Haley said with a grin.

Moreau chuckled and said, "Very good. So, let us have the meal!"

Room 114, L'hôtel Caraïbe, Île Oiseaux, Îles des Saintes, France
18:17 AST, 30 June

Peter

Why? Why did I pick kids?!

Peter slammed the photo album shut and pushed it away from him across the small table. Gripping the table with both hands, he squeezed his eyes closed and con-centrated on his breathing to quell the nausea. He knew they could monitor the guests in their rooms. It was doubtful they did it continuously, but he couldn't chance them watching him puking his guts out after reviewing what the concierge called la carte des enfants—the "menu" of children.

Because you're an agent and you have to complete the mission and you do anything that reduces the risk of com-pleting that mission. You picked kids because they would be easier to control than an adult when the time came to grab the defector and run. Despite his revulsion, it was the correct decision. A child could be sedated quickly and quietly, whereas an adult would probably put up a fight, and maybe even need to be killed to avoid triggering an alarm. But still...

The binder was divided into sections, each devoted to a particular child. The sections included a name, probably fictitious, the child's age, country of origin, and several pictures in various costumes and degrees of nudity. Each section ended with a thoroughly disgusting standardized list of depravity options, showing which were included, prohibited, or subject to an up-charge. On seeing the first one, he shook his head, thinking, *you just can't make this shit up!*

He had been slowly perusing the binder, feigning a pedophile's arousal and holding his own against his distaste until he reached the twelfth child, a nine-year-old girl. Her stated name was Babette, undoubtedly a pseudonym given her stated birthplace of Tallinn, Estonia. When he turned over the title page to get to the pictures, his blood froze. "Babette" was a beautiful little girl with a shy smile and large pale blue eyes in a heart-shaped face surrounded by wavy auburn hair. She was, in fact, identical in almost every respect to another shy nine-year-old girl Peter had met some years ago—Victoria Carpenter.

He squeezed his eyes closed and fought to remain motionless as the memories of that day flooded back. Julie's apprehension at introducing him to her neurodiverse sister and her relief when he and Victoria immediately hit it off. Their times together as a family, with Victoria alternating between the young girl full of wonder and the intellectual equal with whom he could discuss almost any academic idea. He knew he could not look at the pictures without losing it, so he focused his vision on the table above the binder and unseeingly traced his fingers over the pictures, as he had with the other children. His relief upon reaching the end of section twelve was palpable.

There were thirteen more children to view, but he needed a drink to continue. He stood, walked briskly to the bar, poured himself a quarter-glass of Jameson's, and downed it in a single gulp. He wiped his mouth with the back of the hand holding the glass and gripped the armoire with his other hand as the nausea and warmth from the whiskey fought for control over his stomach. Fortunately, the whiskey won this round.

Peter poured himself another half-glass, then held the bottle before his face and said aloud, "This far, and no farther." The drink would be waiting for him when he completed his ordeal. He trudged back to the table, sat before the open binder, and finished his grim task.

After closing the binder, he took another swallow of the whiskey and stared at the piece of paper on the table in front of him. It was the "order form" on which Declan Shea would specify his desires for entertainment on the following evening. *Leave it to these monsters to have a form for this, like you were ordering a custom computer to be built. They probably hold on to them in case they are needed later for blackmail.* Even knowing he would not actually be carrying out the inhuman acts did little to ease the horror of selecting a child and checking the various blocks. *This is it. This is the last time. I'm out. When I get back from this one, I'm putting in my papers.*

He took another swallow of the Jameson's and as the warmth spread through his body, the reality of the decision took hold. *Yes, this is the last one. So, if I step outside the lines, what are they going to do, take away my birthday? Friend, it's time to go out in style!* He looked at the binder sitting on the table as the idea coalesced. It was crazy and would probably get them all killed. He desperately wanted to save them all, but it was impossible. However, he might just be able to bring one out during the exfil.

He smiled sadly, took another swallow of the whiskey, picked up the pen, and wrote "12" on the line after the word "Selection."

Marine Nationale FS Frimaire, Moored, Port de Basse-Terre, Basse-Terre, Guadeloupe, France
22:14 AST, 30 June

Ben

Chef has a rival, Ben thought while he followed Haley and LeClerc through the interior passageways toward *Frimaire*'s quarterdeck. The food was delicious and plentiful, with the bonus of a couple of glasses of fine wine. He would have limited himself to one had he known of all the toasts with Madeira that were to follow the meal. He was definitely feeling the effects and suspected his companions were as well. *One or two more toasts and we'd have to call Drake and Bondurant to carry us back—wouldn't* that *look good in the trip report!*

Having an English speaker like LeClerc around to see them off was a godsend. Any chance of Ben's remembering, much less delivering, the French version of "Permission to leave the ship, sir?" had vanished with the third toast. He would have been surprised if even Haley could have managed it, considering she had matched them drink for drink.

As they passed outside into the warm and humid air, Ben could hear the distant sounds of music and traffic going on in the capital city, just off the small port reservation. They finally arrived at the quarterdeck, and Haley and Ben shook hands and shared goodbyes with LeClerc. Much to Ben's relief, Haley saluted LeClerc and said, "Request permission to leave the ship, sir."

"Permission granted, madame," LeClerc replied with a salute.

Haley stepped just over the side onto the brow to await Ben. After he completed the ritual and joined her, they both set off down the brow, their footsteps thudding loudly on the metal plate. As soon as they were out of earshot, Haley whispered, "How are you holding up, Ben?"

"I sure as hell won't be driving anywhere tonight, skipper," Ben whispered back.

"Same here. If it looks like I'm going to fall over, be sure to grab me."

"Same here, *mon Capitaine*!"

USCG Cutter Kauai, Moored, Port de Basse-Terre, Basse-Terre, Guadeloupe, France
06:05 AST, 1 July

Ben

Ben had dragged himself out of his bunk a half-hour previously to get in a quick shave and don his exercise gear for a morning run. He took a quick tour around the decks to check the rigging for dressing the ship, a form of rendering honors in which *Kauai*'s signal flags would be hung in the prescribed rainbow pattern along a wire running from the jackstaff on the bow up to the top of the mast and then back down to the flagstaff on the stern. When the ensign and union jack were raised for morning colors, crewmen would pull the lines of signal flags into place. It was another of those administrative details that ate up time and effort and, as he had done countless times before, Ben thanked God he had Hopkins around to handle it.

He had just started stretching for the morning run when Lee, Chen, and Bunting arrived to join him. "Hi, guys," Ben said, managing a weak smile despite the throbbing in his head. "How is everyone on this fine day?"

"We're tip-top, XO," Lee replied with a grin. "How's your head? We heard you and the C.O. drank the Frenchies under the table last night."

"OK, for the record, no one drank anyone under the table last night. However, an important lesson for you boys and girls is that it's important to do a little research into foreign customs before you experience them. That way, you might avoid waking up the next morning feeling like you've been dragged through a grommet."

Lee turned to the others and said, "On three, everyone. One...Two...Three!"

"YES, MISTER WYPOREK!" the three petty officers shouted, then broke into laughter.

"Alright, alright, children." Ben straightened up. "Let's hit the road. Who wants the lead?"

"I nominate Lil Boats!" Chen said.

Ben glanced at Lee, who said, "Watch it, Boot! Keep in mind the advantage of being petite is that my big toe will hit peak upswing about the time it contacts your balls!" After another round of laughter, Lee said, "XO, you probably want to set the pace after last night, so I cede the lead to you. We, your loyal minions, will follow."

The run was exactly what Ben needed to blow the cobwebs out of his brain and get back to fighting trim. It was warm and humid, but a fresh breeze from the southeast kept things from getting too uncomfortable. Ben took them on a scenic two-mile tour of the architecture of the capital, past the Cathédrale Notre Dame and around the Palais d'Orléans before returning to the port and *Kauai*.

After sharing breakfast with his running mates, Ben grabbed a quick shower and then changed into his service dress whites for the upcoming ceremony. He met up with Haley, who looked none the worse for wear after the hard night and was also already in her whites for the day. "Back in the land of the living, skipper?" Ben asked.

"Barely," she answered with a grimace. "How 'bout you?"

"Pretty rough getting up, but I had a good run downtown with the crew that got me back in the game."

"Wish I could have joined you, but that would have been a little above and beyond today," Haley said. "I just got a call from Captain Moreau. He'll be coming over for his tour in about fifteen minutes. Could you tell Lamonde to stay out of sight and have Chief fire up the FC3 for an unclassified demo, please?"

"On it. Do you want me along for the tour?"

"If you don't mind. I can handle the technical questions, but if he wants to know anything about unit history, you'll be the guy."

"Roger that."

"Also, I know COB will run the main control tour, but I would like him to avoid mention of our battery capability. If Moreau asks directly, well, I don't expect COB to lie about it, but I have a strong preference the French not be aware we can cruise silently until after the mission tonight."

"I'll let him know, Captain. COB has a way with things. It should be OK."

Île Oiseaux, Îles des Saintes, France
10:22 AST, 1 July

Peter

Today was the day. Peter did not like to leave things like finalizing an escape plan until the last minute, but with defectors, you do what it takes. The physical location for the rendezvous had been arranged before he had departed Ireland, and he made sure to visit it from different routes during the preceding two days. Peter was still alive because he never took things on faith and did not show up for a meeting in a place he had not scouted beforehand. He took a third route to the location this morning as an added precaution and walked a circle five hundred feet wide around the spot, looking for evidence of surveillance. It was clean, and he settled in the spot, sitting on a boulder in the center of the clearing, pretending to adjust his camera while he waited.

There was a snap of a twig from his right and Peter slowly turned in his seat while gazing at the camera in his left hand, his right moving to a spot next to the combat knife hidden in his boot. After some more rustling and the sound of footsteps, a figure emerged from the line of trees and approached his position. It was a young man, white with purple-dyed hair and glasses, wearing an over-sized t-shirt and jeans that revealed a scrawny body. He was looking around fearfully as he approached. *My God! If they had gone to central casting in Hollywood, they could not have come up with a more quintessential geek!*

Peter smiled and said with Declan Shea's Irish accent, "G'day, friend. Out to see the birds? The doves are especially active this morning." It was the agreed-upon challenge that identified him as the American agent and indicated no danger.

"I do not know, it seems a little hot for doves," the man said, using the correct non-distress countersign.

Peter nodded. "Right. When do we go and how do I get out of the hotel without bringing every goon on the island down on us?"

"We go at 22:23. I will deactivate the alarm on the emergency exit door on the southeast corner of the building for one minute, starting at that time. At 22:27 exactly, I will trigger the fire alarms throughout the hotel. There are nearly three dozen guests. It should create quite a distraction."

"Sounds good. Let's synchronize time." Peter pulled his micro-chronometer from his wallet—it looked like two credit cards stuck together until you pressed at a certain spot for two seconds, triggering a time display to appear. "Give me a count to the next even minute."

The man looked at his watch, a cheap digital with a garish orange band. "Ten twenty-six in ten seconds...five seconds...now."

Peter reset the chronometer to 10:26:00 and then returned it to his wallet. "We will meet up at point B for the exfil. Make sure you have the goods or you get left behind. Understand?"

"Yes, I will have them both."

Both? "Good. We will meet another operative there who will escort us to the boat."

"Then I will get my money, yes?"

"Yes. We keep our promises. And I mean both ways—you screw with us and we'll leave you behind, gift-wrapped for your *friends* to find. Clear?"

The man visibly gulped. "Yes."

"On your way then. I will see you tonight."

"Yes." The man nodded vigorously, then turned and almost ran back into the bush.

Peter stood and then turned in the opposite direction to resume his walk. *Scumbag! What the hell did he mean 'both'?* He shook his head and started scanning for suitable bird subjects to photograph.

Palais d'Orléans, Rue Lardenoy, Basse-Terre, Guadeloupe, France
13:53 AST, 1 July

Haley

Haley and Ben were near the end of a long queue of dignitaries, senior military officers, and wealthy citizens waiting to greet the new Prefect of Guadeloupe. The inauguration ceremony had been very similar to the Coast Guard changes of command she had attended, with martial music, parading of colors, awarding of medals, and long speeches that probably would not have been any less boring had they been in English instead of French.

The major headache from the hangover afflicting her that morning had faded away. Haley had been relieved to find out that the ceremony was being held inside the air-conditioned Prefecture building rather than outside in the mid-day sun of a tropical island in summer. She envied Ben—although he was stuck wearing a high "choker" collar, he only had to wear the coat, whereas she was laden with a coat, shirt, and tie. At least she had the discretion to wear pants and normal shoes for the ceremony rather than the skirt and pumps she thoroughly hated.

When they finally reached the head of the receiving line, Haley whispered her identity to a waiting aide, who, when the new prefect had finished with the man ahead of her in line, announced, "*Lieutenant de vaisseau* Haley

Reardon, *La Garde côtière des États-Unis, le commandant le navire Kauai!*"

The prefect, a slim, balding, middle-aged man slightly shorter than Haley, wearing dark gray morning dress and a tricolor ribbon of office, turned with a beaming smile and outstretched hand. "Welcome to Guadeloupe, *Capitaine!* I am pleased you were able to attend."

Thank God we are doing this in English! As they firmly shook hands, Haley said, "Thank you, Your Excellency. We were honored by your invitation."

"You are most welcome." He turned to a striking woman with dark, graying hair in a formal dress to his left and said, "*Chère, puis-je vous présenter le capitaine Reardon*? *Capitaine*, my wife, Suzanne."

As Haley lightly took her hand, the woman said, "*Enchanté. Bienvenue en Guadeloupe, Capitaine.*"

"*Je suis enchanté de faire votre connaissance, madame.*"

And so it went down the line with the outgoing prefect and his wife, the President of the Departmental Council and his wife, and the mayor of Basse-Terre and his wife. Haley was grateful, finally, to reach the end of the receiving line—all this smiling was bringing back her headache. She waited for Ben to clear the line, and then they walked together into the next room, where refreshments were being served. It was another large, ornately decorated room where several dozen people were mingling and drinking punch. She recognized Moreau and his XO, Dumas, standing at a small bar table in their dress white uniforms, and, after sharing a wave, led Ben over to join them.

"We meet again, *Capitaine*, Lieutenant. You seem to have come through the gauntlet well," Moreau said with a warm smile.

"Not a small challenge after last night," Haley replied with a grin.

"Yes, I share the malady. May I suggest what you call 'the hair of the dog' as a restorative?" he asked, holding up his glass of punch.

"No, Commandant, we'll be sticking to Perrier today." Haley shook her head. "That cure has never worked for me. Besides, Ben and I need to stay clear, as we sortie in just a few hours."

"Oh, I am both surprised and sorry to hear that. I would have hoped you would have more time to enjoy the port call," Moreau said, looking at Ben.

"We are supporting a geological research team on St. Ignatius," Ben replied. "We can't be absent for too long."

"Yes, I suppose that is one of the hazards of being a special purpose vessel," Moreau said, his smile fading.

There was something about the exchange that bothered her. She couldn't put her finger on it, but it was like Moreau knew something was going on. Well, it couldn't be helped. She put on her best disappointed look and said, "It's regrettable. Hopefully, we will be able to put in for enough time for a proper visit on our next call."

"Agreed," Moreau said.

The polite conversation continued for several minutes when a boisterous conversation across the room drew their attention. A short and stocky man with dark, slicked-back hair in a gray Amani suit was lecturing a small group of men and women. The man was enjoying the attention and laughing at what Haley assumed were his own jokes, while the other people smiled politely. Haley turned back to Moreau, whose face was a dark storm of unalloyed hatred. "*Sac à merde*!" he said under his breath.

"Who is that man?" Ben asked.

"Laurent. A local gangster who was thrown out of *la Légion étrangère*," Dumas answered, looking like he had just discovered a fly in his wineglass. "He is rich and well-connected, so he must be tolerated."

So that *is Laurent. Behold the werewolf! Looks more like a gauche Joe Pesci wiseguy knockoff*, Haley thought. Their companions were clearly humiliated that someone on the fringes of the law could be powerful enough to make a spectacle of himself at an official government function. In sympathy, she said, "I wish we could say we don't have such in the States, but they can be found anywhere."

"True indeed," Moreau said, recovering his good humor. "Let us not let that pig ruin our day. May I get you another Perrier?"

"No, Commandant," Haley said sadly. "Ben and I must return to *Kauai* to prepare to sortie. I would like to say it has been a delight to meet and associate with you on this trip. Thank you for your hospitality."

"Oh, it was nothing," Moreau said. "It is we who have you to thank for the pleasure of your company and many future toasts with your wonderful gift. Not so, Andre?"

"Most definitely, Commandant!" Dumas answered with a smile.

As they all shook hands, Moreau clasped Haley's with both of his, gazed into her eyes, and said, *"Bon chance, Capitaine. Au revoir."*

Haley and Ben walked in silence out of the building and hailed one of the waiting taxis for the short drive back to the harbor. Once they were inside the gate and walking toward *Kauai*, she asked, "Was it just my lingering hangover, or did it seem like something was up with Moreau?"

"I thought so too, skipper," Ben replied. "You don't suppose there's been a leak somewhere, do you?"

"Whether there is or isn't is academic at this point, but let's hope not."

"Yea verily, boss."

Chapter 16

Exfiltration

USCG Cutter Kauai, underway in the Dominica Passage, 5.3 nautical miles east-southeast of Île Oiseaux, Îles des Saintes, France
21:37 AST, 1 July

Ben

It was dark, a new moon night, with sky clear and bright with stars and the occasional meteor. Ben liked being out in the open air of the afterdeck, enjoying the cool breeze and the view of the stars as *Kauai* cruised slowly through the calm sea. Looking south, he could see the dense cluster of stars comprising the Milky Way, visible in the absence of light pollution from the shore. He sighed to himself, wishing he could share the view with Victoria, who was fascinated by all such wonders.

The quiet laugh from behind brought him back into reality—Lee, Chen, and Bondurant were gathered by the crane, sharing some story or joke he couldn't make out from where he was standing. Ben and the boat crew were in combat gear and had just finished their final briefing on the afterdeck when Lamonde arrived. His clothing and night-vision goggle-equipped helmet were like Ben's, only all black. Ben could see that, unlike the others, he was slinging a Chinese type 95 assault rifle and there was no doubt his sidearm was of Chinese origin as well. When Ben discovered them during Lamonde's check-in, he had explained that if any shooting became necessary, it was important that the forensics pointed to the Chinese rather than the U.S.

They had reviewed the latest intelligence passed from Pete and other sources before going to general quarters ten minutes previously. The plan of approach, rendezvous, and egress were unchanged. "Do you have any questions or comments, Captain Tucker?" Ben asked.

"No, Lieutenant. Good to go."

"Right." Ben turned to Lee, Chen, and Bondurant, who would be operating the crane. "Could you guys excuse us for a minute?"

"Yes, sir," Bondurant replied, then led the others away.

Once they were out of earshot, Ben turned to Lamonde and whispered, "It has been suggested that you may have secondary orders to dispose of Agent Simmons. I hope that is not the case, but whether or not it is true, know this. If you appear on that beach without Agent Simmons alive and well, I will tell the boat crew that the mission has been compromised and order them to return to the ship without you."

Lamonde scoffed. "This is an op, Lieutenant. *Things* happen on ops. I can't be held responsible if Simmons cocks it."

"Oh, but you can and you will," Ben replied. "If you believe nothing else I ever say, believe *that*. Am I clear?"

"Yes, *Lieutenant*," Lamonde sneered.

"Very well." Ben nodded, then turned to the others. "OK guys, let's go."

As they walked over to the RHIB, already lowered to the level of the afterdeck, the rumble of *Kauai*'s engines vanished, replaced by the low hiss of the water sliding by the ship. The engines were secured, and placed in immediate standby while the cutter continued the rest of the approach, with just batteries powering the electric motors. As always, the cessation of noise and vibration led to a chill running up Ben's spine. He stepped into the RHIB after Chen and Lee, and, followed by Lamonde, sat behind Lee at her helm station. Within a minute, the RHIB was cruising quietly at low power alongside *Kauai*'s starboard side.

Through his night vision goggles, the stars glowed brightly against the dark background of the sky. He could make out the island a few miles ahead, the lights from the hotel complex creating a soft glow. As they neared, he could see details of the shoreline, with the occasional wave breaking on the lightly tinted beach. They were within a quarter mile now and *Kauai* fell behind as she idled in position, awaiting their return.

Two minutes later, they were quite close to shore, and Lee slowed the engine, then went to idle, and the RHIB ground to a stop. Ben turned to Lamonde and said, "Go. Good luck."

Lamonde said, "Right." He then turned and dropped over the side, wading to shore through the knee-deep water.

The RHIB refloated once free of Lamonde's weight, and Lee put the engine in reverse to back off the beach. They would await the agents' return offshore, about halfway to *Kauai*'s idle position. It would have been more convenient to remain on the beach, but they couldn't risk a roving patrol stumbling across them and sounding the alarm.

As they reached their holding position and came to idle, Ben turned to look at *Kauai*, visible in his goggles only as a dark silhouette in the background of stars. He imagined Haley on the bridge, watching the screen from the electro-optical camera in its low-light mode. He could feel for Haley, her anxiety doubled with not only the boat's crew to worry about, but her significant other as well. Ben turned back to look at the shore. *We've done everything we can. Now, as usual, the damn wait!*

Room 114, L'hôtel Caraïbe, Île Oiseaux, Îles des Saintes, France
22:00 AST, 1 July

Peter

The knock on the door sounded promptly at ten p.m., right on schedule. Peter had dressed himself in the manner he assumed would be favored by a creepy rich Irish pedophile—a white silk shirt, half unbuttoned, loose-fitting khaki pants, and topsiders without socks. He had expended about a quarter of the bottle of Jameson's rinsing out his mouth and daubing inside his clothes to achieve the odor of raw liquor. As he stepped to the door, he gathered himself for the performance of his life, hopefully for the last time.

He opened the door to find two men in hotel livery standing on either side of the child. She was dressed in dark street clothing and athletic shoes as Peter had specified in his "order", which was as close to ideal for a night escape as he could come. He was struck by the way she had her dark red hair pulled back into a ponytail, almost exactly the way Victoria favored her hair. Peter couldn't see her eyes—she was head down, staring at the floor.

"Your order for the evening, *Monsieur* Shea," the man standing on the right said. "An excellent choice. She will provide a very satisfying experience for you."

Peter stared at the man and put on a lascivious smile, thinking, *How I wish I could snap your scrawny neck, you slimy bastard!* Aloud, he said, with a slight slurring of his words to complete the simulation of partial intoxication, "Fantastic! I've been looking forward to this for weeks now." He reached down and lifted her head. She had the same look—an identical twin to the nine-year-old Victoria, except for her pale blue eyes. Her mouth was quivering and her eyes showed the deep fear of someone facing a terrible ordeal. *Steady!* The sight generated a deep ache in his chest and he had to concentrate on his character to continue the charade. "Yes, she's perfect!"

"*Bon*," the man on the left said. "She is yours until six a.m. If you tire of her earlier, simply ring the concierge and we will send someone to fetch her."

"I'm sure I'll have no need for that," Shea/Peter slurred. "Thanks, friend!" He put his arm around the girl's shoulders and pulled her into the room.

"*De rien, monsieur*. Enjoy your evening."

The two men turned away, and Peter locked the door. He pulled the girl into the doorway between the main sitting room and the bathroom and then released her to open the faucet into the bathtub. He had done a thorough survey of the room over the past couple of days, evaluating blind spots for the cameras he knew would be pointed at the bed and recliner in the sitting room. There was only one other camera location that could cover the bathroom door, and he had "accidentally" left his backpack blocking it.

When he returned, she was standing there, stiff, with her arms at her sides and her head down as before. Peter kneeled before her, raised her face to his, and whispered, "Do you speak English?" After the girl returned a dull look, he continued, "*Parle-vous Français?*" Another dull look and head shake drew a sigh from Peter. "*A ty govorish' po russki?*"

The girl's eyes locked on his. "*Da.*"

Better than nothing, he thought, then continued in Russian. "I am an American agent, and I will leave in a few minutes. You may come along with me if you choose, and I will see that you get to the United States. The escape will be dangerous, so you can remain here if you prefer, but I will have to give you something that will make you sleep for a short time. Do you understand?"

"Yes. If I go, what will become of me in America?" she asked in heavily accented Russian.

"We will care for you as a child should be cared for. If you wish to return to your home and family, that will be arranged."

"No!" Her eyes grew wide. "They are as bad as here. Worse, even. If I go, I stay in America. Yes?" she pleaded.

"Yes, of course. We have many people who can care for you, and you will not be sent away unless that is what you wish." He could see the glimmer of hope in her eyes, hope that this was not just another pervy game. It was heartbreaking to imagine a home life so horrific that any child would prefer to continue in sexual slavery.

"Yes. I will go with you," she said finally.

"Good," Peter smiled. "Now I know your true name can't be 'Babette'. Can you tell me what it is, please?"

"Tamm, Lenna Tamm."

"Thank you, Lenna." He pulled the micro-chronometer out of his wallet and checked the time—22:08. "We go in fifteen minutes." He put the card in his shirt pocket and nodded toward the toilet. "It may be some time before we can use the bathroom again. Do you need to go?"

The girl shook her head. "I do my business before I go to the rooms."

Peter thought, *I hope she is telling the truth and not just putting up a defense against perverts who like to watch.* He nodded and said, "Very well. We will not speak again until we leave. OK?" She nodded, and he said, "Go sit on the bed now and try to stay calm." After she walked off. He went into the bathroom to close the faucet, then came out, poured himself another half glass of Jameson's at the bar, and sat in the recliner. The girl stared at him from across the room and he smiled slightly and pretended to drink.

At 22:20 on his chronometer, he stood and walked over to the dresser, pulling off his white shirt and dropping it on the floor. He pulled on a black, long-sleeved turtleneck, then reached behind the drawer, pulled out his silenced pistol, and checked the magazine and chamber. He pulled open his backpack, opened the hidden compartment inside, and pulled out a night vision ocular. Its small Lithium battery would only last about half an hour, but that would be enough. He motioned to Lenna, who jumped off the bed and joined him at the door.

He kneeled and whispered in Russian, "When we leave, I want you to hold my hand as if we are going for a walk together. If anyone challenges us, I will have to kill them with my gun. If that happens, you mustn't cry out. Do you understand?"

Lenna's look was more determined now. "*Da.*"

Peter smiled back, trying to convey a level of confidence he wished he had. At 22:22, he opened the door, verified no one was in the hallway, then took Lenna's hand and set out at a brisk pace down to the left. They ducked into an alcove with a sign labeled "Sortie" and waited in front of a solid door with a crash bar. When his chronometer ticked over to 22:23, Peter turned to the box above the door. A few seconds later, the red LED light went out, and he opened the door and led the girl outside.

Peter briefly checked the lighted walkways in all directions and, verifying they were clear, set off with Lenna in hand down the walkway leading to the path they would take to the rendezvous. They had walked some distance and rounded a corner to find a man dressed as a security guard.

"*Qu'est-ce que tu fais ici?*" He was not carrying an automatic weapon, just a holstered pistol. He was part of the roving hotel security patrol, intended to prevent guests from wandering around and getting hurt rather than as a defense of the compound.

"My sweetie and I are just out for a walk, friend," Peter said, pulling the girl close with his left hand while thumbing off the safety of the pistol he held behind him with his right. When the sudden wail of an alarm from the direction of the hotel drew the guard's attention, Peter brought up the pistol and shot him through the forehead with an audible "pop." As the man tumbled backward off the walkway, Lenna gasped but did not cry out. Peter thumbed the safety back on, tucked the pistol into his waistband, and then strode over to drag the body into the bushes.

Once the body was out of sight, Peter returned and led the girl down the walkway to where it joined the path to the rendezvous point. He leaned down and whispered in Russian, "I have a device that lets me see in the dark, so I need to carry you from here. OK?"

"*Da,*" she replied, then put up her arms.

Peter donned the ocular and switched it on, then picked up the girl and strode quickly down the path into the wood. The lack of moonlight made it difficult to see, even with the ocular, and he nearly fell several times after stumbling over roots or fallen branches. He was relieved to break into the clearing where he would meet the defector. After lowering the girl to the ground, he sat heavily on the boulder in the center of the clearing, watching in the direction from which the defector had come during the earlier visit.

Within two minutes of their arrival, he caught sight of intermittent flashes of light from that direction. He pulled the girl over and down behind the boulder, then brought the pistol up and sighted on the flickering light. *It has to be him. No security guy would be stupid enough to patrol with a lighted flashlight!* There was rustling and the snap of a branch, then the man stumbled into the clearing, his face visible in the ocular. "Turn that light off, you dumbass!" Peter whispered urgently.

The man jumped and then switched off the penlight he was carrying. Peter stood, picked up the girl, and then stepped over to the defector. "I have a night vision device I can use to see the trail," he whispered. "You grab hold of my waistband and follow behind."

"What's she doing here?"

"She's coming with us."

"That wasn't part of the deal!"

"It is now! Now shut up, unless you'd like a broken jaw!"

Peter turned and, when felt the defector take a good grip on his waistband, started at a slow pace down the trail to the rally point. The traveling was difficult enough when it was just him and the girl. With an inexperienced man in tow, it was a nightmare and Peter lost count of the times the man went down. As they approached the rally point, Peter heard a soft whistle from ahead. He answered with three equally soft, short whistles.

"Shaft!" whispered a voice from the darkness.

"Crank!" Peter whispered in return, then crept into the next clearing. He could see the figure straightening up in the darkness, pistol in hand and submachine gun slung on his left shoulder.

"About damn time!" Lamonde whispered. "Who the hell is this?" he asked, pointing at the child with his pistol as Peter lowered her to the ground.

"Never mind. She's with me. Let's get going."

"First things first," Lamonde said. He turned to the defector and holstered his pistol. "I need to see the goods."

"I have them!" the man replied.

"Fine. Let's see them," Lamonde said.

The defector reached into his pocket and drew out two objects. "This thumb drive has the Chinese data, and the portable drive has the rest," he said and handed them to Lamonde.

Lamonde looked each over carefully, then pulled a gallon-sized ziplock bag out of his pocket, dropped both drives in, and zipped it shut. He glanced again at the defector and said, "What about the source material?"

"There are two racks with RAIDs in separate buildings. They are both equipped with degaussers in case we get raided." He giggled at his own joke. "I activated the kill switch on both systems before I bailed. It's all gone by now."

"Most satisfactory." Lamonde nodded. He casually put the bag in his vest pocket and zipped it closed, pulled his silenced pistol from its holster, and shot the defector in the head. The man fell backward with a thud and no other sound.

Peter had already been lifting his pistol when Lamonde was pulling his and audibly thumbed off his safety as he aimed at the man's face. "Toss it or die!"

"Relax," Lamonde said, holding up the pistol by a single finger through the trigger guard. "Your boyfriend on *Kauai* made it clear that he'd burn me if I showed up without you."

"Toss it. Do it now!"

"Fine," Lamonde said, tossing the pistol aside.

"Now toss the other one. Slow and careful."

"What if we run into a patrol?"

"I'll take that chance. Toss it now! By the sling, asshole!"

Lamonde shrugged, unslung the assault rifle, and flung it to the side.

"Why?" Peter asked, keeping his pistol pointed at the other agent's head.

"Did you really think we were going to pay that piece of shit twenty million bucks and set him up somewhere he could do it again? Who did you think was behind this scam, that throwback Laurent?"

Peter swallowed and said, "Alright, let's go. You lead. If I even see a twitch, I'll blow your head off. Move!" After Lamonde turned and started walking toward the shore, Peter picked up the child, who was shaking like a leaf. "Don't worry, little one," he whispered to her in Russian. "We'll be among friends soon." She put her head down on his shoulder and he gave her a soft, reassuring squeeze.

Ben

The wait in the RHIB had been interminable and Ben wanted to cheer when his headset finally crackled with the low-power transmission from *Kauai.*

"One, this is Orchid. Friendlies in sight, negative bad guys. Cleared to move in," Bunting's voice said.

Ben pressed his transmit button and said, "Confirm Simmons in sight."

"Affirmative. Positive ID."

Ben exhaled with relief and clicked his transmit switch twice in response. He could barely make out features on the coast with his NVGs at this distance, but *Kauai*'s camera could pick out the buttons on the men's shirts. He turned to Lee. "Take us in, Shelley."

"Roger that, sir," Lee replied, shifting the thrust lever out of neutral and turning the rib toward the shore. Even at the low power setting, it only took three minutes to reach the water's edge and Chen jumped off to wade ashore as the bow touched the beach.

Ben could see the two men approaching now, the one in the rear apparently carrying a child. *What the hell, Pete?* As they neared, Ben asked, "Where's the defector?"

Pete replied, "Dead. I'll debrief you on the boat."

"Right." When they reached the boat, Ben reached over and gave a hand to help pull up Lamonde. After he was seated, Ben took the child from Pete and sat her on the deck next to Lee. When he turned around, Pete had already pulled himself in and Chen was pushing the RHIB off the shore. Once he had boarded, Lee turned the boat toward *Kauai* and advanced the throttle.

The trip to *Kauai* took about ten minutes. Ben gazed in curiosity at the child, a girl, by appearances, her arms wrapped around Pete's leg as she sat on the float with her face buried into his thigh. His hand was on her back, between her shoulders. Ben turned to Lamonde, who was sitting impassively on the float across the RHIB from Pete, staring straight ahead.

As they climbed out of the RHIB, Ben's headset crackled again. "XO requested on the bridge."

Ben clicked his transmit button twice and turned to Lamonde. "I'm needed on the bridge."

"I'm coming too," Lamonde said firmly.

"Alright," Ben said, then turned to Pete. "We need you two out of the way. Wait on the messdeck."

Ben was turning back when he was stopped by Pete's hand on his shoulder. They locked eyes, and Pete squeezed his shoulder and said, "Thank you, Ben."

Ben nodded, then led Lamonde up on the boat deck, then up the ladder and onto the bridge through the starboard door. Something was wrong. They were still making an extremely slow speed, whereas they could cruise at up to twenty knots on the batteries. Ben stepped over to Haley, sitting in the command chair, and said, "Captain?"

"Ben, welcome back," Haley said with a smile, giving him a hug across his shoulders. She turned to Lamonde, "Captain Tucker."

"Captain Reardon," Lamonde answered with a nod.

Haley turned back to Ben. "We've got company. Confirmed Furuno navigation radar." She nodded toward the FC3.

Ben turned to see Williams gazing at the screen, which was displaying the Electronic Warfare data page. "One of the gang's response boats?" he asked. Furuno radars were common across many classes of ships, large and small.

"No," Haley said. "It's a DRS12A, one of the big ones."

Williams turned suddenly. "It's *Frimaire*, Captain. Confidence high." *Kauai*'s new EW gear had completed the analysis of the radar's unique electronic signature and found a match to the French frigate in the database.

"Shit!" Haley said. "He is coming around the headland now, but he's only doing ten knots. We don't think he has us. We are maintaining bare steerageway and keeping the same aspect in hopes he won't pick us out of the clutter."

Ben glanced at the navigation screen. They were a little over two miles off the beach of Île Oiseaux right now. The territorial sea only extended about six and a half miles offshore here, because of the proximity of Dominica across the channel, but four miles was not fudging distance and they couldn't claim "innocent passage" the way they were operating. In short, they were on the verge of creating an international incident, which, bad as that was, would be made infinitely worse by the fact that the two agents had left a dead man ashore.

"You can't let them take us, Captain," Lamonde said firmly, obviously having the same thoughts as Ben.

"I'm doing what I can here, Mister Tucker," Haley answered, her eyes fixed on the tactical screen. *Kauai*'s radar, like all other gear that emitted trackable radiation, was shut down, but the EW system produced an approximate bearing and range that was displayed on the tactical screen.

"You can turn and run. You have a ten-knot speed advantage."

"With three diesels on line, yes. But it will take us at least a minute to light them off and we'd have to turn broadside to run, which will provide enough cross-section for their nav radar to pick us up. Now kindly be silent and let me do my job." She turned back to the FC3 console. "Report, Williams."

"Yes, ma'am. Target bears three-five-four relative at four-point-three miles. Estimated course one-nine-five at ten. Estimate we are on his two-four-five."

"So far, so good," Haley said.

On most ships, radar performance decreased as the target passed behind because of interference from the superstructure. With luck, they could soon kick in some speed and scoot out to the open sea without detection. The tension had continued for another half minute when Williams suddenly sat up and said. "Target angle change. Target turning left, pulse amplitude increasing."

Suddenly the screen lit up with the announcement "Target Warning." Williams turned and said, "Fire control radar lock-on. They've got us for sure, Captain!"

Haley jumped out of the command seat. "Chief, all diesels emergency light-off now!"

"Aye, aye, ma'am!" Hopkins replied, then turned to the intercom to engineering.

"Bunting, nav and stripe lights on now!"

"Yes, ma'am!" Bunting replied, then reached up and flipped the switches to the navigation lights and the floodlight illuminating their red hull "racing" stripe to "on". "All lights on," he said as the whine of a diesel engine starter followed by the loud growl of the starting engine passed up from below.

"Lights on? Are you crazy? You're making us an easy target!" Lamonde cried.

"We're already an easy target! Now SHUT UP!" Ben said, stepping between Lamonde and Haley.

The bridge was suddenly bathed in bright white light. *Frimaire* was illuminating them with its powerful search-light. Ben swallowed hard. *That's it. They've got us. They won't be shooting, of course, just documenting the crap out of our violating their sovereignty before they haul us in!* Ben glanced at Haley, whose face was a cold, expressionless mask. Like him, she was waiting fearfully for what was about to follow.

Just as suddenly as the searchlight appeared, it was switched off. A few seconds later, Williams announced, "Fire control radar secured, Captain! I'm just picking up their nav radar now."

"Get the camera on him!" Haley replied. Within five seconds, the camera was showing a dark silhouette against the stars.

"Track change and amplitude shift indicate target has shifted turn," Williams said. "He's turning away, Captain."

Ben watched the screen in wonder. A much less intense light began flickering over the water from the silhouette of *Frimaire*—a signal lamp. Ben's morse was too rusty to read it in real-time, but Zucarro was fresher, as she was just a year out of school. "Did you read that Zucarro?" Ben asked.

She turned and said, "Yes, sir, but it doesn't make sense. It just said, 'Bon chance'."

Ben turned to Haley with a grin. She sat heavily in the command chair, took a deep breath, and said, "No, Zucarro, it makes perfect sense. Chief, let's not push our luck anymore. Give me twenty-four knots to San Juan, please."

"Aye, aye, ma'am!" Hopkins said.

"Williams, let's secure from EMCON. Get the nav radar on before we run into something."

"Yes, ma'am," Williams replied, turning back to his console.

As *Kauai* turned on course to the north-northwest and Hopkins brought her speed up, Ben turned to Haley and asked, "Captain, what just happened?"

She smiled back and said, "I don't know how XO, but it looks like the fix was in."

******

They had secured from General Quarters and Ben had made his way to the messdeck, where Bryant was examining the child Pete had brought aboard. As Ben approached them, the girl, who was gripping Pete's right arm tightly with both hands, turned toward him and he froze in shock. Pete looked up, smiled, and said, "Yes, you see it too, don't you?"

"My God! They could be sisters! Twins even!" Ben shook himself and said, "You've got some 'splaining to do in a minute, brother." He waited until Bryant was done and asked, "Do we need to do anything, Doc?"

"No sir. Physically, she's fine. I expect she's about as twisted up psychologically as a kid can be, though, given where she's come from." He turned toward Pete. "Dr. Simmons, do you think you can stay with her for now? I think peeling her off would just cause more trauma."

"No problem, Mike. She can hang on as long as she likes."

"Thank you." He turned to Ben. "We need to keep a close watch on her, sir. It's just like the *Miho Dujam*."

The *Miho Dujam* was a 252 Syndicate arms trafficking freighter the crew abandoned when their engine quit while trying to outrun *Kauai*. They had left it sinking and Ben and his crew had boarded to make a sweep for evidence before it went down. They discovered twenty-two female human trafficking victims locked in two wooden cells and left to drown when the ship sank. The physical and emotional trauma the women and girls had suffered at the hands of the gang beggared belief.

"I'll see to it. Thanks, Doc," Ben said.

"Sir," Bryant said, then turned and left the messdeck.

Ben sat across from Pete and said, "OK, Pete. Can we talk?"

Pete nodded and said, "Yes. Let me introduce you. This is Lenna Tamm. She doesn't speak English, only Russian, and it's not her first language. She's from the Baltics, I think, maybe Estonia." He turned to the girl and spoke something in Russian, none of which Ben could understand other than his name.

"OK, kudos for getting her out of there. But doesn't that jam you up?"

"Who cares? I'm getting out, anyway. I went in thinking I could order up a kid off their menu, drug him or her, and then slink out. Needless to say, that cowardly plan went into the shitcan as soon as I saw her picture. We'll get her fostered on some sort of material witness deal. She's terrified we're going to send her back to her family. They probably sold her into slavery."

"Jesus Christ," Ben said, shaking his head. "Is there no end to this horror?"

"No, I think not," Pete said. "Saved one, though. Maybe twenty-three of her mates, if we're lucky."

"OK. So what happened with the defector?"

"Lamonde murdered him. In cold blood."

Ben looked into his eyes and said, "Then you were right."

"Yes, about everything. He would have capped me and her too if you hadn't dissuaded him. Thank you again for that."

"So it was just a murder jaunt?"

"No, the blackmail scenario is legit, but it goes deeper than we were led to believe. The defector had two USB drives with him. One's the Chinese kompromat, but the other's something bigger, maybe everything the gang's collected."

"No wonder Lamonde was so worked up about our getting caught by the French. And they had us dead to rights, by the way. One of their frigates had us pinned to the shore of Île Oiseaux, but they let us go. You know anything about that?"

Pete smiled, "Let me paraphrase Chief Drake by saying 'I know some guys' in *Direction générale de la sécurité intérieure*, French internal security, who know some guys in *Marine nationale*, who might have influence on certain frigate skippers to not see certain things at particular times. With that kind of daisy chain, it was not a sure thing, so I didn't want you guys planning on it. Sorry about that."

Ben raised an eyebrow and said, "Took a few years off my life, but probably better we didn't know. How did you persuade them?"

"I told you they were madder than hell that a scumbag like Laurent was running a slave operation on French soil with impunity. They knew they couldn't break his hold on the government, so they gave us a shot. We'll send them a copy of the French portion of the kompromat data—that should shake them up as to the security risk Laurent poses and get them to clean him out for good. Being a paedo-peddler is one thing, threatening the security of *La Belle France*, well, that's different. At least Laurent is out of the blackmail business. If the defector was telling the truth, he wiped all their hard drives on the way out the door."

"Good, good," Ben said, putting his head down. "Everybody likes a happy ending."

"Maybe. Maybe not."

"What do you mean?"

"The other portable hard drive. I think Irving sent Lamonde to get it. Once she has it, she will have a lock on the DNI job, maybe for life."

"You are nuts! How would she pull that off?"

"Think J. Edgar Hoover. You have some compromising material that gets you in the door and compounds over time as you selectively leverage it. Pretty soon, everyone knows you have 'the files', but they're afraid to do anything about it. Eventually, the higher-ups rationalize it by saying yes, she's the devil, but at least she's *our* devil."

"You have slipped some gears, you know that? I'm glad you're getting out. What are you going to do?"

"Don't know. Can't go back to Princeton. I guess I'll have to think of something else."

Ben nodded. "Well, tomorrow's another day." He looked at the child, nodding off on Pete's arm. "Why don't you take her to my cabin? You can put her in the upper bunk and stay with her tonight."

"What about you?"

"I'll suck it up. We should be tied up in San Juan by fifteen hundred tomorrow. It's only one lost night of sleep. Not my first, won't be my last."

"You twisted my arm." Pete stood and picked up the girl in his arms. She looked anxious until he murmured something to her in Russian, after which she closed her eyes and rested her head on his chest. "Lay on, Macduff," he said with a smile.

It was a quick trip to Ben's stateroom. After laying the girl on the top bunk and pulling up the retaining rail, Pete turned and drew Ben into a hug. "Thanks, brother."

"Don't mention it," Ben replied and returned the hug. He grabbed some folders off his desk and headed to the messdeck for some St. Ignatius coffee.

It was going to be a long night.

Chapter 17

Inferno

William F. Baker Airport, St. Ignatius, U.S. Virgin Islands
03:07 AST, 2 July

Marcus

It started with a low, soundless vibration, like all the previous tremors, increasing in intensity second by second. Eventually, the tremor became audible, a rumble, like a constant distant thunder moving ever closer. The rumble was then overtaken by the rattle—the ringing, clanging, and clattering of unfixed objects on shelves and tables and in closed drawers.

Unlike the previous tremors, it did not subside.

Marcus was shaken awake in the camp cot they had set up in one of the offices. He had only been asleep an hour, having fallen into the cot after he, Lincoln, and Deffler had serviced and relaunched the UAV. None of them had had any good sleep for the last couple of days and

331

pounced on any chance to shut their eyes, even if it was only for a few minutes.

He remained in the cot, desperately tired, yet too fearful to go back to sleep. His fear grew with the intensity of the tremor and when it did not go away as the others did, he knew the time had come—this was the eruption. He threw himself out of the cot, pulled on his boots, grabbed his survival bag, and loped to the door, nearly colliding with Lincoln as he hurried to the office housing the control console.

When they reached the office, Deffler turned from the panel and shouted, "Linc, get the generator turned over. Marcus, take over the controls while I man the camera!" He slid over and Marcus plopped into the right seat. "We're on automatic, orbiting the field at one mile, altitude three thousand."

Marcus scanned the instruments and oriented himself to the current operating state of the aircraft. Within ten seconds, he was comfortable enough to say, "I have the controls, orbiting at three thousand." He focused on the panel, concentrating on the instruments to avoid thinking about being inside of a building being shaken with a cacophony of rattling, with its lights flickering and dust and paint flecks falling from the ceiling.

Lincoln returned a few minutes later, towing several extension cords. "Generator's up, Chief!"

"Right, plug in the UPS right now. Then take that other cord over to the rock heads." The UPS, short for uninterruptible power supply, was a combined battery, surge protector, and current splitter that powered the UAV's ground control station and transmitter. The battery could keep it running for about fifteen minutes in the event of a power loss, long enough for a controlled landing.

As Lincoln was switching the UPS from the wall outlet to one of the extension cords, Dr. Hernandez poked her head in and said, "Keep an eye on the peak! We're reading increasing magnitude and shallow harmonic tremor!"

"On it, ma'am!" Deffler replied, swinging the camera lens toward the summit of Mt. Acadia. To Marcus, he said, "Keep her in orbit over the field for now."

"Yes, Chief," Marcus replied. About five minutes later, the vibrations and rumblings tapered off. *Thank God! It's ending. It's not the big one,* he thought.

He was about to exhale in a sigh of relief when Deffler suddenly sat erect beside him. "Whoa!"

Marcus glanced over to the camera screen to see an expanding, white-hot ball where the peak of Mount Acadia used to be. Then the floor seemed to jump up several inches, followed a few seconds later by the loudest bang he had ever heard, accompanied by a jolt that shook the building to its foundation. It felt like a giant hand had just slapped the building, shattered the windows, and knocked out the lights. The air was thick with dust and as they all began coughing, Deffler shouted, "Goggles and respirators, now!" After they had all donned the protective equipment from their bags, Deffler continued. "Linc! Go next door and tell Doc Hernandez that Acadia just blew its top and we have the explosion and vent on visual!"

"Yes, Chief!" Lincoln shouted, then scurried off.

Marcus glanced over at the camera screen and his mind briefly struggled to comprehend what he was seeing. The ball of fire was gone, replaced by a fountain of smoke interlaced with red, yellow, and white glowing clouds roaring skyward. As Marcus watched, the rapidly rising and expanding cloud was streaked and strobed with flashes of volcanic lightning. The explosions from the mountain were almost continuous now, although only a small fraction of the intensity of the first one that knocked out their lights.

The lead USGS man came into the room and said, "This is definitely the first act. We've got harmonic tremor out the yin-yang. I'd like to beat feet right now, but the last ferry won't be here for another three and a half hours." He glanced grimly in the direction of the mountain. "If ever."

"We are ready to run," Deffler replied. "But we'll stay in the air as long as we can. Is there anything you need to see?"

"Just monitor the summit vent for now. If you see any changes, let us know. The big danger would be another vent popping off. If we see anything on the sensors, we may need you to get over quick for a look."

"We'll keep her orbiting over the field," Deffler replied. "We can see the top well enough from here."

"OK!" the man said on his way out the door.

As Marcus listened to the conversation, he felt a looming sense of dread building up inside, a dark, unreasoning monster, repeatedly broadcasting a single command to his brain: RUN! He focused on the instruments, hoping his uncle would order him to take the aircraft off automatic so he could concentrate on doing something, anything, but just sitting here thinking about the current situation.

Nearly everyone on the island had been evacuated by earlier ferry runs. The last ferry, one of those run by a makeshift crew of coastguardsmen, would arrive in three and a half hours, as the USGS man noted. Besides the three members of Marcus's team and the five volcanologists, they were down to about half a dozen civilians, two policemen, and Isabelle. When they got the radio call from the ferry indicating they were heading in, the UAV team would recall the aircraft, hurriedly remove the expensive camera and electronic boxes, and leave the airframe and catapult behind—there was no time to disassemble and pack them and no time to transport or load them, even if there was room on the ferry to carry them. Marcus thought it was a sad end for a fine bird, but the orders had come from Admiral Pennington personally—the materiel was expendable, and the crew was to take no risks recovering it.

Marcus was seriously worried that Isabelle was still on the island and torn between anger over her decision and admiration for her courage to remain behind. He was angrier still at Adelaide, who refused a slot on an earlier ferry out of a sense of what Isabelle referred to as "noblesse oblige." Isabelle could hardly run while her grandmother remained behind, so she volunteered to be the administrator staying to the last, allowing Thomas to depart with his family. The good news was they would be together for the long ferry trip to Charlotte Amalie, but Marcus would have gladly traded all their time together for the knowledge that she was safely out of harm's way.

His uncle seemed to read his mind again. "Get a good instrument scan going. In a couple of minutes, we'll take her off automatic so you can get the feel for the controls. I don't want you playing catch-up when we have to run something down."

"Yes, Chief," Marcus said, breaking free of his gloomy fixation. He suddenly realized he had been staring unseeingly at the airspeed indicator for quite a long time. *Snap out of it, boy! You have a job to do here!* He shook himself, then began the methodical process of using the instruments to build and maintain in his mind's eye a picture of what the aircraft he couldn't see was actually doing. As his eyes began the scan, he concentrated on the drill, *Attitude; Altitude; Vertical Speed; Attitude; Airspeed; Engine Tachometer; Attitude; Heading-Turn Indicator; Attitude...*

USCG Cutter Kauai, underway in the Caribbean Sea, thirty-one nautical miles

**west-southwest of Montserrat
03:48 AST, 2 July**

Haley

Haley was still tossing and turning when the phone above her bed rang. She picked it up before the second ring. "Captain."

"Ma'am, this is the O.O.D.," Lee's voice said. "Could you come to the bridge, please?"

"Of course," Haley said as she swung her legs over the side of her bunk. "What's going on?"

"We just received a report on chat that the volcano on St. Ignatius is erupting, ma'am. I don't know what to do."

"Start heading that way and get Main Control to put the third engine on line. I'll be up in a minute."

"Aye, aye, ma'am!"

Haley clicked the flash switch and started to dial Ben's number, then remembered he had given up his stateroom to Pete. She clicked flash again and dialed the messdeck.

"Messdeck, XO."

"Ben, head to the bridge. St. Ignatius is erupting. I'll meet you up there."

"On the way, boss!"

Haley pulled on her pants and was doing the same with her boots when the sound of a diesel engine starter drifted up from below. As she stepped out of her cabin, she almost collided with Pete stepping out of Ben's stateroom and froze in shock.

It was her first sight of Pete since they parted before the mission. Her relief upon learning he was safe and alive earlier in the evening had been more intense than she had thought possible. In the aftermath of the encounter with the French frigate, her mind was free to think about him, but she had to keep her distance, for appearances' sake. When she retired to her cabin shortly afterward, sleep would not come, knowing he was mere feet away in the next room. She wanted to hold him, be with him, just talk with him. But she was the captain, and captains couldn't indulge themselves on their own ship.

Pete, clearly affected as well, broke the silence. "Captain, what's happening?"

Haley swallowed and replied, "Looks like St. Ignatius is erupting. We may have to divert in case we're needed."

Pete reflexively glanced back into the stateroom at the girl sleeping in the top bunk, then turned back. "I understand. Is there anything I can do?"

"Just keep your side of things under control." She reached out and squeezed his arm. It was little enough but would have to do for now. "We'll talk later."

"Yes." He nodded, then said, "Good luck."

"You, too. Now, please excuse me." She continued past him toward the bridge as he stepped back into Ben's room, finally remembering to breathe. Haley rounded the corner and bounded up the ladder to the bridge, finding Ben already seated at the FC3. She immediately waved off the call to attention and stepped alongside Ben as he stood from the console. "What's the situation?"

"The evacuation is nearly complete. Nine civilians, the five USGS folks, including Dr. Hernandez, and our three UAV guys are all that's left. The last ferry should arrive in about three hours. It's one of the old ones that was condemned before we took it over."

"How soon can we get there at max speed?"

"Four hours and twenty minutes, but ma'am..." Ben said with a look of concern.

"But what, XO?"

Ben nodded toward the starboard bridge door and then turned and walked in that direction, with Haley close behind. Once they were out of earshot on the starboard bridge wing, Ben turned and said, "We're at forty-five percent fuel right now, Captain. If we haul ass for four-plus hours, we'll be down to around ten percent when we get there. We couldn't make it to San Juan, much less Mayagüez, with that residual. It would be a nail-biter to make it to St. Thomas. And if they and St. Croix get clobbered like everyone's saying, we might be out of options."

It was that same ice ball in the gut feeling again. They had to run at flank speed to the island if they were to be there in time to do any good. But if they did that and the harbors at St. Croix and St. Thomas were closed by ashfall, it might be days before they could get in for fuel, and by that time, they would run short of water as well. She put her head down and squeezed her eyes shut. *If they aren't wiped out by tsunamis, that is. What then? And that's* after *the eruption. What happens if that thing goes nuclear, as Dr. Hernandez feared?*

It was the search and rescue dilemma. Should she risk sixteen lives, *nineteen*, she corrected herself, to save seventeen? Haley looked up at Ben and did what she swore she would never do. "Ben, you know the stakes. What would you do if you were C.O.?"

Ben stared back for a few seconds, then said, "Captain, you have my support, whatever you decide. But if I had to make the call, I'd go. Maybe they won't need us, but I just couldn't leave those people with their only hope of not getting burned alive dependent on a rickety old ferry."

"Oh, Ben. Here I was, hoping you weren't as crazy as me. We're going in."

Ben smiled sadly in return. "Yee-ha."

She smiled back, reached out, and squeezed his arm. "Thank you, XO. Now I need to figure out how to break it to the crew. God help us!"

Ben nodded sympathetically as they stepped toward the door. "We'll need His undivided attention, that's for sure."

Peter

Peter's heart was still racing from the encounter in the passageway. He had been dozing in the chair by Ben's desk—he did not want to lie down in a bunk in the same room with a child just rescued from sexual slavery—when the sound of the diesel engine being started awakened him. Peter knew from his previous trips aboard *Kauai* that a third diesel engine being started meant some sort of action requiring full speed was imminent. He had gotten up in curiosity and, after checking that Lenna was still asleep, was heading to the bridge to inquire what was going on when he blundered into Haley.

Her hair was down around her shoulders like she normally wore it when they were together. There was some urgent issue demanding her attention, otherwise, she would have taken the time to put it in the tight bun she always used when in uniform. Her hair was not only down, but uncombed and untamed, framing her face and the graceful lines of her neck. Her dark blue tee-shirt, looking black in the red light of the passageway, emphasized her well-defined chest and shoulders and the gentle curve of her bust. It was like the first time they met, at Ben and Victoria's wedding, when she wore that sexy cocktail dress that made the most out of every detail of her athletic body. The sight of her in the tight clothes and wild hair had taken his breath away.

Returning to the chair by the desk, he reminisced about that first meeting. He had learned of Haley's role in the Haiti mission from his friend and mentor Art Frankle, how she had violated orders and risked her and her crew's lives to come to recover him, his team, and two rescued kidnap victims. Impressed by the physical and moral courage inherent in this act, Peter had decided this was a Coast Guard officer he wanted to meet. He had been taken by surprise by how beautiful she was in person, even though Frankle had passed on that she was a "looker." Better still, she was intelligent, charming, funny, and both knowledgeable and understanding of who and what he was.

After a promising start, he had been both stunned and dismayed by their brush with a breakup at the beginning of the mission. It hadn't occurred to him that her feelings for him were as strong as his for her and had mistakenly been playing things cool. He was doubly grateful to Ben for his innocent gesture of a meal together, providing an opportunity for Pete and Haley to pull their nascent romance out of the crapper. Their second sojourn together allowed them to clear the air about how they felt and where they wanted to go.

He turned and scanned the pictures Ben had mounted over his desk, pictures of Victoria and him and her together. Getting them together had been the most satisfying experience of Peter's life, although their initial meeting had been completely by accident. Victoria, who looked so much like the young girl sleeping in the bunk across the room when she was that age, had been his responsibility since Julie's death. He had fulfilled that responsibility joyfully, looking after her while she blossomed into a beautiful and brilliant young woman and finally married the finest man he had ever known. Peter had envied Ben his good fortune in finding a partner of such mutual devotion. He had had that experience before with Julie and had believed no woman could persuade him to move on, but he was wrong—Haley Reardon was that woman.

Peter stood and checked on Lenna again—she was curled up fast asleep, a look of innocence on her freshly scrubbed face. *You poor kid. I hope they can bring you back from the hell you've been through.* He reached down and pulled the covers over her. He sat again, put his head down on his arms folded on top of the desk, and drifted to sleep.

******

"Attention all hands, this is the Captain."

Peter jolted awake to the sound of Haley's voice coming through the overhead speakers. He glanced at the clock, 06:00, sat back in the chair, and rubbed his eyes as Haley's speech continued.

"A little before oh-four-hundred, we received word that the volcano on St. Ignatius had erupted. This was not unexpected, and efforts have been underway since we departed a few days ago to evacuate everyone from the island. This has largely been accomplished, and only seventeen people, including Chief Deffler, Cadet Porter, and Petty Officer Lincoln, remain on the island. An interisland ferry manned by Coasties is en route to complete the final evacuation and should be there in about an hour. We are hauling ass to the island to stand by in case they need support and will be there in around two hours.

"This is a dangerous mission. You have been trained on the hazards the volcano poses and are probably a little anxious right now. Join the club. However, some people may need our help, including some of our own shipmates, and we will not let them down. Let's look to each other and get through this together. Thank you and good luck!"

Peter stood and stretched. Sleeping in the chair hadn't done his back any good, but he'd had worse. He was turning to check Lenna again when he was startled by a pounding on the door. He stepped over and opened it to find a wild-eyed Lamonde standing there.

"She can't do this!" he blustered. "The mission is to get us to San Juan!"

"Be quiet, you idiot!" Peter whispered fiercely before pulling him into the room.

"These guys are crazy! They're going *to* an erupting volcano?" Lamonde said in a much quieter tone. "We need to go up there and remind them who they're working for!"

Peter leaned in. "First, as I'm sure Ben mentioned to you, they were ordered to conduct our extraction from Île Oiseaux. Mission accomplished. Second, you don't really think they would abandon those people to their fate just to get your ass to San Juan earlier, do you?"

Lamonde's face clouded into a sneer. "We've got guns. We can use those to *remind* them of their duty."

Peter stepped back in astonishment. "You *are* psychotic. Even if I were inclined to overrule a rescue mission, which, by the way, I'm not, I wouldn't help *anyone* commit an act of piracy, least of all you. Now I suggest you suck it up and either pitch in or stay out of the way."

Peter was tired and still waking up from an uncomfortable sleep. If he had been at the top of his game, he would not have turned his back on Lamonde when Lenna cried out in her sleep. When he stepped over to check on her, his vision seemed to explode in stars and then went black.

Haley

Haley had returned to the command chair after completing her address to the crew and was now sitting and staring at the tactical screen on the FC3. There was nothing on radar right now, no ships and their destination was still over the horizon, fifty-five miles distant. Lee was still on watch as O.O.D. and would be until seven forty-five. Smith had the helmsman watch and Zucarro was on the FC3.

Ben had just departed to make a round of the ship, looking over what he described as the three Ms: machinery, materiel, and morale. He had a knack for the personal touch Haley wished she had. He would talk to people, joke around, give encouragement, whatever was needed to get them through the next challenge. The crew liked and respected him, but most of all, they trusted him, and through him, they trusted her.

The sun had been up for around twenty minutes, and the sky over the Caribbean was clear and azure blue almost all the way around the compass except for the northwest. Haley lifted her binoculars to her eyes. The break in the sky blue was not the white clouds one would normally expect, but a dark smudge of grayish brown. It was the ash cloud from Mount Acadia, now reaching into the stratosphere and visible even from this distance, an omen of what lay ahead.

She had lowered her binoculars and caught sight of Lamonde as he strode into the bridge, looked around briefly, and then stepped immediately toward her. *Great, this is just what I need right now.*

"Captain, I need to speak to you," he said with a firm voice.

"Yes, Mr. Tucker?" Haley said, turning toward him.

"I must insist that you turn back toward San Juan and complete your mission."

Haley sighed. "Mr. Tucker, first of all, there is only one person aboard this vessel who can insist on anything, and that's me. Second, my mission was to support you and Dr. Simmons in your expedition to Île Oiseaux. That mission is now complete. Finally, even if that mission was incomplete, search and rescue would take priority."

"You need to contact your headquarters, Captain. They will clarify that my mission takes precedence."

"No."

"What?" he asked incredulously.

"I said no. The decision is made. Now please leave the bridge."

"Captain, I don't think you realize what you are dealing with here."

"In fact, I do, Mr. Tucker. This is your last chance. Leave the bridge now or I will have you placed under arrest."

"I don't think so." Lamonde reached behind him, drew a pistol, and pointed it towards Haley's face. "Everyone, stay exactly where you are and put your hands up!" Everyone on the bridge had been staring at the escalating conversation and immediately raised their hands.

Haley briefly froze, then slowly raised her hands, her eyes fixed on the muzzle of the gun inches from her face. She instantly recognized it as a Sig Sauer nine millimeter, but at the moment, when everything but the muzzle faded into a blur, she would have sworn it was a *ninety* millimeter. Her heart was pounding, and she had to concentrate to breathe, finally saying, "Mr. Tucker, what do you think you'll accomplish with this?"

"I am restoring order to the situation," he said. He glanced briefly at Zucarro, gaping at him from her seat at the FC-3 console. "You, girl. What's the heading to San Juan?" After she sat frozen for a few seconds, he shouted, "Get me that heading or I'll blow her brains out!"

Zucarro jumped in her seat and then glanced at Haley, who nodded slowly. She turned and typed briefly at the keyboard, then turned back. "Th-Three-four-eight magnetic."

Lamonde turned back to Haley. "Give the order, Captain."

Haley blinked and then swallowed hard. "No."

Lamonde cocked the hammer of the pistol. "Do you think I'm screwing around here? Give the goddamn order!"

Haley took a deep breath, then said. "No. You can kill me, but you will not get me to hand over my ship."

Lamonde sneered and said, "We'll see about that." He glanced around at the bridge crew. "You may not give a shit about dying, but what happens when I start executing your crew." He stepped back and pointed the gun at Lee. "Let's start with her!"

Haley was opening her mouth to say "No!" when a deafening shot rang out and Lamonde fell to the floor face down. Haley looked up to see Pete standing on the other side of the bridge, his pistol held in both hands, still aiming at Lamonde. She stared open-mouthed while he stepped unsteadily toward the body, blood running down from a wound on the side of his head. Upon reaching it, he kicked the pistol away from the dead man's outstretched hand, then kneeled and flipped the body over. Pete pressed his left index finger against Lamonde's carotid artery, still aiming the gun at his head with his right hand. It was an unnecessary precaution—blood was already pooling from the head wound a few inches to the left of Lamonde's sightless eyes. Satisfied, Pete dropped his head, leaned onto his left hand, and held up his pistol by the trigger guard with his right as Ben, followed by Bondurant, thudded onto the bridge.

Ben moved quickly to Pete, grabbed the pistol, and handed it to Bondurant. He caught sight of Lamonde's pistol and picked it up, ejected the magazine, and cycled the slide to remove the chambered bullet. He then turned to Haley and asked, "Captain, are you alright?"

Haley looked up at Ben and nodded, unable to find speech. He glanced across the bridge at Lee, still gaping at the body, and said, "Bondurant, relieve Lee of the O.O.D."

"Yes, sir."

There were more footsteps from the ladder and Bryant trotted onto the bridge, carrying his EMT bag, followed by Williams. Ben glanced over and said, "Doc, see to Dr. Simmons. Don't bother with Tucker, he's dead."

"Yes, sir," Bryant replied, stepping over to and squatting beside Pete.

"Williams, take over for Zucarro."

"Yes, sir." He sat down next to Zucarro, who had her head down and face in her hands.

Ben turned back and whispered to Haley. "Captain, can you tell me what happened?"

Haley nodded, finally able to speak, and whispered back, "Lamonde pulled a pistol and tried to take over. He wanted us to take him to San Juan. He was about to kill Lee when Pete shot him." She turned to Bryant and spoke out loud. "How is he?"

"Blunt force trauma, ma'am. He's probably concussed, but I don't think it's a skull fracture," Bryant replied.

"Can you get him down to my stateroom on your own or do you need help?" Ben asked.

"Let's see, sir," Bryant asked. "Doctor, can you stand up?" Pete nodded and then slowly rose to his feet. Bryant pulled Pete's arm over his shoulder and said, "We'll be OK, sir."

"Right. Take him down. Call us when you know any-thing."

"Yes, sir." He started to turn away, but Pete stood fast and turned to look Haley in the eye.

"Thank you, Doctor," Haley murmured, trying to keep her voice steady.

Pete nodded, then turned along with Bryant and they both departed the bridge. Ben turned to follow when Lee stepped up to him. "Can I talk to you, sir?"

"Of course. First of all, are you OK?"

"Yes, sir. I mean, I really am, sir. I don't need anybody taking my watch."

Ben continued. "Shelley, you just had a loaded gun pointed at you by a murderer. It's OK to be shaken up by something like that."

"I'm not saying I'm having my best day, sir, but I can do my job." She glanced at Lamonde's body. "Besides, I'm sure there are other things John could do right now."

Ben smiled ruefully. "Yes, I suppose you're right. You sure you're going to be OK?"

"No question, sir."

"OK." He turned to Bondurant. "Belay my last order, Boats. Go find Chen and have him document the scene. We need to remove the body as soon as practicable."

"Yes, sir. I'll see to it." The big boatswain nodded and then set off.

Ben turned back to Haley and then leaned in. "Captain, I think you should go below. I can handle things here," he whispered. When she looked up at him, he continued. "Go to him. It will be OK."

Haley could barely conceal her surprise. *He knows! How?* She took a deep breath, then said, "Very well." She turned to Lee across the bridge and added, "Petty Officer Lee, I'm going below. Call me if there is any change."

"Yes, ma'am!"

Haley stood slowly and waved Ben off when he offered his hand. She hurried out of the bridge and down the ladder to the main deck. After pausing briefly at the closed door to Ben's stateroom, she continued into her cabin and shut the door. Stepping over to her sink and mirror, she was shocked to see red specks of blood, Lamonde's blood, on the side of her face. A sudden wave of nausea swept up and before she knew it, she was throwing up into the sink.

The nausea passed as quickly as it had come, and Haley rinsed the sink, then splashed water on her face to clean up. She gazed at her hands, which were still shaking, thinking, *It's shock. I have to shake it off.* Haley rubbed her hands briefly, looked in the mirror again, and satisfied she had herself under control, walked out of her cabin and knocked on Ben's stateroom door.

Bryant opened the door and, seeing it was Haley, stepped into the passageway, closing the door behind him. "Yes, ma'am?"

Haley nodded and said, "Let's have it, Bryant."

"Dr. Simmons has a contusion, which I have bandaged, and a concussion, but it isn't severe, as far as I can tell."

"What does that mean, exactly?" she asked.

"Ideally, we'd do a CT scan to be sure, but I've run a full battery of field tests. There are no signs of an internal bleed and all his neurologicals are within the normal range. He needs to rest, but otherwise, I think he'll make a full recovery."

"Good. Is he OK to talk?"

"Yes, ma'am."

"I mean, can I talk to him in private?"

"Yes, ma'am. That is, as private as it can be with that Estonian girl in the room."

"She's still in there?" Haley asked incredulously.

"Yes, ma'am. She's kind of attached to him in a post-traumatic way. I thought it would be better to just leave her be than haul her off kicking and screaming. Besides, she did the first aid that brought him to consciousness after Tucker attacked him."

Haley shook her head. "Unbelievable!"

"Yes, ma'am. Like I said, you can go on in. If you need me, I'll be on the bridge helping out."

"Thanks, Bryant."

Bryant nodded, then turned and headed for the bridge. Haley knocked, opened the door, and stepped into the stateroom. Pete was lying on the bottom bunk with a bandage around his head. He smiled and started to sit up when he caught sight of her, and Haley reached over and gently pushed him back down. She looked up to see a young, red-haired girl seated on the top bunk staring wide-eyed at her. "Who's this?" Haley asked.

"Lieutenant Haley Reardon, Miss Lenna Tamm." He looked up and said something in Russian. The girl smiled and then laid back down.

"What did you tell her?" Haley asked.

He grinned and said, "I told her you were my girlfriend and to ignore any sights or sounds for the next few minutes."

"Funny, asshole. What did you *really* tell her?"

His smile faded. "I told her you are the brave captain who came to save us."

"Oh. Feeling a little sheepish about the asshole thing all of a sudden." She reached out and took his hand. "Now, how are you?"

Pete rolled his eyes and said, "I don't know which hurts worse, my head or my pride. I can't believe after everything that's happened, I let that scumbag get the drop on me."

"Why didn't he shoot you or cut your throat or something? No offense, but I'm puzzled he left you alive."

"The shot would have been heard—you saw how quick Ben was on the scene after I dropped him. If he'd cut my throat, he would have been covered in blood. No, he needed to get near to you without tipping off his intent. He did a good job of getting me out of the way. If it hadn't been for Lenna improvising a cold compress from Ben's washcloth, I'd have been knocked out on the floor here when he shot Lee and who knows who else."

"Why did he do it?"

"Mainly because he was a coward and thought you'd gone nuts, sailing into a volcanic eruption. You haven't gone nuts, right?" Pete said, glancing at the top bunk.

"Maybe I have. I'm here with you, aren't I?"

"Touché." He glanced upward at the top bunk and then back to Haley. "I'd like to give her a heads-up on what's coming, if you don't mind."

"Right. It's going to be big, the question is how big. We'll avoid going in unless we have to. If we do, we have to worry about pyroclastic flow cooking us, ashfall capsizing us, or a steam explosion swatting us like a fly. Believe me, I thought hard about giving it a pass, but there are seventeen people left, three of them our guys."

"I get it. You *are* crazy." He grinned again. "But that's OK. I *love* crazy."

"Good to hear." She smiled and then looked away. "I better get going before people talk. By the way, I think Ben is on to us."

"I'd be surprised if he wasn't. Victoria probably figured it out at that dinner, if not before, and told him."

"I thought she was bad at reading people."

"She is. But she is hyper-observant and has an eidetic memory, basically, a human polygraph with playback. She can tell when people are experiencing emotion by changes in their body movements, micro-expressions, voice changes, *et cetera*. She just can't figure out what it means."

"Well, that's...*disturbing*."

Pete squeezed her hand. "If she were someone like Lamonde or Irving, you'd be right to be concerned. But she's not. She isn't even like you or me—the thought of using her talent against anybody is just not in her wiring. So don't worry."

"If you say so." Haley stood, leaned over, and gave him a long kiss. "I'm glad you're back. Now, it's my turn."

Pete caressed her shoulder. "I can't believe I'm the one saying this, but please be careful."

She stood, stepped over to the door, and, on her way through, smiled and said, "*Semper.*"

Chapter 18

Catastrophe

***William F. Baker Airport, St. Ignatius, U.S.
Virgin Islands
06:47 AST, 2 July***

Marcus

They had just heard from the ferry, making the call from ten miles out, thirty minutes more or less. They'd give it another ten minutes, then recall the bird, grab the electronics, and beat feet. With the tremors and explosions seeming to taper off for the first time this morning, Marcus was starting to be confident they would get out in time.

"Hey guys," the lead USGS guy said when he walked into the room. "We're getting a lot of activity in the uplift area off the northwest shore. Can you pop over there for a look?"

"Sure thing," Deffler said. After looking at the tactical screen for a few seconds, he said, "Three-one-five, Mr. Porter."

"Three-one-five, Chief," Marcus repeated back, then pushed the joystick to the right to bank the aircraft into a right turn. After the UAV had completed its slow turn, he reported, "Steady on three-one-five, Chief."

"Roger that. OK, nothing on visual right now, let's switch to IR." Deffler tapped a selector on the panel and, after a few seconds' delay, the display appeared on the screen. "Holy crap! Look at that!"

Marcus glanced over to see a large bright area on the ground stretching to the coast. The water offshore was showing the heat as well, though not as hot as on land. As they watched, the bright spot seemed to leap up and swallow the screen. Deffler hit the selector to switch back to the visible camera, and it switched just in time for them to see a gigantic explosion of black clouds laced with red and yellow. Marcus yanked the stick over, but it was too late. The screen went black, flashed twice, and then was replaced by a blue screen with a single message.

SIGNAL LOST

Marcus moved the stick and shifted the throttle, and Deffler pressed the selector for the alternate radio channel. It was useless. Instrument readings were frozen in place, and no change on the viewer. His uncle broke the silence. "Shame. She was a good bird. Alright, guys. Time to move!" They pulled off their headsets and began pulling plugs for the console when the shock waves hit.

Marcus felt like the ground jumped up and then fell two feet. A cacophony of crashes followed the jolt. "Everybody out! Out, out, out!" his uncle screamed, and they all ran through the office door and out of the building. Marcus was momentarily startled by how dark it was outside the building, both sun and sky blotted out by the ash cloud spreading high above them. He saw Dr. Hernandez and the other USGS men had already run outside, along with Lincoln. As they gathered together, the air shock wave hit, an enormous thunderclap stronger even than the one that blew out the windows earlier. Marcus's ears were ringing, and he glanced back in horror to see the building they had just occupied collapse into rubble. His uncle paused only for a second, then shouted, "Get to the cars! Dr. Hernandez, you're with us!"

They found the windows in both SUVs had been smashed. "Goggles, everybody!" his uncle shouted as they approached. When they reached the UAV team car, he said, "Linc! Get it started! Marcus, help me with the windscreen!" The front windshield was virtually opaque from cracks but held in place by the polymer coating. Marcus grabbed a rock and smashed in one side, while his uncle retrieved a towel from the back. Using the towel to grip the broken glass without shredding their hands, they peeled the windshield off and tossed it aside.

Marcus jumped into the backseat next to Dr. Hernandez as his uncle climbed into the front passenger seat. Lincoln shifted into gear and hit the accelerator, and the SUV leaped forward with a loud crunching of gravel. The other SUV with the USGS team had preceded them onto the road toward town, and Lincoln kept pace as large fragments of ash began falling around them.

Despite the darkness and degradation of visibility caused by the falling ash, the two SUVs reached the outskirts of Jamestown in ten minutes. It took another ten to thread through the wreckage from fallen buildings and power polls, but they reached the harbor to find half a dozen people huddled under a tin lean-to structure at the land end of the mole. The two SUVs skidded to a stop and Marcus jumped out, ran up to Isabelle, and swept her into a hug.

After a few seconds, she pulled back, and Marcus could see that she had been crying. "Oh, Marcus! Thank God you are alright!"

"Same here!" He looked around. "I thought there would be more here."

"Yes!" Isabelle sobbed. "Gran didn't show up—she should have been here hours ago. Neither did the Evans's. We tried calling, but the phones were out. Marcus, I'm so frightened!"

Marcus glanced over at the harbor. He couldn't see the ferry yet in the restricted visibility of the ashfall but knew it was only minutes away. He turned as Dr. Hernandez ran up. "Doctor, how long do we have before things go to hell?"

Hernandez glanced briefly toward the mountain, then turned back and shrugged. "Could be hours, could be minutes!"

Marcus turned back to Isabelle, saw the pleading look, and then shouted, "Chief! There are four civilians about half a mile from here. I'm heading out for them!"

"The HELL you are!" his uncle shouted.

"Chief, one of them is a kid!"

Deffler's face contorted in anger for a few seconds, then he shouted, "Dammit! Alright, we'll go! Linc! Hold the boat for us!"

"Yes, Chief!"

Deffler climbed into the driver's seat and Marcus gave Isabelle a quick hug, then climbed into the front passenger seat. They were just shifting into gear when the back door slammed, pulled shut by Isabelle in the back seat. "What the hell are you doing?" Deffler shouted.

"I'm responsible for the citizens here. You go, I go!" she shouted back defiantly.

"Dammit!" Deffler repeated as he stepped on the accelerator and the SUV launched forward. Fortunately, the main road toward the mountain was mainly clear, and they were able to dodge the few fallen trees without slowing too much. After a few minutes' drive, they reached the Jones house—it was still standing, despite several fires along the driveway and woods.

"Drop me here," Isabelle said. "I'll fetch Gran. The Evans's house is around that bend."

"Right," Deffler said, hitting the brakes. After Isabelle had jumped out and shut the door, Deffler set out again onto the road. As they rounded the bend, Marcus was horrified to see an enormous fire ahead where Isabelle had said the Evans's house stood.

As they pulled up, Marcus cried, "No! No, no, no!" and jumped out. "Percy! Percy!" He ran around the burning wreckage, looking for some sign, any sign the inhabitants had escaped. There was nothing. Marcus felt like his insides had just been ripped out. As he approached the SUV, he fell on his knees, put his face in his hands, and sobbed. After a few seconds, he felt his uncle's arm around his shoulders.

"I'm sorry, son. We have to go now," his uncle said quietly.

Marcus nodded, wiped his eyes, then stood and headed toward the SUV. He could only see a blur because his eyes had teared up again, felt the SUV move forward and turn back toward the Jones house. As they rounded the bend and slowed, his uncle suddenly said, "Who's that?" Marcus wiped his eyes again, expecting to see Isabelle with her grandmother. Instead, she was standing outside the front door, holding the hand of a small child.

Marcus did not wait for the SUV to stop before jumping out and running over to them. "Oh, Percy! I'm so glad to see you!" he said, lifting and hugging the child.

"Marcus, I knew you would come!" she replied.

Marcus looked at Isabelle, who said, "When their house was hit, Percy got out and ran over here."

Marcus hugged her again. "Clever girl!" He then glanced at Isabelle and asked, "Her parents?"

Isabelle looked down and shook her head.

"Oh," Marcus said. "I'm sorry. We need to roll. Where's Mrs. Jones?"

Isabelle looked up again with a desperately sad expression. "She won't come."

"*What?*"

"She says this is her home. She won't leave it."

Marcus glanced at the house, then back at Isabelle, a feeling of anger rising. "Percy, I want you to go with Izzy now and get in the car. I'll be along in a minute."

"Yes, Marcus," the little girl said as he put her down.

Marcus clenched his fists and strode into the house through the open door. He found Adelaide standing with her hands behind her back, gazing at her wedding picture. "I'm sorry, but time to go now, ma'am."

She turned and said, "No, young man. My life is here. There is nothing for me anywhere else."

"There's your granddaughter, who loves you more than anything. What about her?"

"She'll come to terms with it and move on." She turned back toward the picture. "That's my final word. Now please get her and the child to safety."

"No, ma'am. Do you know what will happen when that mountain goes? You're not just going to lie down and die—you'll be burned alive. Isabelle knows that, and I...I love her too much to have that picture in her head. So, here's the deal, ma'am. You walk out of here with me, or I'll sling your ass over my shoulder and carry you out!"

"You are an insolent bastard, aren't you?" she said with an angry expression.

"There are times and needs that transcend good manners, ma'am."

Her face softened. "Well, given the choice, I suppose I elect to preserve some dignity. Give me your arm."

"Thank you, ma'am!" Marcus said as she took hold of his outstretched arm with both hands. They hurried to the SUV, already running, and Marcus helped her into the back seat with Isabelle and Persephone. He slammed the door after climbing in, and his uncle gunned the SUV out onto the road headed for town. They had just turned on the main road when there was another giant explosion, followed by the hisses and thuds of volcanic blocks and bombs, invisible in the near darkness enclosing them. Marcus glanced upward nervously—the thin roof would be scant protection if one of those falling rocks struck the SUV.

As they pulled within sight of the harbor, there was an ominous cloud of smoke billowing up from the side of the mole. A few seconds later, Marcus caught sight of the source as the SUV stopped in front of the lean-to. "Oh My God!" he said in horror.

The source of the smoke was the ferry boat, burning and lying half-submerged on its side beside the mole.

Marcus jumped out and grabbed Lincoln, standing still, staring at the sunken boat in shock. "Linc! What happened?" Marcus asked.

Lincoln answered slowly, as if in a trance. "They had just pulled in and put over the lines when it hit. A volcanic bomb. It tore through the port side and ripped open the tanks. She went down in seconds!"

"What about the crew?" Marcus asked, his head spinning.

"One's gone, blown to pieces. The engineer is still on board, trapped inside. Dead, I hope. The other two are there," he said, pointing to two men sitting on the ground, one sobbing and the other trying to console him.

The other occupants of the SUV had climbed out and joined the others in the lean-to's shelter. Marcus gazed around, face to face, seeing the same mixture of fear and dejection. No one was talking because everyone knew what this meant. They were about to die.

Marcus turned to his uncle, and they looked into each other's eyes for a few seconds, then hugged. After a brief pause, his uncle turned to Dr. Hernandez and quietly asked, "The end, Doc. How will it come?"

She looked up at him, then looked straight ahead out in the distance toward the mountain. "The main vent at the summit is the strongest now, but the secondary vent is catching up. Soon the eruption column from the summit will be robbed of pressure and partially collapse, sending a strong pyroclastic flow through the draw, straight at the town." She put her head down. "And us."

"Shouldn't we seek shelter in the buildings? A basement or cellar?" he asked.

She shook her head. "No point."

Marcus was aghast. Nothing had prepared him for this moment. He had been in danger before, but there was always something that needed to be done, something to keep his mind off the terror of the situation. It wasn't fair. There had to be something he could do rather than just stand here and wait for it!

There was a tug at his hand, and he looked down to find Persephone looking up at him with a pleading face. "Marcus, I'm scared!"

Marcus swallowed and forced a smile, then reached down and picked her up. After she put her arms around his neck, he said, "Percy, can you help me with something? I need to keep watch, but I can't look in all directions at once. While I watch the town, could you look over my shoulder and keep an eye out for the next boat, please?"

"Sure!" she said, leaning into his shoulder. "I love you, Marcus."

Marcus's eyes welled up again, and he said, "I love you too, honey." *OK, she won't see it coming and it will be over before she knows it. That's something.* He felt a touch on his arm and looked down to see Isabelle sitting beside him. He reached out to her, and she took his hand, kissed it, and held it against her cheek. They locked eyes and Marcus silently mouthed, "I love you, Isabelle."

She nodded, crying without a sound, and also mouthed, "I love you, Marcus."

This blessed, shared moment, which seemed like it could continue without end, stopped when Persephone suddenly raised her head and said, "Oh, there it is."

Not looking away from Isabelle's eyes, Marcus said, "What's that, honey?"

"Your boat."

Marcus's eyes grew wide, and he spun around. At first, he couldn't speak, just a gasping "Huh!" Then he took a deep breath and cried out, "Chief!"

Through the darkness and brownish-gray haze of falling ash, a mixture of white and red was taking shape—USCGC *Kauai* was racing in from the sea.

USCG Cutter Kauai, underway in the Caribbean Sea, 4.1 nautical miles east-southeast of Jamestown, St. Ignatius, U.S. Virgin Islands
08:02 AST, 2 July

Haley

Haley had hoped they would have settled into a waiting posture at this point, idling a few miles off the island while awaiting the reappearance of the ferry. The mountain was obscured by a curtain of falling ash, but the loud claps and rumbles of the intermittent explosions assaulted the ears like an artillery bombardment on some past battlefield. It had become progressively darker as they approached the island and despite being over two hours since dawn, it was more like twilight.

Chat with the coordination center was intermittent at this point, apparently because of interference in the communication satellite signals from the thickening and spreading ash cloud of the eruption. The last report they had received was that the ferry *Tarpon Sun* was in radio contact with the UAV team and making its approach to the harbor.

"Motor Vessel *Tarpon Sun*, Motor Vessel *Tarpon Sun*, this is Coast Guard Cutter *Kauai*, Channel sixteen. Please respond. Over." Williams had been repeating this call for the past five minutes with no response. There was no question the vessel was in some sort of trouble. It was manned by coastguardsmen, and they would never have left the radio unattended.

"Williams, anything on radar?" Haley asked hopefully.

"Negative, Captain, just the island," Williams replied without turning from his panel.

They were already at Rescue and Assistance detail with most crew committed to the deck operation of boarding and attending to the survivors. Everyone was in combat helmets and vests for whatever protection they could provide against the larger eruption fragments and were wearing goggles to keep the ash out of their eyes. Besides Haley, only Hopkins, Williams, the helmsman Smith, and Ben remained on the bridge, and Ben would head down to lead the deck operation momentarily.

Haley bit her bottom lip. She hated having to make the decision that would risk her crew and boat, but any doubt that *Kauai* was the last hope for the people ashore was virtually gone. "Alright, we're headed in. Chief, keep up the speed as long as you dare, then stretch it a bit more."

Hopkins nodded back. "Aye, aye, Captain!"

"Williams, our asses are hanging out here. Anything that has even a whiff of being a contact, you call a crash-back."

"Yes, ma'am! Dropping to four-mile scale now," Williams replied, switching the radar display to short range and high resolution.

Haley turned to Ben. "XO, time is our enemy. You know the feel of the boat and can gauge the motion as well as we can. Handle the lines at your discretion. Don't wait for orders."

"Understood, Captain," Ben replied with a nod. "By your leave?"

Haley held out her hand, and Ben gripped it for a firm, warm handshake. Haley was investing a great deal of discretion in him, but his performance was the factor in which she had the *most* confidence under the circumstances. "Stay safe and good luck, Ben."

"Thanks, ma'am. Same here." And then he was gone.

"Picking up the harbor on infrared ma'am," Williams said. "Lots of fires around. I'm picking up a big one alongside the mole, near the shore. I don't have the ferry on radar or IR."

Haley was about to comment on the need for caution when she saw Hopkins was already pulling back the thrust levers to slow their approach. She just closed her mouth and smiled. *Hopefully, that ferry isn't sitting on the bottom in our path waiting to rip our hull open!*

"Getting a visual on the harbor now," Williams said. "Oh, holy shit! Um, excuse me, ma'am. I can see the ferry now. She's partially capsized and on fire beside the mole, close to shore. Looks like one-hundred-fifty to two hundred feet of good space for the approach."

Haley leaned forward and Hopkins stepped over to gaze at the screen. The urban landscape looked like a war zone, with many buildings collapsed and some burning. The picturesque Caribbean town was gone forever, as sad a sight as Haley had ever beheld. What was left of the ferry was largely obscured by the smoke from her fuel fires. Haley lowered her head. *No way they escaped casualties from that.*

"Captain, I intend to bring her in starboard side to, one hundred feet down from the ferry," Hopkins said, after checking the camera screen.

"I concur, Chief," Haley replied, raising her head. After Hopkins turned to stand by the thrust levers on the starboard side of the bridge, Haley turned to Williams. "Williams, send the following message by burst every thirty seconds until acknowledged: 'Ferry *Tarpon Sun* is sunk dockside Jamestown, am moving in to pick up survivors.' Got that?"

"Yes, ma'am," Williams said and typed furiously at his keyboard.

Haley turned back to the screen. There were four men in Coast Guard utilities running down the mole to serve as line handlers. A large group of people were following more slowly behind. It was impossible at this distance to identify anyone specifically. A fifth man in a Coast Guard uniform halted the group just clear of the end of the burning ferry. *Good, good! Somebody's using their head down there!*

Haley stood and walked out onto the starboard bridge wing to get a good view. Ben was walking back and forth, passing instructions and encouragement to the line handlers. Haley glanced aft to see Bondurant and Lee on the afterdeck, ready to put over the brow, the cutter's boarding ramp, as soon as she settled into position.

They were in their final approach now and Hopkins was using engines and rudder to walk *Kauai* sideways into position alongside the mole. On Ben's command, three heaving lines simultaneously arced over to the blue-clad men ashore, who quickly pulled over the mooring lines and dropped the eyes of the lines around bollards on the mole. Within a minute, *Kauai* pressed against the fenders Ben's deck crew had hung over the side, and the mooring lines were belayed to hold her in place. Ben shouted a command aft and Bondurant and Lee quickly put the brow over and tied it in place.

"Come on! Come on!" Ben shouted at the people waiting down the mole, making a beckoning gesture with his left arm. The crowd on the mole started moving, slowly at first, then picking up the pace as the thunderclap of an explosion rattled the cutter's windows. The crowd formed into a line as they approached the brow and soon the first person crossed over. Within a minute, the last of the civilian crowd was on board and moving forward along the port main deck toward the door into the messdeck.

"Stand by on the brow!" Ben shouted. "Ease all lines! On the mole! Take off the lines and get your asses on board!"

The men on the mole pulled the lines off the bollards and tossed them toward *Kauai*, then ran to the brow and scrambled on board as *Kauai* started drifting away. Ben was turning back and forth as the line handlers frantically pulled in the mooring lines. Finally, he turned and gave a thumbs-up to Haley. "All lines aboard! Ready to maneuver!"

"Cleared to maneuver, Chief!" Haley repeated to Hopkins.

"Right full rudder!" Hopkins shouted at the helmsman as she used asymmetric thrust from the motors to move sideways and pivot. When the stern was pointed out of the harbor, she commanded, "Rudder amidships," and went to back full on the motors. Once she had sea room, Hopkins used full rudder and asymmetric thrust to pivot *Kauai* one-hundred-eighty degrees and then finally went to full speed to escape.

Haley had been watching the maneuver from the bridge wing, willing it to go faster. Hopkins had just completed the turn and was bringing *Kauai* up to speed when a colossal blast from the volcano, far louder than any they experienced before, shook the ship. A few seconds later, Haley's attention was drawn skyward by a strange ripping sound, as if someone were tearing a giant bedsheet. The sound became louder until Haley caught a glimpse of a large rock, perhaps thirty feet across, an instant before it plunged into *Kauai*'s wake with a tremendous splash.

Haley stood frozen in shock. Had that rock fallen just five seconds earlier, it would have disintegrated the patrol boat.

"What was that, Captain?" Hopkins shouted from inside the bridge.

Haley turned slowly and reeled onto the bridge. "You don't want to know, Chief," she said, shaking her head. She stepped over to the command chair and was sitting down when Ben called up from the messdeck on the tactical radio net.

"Captain, all survivors are on board and being settled in. Final count is seventeen, including all the UAV team. Two of the ferry crew and two civilians were killed during the eruption, and we have four minor injuries among the civilians we are dealing with now," Ben reported.

"Well done, XO!" Haley said. "Keep me informed." After getting two clicks in acknowledgement, she turned to Williams. "New message, report 'Have cleared Jamestown harbor with seventeen survivors.' Keep repeating that until it's acknowledged."

"Yes, Captain," Williams said.

Haley nodded and turned to Hopkins. "Chief. Just confirmed by the XO, the UAV team are all aboard and unhurt."

Hopkins exhaled with relief, then said, "Captain, our fuel is critical. We're down to ten percent. I recommend we throttle back."

Haley shook her head and said, "No, we need to put some distance between ourselves and the island. I expect a pyroclastic flow anytime now."

"It will stop when it hits the sea, right?" Chief asked.

"Dr. Hernandez told us it may, but they have also been known to travel for miles over water, borne by a cushion of steam from the seawater heated to boiling."

"But we'll be OK as long as we're inside the ship, won't we?" Hopkins asked.

"Chief, the temperature inside a pyroclastic flow can top a thousand degrees Celsius. It will ignite our paint and melt the windows. By the time the fuel and ammunition explode, we'll all be roasted alive. So keep her wide open for now."

"No problem, ma'am," a wide-eyed Hopkins replied.

"Captain, I'm picking up something on radar. Moving off the island fast," Williams called out in alarm.

They crowded around the console to look at the screen. What looked like an enormous bulge was hurtling off the island, thrusting eastward along a line to the north of their position, but spreading rapidly. "That's it! That's the pyroclastic flow! Turn thirty degrees to starboard, Chief!" Haley ordered, guessing turning perpendicular to the wave front gave them the best chance of escape. As Hopkins gave the order, Haley stepped to the closed starboard bridge door and gazed aft out the window. The flow was coming into sight now—a great, roiling mass of black and gray clouds, with flashes of glowing red within, like Hell itself was boiling out of the Earth. Haley could only gape speechlessly at this vast, monstrous horror, rushing in from behind to consume them, wanting to run, yet unable to look away.

Her mind fought to keep control, to focus on a task, but there was nothing more to be done. *Kauai* was running at maximum speed, planing over the surface of the Caribbean at thirty knots, with her wake of white foam spreading out behind. Yet, the vast burning devil loomed larger and closer with each passing second. *Go, go, go, girl! It's up to you now!*

Haley was feeling the heat from the thing. *It must be psychosomatic—I can't be feeling the radiant heat through a window and steel door. Can I?* Suddenly, the approach of the cloud front seemed to slow, then stop, and finally receded behind them. *Am I seeing things? Wishful thinking?*

"Captain, we are outrunning the wave front!" Williams shouted. "Range three hundred fifty yards and increasing!"

Thank God! Haley lowered her head and took some deep breaths, then turned back to Hopkins. "Throttle back to twenty knots, Chief. I know we're short of fuel, but we've got to get out from under this ash cloud."

"Yes, ma'am," Hopkins replied.

"Williams, any acknowledgement of our messages?"

"No, Captain. Nothing's coming over the net."

Damn! "Very well. Set up an automatic message to transmit our position, course, and speed every sixty seconds. Include the following free text block, 'Thirty-five souls on board, fuel critical, request immediate assistance.'"

"Yes, ma'am," Williams replied, and then turned to typing the message. "Message is auto-generating now, ma'am."

"Very well. How far offshore are we?"

"Four point nine miles, ma'am. Whoa, what the hell..." He was cut short when *Kauai* seemed to jump up two feet and a loud "thud" came from the hull.

"Did we hit something?" Hopkins asked in alarm.

"Look at that!" Williams cried.

Haley glanced at the tactical screen to see another wave approaching from the island, only much faster than the pyroclastic flow. In one radar sweep, it had closed half the distance to *Kauai*. Haley ran to the bridge door to look aft and gasped. A solid wall of white fog was hurtling toward them from behind. "Sound Collision! Hit the deck!"

Hopkins pulled the lever on the collision alarm, and she and Haley were diving for the deck when it hit. Haley felt like she had just fallen off a building flat on her face, and her view of the bridge disappeared into a kaleidoscope of fog and shattered glass. She could not remember any particular sound, just one instant the wail of the collision alarm, and the next a continuous shrieking accompanied by a feeling like someone had shoved a knife into each of her ears. Momentarily stunned, she rolled on to her side with her back against the wall of the bridge. The fog had cleared, but she could see smoke seeping from the vents and seams of the FC3 console. *Fire!* She tried to push herself upright and then screamed in pain as a shard of glass pierced her palm, except there was no scream—no sound beyond the terrible shriek in her ears.

I have to do something, I have to do something! My ship! She was crying now, from shock and pain, her view of the wreckage of the bridge blurring. She was reaching upward for the railing above her head when she felt rather than heard the pounding of footsteps. A dark shape appeared before her and she blinked away the tears, her vision clearing to focus on a familiar face.

It was Ben.

Thank God, Ben is alright! He's saying something to me. I can't hear. I can't hear! She squeezed her eyes closed for a second, then opened them wide. Ben had stopped speaking and was looking at her with a face as grave as she had ever seen. She took a deep breath, the pain in her chest briefly overriding that from her ears, gripped his arm with her uninjured hand, and shouted, "I can't hear! Ben, take command!"

He nodded vigorously, mouthed something, then turned to speak to someone else. Ben disappeared and Bryant replaced him. Haley could feel her helmet being removed and her head laid on some sort of cloth. She was growing dizzy and closed her eyes, close to passing out from the pain, when she felt herself gently lifted and then cradled in someone's lap and arms. Haley opened her eyes to see Pete looking down at her, saying something she couldn't hear. She looked into his eyes, did her best to smile, and then the world went black.

Chapter 19

Uncertainty

45 Constellation Avenue, Middletown, Rhode Island
07:47 EDT, 2 July

Victoria

Victoria was worried, fearful even, after reading the message she had received that morning. She knew Benjamin would call her whenever _Kauai_'s operations permitted and that a lack of communication did not imply trouble. But Victoria was a genius at data science and had created bots to crawl the internet in background surveillance for any news about _Kauai_ or St. Ignatius. Several had reported back to her this morning—a volcanic eruption was underway on the island.

She was sitting in Joana and Samuel's living room, gripping Joana's hand with both of hers, watching the television coverage of the eruption. It featured a background video of the enormous gray and black clouds of ash spewing skyward from the mountain on the island, relayed from an Army Gray Eagle UAV orbiting at a distance of ten kilometers. She was ashamed to admit that she found the visage both fascinating and beautiful, like a majestic fountain of fire and smoke, traced with frequent flashes and streaks of volcanic lightning. Her guilt came from the knowledge provided by the chyrons and commentators that rescue operations were still underway. Her fear stemmed from her knowledge that if people were in harm's way, Benjamin and his crew would be there trying to help them.

Samuel was in the playroom with the children—he, more than anyone else, understood the gravity of the situation and was determined to help however he could. Victoria glanced at Joana, grateful for her presence and yet worried that she was asking too much of her friend. "Joana, I will be alright. I do not want to keep you from your family."

Joana smiled back. "I *am* with my family, Victoria, and I am exactly where I need to be right now."

The answer made Victoria's eyes well up. Unable to speak, she blinked away the tears and turned back to the screen.

It had been a wonderful vacation so far, enjoying beautiful weather in a fascinating place with her best friend in the world, not counting Benjamin. Victoria had met Joana Mendez Powell a little over a year ago, in that terrible time when she had flown to Miami to be with Benjamin after he was wounded in battle. Victoria was as fearful as she had ever been, not knowing if this man she loved so dearly would even survive, much less recover, and dreading waiting in a room crowded with strangers.

Joana had come up and introduced herself when Victoria arrived at the hospital, talked to her, and consoled her during the long wait for the result of Benjamin's surgery. Victoria knew of her before, of course, from the many stories Benjamin had shared. Joana was married to Samuel Powell, Haley's predecessor as Benjamin's commanding officer on *Kauai*, and Benjamin was effusive with praise for her charm, intelligence, humor, and beauty—she and Samuel were like family to him. By the end of that first day, Victoria could say the same about Joana.

The strength of their friendship was surprising given the fact their backgrounds could not have been more different. Victoria was the child of two Princeton professors, raised in the cloistered environment of the university and living a quiet and unsocial life because of her autism condition and the personal tragedy of her parents' and sister's deaths. Benjamin had been the first intimate friendship she had experienced.

Joana was the elder child of two "Marielitos" who, as children, had fled Cuba with their families and settled in the U.S. A highly gregarious child, she had proudly followed her father into the U.S. Navy after high school. After serving an enlistment as a Public Affairs Specialist, she left the Navy to put herself through Eastern Connecticut State University with a bachelor's degree in Computer

Graphic Arts, while living at her parents' home in Gales Ferry. It was there that she met Samuel, then completing his officer candidate training at the Coast Guard Academy with her younger brother Eduardo. They married, and she had become a work-from-home wife and mother of two children, with a successful career as an online computer graphic artist, living in Hawaii and then South Florida as Samuel continued in the Coast Guard.

Victoria was dazzled by Joana's charm and compassion for a woman she had never met before and admired and envied her ability to create beautiful art on the computer. Joana succumbed to Victoria's openness and honesty, and her intense curiosity that made whomever she was talking to feel like the most important person in the world. They had grown very close in the months following Victoria's move to Florida and the hole in her life left by Joana's move to Rhode Island had only partially and un-satisfactorily been filled by phone calls, IMs, and the occasional Skype video chats.

Samuel had taken a break from his studies at the Naval War College to spend what he called "Dad Time" with their children, Robert and Danielle, over the past few days. Joana and Victoria took full advantage, driving all over New England to visit interesting places and bask in the beautiful scenery. After a few days, it was apparent even to Victoria that Joana was missing her family and, yesterday, they decided to return. Victoria did not mind—Newport was lovely, and she was almost as fond of Samuel, Robert, and Danielle as she was of Joana.

The change from an idyllic holiday to a fearful vigil had occurred like the flipping of a light switch when Victoria read the messages on her phone this morning. She had dressed hurriedly and rushed downstairs from the guest bedroom to find Joana and her family at breakfast. Victoria was far too upset to eat anything and the cup of tea Joana had prepared for her lay untouched on the coffee table. She knew she should eat and drink something, but her insides were roiling so much she was afraid she could keep nothing down. Instead, she gazed at the readout of distance from the UAV on the television screen as it ticked down from ten to seven kilometers. The operators were apparently trying to overcome the obscuration from falling ash by moving closer to the island. None of the commentators noticed, they simply continued reciting the same meaningless trivia and *non sequitur* conclusions. She hated the way they just prattled on but understood that it was expected of them not to allow "dead air."

There had been a series of larger explosions earlier, notable by flashes in the increasingly fuzzy camera feed. Her reading of volcanology suggested these were expected, as pockets of gas in the magma were exposed by the vent. The last one was substantial, throwing off large fragments visible even with the obscuration and distance. Afterward, the flow of material appeared to increase, which Victoria knew was caused by the wider opening reducing pressure and allowing more gas to come out of solution in the magma. The metaphor Victoria had read was shaking and opening a soda bottle, although she was at a loss for why anyone would do something so foolish.

Victoria was about to comment on this to Joana when it happened. There was the beginning of an enormous upheaval of earth, immediately vanishing behind an expanding opaque white cloud. Victoria stood without thinking, Joana following, gaping as the cloud approached the camera. It struck the aircraft with a visible jolt and explosion of static on the screen, followed by a couple of brief flashes of light and dark, ending with a blue screen with a single message.

SIGNAL LOST

Samuel heard the women gasp and came running into the room with Robert on his heels. "What happened?"

"We don't know," Joana answered. "The UAV feed just quit."

Joana was wrong—Victoria knew exactly what had happened. The last explosion had triggered something, a landslide or some fracture in the Earth that had opened the magma chamber to the sea. All the water rushing in would have flashed instantly to super-heated steam on contact with the magma, creating pressures the chamber could not contain and triggering an explosion that shattered the island. The blast wave from the explosion probably snapped the wing spar of the UAV, knocking it out of the sky.

Joana was saying something, but Victoria was not paying attention, her mind locked on calculating the force of the blast from what she had just seen. Based on the distance shown on the UAV readout at the beginning of the explosion and the time it took for the blast wave to reach the aircraft, she calculated the force of the explosion was between ten and twenty million tons of TNT. She had read classified reports on nuclear weapons tests, and knew if *Kauai* had been within three miles of the island at the time of the explosion, she would have been obliterated by the blast wave. With the calculations resolved and that thought now firmly in her mind, Victoria fainted.

******

Victoria's eyes fluttered open, and she found herself looking up at the ceiling of the bedroom. Momentarily disoriented, she turned to the side to see Joana sitting on the bed next to her with a sad smile on her face. "What happened?" she asked, feeling like a fool as soon as she said it.

"You fainted, honey," Joana said, putting her hand on Victoria's cheek. "Sam carried you up here."

"Oh, yes. I remember now." She squeezed her eyes shut, trying to block the memory of the televised explosion. "Where is he?"

"Sam? He's downstairs with the kids. He's got calls out to the Miami Op-Center to get some information on *Kauai* and to the Naval Hospital to see if we should bring you in."

"No. No, no, no. I do not need to go to a hospital!" The idea of being confined to a military hospital room filled her with horror.

"OK, but here's the deal. You drink some water right now and we'll negotiate from there."

"Yes, I will," Victoria said and sat up in the bed. Joana was correct, she had to see to her own health or it would just add to her difficulties. She took the proffered glass of water and drank several swallows.

A few minutes later, there was a soft knock at the door, and Samuel stepped in. "Are you OK, Victoria?" After she nodded, Samuel looked at Joana and said, "I have some news." After Joana took Victoria's hand and nodded back, Samuel continued. "I talked to Captain Mercier. She said *Kauai* was at the island. The last thing they have from her is a message fragment saying they had cleared the harbor with seventeen survivors on board. The ash cloud is apparently scrambling satellite and HF communications and there are no ships or aircraft in the area for line-of-sight radio. I'm sorry I can't bring you more, but I was lucky to get her on the phone at all. All hell is breaking loose down there."

"What's happening?" Joana asked.

"The ash is coming down heavy across the Northern Antilles and there are reports of tsunamis in the Virgin Islands and Puerto Rico. I'm sorry, Victoria, I know how this must sound."

Victoria felt remarkably calm under the circumstances. The fact *Kauai* was not in the harbor at the time of the explosion gave her some hope. "I will be alright, Samuel. Thank you for checking. I am relieved they have cleared the island, at least. And the ash cloud explains why they are out of contact."

"Good girl. Ben and his crew are the best there is. And *Kauai* will see them through." He forced a smile. "If you'll excuse me, I need to get back to the kids."

"Yes, of course. Thank you again, Samuel." After he left, Victoria looked up at Joana. "You should go as well, Joana. I will be alright."

"Not a chance in hell, girl. We'll sit and talk this one through, just like last time. Remember?"

"Yes, I do." *The circumstances were different that time*, Victoria thought.

USCG Cutter Kauai, underway in the Caribbean Sea, position uncertain. 11:37 AST, 2 July

Ben

Ben contemptuously tossed the dividers onto the nautical chart lying across the chart table in the rear of the bridge. The best that he could estimate, based on dead reckoning, was that they were about twenty-two miles south of St. Ignatius. That is, they were that far from where St. Ignatius used to be.

According to Dr. Hernandez, it was highly likely that the last blast was a phreatomagmatic explosion that reduced the island to a caldera, with little or nothing remaining above the surface. Ben walked over and glanced out of the starboard door aft of the ship. The window in the door was gone, shattered by the blast wave along with all the other windows of the bridge. From the west around north to northeast, the horizon was dark, like an approaching squall. They had emerged from the ashfall about half an hour ago, still doing twenty knots. Ben hated burning fuel like that, but they had to get clear—with their fuel nearly gone, so was their margin of stability, and any additional top weight from accumulated ash was dangerous.

Once satisfied they were clear, Ben ordered a step down to one diesel generator and bare steerageway. He set everyone to work who had the appropriate protective gear pushing the ash overboard. About fifteen inches had built up during their time under the cloud.

He turned again and looked across the bridge. Lee had the O.O.D., quietly and methodically scanning the horizon with her binoculars. Pickins was on the helm and Farnell, one of the crewmen from the sunken ferry, was standing lookout on the flying bridge. Ben stepped over to the open rear access panel of the FC3, where Bunting was probing with a flashlight and screwdriver. "What do you think, Bunting? Any hope?" Ben asked.

Bunting pulled out and sat back. "No, sir. We've got a few replacement boards down in stores, but everything in here needs a complete rebuild."

Ben was disappointed, but not surprised. From what he could see through the open panel, the insides were a charred mess. The blast had shaken loose several connections among the modules that controlled everything from radios and radars to computers and displays. That and the intrusion of ash created short circuits and an electrical fire that consumed the delicate electronic components before Ben's rescue party could put it out. Even if its innards had not been trashed by fire, every screen on the panel had been cracked by the shock wave. The FC3 was now about two hundred pounds of smashed and melted junk and, electronically, *Kauai* was deaf, dumb, and blind.

Ben patted him on the shoulder. "About what I figured. Thanks, Bunting. Now head down and get some chow."

"Yes, sir," Bunting said, then stood and gathered his tools.

Ben turned to see Drake and Bondurant coming into the bridge and turned to meet them.

"Cleanups are complete, sir," Bondurant said. "I've been over every inch. We could use a good wash-down, but anything loose is gone."

"Good job! Thank everyone who took part for me, please. I know it was a dirty job."

"Will do, sir."

"Now, I want you to head down and breakout and light off the EPIRB," Ben said. The EPIRB, short for Emergency

Position-Indicating Radiobeacon, was a battery-powered transmitter that sent distress data readable by a constellation of sixty-five search and rescue satellites spread between low to geostationary orbits. It was the last resort in terms of distress, but between their fuel state and Bunting's grim report, they were down to the last measures.

"Yes, sir. I'm on it," the big boatswain said, then turned and made his way aft.

"Your turn, COB," Ben said.

"We're down to the feed tanks, Captain. We'll need to secure number two in about ninety minutes or risk damaging the injectors. I've got the boys clearing the intake plenums of ash and replacing the air filters on one and three. We'll do the same with number two once it's shut down."

Captain. My dream come true! Ben thought bitterly. Out loud, he said, "I appreciate your optimism."

"You'll get us hooked up with a handy medium endurance cutter and then we'll be in fat city," Drake said with a smile, then scanned the bridge. "Gonna be a big job in the yards."

"Yep. That's pretty far down on my list right now. I'd better head down to deal with the personnel overflow situation," Ben said as he started to step away.

"No, you don't," Drake said, gently grasping and holding his arm. "Fritz Deffler and I will herd those cats. You need to keep the big picture. We'll let you know if there's anything that requires your attention."

Ben almost sighed with relief. He had been dreading the task of explaining to a dozen civilians what being in a survival situation meant. Water was the critical factor. It was going to get unpleasantly hot on a July day in the Caribbean. When the last generator is shut down in an hour or so, they would only have the batteries. They wouldn't last more than a day, even if he shut down the air conditioning at night. Ben shuddered to think what could happen if help did not arrive soon after that. "Thanks, COB. That takes a huge load off."

"Yes, sir."

They both turned as Chen came up the ladder. "XO, Doc sent me. The captain's recovered consciousness."

"On the way," Ben said, then turned. "Lee, I'll be on the headset if you need me."

"Yes, sir. Good luck, sir!"

It was a quick trip down to Haley's cabin, and Bryant was standing outside. "Doc, how is she?" Ben asked.

"Pretty rough, sir," Bryant replied. "She's in a lot of pain from the ruptured eardrums and she has severe tinnitus. I stitched up and bandaged the laceration on her left hand. With her hearing gone, I've been talking to her through her tablet."

"What do you think?"

Bryant shrugged. "I don't know, sir. I've dealt with blast injuries before, but this is new to me. Sorry, I just don't know what to say."

"That's alright. We're all figuring it out."

"Yes, sir. If you'll excuse me, I have to continue rounds. Doc Simmons is in there with her. He knows what to do."

"Thanks, Doc. I'll be on the headset if you need me."

"Yes, sir," Bryant said, then walked off.

Ben knocked on the door, then opened it and stepped in. Haley was lying on her bunk, just wearing her dark blue tee-shirt and utility pants. Her ears were covered with taped gauze and her left hand was bandaged. When she looked up and saw Ben, she gave him a pained smile that made his heart ache and reached up with her right hand. Pete, who had been sitting in a chair beside Haley's bunk, stood when he came in, and Ben clasped Haley's hand, gave her a forced smile, and sat down. He turned to Pete and said, "Hello, Pete. How's the head?"

"Splitting. How's yours?"

"Pretty much the same." He looked across the room to see Lenna sitting in the other chair, a wary look on her face. "Shouldn't she be with the others?"

Pete shook his head. "No one speaks her language and there's a young child there. After what's happened to her, it's too risky to leave her with other children until she's been evaluated."

Ben closed his eyes and shook his head. *It never ends.* "OK, I understand we're using a tablet."

"Yes, here it is," Pete said and handed it over with a grim look. "Give it to her straight."

"I plan to." Ben turned to Haley and said, "Hello, Captain."

Haley answered loudly, "I'm glad to see you, Ben. Tell me what's happening, please."

Ben nodded, released her hand, and typed on the tablet: "Our position is about 20 miles south of St. Ignatius, doing steerageway to the southwest. We came out of the ashfall about an hour ago and I have cleared the decks. We're running on #2 only and I have to shut that down for fuel in about an hour. Hull's OK, but the bridge is a wreck and all electronics are down except the handhelds. I've activated the EPIRB."

Haley took the tablet, read it, and then said, "Good job. What's the personnel situation?"

Ben took the tablet back and wrote, "The bridge crew all have concussions, lacerations, and ruptured eardrums. Hoppy has a simple fracture of her left forearm. Doc has set and splinted it. Two civilians got banged up in the blast, but nothing serious. Everyone else is fine."

After reading the latest entry, Haley said, "I'm sorry you're stuck with this, Ben. Get Drake to help you and turn over as much as you can."

Ben nodded and started typing again. "He's already on the job. Chief Deffler is pitching in too." He looked at Haley, then continued. "You sit back and let us take care of things for you. I need you back ASAP, skipper. This C.O. gig sucks!"

Haley read the tablet, chuckled, and then stopped in obvious pain. When Ben leaned over with a worried expression, Haley managed a smile and then reached out and briefly cupped his face with her hand, then moved her hand down and squeezed his shoulder. "Thank you, Ben."

Ben nodded and stood up and said, "Pete, can I see you outside for a minute?"

"Sure."

Ben reached down, gave Haley's hand a last squeeze, and then led Pete out into the passageway. "I appreciate you staying with her, and so does everyone else. Don't worry about how it looks."

"I would only worry for her, not me, but thanks. Speaking of worried, you look like hell. Is there something I don't know about? My understanding is you light off an EPIRB and everybody comes running."

"They do if they hear the signal, which I'm not 100% sure of with this ash cloud, and if they have the resources available, which, with everyone around getting clobbered by ashfall and tsunamis, I'm really not sure of. So, yes, I'm pretty worried. No need to share that with the patient."

"Got it. Anything I can do to help?"

"You're doing it, thank you." Ben gazed at his face. "What about your mission?"

"Oh, yes, that." He reached into his pocket and pulled out the package holding the thumb drive and portable hard drive. "I liberated these from Lamonde's body. I hope you don't mind."

"Whatever," Ben said.

"Right. This thumb drive contains the information on the government officials compromised by the Chinese. That one's a keeper." Pete resealed the thumb drive in the bag and put it in his pocket. "This one," he said, holding up the portable drive. "Is the most dangerous cache of information in the world. Now, let's step outside for a minute and, if you don't mind, I'd like a second witness."

Chen happened to be passing and Ben said, "Chen, come with us, please."

"Yes, sir."

The three stepped out into the sun and heat of the main deck and Pete said, "Gentlemen, please note the time." After the other two glanced at their wristwatches, Pete said, "Now, observe, in my hand, I have a portable drive." After they both looked and nodded, he continued. "And I do this!" He pulled his arm back and threw the drive a good twenty yards into the Caribbean, where it disappeared after the splash. "I don't expect they'll ask you about it, but just in case."

Ben glanced at Chen and said, "Thank you, Chen, that's all."

"Yes, sir," the perplexed petty officer said before turning and walking away.

Ben turned to Pete. "Well played, sir. I'm proud of you."

"That means a lot to me, thank you. Now do me a favor and take it easy, will you?"

"No promises," Ben replied with a grimace.

Marcus

The elation of *Kauai*'s surprise appearance and their escape from the island had rapidly regressed into worry.

When he boarded after completing his line-handling task, he sought out Persephone, Isabelle, and her grandmother. The crew had settled them into a vacant four-man berthing area, along with Dr. Hernandez. Marcus could sense they were running for their lives by the motion and the sound of the engines, but kept it to himself, and just engaged in chit-chat.

The throttle back had lulled him into a belief that the danger had passed, and he made his excuses, gave Persephone and Isabelle each a warm hug, and then left to seek his uncle to report for duty. He found Lieutenant Wyporek on the messdeck trying to organize things and reported to him instead. They were shaking hands when the collision alarm sounded and the blast hit—Marcus had never been shut inside a trash can that got hit by a car, but guessed that is what it would feel like. Men were shouting and picking each other off the deck, and the lieutenant was frantically calling the bridge.

After a few seconds, he shouted, "Deffler, take over here! Bondurant, Doc, Bunting, and Mr. Porter, with me!" They turned and ran toward the bridge. They were approaching the bridge ladder when a woman's scream echoed down that froze the blood in his veins. Marcus hesitated for a moment, then vaulted up the ladder. The bridge was wrecked, with broken glass everywhere from the shattered windows and smoke pouring from the smashed FC3. Marcus was aghast to see bodies on the deck.

"Bunting, hit the circuit breakers and then get on that fire! Mr. Porter, take the helm, keep her heading south! Doc, triage, captain's first!" Lieutenant Wyporek shouted, then ran to the captain, lying on the deck by the starboard side.

Marcus pulled the body of the helmsman aside and then grabbed the helm tiller. They were heading one-nine-six magnetic, so it only required a slight amount of rudder to bring them to one-eight-zero, straight south. With the FC3 down, there was no digital feed of the gyro heading available, and Marcus hoped the magnets in the compass had not been knocked awry by the shock of the impact.

Bunting had already subdued the fire in the FC3 with a portable CO2 fire extinguisher when Marcus had settled on the new course. He gazed around the bridge to take stock. The bridge crew were all down and bleeding from their ears. Lieutenant Wyporek was moving from person to person, checking them out, and Marcus was surprised to see some guy in civilian clothes with a bandage on his head holding the captain.

"Are you alright, Mr. Porter?" the lieutenant said, suddenly.

"Yes, sir. Steady on one-eight-zero magnetic. The bridge crew, sir. Are they...?"

"Dead? No, just beat up. You keep the helm for now. I'll get someone to relieve you shortly."

"I can manage for as long as you need me, sir," Marcus piped up.

The lieutenant smiled sadly and said, "Thank you. Hang in there."

The next few hours were a flurry of activity. He was relieved of the helm after thirty minutes and helped settle the survivors in and distribute water. When the call came for volunteers to clear off the ash, he stepped up and grabbed one of the shovels. It was hard work. The word ash was deceptive—it was nothing like wood ash, but more like mixed-grade sand. He'd been at it for over an hour and was exhausted and dripping sweat in the heat when Petty Officer Bondurant said, "That's it for you, Mr. Porter. We've got it from here."

Marcus did as he was told, handing off the shovel to one of the ferry survivors as he headed in to report to his uncle. He found him assisting with one of the injured civilians. After he stood and turned, Marcus said, "I'm officially done outside, Chief. Is there anything I can do?"

His uncle shook his head and said, "No, you've done enough for now. Get some rest."

"Thanks. How's Chief Hopkins?"

He shook his head. "Doc has her knocked out right now. He says her arm will be OK, but he doesn't know about her ears." He smiled when he saw Marcus's expression. "Don't worry. She'll be OK. The ladies are down in forward non-rate berthing. How about you make sure they're OK."

Marcus smiled in return. "Can do. Thanks, Chief." He stepped up to Hebert, handing out water bottles from a cooler. "Chef, have you hooked up any of the survivors in the berthing areas yet?"

"Nope. Mind taking a few on your way down?

"No problem." Marcus gathered five bottles in his arms and headed down to the berthing area. Persephone and the women were delighted to see him with his gift, although the girl was not impressed by his appearance.

"Ew. Marcus, you're dirty."

"Yes, sweetie. I had to help clean all the dirt from the volcano off the ship."

Isabelle smiled and stepped over to him. Cupping his face in her hands. "Don't worry. I'll take you however I can get you, flyboy." She then gave him a kiss that rivaled the one from the park several days before. She stepped back and said, "Is there anything you can tell us? Why have we slowed down?"

"I don't know. Saving fuel would be my guess. I haven't been in the loop for a couple of hours. The boat is OK, although the bridge was wrecked by the explosion. The captain was hit and Mr. Wyporek is in temporary command. That's all I know. The lead boatswain and my uncle told me to knock off and take a break, so here I am. If you don't mind, I'd like to get off my feet."

"Of course. You sit here," Isabelle said, pointing at a spot on the floor.

After he dropped into the spot and stretched his legs out, Isabelle pulled up a chair behind him, sat, and began rubbing his shoulders. It was heaven. "You don't have to do that," he said.

"You want me to stop?"

"Heck, no!" he said, catching himself from saying "hell" in front of Persephone.

"Right then. Shut up and relax."

"Yes, ma'am."

Isabelle gave him a playful slap and then continued the massage. Dr. Hernandez was holding forth on her volcanoes while Adelaide and Persephone listened. Marcus tried to pay attention, but the fatigue of non-stop operations over the last few days was catching up with him. Between that and the release of tension from the massage, his head lolled against Isabelle's leg, and he fell fast asleep.

Chapter 20

Recovery

***USCG Cutter Kauai, underway in the
Caribbean Sea, position uncertain.
01:33 AST, 3 July***

Ben

The ship was rolling, capsizing, and he was climbing from handhold to handhold as the room turned upside down. Water was now pouring in through the cracked windows onto what had been the ceiling, swiftly filling the room and compressing the air above it. He was running out of space to breathe—there was only about two feet of air left. He had to get out, saw, and made his way to the door. The water was reaching the top of the door and now he could open it. He took a last deep breath and dived. He found the door handle, turned it, and pushed.

The door did not open.

He turned the handle again and pushed. Nothing. He looked around, set his feet against a beam for leverage, and pressed again and again and again. The ship was sink-ing, and he had to get out. He had to get out! HE HAD TO GET OUT! Sir! Sir!

Ben's eyes flew open, his heart pounding, gasping for breath.

"Sir!" It was Chen, shaking his shoulder, the light from the passageway shining in through the open door creating an eerie red image of his face.

Ben blinked twice, then sat upright in his bunk as Chen stepped back. The nightmare reprised the one he experienced in real life aboard the smuggling vessel *Miho Dujam* last year. The ship had been deliberately sabotaged by the crew before they fled and Ben had been trapped in-side the bridge when it suddenly capsized. Unlike his re-cent dream, he had escaped, barely, but it had been the most terrifying experience of his life and still haunted him as an occasional night terror.

He wiped away the sweat dripping from his forehead and looked at the clock on his desk. It read 01:34. "Yes, yes. What is it?"

"I'm sorry, sir. I came down to get you and you were calling out in your sleep."

"Came to get me for what?"

"We can hear an aircraft, sir. It sounds like an H-65."

Ben jumped out of the bunk, bent down, realized he was still wearing his boots, and then darted out his door. A few seconds later, he was pounding up the ladder and onto the bridge. Lee turned and greeted him with a smile. "Aircraft anti-collision light in sight, sir!" Ben could hear it now, the distinctive whine made by the ducted tail rotor of a Coast Guard MH-65E helicopter. Ben jogged over and grabbed one of the hand-held VHF-FM radios off the charging rack, turned it on, and moved the selector to "CH16".

"...Seven, do you read me? Cutter *Kauai*, Six-five-three-seven, do you read? Over."

Ben took a deep breath and pressed the transmit button. "Six-five-three-seven, Cutter *Kauai*, read you loud and clear! Over."

"*Kauai*, Three-seven, have you the same. What is your situation? Over."

"Three-seven, *Kauai*. We are out of fuel. Hull is intact, but electronics are all down, one hundred percent. I'm talking on a hand-held here. We have thirty-five souls on board. Ten are injured and require medical attention. We need fuel, water, medical assistance, and an escort to port. Over."

"*Kauai*, Three-seven, roger, copy all. We are from Cutter *Seneca* and she is about forty miles behind us. ETA two-plus-ten. Over."

Ben lowered his head, his eyes tearing up with relief. *Thank God, Thank God!*

"*Kauai*, Three-seven, did you copy? Over."

"Three-seven, *Kauai*, roger, copy. Sorry, we're a little choked up here. Thank you, guys! Over."

"*Kauai*, Three-seven, we are going to loiter here until Mother has you in sight. While we are waiting, can you provide details on casualties we can relay? Over."

"Three-seven, *Kauai*, affirmative. Give us a few minutes to get our HST up here. Over."

"*Kauai*, Three-seven, roger, standing by. Out."

Ben turned to Chen. "Jimmy, find Doc and tell him to report to the bridge with his notes ASAP. Then pass the word, *Seneca*'s coming and will be here in two hours. Tell COB to rig for refueling."

"Yes, sir!" Chen responded, then turned and bounded toward the ladder.

Ben wiped his eyes, then stepped over to Lee and smiled. "So, Petty Officer Lee. How are things going?"

Lee grinned back. "Oh, you know, sir. Same shit, different day!"

45 Constellation Avenue, Middletown, Rhode Island
02:03 EDT, 3 July

Victoria

Victoria was sleeping fitfully, having succumbed, finally, to exhaustion an hour previously. She was startled awake by a knock on the bedroom door. "Yes?" she said groggily.

The door opened and Joana and Sam were standing there. Victoria's eyes widened, and she sat up abruptly. "Captain Mercier is on the phone, Victoria," Joana said. "She wants to talk to you."

Victoria did not respond, just held out her hand. Joana stepped in, sat next to her on the bed, and put her arm around her shoulders. Victoria's hand was shaking when she took the proffered cell phone from Samuel and put it to her ear. "Hello?"

"Mrs. Wyporek? This is Jane Mercier."

"Yes, Captain?" Victoria said, her voice quavering.

"I have wonderful news! Ben is alive and well. The helicopter from the cutter we assigned to search for *Kauai* has found her intact. This is absolutely official. The pilot talked to Ben personally."

"Ahhh," Victoria could scarcely breathe. She swallowed and said, "Thank you, Captain. What about the rest of the crew? Can you tell me anything?"

"Yes. Captain Reardon was injured, and Ben is in temporary command. Chief Hopkins, Petty Officer Williams, and Seaman Smith were also injured. None of the injuries are life-threatening."

"That is wonderful news, Captain. I know you are very busy and I deeply appreciate you taking the time to call me."

"Not at all. I'm happy to be able to pass on some good news for a change. Now, if you'll excuse me, I need to get back to it."

"Yes, of course. Thank you, Captain. Goodbye." Victoria handed the phone back to Samuel, then turned to hug Joana. "Benjamin is alive and well. He is alive and, and..." Her voice broke at that point and she could only sob quietly, her face buried in Joana's shoulder.

USCG Cutter Kauai, moored, Pier C, Naval Station Guantanamo Bay, Cuba
10:29 EDT, 5 July

Ben

There were advantages and disadvantages to being the "go-to" cutter for special missions. The disadvantages in terms of threats to personal and unit safety were obvious. The advantages were that when you got roughed up in a scrape or needed items that were out of the ordinary, things happened quickly.

They had barely finished securing the mooring lines and engines when the first of the trucks arrived with replacement windows for those smashed by the explosion and a new Furuno 1815 maritime radar, a temporary fix that would give them "eyes" for the trip home. Another van arrived shortly afterward, carrying Lieutenant Lena Huang, their platform manager, and Drake's "I know a guy" at the Surface Force Logistics Center in Baltimore, Maryland. She would conduct a comprehensive inspection to ensure *Kauai* was seaworthy enough to return home and compile a list of items to be completed when she entered the shipyard for permanent repairs later. It was not her first such trip in the two years she had been associated with *Kauai*.

The repair force had to wait while ambulances and vans removed their casualties for transport to the Naval Hospital. The prognosis for the bridge crew was uncertain, as Bryant had neither the equipment nor training to do a proper evaluation of the ear injuries they had sustained. Hopkins's arm injury, acquired when she was thrown into the FC3 panel after activating the collision alarm, was more straightforward, and Bryant expected her to fully recover. Deffler, Pete, and Lenna Tamm were among those traveling to the hospital, Deffler to look after Hopkins and *Kauai*'s other survivors and Pete to get the initial psychiatric evaluation and support for the young girl. Ben had no doubt he would also look in on Haley while he was there.

Ben and Bondurant had overseen the offloading of their passengers. The now-homeless survivors of St. Ignatius would be housed in unaccompanied personnel quarters until a more permanent solution could be devised. The USGS team and Dr. Hernandez had departed for the airfield across the bay at Leeward Point. They would hitch a ride back to the U.S. aboard one of the many military cargo planes shuttling in relief supplies and support personnel.

Dr. Hernandez was the hero of the hour—as bad as things were, they would have been orders of magnitude worse without her timely warning of the eruption. She had a top priority for any flight to get her to the mainland as soon as possible, then onward to the U.S. Southern Command headquarters in Doral, Florida, where her expertise would be invaluable to the St. Ignatius crisis management team established there. Her departure was a tearful one, with hugs from Ben and Drake and a large sack of her beloved beignets from Hebert.

The journey to Guantanamo Bay from their distress position south of St. Ignatius was one of almost seven hundred miles. Plodding along under escort of the medium endurance cutter *Seneca* at fifteen knots had taken two full days, but Ben preferred that to finding their way on their own without electronic navigation systems or radar. *Seneca* was nearby at Pier B, refueling and taking on relief supplies and support personnel for delivery to the U.S. Virgin Islands. *Kauai* had taken the first blow in this effort, and her fight was over. For *Seneca* and the myriad of other cutters and naval vessels gathering here, the fight was just beginning—a long and grueling struggle to help hundreds of thousands of people whose lives had been shattered by the catastrophe.

Ben was running ragged just trying to stay even, much less get ahead of the administrative avalanche that greeted him after mooring. He was functioning as both commanding and executive officer while Haley was laid up, and unlike normal times when Drake and Hopkins could help shoulder the load, Drake was tied up with the inspection and Hopkins was in the hospital. When the phone on his desk rang, his first thought was *Oh, God! Now what?* He picked up the phone and said, "XO."

"Sir, this is Seaman Pickins on the quarterdeck. There's an officer here to see you."

Of course there is! Ben sighed and said, "I'll be right there." He glanced forlornly at the pile of papers on his desk, then grabbed his cap and headed out of the room. It was a quick trip to the quarterdeck and a pleasant surprise when he saw a familiar face. "Talesha!" he called out when he caught sight of Lieutenant Junior Grade Talesha Gibson standing next to Pickins.

Gibson was one of the junior members of Captain Mercier's operations staff when she was Chief of Response at the Seventh District in Miami, before her fleeting up to Chief of Staff. Mercier had assigned then-Ensign Gibson to fill in for Ben as XO for a few weeks while he was convalescing from his injury in the Barbello operation. Her performance was superb, and Ben suggested she would make an excellent successor for him as second-in-command. "Sir!" she said, rendering a crisp salute.

Ben returned the salute and then shook her hand warmly. "Talesha, it's great to see you. What are you doing here?"

"Once again, I'm sent out into the cold, cruel world to do your job, sir," she said with a smile. "Captain Mercier thought I might be able to take some of the load off your shoulders."

"OK, two things. First, it's still Ben, and second, Thank God! Quick! Get inside before one of these other ships steals you away!"

"Right. Let me grab my bag." As they made their way to Ben's stateroom, Gibson asked, "What the hell happened to you guys?"

"What have you heard?"

"The usual Captain Mercier pep-talk: '*Kauai*'s coming into Gitmo banged-up with the CO injured, and you need to fill in as XO. Your plane leaves from Opa Locka in two hours. Make sure your ass is on it!'"

"Oh, you must be special to get one of her *nice* pep-talks," Ben quipped, drawing a hearty laugh from the other officer. "You know about St. Ignatius, right?"

"Who doesn't? Wait, you guys were involved in *that*? Holy shit!"

"Yeah. We were down doing one of our special *things*," he began. "Our cover was support for a geological survey of the volcano on St. Ignatius. Well, surprise, surprise, it turned out that damn thing was ready to erupt. We were on our way back from the primary op when the eruption started, so we diverted to the area. The last ferry they had to pick up the stragglers and our UAV team got hit by a volcanic bomb and sunk, so we had to go in.

"We got everybody off and were hauling ass when the damn thing blew. We took a helluva whang, even though we were five miles out by then. The bridge was wrecked and Haley Reardon, our new CO, Hoppy, Joe Williams, and Smitty all got clobbered."

"God! How bad?"

"Bad. They're all up at the hospital now. Doc did what he could, but they all have broken eardrums from the blast wave, something he wasn't equipped to handle. Hoppy has a broken arm too, but he was able to set that. I need to get up to the hospital and find out their status so I can report back, but I've been buried."

"That's what I'm here for. Let's do the hand-off so you can get going."

"Thank you, Talesha!"

******

Deffler met Ben at the Naval Hospital's main admitting to go over what he knew. The surgeons in attendance at the hospital were not otology specialists, so they could not make a final prognosis on whether surgery would be needed on any of the patients or even if their injuries would be medically disqualifying for further service.

Ben met with the lead physician to see when a specialist could be brought in and was appalled to get a shrug in return. He was told a hospital ship was due in a week and that the staff would likely include the required specialists. Ben pressed to see if *Kauai*'s casualties could be evacuated by air and got a definitive no. Even within a pressurized aircraft, the changes in cabin pressure would cause extreme pain and possible further damage.

Ben was furious after the meeting and had to take a few minutes to calm down before he met with Haley. When he went to her room, he was not surprised to find Pete there as well. "Hello, Skipper! Any better?"

"A little," Haley answered, still too loudly for Ben's peace of mind. "The tinnitus is still pretty bad, but I can make out some things now."

"Good. If you're up to it, I think you should come back with us in a couple of days. They can't fly you guys out and it could be weeks until they can ship you out. I think this place is about to become a zoo and I don't want to leave you behind."

"I'm one hundred percent for that, but I doubt the Navy guys will agree."

"We'll see about that. I know a guy with two stars in Miami, who knows a guy with four stars in Doral, who just happens to be the big boss down here."

Haley smiled and said, "You are quite an operator, aren't you?"

"I learned from the best."

"Nice. Now tell me about the boat."

After half an hour of briefing Haley on *Kauai*'s status, Ben excused himself and stepped out of the room with Pete. "What do you think, Pete?" Ben asked.

"We'll hope for the best, but ears are tricky. I've seen guys deaf as a post with blast injury who were completely normal in a month and others with less immediate damage who never got better."

"Yes, I see," Ben said, thoroughly depressed now. "Oh, I meant to ask. What happened with Lenna?"

"I was able to pass the torch to people who know what they're doing, I'm happy to say. And the DIA is going to see that she sticks around as a material witness for whatever legal action follows in the Kompromat case."

"Finally, some good news."

"Yes, it is." He reached out to lay a hand on Ben's shoulder. "Try not to let it get to you. Things will work out for the best. In any case, you did real good, brother. Always remember that."

Ben nodded. "Thanks, mate."

3532 Slidergate Drive, Rockledge, Florida 20:28 EDT, 5 July

Victoria

Victoria was glad to be home, as wonderful as the visit with Joana and her family had been. Her apartment in Maryland when she was working for the DIA had been functional, a place in which she ate, washed, and slept. The house on Slidergate was the first time she had made an emotional investment in a home, and she was surprised to find that even with the heat of the Florida summer and the lack of companionship, she preferred to be here rather than elsewhere. There was something strangely comforting about being among her own things and those she shared with her husband. More importantly, she knew *Kauai* would reach Guantanamo Bay this morning and when Ben called her this evening, she wanted to be able to answer that call in their home.

She knew Benjamin would be terrifically busy with both Haley and Emilia injured and in the hospital, and was wondering if he just did not have the time or access to a suitable telephone when her cellphone rang. She checked the calling number—it began with 011-, an area code with which she was unfamiliar, undoubtedly foreign. One of Victoria's phobias was ending up on a call with some stranger. She had enormous difficulty shutting people down and so almost always let incoming calls from numbers not known to her roll to voicemail. It was not Benjamin's number, but he was at Guantanamo and probably had no cell service. She took a chance it was him and answered the phone. "Hello?"

"Hello, Victoria. How was your day?"

It was his voice, loud, clear, and healthy, giving the greeting he knew she treasured. Her voice caught at first with the release of emotion. "Hello, Benjamin. I am so...Hearing your voice...Oh, what is wrong with me?"

"Nothing. There can be absolutely nothing wrong with you," he responded quickly. "I can't seem to find the right words, either. Just hearing your voice again has my brain in a spin. I presume you have seen the news on St. Ignatius. What did they tell you?"

Victoria took a deep breath and steadied herself. Benjamin's question had focused her mind, and she said, "Samuel called Captain Mercier shortly after the explosion. She revealed you had been at the island and that they had received a partial message that you sailed, but nothing more. She called us when the helicopter found you to let us know you were alright, but that Haley, Emilia, Joseph, and Phillip were injured."

"Oh, Victoria, I'm so sorry you had to find out that way. I would have given anything to call or at least pass a message to you. But between the ash cloud and damage to the bridge, we couldn't talk to anyone."

"Please do not worry about that, Benjamin. I understand completely. I need to be sure—are you alright?"

"Not a scratch this time, although I'm feeling guilty about the others."

"Benjamin, I know that is how you process things, but you do know you are not to blame, correct?"

"Yes, I know."

"Good. I share your worries about them. Can you tell me anything about their injuries?"

The conversation went on for almost an hour, Benjamin sharing details of the mission that he could and Victoria the experiences on her visit with Joana. She caressed the frame of his picture while he talked, imagining his smile and the sparkle of his eyes.

"So, if everything goes according to plan, we should be able to depart the day after tomorrow," Benjamin said. "Then a day and a half and we'll be home."

"That will be wonderful! I cannot wait to see you again!"

"Same here, my love. Well, I am on my last legs here. Can I get a phone date with you for tomorrow evening? One nice thing about being the skipper is I have some control over my schedule!"

"Of course! I will wait for your call. Please thank Talesha for me. I appreciate what she has done to help you."

"Will do. Goodbye, Victoria, I love you.

"I love you, Benjamin. Sleep well."

USCG Cutter Kauai, moored, Pier C, Naval Station Guantanamo Bay, Cuba
11:32 EDT, 7 July

Marcus

It was Marcus's first dockside farewell. His orders were to return to *Kauai*, supplementing her crew that had a quarter of their number disabled by injury. Isabelle, Persephone, and Adelaide were remaining at the Navy Lodge on the Naval Station. Not that there were not opportunities for them to fly out on one of the many military and contracted cargo planes returning to the U.S. after unloading. There was simply no place for them to go. Eventually, arrangements would be made for the hundreds of people displaced on St. Ignatius and thousands of people in the rest of the Virgin Islands, but officialdom had not yet caught up to the scope of the tragedy.

The night before, Lieutenant Gibson had cut him loose early, giving him much the same advice as his uncle had before his dinner with Isabelle and her grandmother. Marcus had broken out the credit card his father had given him for just such emergencies and used it to treat Persephone and the two women to dinner at the Windjammer Club and a couple of lines of bowling at the Marblehead Center across the road. Marcus was a lousy bowler, and the others were hopeless, but for that brief time, the world was forgotten, and even Adelaide found herself unable to help laughing at the ensuing antics.

The time had come for him to board *Kauai,* and Marcus was beset by guilt at leaving them behind. He shared this with Isabelle, who responded, much to his surprise, in a half-serious, half-bemused way. "Look, flyboy, we're no longer damsels in distress here. I've been on my own for quite a while, and Gran used to run her own company. We can look after ourselves and Percy. You need to focus on getting you and your crew home safe."

Reality was setting in, not like a bucket of ice water, but more like that first chill breeze off Lake Huron at the end of Labor Day weekend that hinted at the winter to come. The moment of desperation had passed, and Isabelle was gently re-establishing some boundaries. Marcus understood, but it hurt.

Persephone was crying and sniffling quietly. Marcus picked her up and held her gently with her head on his shoulder for a minute. He then held her out to look her in the face. "Percy, I need you to help take care of Izzy and Mrs. Jones for me. Can you do that?" After she nodded, he continued. "Good girl. Remember, we have a date in twelve years."

"I'll remember, Marcus," she said, giving him one last hug.

Adelaide surprised him by pulling him into a hug and kissing his cheek when he offered her his hand. "You are a fine young man. I will miss you." It was probably the last thing he expected her to say, given how rudely he had convinced her to leave her home.

"Thank you, ma'am. Please take care."

Adelaide led Persephone off down the dock, and despite the bustling going on around them, it was like he and Isabelle were the only people in the world. "Please call me when you know anything," he said. "Or if you just want to talk."

She nodded, and Marcus could see she was tearing up. She stepped up and embraced him in a tender, lingering hug, leaning her head on his neck and shoulder. As the embrace went on, he could feel her shuddering, almost imperceptibly—she was crying. Finally, she wiped her eyes and cleared her throat, pulled back, and said, "Keep your nose to the grindstone. I want regular reports, especially with the flight selection panel. I don't want to have to find another nickname for you, flyboy."

"Deal," Marcus said, as they came together to share one last warm kiss. After they finished and pulled apart, Marcus looked into her eyes and said, "Goodbye, Isabelle."

Isabelle took a last deep breath and said, "Goodbye, Marcus." She slowly turned and walked down the pier until she disappeared among the crowds of workers.

Marcus watched until she was out of sight, then lowered his head. He was hurting, a lot—a crushing ache that pressed on his chest. After an uncertain amount of time, he felt a soft touch on his shoulder and turned to see his uncle smiling sadly at him.

"I'm sorry, son. It's time to get on board."

"Yup," Marcus said with a nod, turning to follow him to the brow. "Looks like you were right after all."

"I wish I weren't."

"I know." Marcus swallowed hard and managed a smile. "Hey, it could be worse. We're on our way home safe."

His uncle shook his head. "Speak for yourself, young-ster. When your mother hears about what I dragged you into, she's going to drive down to Jax to kill me."

Chapter 21

Resolution

***Executive Conference Room A, Office of the
Director of National Intelligence, McLean,
Virginia
19:48 EDT, 7 July***

Peter

Peter had been waiting for a little over half an hour for his turn to debrief the DNI. He had only left Guantanamo Bay that morning after seeing Haley safely aboard *Kauai* for her return home. They had shared a brief kiss while Ben had stood guard outside the door, as even under these extraordinary circumstances, it was important to Haley to keep the nature of their relationship from the crew. Not that they could have done much else, both of them concussed, their heads bandaged, and, in Haley's case, with ear stabilization. *What a pair we make—we literally share the pain*, he thought with a wry smile.

419

Travel was not a challenge for once, with heavy transport aircraft shuttling in almost every hour to Leeward Point Field with more support personnel and critical supplies. Peter was able to grab a troop seat on a C-17 returning to Dover Air Force Base in Delaware and rent a car there for the two-hour drive to the Liberty Crossing Intelligence Campus housing the Office of the DNI. He traveled under one of his aliases in case Irving had backup plans for him and did not reveal his true identity until checking in at the security desk. Like most intelligence operatives, he rarely questioned whether he was being paranoid, rather, was he being paranoid *enough?*

Peter ducked into his small office to change into the suit and tie he kept there, then made his way to the main office, where the DNI's swing shift administrative assistant took him to the conference room. He was no stranger to waiting on executives—DIA Director Irving was legendary for keeping field officers on hold just to show her importance—but he knew that if Kevin Welles had him cooling his heels, there was a good reason. Peter genuinely liked and admired Welles, whom he regarded as a fair man and a dedicated and skillful leader. He was deeply grateful for the cover the Director had provided for him during his conflict with Irving.

The door opened and Welles strode in, accompanied by his executive assistant Paul Doogan. "Pete, it's good to see you back!" Welles said with a warm smile and outstretched hand. After the two men had shaken hands with Peter, he continued. "I just got off the phone with

General Miller, the SOUTHCOM commander, and Admiral Pennington. They took a break from the Virgin Islands disaster relief effort to carve me a new asshole over the Guadeloupe operation. You can imagine my surprise when the word 'piracy' was actually used." He gestured to Peter's chair and, after they were all seated, continued, "What the hell happened down there?"

Peter leaned forward in his chair. "I'll begin by saying this mission was not what we were led to believe, at least not completely. You were told we were grabbing a defector and some data on government officials compromised by the Chinese. Nothing more, correct?"

"Yes," Welles answered warily.

"Well, it was a good deal more than that. What we had was a high-stakes play by the Director of the DIA to gather a trove of Kompromat information under cover of a counterintelligence operation. When I met the defector, he had two data drives, one with the counter-intel we expected and the other a dump of Laurent's entire blackmail database. I have to assume whoever held that data would have tremendous power over the U.S. government and probably several others."

"My God! It's Hoover all over again!"

"Exactly, sir. I played along until we met up with Irving's man Lamonde during the exfil. As soon as he had the drives in hand, he murdered the defector. He would have rung me up too if *Kauai*'s XO hadn't threatened to burn him if I didn't show up alive and well. Their plan might have worked if that volcano had not blown up.

Kauai's captain diverted to assist, and Lamonde was not having that. He tried to get me to help him take over the boat. I told him where to shove it and he gave me this for my trouble." He pointed at the bandage on his head. "Fortunately, I came to in time to shoot the son-of-a-bitch before he started murdering Coasties."

"Shit," Welles said. "What happened to the drives?"

Peter pulled a thumb drive out of his pocket. "I have the Chinese Kompromat here. Alas, the hard drive with the big cache was lost overboard in the Caribbean Sea."

"Where?" Doogan broke his silence.

"About twenty yards away from wherever *Kauai* was about noon on the 2nd."

"Why twenty yards?" Doogan asked.

"Because, with a severe concussion, I couldn't throw it twenty-five yards," Peter answered with a determined look.

"Best that one was 'lost', however it came about," Welles said, taking the thumb drive and handing it to Doogan. "Get the full set into the database with copies for yourself and me. Do an extract of the Americans on here and send it to the NCSC Director for action."

"Yes, sir," Doogan replied. He stood and left the room.

After the door closed, Peter asked, "What happens now, sir?"

"I'll have a look at the files on the thumb drive and pass along the relevant ones to my counterparts among the allies. That assumes *they* aren't implicated, of course, in which case I'll have to figure out something else. It may be enough for the French to go after Laurent and close down his operation, but no promises.

"The sticky problem is the DIA. Your XO buddy on *Kauai* reported the incident with Lamonde up his chain. He has kept it quiet otherwise, but this one is not going away. Miller and Pennington have had their fill of Irving after the past year, and this was the final straw. They promised they will go public with charges of suborning murder and piracy if she isn't removed, regardless of the blowback on themselves, and I believe them. The President despises her as well, but politics is politics and he had given up hope of *not* appointing her to succeed me. I'm sure he'll jump at the chance to persuade her to accept an honorable retirement and follow-on career as a cable news national security consultant instead of an ugly, very public dismissal and a court-martial.

"Now, how about you? I guess you'll be heading back home to DIA soon."

"No, sir," Peter said, shaking his head. "I'm done."

"*What?*"

"I came in to fight the 252s, sir. That work is done. Even if the next director isn't a power-mad creep, there's nothing left but dirty jobs like this one. I'm out."

"We can't afford to lose people like you. What would it take to keep you in the fold?"

Peter sat back and appeared to ponder the question for a few seconds. He had been thinking about it throughout the downtime he had aboard *Kauai* after the explosion. "I would consider staying on if it meant joining a task force that goes after the human traffickers and their clients."

"You know there's no appetite for that. I could never sell it on the Hill or in the White House. Too many well-connected people are involved at various levels. Hell, even the media knows better than to touch this stuff and comes down hard on anyone who does."

"Point out that the Chinese almost turned D.C. into a molehill using one of these bastards. It's become a national security issue. Tell them our focus will be on taking out the high-threat traffickers and we'll strive to keep 'collateral damage' to a minimum."

Welles smiled. "I may be able to work with that, but I need to come in with a plan. Who will lead it? You?"

"Hell no. I'm an idea man, not a cat-herder. I was thinking of Art Frankle. You know him?"

"I know of him. He led the Haiti operation, right?"

"Correct. He's an outstanding leader who's very like-minded about this stuff and getting too long in the tooth to stay in the field. I'm sure he'll take it if it's a serious offer. As for the rest, we'll want to keep it lean so it stays off the radar. I see this as principally a digital 'connecting the dots' effort, with very limited, highly targeted field operations. We also need to keep it insular to avoid would-be sycophants snooping around and tipping people off to curry favor. We'll set it up outside of D.C. on a military base that doesn't house a combatant command, so we can stay on the down-low without a lot of security overhead."

"Sounds interesting. You'll need sharp people in each of those roles. Do you have some in mind?"

"I do. I'll need to talk to them first. As you pointed out, none of the big people will like this idea, so getting involved with it is unlikely to advance careers. I believe the folks I'm thinking of will be OK with that, but I need to check before I put them on the spot."

"OK. Can you get back to me with a plan within a couple of weeks?"

"Will do, sir."

Welles stood and shook Peter's hand. "Good. I hope we can work it out. I hate to think of the alternative."

"Thank you, sir."

Trident Wharf, Port Canaveral, Florida
09:23 EDT, 9 July

Victoria

Victoria and Peter were standing near the warehouse buildings, watching as *Kauai* completed her pivot to approach and moor pointing outbound, tying up at the north end of the long wharf. She ran her eye over the exterior of the small cutter, looking for evidence of the ordeal she and her crew had been through. Superficially, there was not much to note. Neither of the radar antennas on the mast was rotating, indicating they were probably damaged and unserviceable. Benjamin had mentioned that they were shipping a temporary radar for safety of navigation, but it was not visible from where they stood. By and large, the maneuver proceeded as quickly and efficiently as usual, and Victoria and Peter stepped out to meet the ship.

Peter's visit had come as a surprise so soon after their last meeting. He had phoned late in the evening on the 7th to say he would fly down from Washington the next day and ask to meet her at her home for dinner. She had pointed out that Benjamin would not arrive until the following morning, but he had said he wanted to discuss an important matter with her first.

As usual, she was delighted to see him. After some wine and a simple dinner of risotto with mushroom sauce, he had asked if she would like to come back to work for the government, this time as part of a special team working directly for the Director of National Intelligence. She would do work similar to what she had done in her former DIA job, trawling the Internet for data, then correlating it to reveal the presence and intentions of human traffickers, "connecting the dots" as Peter colloquially put it.

Victoria was intrigued by the offer. She liked her job at Vectorsonds—most of the people there were friendly, and the work was pleasant, although not as challenging or satisfying as what she had done for the DIA. Returning to that sort of work, particularly when it was focused on liberating women and children from slavery, had enormous appeal. But she clarified she would not move to Washington, D.C., or anywhere else for that matter if it meant separation from Benjamin. Peter had smiled and said that he had expected that and was prepared to set up the office either at Patrick Space Force Base or on the Cape Canaveral Space Force Station.

"And when Benjamin completes his tour of duty and is transferred elsewhere, what then?" she had asked.

"If you are still interested in working with the team, we will find a way to keep you connected, wherever you go," he had responded. "Not asking for an answer right now. I understand you need to discuss it with Ben. Also, it's sort of close hold, like the other stuff we used to do in the old days, if you'll remember."

"Of course I remember, Peter. You know I will always be discreet."

She was very excited at the prospect, even though it would mean less income, and was sure Benjamin would concur. She knew he felt strongly about the human trafficking problem and had risked his life on more than one occasion to help save victims of it.

Lee was supervising the rigging of the brow as they approached the patrol boat. "Hey, Victoria, Dr. Simmons," the young petty officer said with a wave as soon as she caught sight of them.

"Hello, Shelley," Victoria answered with a broad smile. "It is good to see you. Congratulations on your promotion! It is very well deserved."

"Thanks, Victoria."

It was a brief wait on the wharf before Benjamin emerged, followed by another young officer Victoria guessed to be Talesha Gibson. Benjamin was smiling, but his face had the familiar drawn and fatigued look it often did after a hard patrol. He dropped his bag and gathered her in his arms for a long, passionate kiss. "Hello, my love," he said afterward. Gesturing to the other officer, who was smiling at the scene, he said. "Lieutenant Talesha Gibson, may I present my wife, Victoria?"

"I'm pleased to meet you, Victoria," she said, offering Victoria her hand.

Victoria shook her hand vigorously. "As am I, Talesha. Thank you for all you have done for Benjamin."

"Believe me, it was my pleasure."

"And, may I present Dr. Peter Simmons of the DIA?" Benjamin added.

"How do you do, Lieutenant?" Peter said, shaking her hand.

"Very well, thank you. Pleased to meet you, doctor."

"Haley's in the cabin, if you care to go on in, Pete," Benjamin said.

"Thank you. If you'll excuse me, please," Peter said, then made his way inside.

"You'll need to excuse me as well," Talesha said. "I have plenty of XO-ing to do. By your leave, Captain?"

"Of course. Thanks for everything, Talesha. You know how to get hold of me if you need anything."

"Natch. See you soon, sir."

After they turned and started walking toward her car, Victoria said, "Captain! I must admit that I am quite thrilled to hear you called that, Benjamin."

He smiled sadly. "Thanks, love. It's only temporary, I hope. I don't want to get the job like this."

"I understand. How are things with Haley?"

"She seems to be improving. Right after the blast, she was totally deaf. Now, she's got some of her hearing back, but the tinnitus is still pretty bad. I'm afraid she'll need surgery."

"Oh, no! At least Peter is here for her. I hope she will recover."

"Me too. Like I said, I'd hate for her to lose her command and her career."

"Yes," Victoria said, her tone subdued.

"Hey, let's buck up. I'm so happy to see you!"

"Me too, Benjamin. I have the most marvelous news!"

"Oh? What's that?"

"You will need to wait until we get home."

"OK, as long as it doesn't get in the way of our normal post-patrol routine," he said with a grin.

"There was never any chance of that, *my captain*!"

✶ ✶ ✶ ✶ ✶ ✶

They were lying together afterward, Victoria with her head on Benjamin's chest, tracing the outline of his pectorals on the opposite side with her fingers, while he gently caressed her spine with his fingertips. "Are you sure that you are OK with this?" she asked.

"You are my wife. You have my unconditional support in whatever you want to do. I just want to make sure you're ready for the emotional cost. Not sure if I could handle it. I mean, dealing with the women in this situation tears me up. When you are talking about kids…" He shook his head.

"I know. But I already know they exist and if I do nothing, I will be condemning them to that existence for the rest of their lives. It is analogous to you and your crew putting your lives in danger to save people in distress."

"Yes," he nodded. "The cruel math of search and rescue." After a few seconds, he continued, "Promise me that if it becomes too much, you'll get out, or at least let me help you get some professional help."

She hugged him again. "I promise."

"I'm very proud of you and I love you more than anything," he said, kissing her forehead.

"My thoughts as well, dearest man. Every hour of every day."

Scotts on Fifth Restaurant, 141 5th Ave, Indialantic, Florida
21:04 EDT, 22 July

Haley

It was a night out to celebrate. It was the joy that stemmed from extreme relief, like a last-minute pardon for a death row prisoner or seeing the light of the search helicopter when you were reaching the end of your energy treading water. The relief in this case was the follow-on evaluation from her ear surgeon—the procedure had been successful, progress exceeded expectations, and full recovery was expected. He signed off on her returning to full duty immediately. He warned her she might have problems later in life, but that possibility was so distant and hypothetical that it could not dent her elation. It had taken every bit of self-control to avoid a rather conspicuous "public display of affection while in uniform" when she returned to Pete, standing by for her in the waiting room.

It was good news across the board for those who were injured. Williams and Smith had already recovered and were back on the job. Hopkins had recovered from her ear injuries, although her forearm fracture would keep her on medical leave for another two weeks. Haley had the worst of them in terms of eardrum injuries, probably because of where she was on the bridge when the blast wave struck. *Kauai* was also recovering from her damage, with Drake and Williams closely supervising the rebuild of the wrecked bridge and FC3.

She had briefly visited *Kauai* after the medical verdict to complete the formal process of resuming command. Haley was delighted to be back on the job with all that meant, but there was a tinge of regret as well. She remembered vividly the pain and the fear after the explosion when she thought *Kauai* was lost and the relief she felt when Ben appeared—*Thank God, Ben is alright!* He had saved the ship and all their lives under impossible circumstances, as she knew he would. He deserved his own command and probably would have one now if he had not volunteered to extend his tour to help her. As much as she feared what it would mean to lose him, she had to do something to get him his own boat.

Talesha had been exemplary as well. Haley knew the XO job could be grueling, and she could not imagine being dropped into it on a unit that had suffered as *Kauai* had in the disaster. Yet, Talesha had hit the deck running and relieved Ben of a crushing burden in his hour of need. She should have her shot as well, not be stuck in a staff job. The urgent need was to get *Kauai* back in the game again, but Haley resolved that as soon as the opportunity presented itself, she was going to request a heart-to-heart with Captain Mercier about moving up the two younger officers.

Back in the real world, she looked across the table at this man who had become such an important part of her life. Pete was wearing an open-collar light blue shirt and a light khaki jacket, his hair and anchor beard neat and trimmed instead of the scruffy look he normally affected because of his work. He was in fine form tonight, attentive at just the right times, and funny at others.

Pete had been there for her throughout her ordeal, by her bedside after the explosion and while she was in the hospital in Gitmo, caring for her at home, driving her to her treatments and physical therapy sessions. Unlike their previous sojourns, this one had been focused on healing rather than excitement. He revealed a very caring side that should not have surprised her, but did. Going out for a quiet celebration in this wonderful little restaurant was his idea as well, to mark the transition back to normal life. Haley had enjoyed getting "dressed up and hair down" for the occasion. She was wearing the sexiest dress she owned and was wearing her hair down in the teased-out way she knew he really liked.

They were seated in a quiet corner of the dining room, out of the main flow, but still engaged in the atmosphere. Haley enjoyed the intimacy of the room, which felt more like an outing with a group of friends rather than dining out. The wall décor and subdued lighting made it seem more like a cozy European restaurant than one you would expect to see on the "Space Coast" of Florida. She thought the food was magnificent—the owner was an award-winning chef who prepared each meal personally, and the Steak Diane she had ordered reflected this attention. Everything was perfect, almost too perfect, which made her wonder if something was going on.

"How did you get on to this place?" Haley asked.

"I asked Ben if he knew of any romantic restaurants in the area and he was hard over on this one. It was at this very table that he and Victoria stumbled through their vaudevillian engagement act." He grinned upon seeing the reaction on her face. "Don't panic. I'm not carrying a ring in my pocket."

"That's a relief," she said with a smile. *Is it though? Would you have turned him down if he had asked?* She had to admit that she did not know the answer. "It makes me wonder, though. What's going on here?"

"What? I can't take you out for a nice romantic meal? I am off the clock, you know."

"Yes, but as I recall Victoria saying, this is one of the best restaurants in Brevard County. You can't just show up at this place expecting a table, much less a table for two. So, give it up, *professor*. What's happening here?"

"Alright, *inspector*, you've got me. I confess there is an ulterior motive afoot here. Do you recall my saying that I was going to pack it in after the last one? Go straight, as they say?"

Oh, God. Here it comes. The great cold hole after hope has been sucked away. 'But honey, they need *me in this job!'* "Yes, I remember," she replied as neutrally as she could.

"I told Welles as much, but he counteroffered I could write my own ticket if I stayed." He reached over and took her hand. "I want to set up a special team to go after these traffickers. It will mainly involve connecting Internet dots and leveraging digital finance to go after their money. The field work will be low, mainly follow-up and joining the Feds or Europol on the occasional raid."

"And you'll lead the team?"

"No, that's the best part. Art Frankle is going to take it. He's done his bit in the field and deserves a less-kinetic job."

"Good choice. I only met him twice, but what I saw was impressive. Have you picked anyone else?"

"Everyone. Investigators, admin, data scientist, the lot."

"Data scientist? You mean..."

"Yup. It's Victoria. She jumped at the chance to get back with everyone."

Haley sighed. "I was getting spoiled having you around. But this really sucks, as I guess this means Ben will be off too."

"No, he won't."

"Um, you don't think he is going to pull a geographic bachelor tour away from Victoria, do you?"

"No need. " He grinned. "Our base of operations will be a lovely suite of offices securely within the confines of Patrick Space Force Base."

Her heart jumped, and she reflexively squeezed his hand. "You jerk! That was a hell of a detail to save for last!"

"I know, I know. I'm so ashamed," he said, putting his other hand to his forehead in mock contrition. "But I couldn't resist seeing the look on your face!" He brought her hand up to his lips and kissed it. "Forgive me?"

"I don't know. I suppose I can be bought. Since you're paying for this, let's ask Kayleigh for the dessert and apéritif menus and you can ply me with confections and spirits. I'll need the carbs for later tonight."

He nodded with a wry smile and said, "Ah, the lady is a cunning negotiator!"

"I didn't make captain because of my good looks, boyo."

Dupont, Jacques. "National Gendarmerie and Navy Raid Caribbean Sexual Slavery Spa." Le Monde. 4 August.

In a bold pre-dawn assault on 3 August, five teams of National Gendarmes, supported by Naval Riflemen and warships, raided a criminal prostitution enterprise believed to be part of *Le Milieu* operating on the island of Île Oiseaux, one of the Îles des Saintes group south of the island of Guadeloupe. The surviving criminals surrendered after a brief firefight and were taken into custody, along with an undisclosed number of suspected clients. Six men, seventeen women, and twenty-three children believed to have been held and forced against their will to conduct sexual acts have also been taken into custody while their status is evaluated.

The prostitution enterprise allegedly operated as a high-end spa called L'hôtel Caraïbe, servicing a select clientele of government and industrial elites from many countries, including France. Inquiries are now underway into how such a criminal organization could operate without official interference on French territory. Authorities are seeking the proprietor of the Spa, an ex-Foreign Legionnaire named Renard Laurent, not present on Île Oiseaux during the raid and still at large...

Malenski, Britney. "Ex-DIA Chief Jennifer Irving Signs as MSNBC/NBC Contributor." The Wrap. September 19.

Former Defense Intelligence Agency director, and retired Navy Vice Admiral Jennifer Irving has become the latest member of the NBC News and MSNBC family, officially signing with the network as a contributor.

Admiral Irving will serve as a senior national security and intelligence analyst for the networks, the company announced Thursday, adding that her first official appearance will come on this Sunday's "Meet the Press". Another person familiar with the matter said she would take the stage at "Morning Joe" on Monday.

The first female director of the DIA, Admiral Irving was appointed to the post after a distinguished career as a naval intelligence specialist that included tours of duty as Commander of the Office of Naval Intelligence, and Director for Intelligence (J-2) in the Office of the Chairman of the Joint Chiefs of Staff.

Whittle, Holly. "Hero Scientist Decorated in White House Ceremony." AP News. October 23.

Washington, D.C. — In a ceremony held at the White House today, President Driscoll recognized Dr. Lydia Hernandez, Professor of Geology and Volcanology at the University of Puerto Rico, for her outstanding contributions to public safety and scientific advancement. Dr. Hernandez was bestowed with the prestigious Department of Homeland Security Distinguished Public Service Award and the United States Geological Survey (USGS) Citizen's Award for Exceptional Service. The awards were conferred in recognition of Dr. Hernandez's groundbreaking discovery and timely warning of the catastrophic volcanic eruption of Mount Acadia on the island of St. Ignatius last July, saving countless lives and exemplifying the spirit of heroic public service.

Dr. Hernandez's pioneering work came to the forefront when she discovered crucial indicators pointing towards an imminent catastrophic volcanic eruption on St. Ignatius, a region previously believed to be geologically stable. Her on-site research, which involved innovative techniques in seismology and geothermal studies, enabled her to accurately predict the scope of the eruption and issue an alert to the local authorities.

Although over 6,000 people were killed by tsunamis and other volcanic effects across the islands of the Northern Caribbean as a result of the eruption, the death toll would have been many times higher without the timely warning her efforts provided. Dr. Hernandez was among the last people evacuated from St. Ignatius, and narrowly avoided death herself when the Coast Guard cutter on which she was evacuated was nearly sunk in the island's explosion.

The Department of Homeland Security Distinguished Public Service Award is one of the highest honors granted by the U.S. government to individuals who have shown outstanding dedication to ensuring the safety and security of the nation. The USGS Citizen's Award for Exceptional Service recognizes individuals outside of the agency who have made significant contributions to the mission of the USGS in the fields of natural resource science and public safety.

Sussmann, Ari. "Boston Financier's Daughter Pleads Guilty in Miami Federal Court for Oil Tanker Bombing Plot." Boston Herald. November 10.

Miami, FL - In a shocking turn of events, Bridget Morehouse, the daughter of Boston financier Jeffrey Morehouse, pleaded guilty in a Miami federal court to a charge of conspiracy to destroy a vessel or maritime facility. Morehouse, alongside her co-defendants Terrell Pollack and the late Lyman Goetz, was involved in a bombing plot targeting an oil tanker off Port Canaveral, Florida, on June 12th.

According to court documents, Morehouse received a $250,000 fine and was sentenced to five years of probation. Her co-defendant, Terrell Pollack, also pleaded guilty and was handed down a five-year prison sentence and a $50,000 fine. Tragically, the third co-conspirator, Lyman Goetz, took his own life while awaiting trial.

The trio were arrested by the U.S. Coast Guard after the explosives-laden, remotely operated boat they were piloting toward the tanker *Paul Morris* exploded upon being hit by gunfire from a Coast Guard cutter. There were no injuries during the incident and no damage beyond the destruction of the converted sport fishing boat used in the attack.

Legal experts have expressed their astonishment at Morehouse's relatively lenient punishment, given the severity of the crime. Many speculate that her cooperation in the ongoing investigation of the Climate Annihilation Response Emergency (CARE) environmental activist organization played a pivotal role in her sentencing outcome. The details of her cooperation agreement remain confidential, leaving the public to wonder about the extent of her involvement in CARE and the information she provided to authorities.

Chapter 22

Coda

Cyril E. King Airport, St. Thomas, U.S. Virgin Islands
12:17 AST, 26 December

Marcus

Marcus had selected the last row of the aircraft when booking the flight on the Department of Homeland Security's official travel system, knowing he needed time to stretch and get his uniform in order before he deplaned. It was never pleasant for someone of his six-foot-two height to twist into a coach-class seat for a flight of any length, even on a reasonably large aircraft like an Airbus A319. This one had taken three hours and twenty minutes to fly non-stop from Charlotte Douglas International in North Carolina to St. Thomas, which meant he was bent into the window seat for almost four hours.

After climbing out through the impossibly narrow passageway between the seats, he stood in the aisleway and stretched, smiling at the bemused flight attendant standing in the rear galley. He reached into the overhead bin to retrieve his carefully folded, navy blue-colored service dress uniform coat and put it on, buttoned it, and tugged it down into place. At last, he retrieved his backpack and uniform cap and, after putting it on, smiled one last time at the flight attendant, then turned forward to leave the plane.

As a rule, Marcus didn't travel in uniform—it wasn't officially prohibited to do so, but the times were such that members of the armed forces were discouraged from appearing in public in uniform as a matter of personal safety. Today, the situation was different. He was here to attend an official function and there was no time to check into a hotel to change. He didn't mind the discomfort of the flight, having to wear a coat and tie outside on a tropical island, or even having to leave his family in the early morning the day after Christmas. All was well with the world, as he was about to spend time with Isabelle Jones.

They had stayed in touch in the months that followed the tragedy, becoming very close in hours spent over the phone, sharing both good news and bad, celebrating or commiserating as appropriate. Celebrating when Isabelle landed a job as a paralegal in Tampa, Florida, and found a home for herself and her grandmother, when Marcus was selected to attend Flight Training after his Academy graduation next May, and when Isabelle's support organization for the St. Ignatius refugees was awarded a large federal grant. They commiserated as her grandmother's health declined, she went into hospice care, and eventually died. The doctors attributed her death to a mishmash of physiological and psychological causes, but Isabelle believed the true cause was a broken heart over the loss of the only home she had ever known.

Persephone was a good news story—Isabelle contacted Laetitia Evans's sister, who lived just outside of Atlanta with her husband and two small children. They immediately took custody of the young girl and were working through the paperwork required to adopt her. Persephone had written Marcus regularly at first, but the letters became more infrequent over time as she settled into her new home. The tapering off of her letters was bittersweet—Marcus missed them, but was glad she was resuming her life as a child.

His feelings toward Isabelle had not cooled over time. In fact, quite the opposite. The more he learned about her through their conversations, the stronger his feelings for her became. He longed to be with her, but she was over twelve hundred miles away and neither of them was able to travel with the demands upon their lives.

Marcus had seen Isabelle face-to-face just once since kissing her goodbye on the dock in Guantanamo Bay. He flew down to Tampa late on a Friday night to attend the memorial service held for Adelaide that Saturday, pitching in however he could as Isabelle coped with her grief and the demands of the event. There was little time to talk with her, as he had to return to the Academy the next day. It was a brief visit dedicated to support, not romance, and

Marcus did his best not to reveal his inner feelings to her. He could only hope that someday the stars would align and he would have his shot.

The orders to fly to St. Thomas had come as a complete surprise shortly before he completed his exams and traveled to his parent's new home west of Charlotte, North Carolina, for the holidays. He was to be the Coast Guard's representative to a sunset memorial service in the Caribbean where St. Ignatius formerly stood, held on the day after Christmas. From their conversations, he knew Isabelle's organization had worked with the Office of the Governor of the U.S. Virgin Islands to set up the event. One of the inter-island passenger ferries had been hired to conduct a select group of survivors and official representatives sailing from Charlotte Amalie that afternoon to the location for the service. Marcus had been requested by name, nominally in recognition of his service during the catastrophe, although he hoped Isabelle was behind it.

As he neared the open door to the plane, he could feel the warm and humid air of St. Thomas, quite a change from the cold December weather in North Carolina. The airport was small, with a single-story terminal, and passengers boarded and deplaned in the open air via stairways pushed up to the aircraft. He followed the other passengers down the stairway and into the air-conditioned terminal building.

It was when they neared the baggage claim that he caught his first sight of Isabelle, staggeringly beautiful in a modest black dress, hose, and pumps, her hair partially up in the dirty ponytail he liked so much. Once he caught his breath, he laughed out loud when noticed the large pickup sign she was holding, white with a border of flowers with large blue print reading, "Handsome Flyboy."

Marcus walked up to her, still grinning, put his backpack down, and said, "I understand you're looking for a handsome flyboy, miss."

Isabelle smiled and her eyes sparkled when she replied, "Yes, I am. Have you seen one, by any chance?"

Marcus tipped his head back and laughingly said, "Owww!"

Isabelle carefully placed the sign down next to Marcus's backpack, put her arms around his shoulders, and said, "Aw! Let me make it better." She then gave him a kiss that nearly made his heart stop. "There. How's that?"

"Seems to have done the trick," Marcus said. "You look beautiful, Isabelle."

She said, "Thank you, Marcus." She then pulled away slightly and, after scanning his uniform, ran her fingers over his ribbons, which included three he had just been awarded for his St. Ignatius service. "You look the handsome hero."

"Please don't put *that* on a pickup sign," Marcus said.

She smiled, then picked up the sign and said, "No, I think this one is a keeper." After Marcus nodded and picked up his backpack, she asked, "Have you eaten?"

"Just a bagel in Charlotte before I got on the plane."

"Good. I know a place downtown where we can grab a bite before we sail."

"I'm in," he said as she slipped her arm in his.

They had a very nice, light lunch at a Caribbean restaurant during which Isabelle explained what was going on and what was expected of him. "I hope you're not expecting some sort of inspiring speech from me," Marcus said. "I'm really, *really* not good at that."

Isabelle grinned in return. "Don't worry. That's why the politicians are here. The last thing they want is a genuine young hero upstaging them with an inspiring speech. Just give up a couple of 'thank you', 'honored to be here', *et ceteras* and everything will be fine."

"Roger that!"

The capital city of Charlotte Amalie was returning to life, slowly but surely recovering from the devastation wrought by the eruption less than six months ago. The proportion of shops still shuttered increased exponentially as they approached the harbor, where the thirty-foot tsunami from the last explosion had done the worst damage. They, along with the enormous piles of cleared ash he had seen near the airport, were reminders of that terrible day.

They parked at the marina and Isabelle retrieved the wooden box containing her grandmother's ashes from the trunk. Marcus was uncharacteristically at sea at that moment, feeling he should say something, but not knowing what. He settled on the very weak, "Can I help you carry that?"

She responded with a sad smile. "No. This one's for me. I would appreciate it if you could clear a path for me, though."

"Of course."

They made their way through the marina security to the dock. Marcus could see the boat was one of the newer ones with a customer lounge for first-class passengers. They presented their IDs and were admitted on board, then went straight to the lounge, where Isabelle gently deposited the box next to several others. She would not be alone in returning loved ones home to St. Ignatius this day.

By the time they settled in, it was about thirty minutes before departure and Marcus was happy to stand along-side Isabelle, smiling, nodding, and shaking hands as she made the rounds of the other guests. Marcus was de-lighted to see a couple of familiar faces, Dr. Hernandez and Sergeant Platt, the former in a subdued dress like Is-abelle's and the latter in his police dress uniform.

"My, my. You sure clean up good," Platt said with a grin, pumping Marcus's hand.

"You too, Sarge. It's good to see you again."

"Miss Jones, you look terrific," Platt said to Isabelle. Before she could answer, there was a commotion on the other side of the lounge as the official party had arrived from Government House. Platt shook his head and said, "Well, fellow swine, are you ready for your ration of pearls?"

"Shhh!" Isabelle whispered while Marcus tried not to smile.

The boat left the dock once the official party was aboard and was soon cruising through the Northern Caribbean Sea at what Marcus estimated to be about twenty knots. Shortly after departure, the Governor of the Virgin Islands provided an introductory speech. Marcus recognized his voice from the phone conferences and admired the way he was able to thread the needle on the tone of the speech, not too light-hearted nor too depressing. He introduced the politicians next, a U.S. Senator, two representatives, and the delegate to the U.S. House of Representatives from the Virgin Islands, each presenting the usual political speech, not bad, but not on the level of the governor's.

The governor introduced Isabelle as the organizer of the event and the leading light of the community. She gave a brief speech full of hope that Marcus thought was wonderful, although he admitted to himself he might be biased. Dr. Hernandez and Sergeant Platt were introduced and said a few words of thanks.

It was Marcus's turn next, and when the governor brought him forward and introduced him as one of the heroes of the day, he was almost disabled by stage fright. It felt like a giant invisible boa constrictor was wrapped around his chest, squeezing the breath out of him. He caught sight of Isabelle in the crowd smiling at him and was finally able to speak. "Thank you for your kind words, Governor Harrison, which I accept on behalf of all my fellow Coast Guard members. It is an honor to be here, representing them, to express our sorrow for those who lost loved ones during this terrible tragedy. Our hearts and thoughts will always be with them. Thank you."

After a final handshake, Marcus quickly stepped away from the center of attention, back to where his friends were standing. "Bang on, son!" Platt said, giving him a fist bump when he arrived. Isabelle cupped his face in her hands, kissed him lightly, and said, "Perfect, flyboy. See? You're a natural."

The rest of the trip down was far less stressful, and he and Isabelle strolled outside in the bright sunshine and cool breeze. About two hours through the trip, they passed to the west of St. Croix. Most of the remaining disaster recovery effort was focused there, as they were by far the hardest hit by both the ashfall and tsunamis. Marcus felt a pang of guilt looking at the smudge of gray in the distance, thinking of the privations the residents there were still experiencing.

The only good thing that could be said about the situation on St. Croix was that they had been spared from hurricanes this season. A direct hit on top of the catastrophe from the eruption would likely have left most of the forty thousand residents dead. Ironically, scientists were attributing the greatly reduced hurricane season of the past year to a "volcanic winter" created by all the ash and sulfur gases injected into the upper atmosphere by the eruption.

Half an hour after passing St. Croix, Marcus could see what looked like a tall cloud coming over the horizon. He was puzzled by it until a voice behind them said, "It's steam from the magma chamber." He and Isabelle turned to see Dr. Hernandez had joined them. "It will continue for at least a year."

"Will it erupt again?" Isabelle asked.

"Probably. But not for some time. Certainly not within our lifetimes. There is no danger, provided we don't sail directly through the plume."

"Does the captain know that?" Ben asked.

"Oh, yes." Hernandez smiled. "I had to do some fancy talking just to get him to go within sight of it."

Within half an hour, they were approaching the site for the service, a mile southeast of where the plume emerged from the water, approximately where Jamestown had been before the eruption. Marcus knew that the geography had changed so much that the land and debris from the town were likely scattered over an area of several square miles. But he also knew the survivors needed a point of reference to give the service meaning, and this location was as good as any.

Everyone gathered on the open afterdeck for the service. The lower limb of the sun was approaching the horizon when the Bishop of the Episcopal Diocese of the Virgin Islands completed his invocation. After the singing of two hymns, the mourners scattering the ashes of their loved ones were called forward. Marcus walked silently beside Isabelle as she picked up her box and awaited her turn.

When her turn came, she stepped forward, took the urn from the box, kneeled, and scattered the ashes over the water, softly whispering, "Goodbye, Gran." Marcus leaned down and helped her to her feet and then put his arm across her shoulders. She was sobbing quietly as they walked back into the crowd. After putting down the box, she embraced him and he held her close as she silently cried, gently stroking her back.

The Bishop of the Roman Catholic Diocese of St. Thomas delivered the benediction as the last limb of the sun disappeared under the horizon. The subdued crowd wandered back into the lounge as the boat turned and started making its way back to St. Thomas. Marcus and Isabelle did not follow but sat on an outside bench on the port side, watching the light fading in the west.

Isabelle leaned into him as they sat in the soft light of the deck lanterns, and he just held her for what seemed forever with neither talking. He was saved from his increasing discomfort of indecision over whether to ask if she was alright when she finally said, "It was a nice service."

"I thought so. Is there anything I can do, Isabelle?"

She nestled closer to him. "You're doing it." After a moment she said, "You know, you're always doing it."

"What?" he asked.

"The right thing. When I need something, you are always there, always doing it. If I need to laugh or to cry or just talk, you are the one I want to call. When I really needed someone to lean on and hold me during Gran's funeral, you were there. And now, here you are, just what and where I need you to be. Do you know what that has meant to me during this time?"

Marcus could not believe what he was hearing. "Um, I don't seem to have the words."

"That surprises me. You had the perfect words a little while ago. And you managed to talk Gran out of her house after everything I laid on her failed. She really liked you, you know, from the beginning."

Marcus managed a sad smile. "I liked her, too."

"Yes, I know. Anyway, I asked her a few months ago how you managed it and all she said was, 'He was very persuasive.' I'm curious. What did you tell her?"

"I pointed out what would happen to her when the pyroclastic flow hit and said she didn't want that picture in your head."

Isabelle nodded. "So that did the trick."

"Not exactly. She answered you would get over it. So, I told her *I* didn't want that picture in your head and if she didn't come voluntarily, I'd throw her ass over my shoulder and carry her out."

Isabelle sat up and gaped at him in astonishment. He was about to blurt out an apology when she suddenly put her head back and guffawed. After a few moments, she calmed down, wiped her eyes, and said, "You told her *that*? I wish I could have seen her face! Marcus Porter, I love you!"

"I love you too, Isabelle."

Her smile faded, and she said, "No, I mean, I am *in love* with you, Marcus."

He had not thought he could have been more surprised by her first admission. He was wrong. "*What?*"

"I know you probably thought I was stuck up. And I guess I was a little when I first met you. I thought, here's a handsome boy who seems a little flustered, but cute. I soon found out you're smart, charming, and funny, well worth knowing. Then the courage started coming out, first in the park, then when you went after Percy and Gran. Finally, we were there by the dock with no hope, dead for sure. I was so scared I couldn't even string a thought together. I could see you were frightened too, but when that little girl needed you, you picked her up and took her fear away. My only thought was, who is this man and how does he do that?

"After that, as I said, you have been flawless. I've been on a few dates since I got to Tampa, but I inevitably end up comparing them to you, and they always come up short. I know we are half a continent apart and we should move on, but I can't. Every road leads back to you." After a few seconds of him staring back in astonished silence, she said, "Please say something."

"Isabelle, I have been in love with you since the park. My uncle warned me it wouldn't work, that I wasn't in your league, being just a student and all, and I tried to walk away. But I can't, Isabelle. I love you."

She stood and pulled him up and then they kissed, long and hard. When it finally ended, she looked into his eyes and said, "Well, Marcus Porter."

"Well, Isabelle Jones."

"Tell me, if you have someone making love to you in your government-funded hotel room all night, will you get in trouble?"

"Nope."

"Good. I would hate to see you get in trouble."

Notes from the Author

None of the characters in this book represent any person, living or dead (you got that, all you lawyers out there?). However, some of the best qualities of the fictional crew members of *Kauai* were inspired by many of the fine people with whom I had the honor and pleasure of serving while I was a member of the U.S. Coast Guard.

USCGC *Kauai* is fictional. There is no "D Class" of the 110-foot patrol boat series, and the last of those built was USCGC *Galveston Island* (WPB-1349). I created a fictitious D-Class to buy some extra margin of verisimilitude and get the nit-pickers off my back. The cutters *Dependable* and *Seneca* are genuine and still in service as of this writing.

The island of St. Ignatius, U.S. Virgin Islands, is fictional. It was inspired by the island of Saba, a municipality of the Netherlands in the Lesser Antilles about ninety miles to the east-northeast of the fictional St. Ignatius. The fictional character of Isabelle Jones was inspired by the real-life politician Esmeralda Johnson, the youngest person ever elected as a member of the Saba Island Council.

The seismic tomography system Dr. Hernandez uses to measure Mt. Acadia's magma chamber is speculative fiction, but inspired by real-life experimentation conducted on the island of Montserrat. Please see the paper "Magma Chamber Properties from Integrated Seismic Tomography and Thermal Modeling at Montserrat" by M. Paulatto, et. al., published by the American Geophysical Union in 2012.

The vignette featuring the rescue of the passengers and crew of the dive boat *Conch Rounder* was inspired by an actual lethal mishap involving the dive boat *Conception*, which caught fire and sank in the Channel Islands off Santa Barbara, California on 2 September 2019. Tragically, rescue resources were not readily at hand in that case, and all thirty-three passengers and one of the five crew members on board perished.

The dialog between the Coast Guard people and in radio transmissions depicted in this story has much more "plain language" than what you would hear during actual operations. Including all the acronyms, jargon, and formal protocols vital for clarity and brevity in real life would have been more authentic. However, it would also be a great deal more tedious or confusing for the average reader. I ask all veterans and any other purists' forgiveness for this compromise for the sake of readability.

Acknowledgments

Many thanks to the highly knowledgeable and dedicated personnel of the U.S. Geological Survey, particularly those servicing the USGS Volcanoes site on X. In addition to their always interesting posts on what's happening in the world of volcanoes, they provided extremely responsive and outstanding advice on resources related to Volcanology and insight into their world of work that was invaluable to the development of this story. I deeply appreciate their patience and professionalism in keeping the public informed and authors like me honest. If you are an X user, I highly recommend you follow them: (https://twitter.com/USGSVolcanoes).

Another shoutout to Chef Scott Earick, who graciously allowed me to use his restaurant, Scott's On Fifth in Indialantic, Florida, as the venue for one of the most important scenes in the story. Scott is a truly fine gentleman and a world-class chef, leading an outstanding crew in the most romantic restaurant in Brevard County, Florida.

Caribbean Counterstrike

The 252 Syndicate has created a new nerve gas far more dangerous than any in existence. But a vicious drug gang/cult has grabbed it along with their converted supply ship lab during a drug war. Can *Kauai* and her crew seize the ship from the gang's heavily fortified base before the 252s retrieve it and market the weapon?

Available in Ebook, Paperback, and Audiobook. Follow this link to find your retailer of choice:

https://bit.ly/CaribbeanCounterstrike

Bravely and Faithfully

Kauai's crew braves a sortie into a major hurricane to rescue a young family from a wrecked sailboat. The action gets *Kauai's* beloved captain, Sam Powell, a well-deserved early promotion and a new assignment. His new, hard-charging replacement, Haley Reardon, has changes in mind, but the DNI has other plans. Her first sortie as CO sees *Kauai* sent to support a Defense Intelligence Agency team infiltrating a Chinese-held Caribbean island.

Available in Ebook, Paperback, and Audiobook. Follow this link to find your retailer of choice:

https://bit.ly/BravelyAndFaithfully

www.ingramcontent.com/pod-product-compliance
Lightning Source LLC
Chambersburg PA
CBHW060723190726
48285CB00001B/50